RUNNING WILD NOVELLA ANTHOLOGY

VOLUME NINE

BOOK ONE

Running Wild Novella Anthology, Volume 9 Book 1

Published in North America and Europe by Running Wild Press. Visit Running Wild Publishing at www.runningwildpublishing.com, Educators, librarians, book clubs (as well as the eternally curious), go to ww.runningwild-publishing.com for tools.

ISBN (pbk) 978-1-963869-05-7

ISBN (ebook) 978-1-963869-45-3

CONTENTS

THE NECROMANCER — 1
by Krista Beucler

THE SPIDER AND THE BIRDHOUSE — 85
by Joel T Blackstock Jr.

THE KITE FLYER AT CHIMERA ISLAND — 149
by Eric St. Pierre

TESTIMONIES AFTER THE FIRE — 215
by Izaskun Gracia Quintana

THINGS UNRECKONED — 283
by David Vonderheide and James Cato

EDGE — 353
by Henry Whittlesey

Author Bios — 463
About Running Wild Press — 467

THE NECROMANCER

BY KRISTA BEUCLER

Silver hated Valentine's Day. It was just another one of those cheap holidays brought over from the mortal world. An excuse to jack up the prices on love potions, beauty spells, and already supernaturally expensive imported chocolate.

People kept bringing flowers into the apothecary and Silver had to smile and tell them, "What lovely flowers!" and "Happy Valentine's Day to you, too!" as she gave them their drink orders.

"Coffee, goblin roast, with a shot of pender tree sap coming up. Always good for the nerves. You planning on popping the question?" The young man in question smiled shyly as she gave him his coffee. She wanted to throw it all over his neatly pressed tunic and leggings.

"We're running out of powdered daisy," Silver told Caton, the young herbalist who owned the apothecary. "Everyone wants it in their coffee this morning."

Caton winked cheekily and pushed a strand of curling, honey-colored hair out of her face. "Love a good aphrodisiac on Valentine's Day, eh? I'll just pop out to the garden and pick some more, shall I?"

Silver turned back to the counter, her customer service smile firmly in place and continued to take orders from happy-go-lucky couples. Sunlight was streaming into the shop from the wide windows, and the scent of coffee and spices hung in the air. Caton had hired some cherubs to flutter about the ceiling and play lutes and tiny harps softly. Periodically, one would throw confetti down upon the heads of whoever was unlucky enough to be standing beneath them. Why anyone thought flying babies were romantic was beyond Silver. She was rather proud of how well she was hiding her hatred.

Aidolyn breezed into the shop an hour late, as usual. Her cloying perfume drifted in clouds about her, and her bright lipstick was faintly smudged, Silver guessed, by the man who was riding a white horse toward the castle down the busy cobbled street outside the shop. She didn't recognize him, but Aidolyn was seeing a different knight practically every week so that wasn't surprising.

"Silvy, my darling!" Aidolyn cooed, giving Silver a kiss on the cheek. "Happy Valentine's Day!" Silver hated when Aidolyn called her 'Silvy,' but she had given up trying to tell Aidolyn that.

"Please be on time every once in a while," Silver said, but for all the notice Aidolyn took, she might have been talking to a hedgerow.

Aidolyn put on an apron and began to make the orders that were backing up: a cup of fairy tea (good for loosening morals and impeding judgment), and two mugs of strong, black peasant coffee with a shot each of wimblenut cream (for the passion).

"Do you have any Valentine's plans? Got a beau?" Aidolyn asked Silver brightly.

"Of course, I don't," snapped Silver.

"Someone's as bitter as coffee this morning." Aidolyn giggled at her own wittiness.

"Maybe if you came to work on time, you'd see me in a better mood."

Aidolyn stuck out her lower lip in a pout. "I tried to be here on time, I really did. But Sir Gladen is, well, something of a romantic." She winked, and Silver rolled her eyes. "You would not believe how hard it was to get out of bed this morning. And he kept hiding my clothes!"

"Ugh, stop. I don't want to hear it."

"He's taking me out on the lake tonight to watch the sunset and drink fine wine," sighed Aidolyn. "But honestly, Sil, you must have some plan for Valentine's Day."

Silver furiously wiped a tankard clean. "If you must know," she said finally, "my parents are visiting."

"Oh, won't that be nice!" cried Aidolyn, her cornflower-blue eyes widening. "After all, Valentine's Day is meant to be a time spent with all your loved ones."

Silver didn't answer. In truth, she was dreading the visit. Her father had business in the city—he carved fine and sometimes magical furniture (it depended on the wood). He and Silver's mother lived in a village at the border between the Kingdom of Meryn and the Wildwood, a day's journey from Ening City, but twice a year they came to the city to sell his work. It was very high quality, and many of the nobles and courtiers of the capital city furnished their castles with his pieces. Whenever they visited the city, Silver's parents always came to stay with her.

Silver liked her parents and had always gotten along quite well with them, even after she had decided to move to the city to study herbs and small magics instead of learning to carve like her big brother, Benjamin (although he made aesthetic, rather than functional pieces).

This time however, Silver dreaded their arrival. Her mother was always reminding her that her uterus wouldn't be young forever and she needed to get cracking before she shriveled up like an old maid. Silver had gotten so tired of this that she had invented a suitor and had written of him dutifully to her family every month, fabricating a romance that would have been worthy of the bard's songs. But now they were coming and the game was up.

"It's your break, luvy," Aidolyn told her and she sighed with relief.

Silver moved into the storeroom behind the counter where Caton kept her potions and herbs and books. The herbalist herself was still in the garden gathering daisies. Silver shooed

Caton's rumpled, one-eyed cat, Growltiger, off the chair behind the table at the center of the room and sat down. He stalked off in a huff.

A book was sitting propped open on the table. It was open to a page on love potions. Now, love potions were no small magic, and Caton was adamant that she did not practice big magic or the black arts.

Silver closed the book to look at the cover. The loopy, gilt script on the leather binding read *Solomon Mea's Guide the Black Arts of Magic*. Silver was impressed. Apparently Caton was more devious than she appeared.

Flipping to the contents, Silver ran a finger down the list of spells and potions. A love potion would do if she could only find someone to use it on. She opened the book back to that page and skimmed the directions. She sighed. She didn't have any bat's wings or phoenix feathers. It was the full moon but she didn't have a month to brew it.

She flipped back to the contents. A persuasion draft? But the sheep's blood had to ferment in an oak barrel, and she didn't have time for that. Perhaps she could turn water to rum. She wondered how drunk her parents would have to be to forget that they had not actually met anyone but would believe her if she insisted they had. But no, it was impractical.

Charming rags to ball gowns and mice into horses: all the godmother essentials, truth serum and all the basic poisons, giving animals the ability to speak... no, none of these would do.

Then Silver's eyes fell on the last spell in the book, labeled simply 'Reanimation.' Now that, she thought, could work.

She thumbed to the correct page. It was faded and there was dirt in the crease—probably, she thought, from the graveyard where the last body had been dug up. She ran an eye over the list of ingredients; it was simple enough, almost deceptively simple, and she had everything in the herbalists' stores. Convenient.

Silver collected the beetle carcasses (to renew the body), the hummingbird wings (to get the heart beating again), the powdered unicorn horn (to rekindle the life-force), and the dragon shinbone (to balance the humors), and dissolved them in a pot of liquid mercury. She worked quickly since she only had fifteen minutes of her break left and who knew when Caton would be back in from the garden? There was a skull on the table with a stuffed raven perched atop it on the other side of her cauldron. There was also a dripping candle. It made her feel very arcane and powerful. Only real witches worked in chambers such as these.

"Silver, honey, bring out some more pender sap when you're done, will you?" called Aidolyn and Silver nearly upended her cauldron.

"Uh, yes, of course," she called back, trying not to sound guilty.

She pricked her finger and let the drop of blood fall into the cauldron, turning the contents magenta. It was the last ingredient. There was an incantation inscribed at the bottom of the page; she would have to do that at the graveyard. Silver poured the purple liquid into several vials (she'd made a triple batch, just in case) and tore the page with the incantation from the book. She hid the two extra vials under the stuffed raven and tucked the third and the incantation into a pouch at her belt. Then she cleaned out the cauldron and generally tried to look innocent when she returned to the bar with more pender sap.

"What's with the grin?" asked Aidolyn as Silver handed her the pender sap. "Aren't you in a bad mood today?"

"Yes," Silver immediately dropped the innocent grin she had been wearing and tried to arrange her features into a more neutral expression.

Silver managed to beg off work a bit early, claiming an upset stomach and a headache. Caton sent her on her way with a poultice for her head and a liquid remedy for the stomach that smelled so strongly of sulfur, Silver suspected it would probably cure anything she had if it didn't kill her first.

Silver walked to the outskirts of the city where there was a little graveyard that was usually empty of mourners and visitors except at night when the grave robbers, wizards, and witches came for more dubious purposes.

She opened the creaking gate, and a chill February wind picked up slightly, sending leaves skittering over the dry ground. Silver felt delightfully excited. She was just like the daring heroines in the dusty, leather-bound books she liked to read so much.

Silver wound her way up and down the overgrown paths scanning the headstones. Some of them were leaning at odd angles, others were crumbling, the words carved into them barely legible. Creeping vines snaked up stones, claiming them for their own. For all of stone's permanence, Silver suddenly felt that nature always took back what is hers.

Eventually Silver found a grave that looked fairly fresh, and indeed, the date of death was barely a week prior. She located a spade and a pickaxe in a gardener's cottage—luckily the gardener appeared to be out—and set to work unearthing Varior Skogil, as his stone proclaimed in tall, austere letters. He was a young man of twenty-four—at least she was assuming he was a man; Varior sounded like a man's name to her—who had died the previous Wednesday. She wondered idly of what he had died.

She had never before considered how deep people are buried. It was hot and hard work. Silver paused to tie up her dark purple hair. After three hours, her boots and the hems of her skirts were muddy and Silver was over the whole digging thing. She stopped to rest and pulled out the page she had torn from the spell book. She flipped it over hoping there might be a helpful grave digging spell there. Someone had written out an incantation in faded handwriting along with the instruction "Bless thy tools."

Feeling a little silly, Silver said the incantation over her spade and pickaxe. Nothing happened. Silver sighed and looked up at the sky. It was already late afternoon. The soil was pretty soft, but it was still going to take forever. She got back to work. It was a few minutes before she realized that the grave was deepening and widening much faster than she was digging. Plunging the spade into the soil felt like dipping it into water. Barely twenty minutes later, she had reached the coffin.

She used the spade to lever off the lid, and the cheap wood and nails gave easily. Varior was rather handsome for someone who was dead. It had been cold and the body had kept surprisingly well.

Silver climbed out of the hole. For a moment, exhaustion and dizziness swept through her. She knew she wouldn't be able to lift him out of the grave on her own, so she'd just have to bring him to life where he was.

"Lords of Winter, Death, and Night," she began chanting a bit nervously. "Release to me this soul, upon lighting and thunder. Though the moon doth howl, let this spirit return to the mortal world to once more inhabit his body. Krewix izseod ab unum sres chanbeo Druzworhot et obetruc!"

Silver opened the magenta vial and poured the liquid over the man's face. To complete the charm, she spat a glob of saliva onto his forehead, above the place right between his eyes. The liquid began to hiss and steam, and Silver hoped she had done the incantation correctly. That last line had included a lot of words she wasn't sure how to pronounce.

Just as Silver was sure it hadn't worked, Varior Skogil

opened his blue, blue eyes. A grin split his face when he saw her.

"Hello, lovely," he drawled, "I didn't know they made witches as pretty as you."

Silver blushed and then hated herself for it. "I'm not really a witch," she said.

"Oh?" Corpse-Boy had stood up in his coffin and was now propping an elbow on the edge of the pit. "Then pray, what are you?"

"I'm a barista."

"How long have I been dead?" asked Varior. "Has the world changed so much that baristas now raise the dead in their spare time?"

Silver offered him a hand and helped him climb out of the grave. His hand was surprisingly warm and alive and she congratulated herself on a job well done. "You died last Wednesday," she told him, deciding not to address the other question.

"Varior Skogil," he said, shaking her hand when he was safely on terra firma.

"Silver Nightbrace," she replied.

"A witch's name if ever I heard one." He had very white teeth, and somehow he seemed to show all of them when he smiled. It was really a very nice smile.

Silver shrugged. "So, how did you die?"

It was Varior's turn to shrug. "Oh, I was murdered. But no big deal. Now that I'm back I can make the bastards pay. I must say," he continued, "you've done a marvelous job. I feel just like new. Do this often, do you?"

"Erm," mumbled Silver, "not really."

He helped her refill his grave, and Silver was slightly nervous that she had brought back such a vengeful corpse. She suddenly realized that she didn't know how to reverse the spell if she needed to.

"So for what dark purpose would a lady such as yourself wish to use a reanimated corpse, especially one so dashing and daring as myself?" he asked as they left the graveyard, both covered in mud.

"Um, well," began Silver. Her planning hadn't included the bit where she asked the corpse to pretend to be her boyfriend to meet her family. And what was she going to do afterward? Let him go on his merry way to take vengeance on his murderers? What if he deserved it? What if he was a criminal?

"I'd like you to meet my parents," Silver said finally.

"Oh," said Varior, "aren't you at least going to buy me dinner first? What was your name again? Copper? Goldie?"

"Silv—" Silver started to say before noticing his sly smile and realizing the joke. "Very funny. Look," she said, "I might have told them I have a boyfriend and they might be visiting tonight and I had to do something."

"Don't you think your methods are a little drastic? Not that I'm complaining, of course."

"I've always been over-zealous," Silver said, waving a hand. "But the way I see it, you owe me. You would still be dead if it weren't for me."

"True enough, fine lady."

"Quit with the fine lady nonsense. You're my boyfriend, you can call me Silver."

"And how long have we been dating, Goldie?"

Silver couldn't decide if she was annoyed about the nickname, so she let it pass. "Five months," she said.

"Five months! And I haven't proposed? You should dump me."

"I will. Later. But I need you tonight."

"Tell me, is it the full moon tonight?"

"The full moon? Yes, why? You're not a werewolf, are you?" Silver asked, panicking. A werewolf. That would be just perfect.

"Oh no, no, of course not. Are you?"

"No!"

"Well, it's worth asking."

"If I was a werewolf, would I be inviting my parents to dinner tonight?"

"You know, that would be a clever hunting strategy." Varior tilted his head, considering.

Silver whacked him on the arm. "Watch it. I got you out of that grave, I can put you back." Though she wasn't actually sure she could.

Varior held up his hands in surrender.

They reached Silver's cottage presently. She lived in a little house on the edge of a field by the palace stables. Apart from the bathroom, the cottage had just one big room, though Silver preferred to think of it as "open-plan." Her bed was tucked into a corner by the fireplace, and the kitchen was grouped around the gas stove on the other side of the room. There was a fine oak table in the center of the room that her father had made. Silver flipped the light switch, which she still found satisfying. Electric lights were becoming more common for private homes in the Kingdom of Meryn, but they were expensive since all the materials came from the mortal world.

Silver and Varior washed up, in an effort to make it appear that they hadn't both just crawled out of a hole in the ground. Varior helped Silver prepare dinner and set the table as they awaited the arrival of her parents.

* * *

It was all going so well: Silver's parents had cooed over Varior and he had simpered impressively, good impressions had been made all around, and everyone was now comfortably tipsy.

Varior clinked his knife against his glass. "Mr. and Mrs. Nightbrace, it's been so lovely to finally meet you both, and I cannot thank you enough for making me feel so accepted into your loving family."

Silver snorted but managed to turn it into a cough.

"Now it seems only right to do this with you present. I've been thinking about it for a long time but," he raised his wine-glass in Silver's direction, "will you marry me and make me the happiest man alive?"

Silver's mouth dropped open in horror as her parents applauded and squealed in delight. "Oh Silver," her mother said breathlessly. "You could wear the dress I wore."

Not that horrid white lace monstrosity, thought Silver.

"You'll be married in the Cathedral, of course," said her father. Silver felt briefly bad for not having been to Mass since moving to Ening City. Then those feelings were overshadowed by panic at how she was going to get out of being engaged to the recently reanimated corpse of a man she had just met.

"Come on now, Goldie," Varior said, smirking. "Don't leave me hanging."

Fortunately, Silver was saved from answering because, at that moment, a pack of goblins broke down the door with a splintering blast. Goblins were only about four and half feet tall, but when twenty or thirty of them were streaming into her house with their slimy gray-green skin and their sharp teeth, all bristling with weapons, they seemed pretty intimidating.

Silver's father screamed and dove under the hefty table he had designed and built, just as her mother leapt onto the top of the table wielding a heavy metal tankard and screaming like a banshee. She brought the tankard down on the head of the nearest goblin, which crumpled to the floor. Immediately, Varior was locked in combat with several goblins, using one of the ornate candelabras they had set out on the table for ambiance.

Silver was frozen in place as fighting swirled around her. Her father grabbed her hand and yanked her under the table beside him. He shouted something that she didn't hear but it was probably along the lines of what she was already thinking: Varior is wanted by goblins? Well, fuck.

It occurred to Silver that she should have been more curious about exactly how Varior had ended up dead in the first place.

In the Kingdom of Meryn, no one messed with the goblins. They ran everything under the castle dungeons. They were crime lords and gangsters and masters of the black market. They let King Festus call himself the monarch, but everyone knew who was actually running the country. Obviously Varior had upset them somehow, and they had killed him for it. Someone must have seen them walking through town earlier, recognized Varior, and tipped them off.

Stupid, stupid, Silver thought. Why hadn't she been more careful? He had been murdered! He told her! She should have realized that if the murderers saw him walking around, distinctly not dead, there would be trouble.

She ran through the possibilities in her head. Goblins were still flooding in through the front door. Her mother–who had jumped to the floor–and Varior couldn't hold them off forever.

"Get ready to run!" she screamed at her father. She surged to her feet, knocking the table over and sending the three remaining candelabras flying onto the bed. Silver grabbed the broom that was leaning against the wall and plunged it into the fire that hissed and spat in the fireplace. When it was blazing, she lifted it to the roof and set the thatch on fire. Last, she threw one of her father's ornately carved stools through the back window.

Varior, Silver's family, and Silver herself escaped out the window as the tiny house went up in flames. Silver's landlord was not going to be pleased. She imagined trying to explain to him what had happened and gave it up with a sigh.

They made it across the field in the darkness, the only spot of light Silver's burning house, and stopped in a glade to catch their breath. Silver's father expressed himself with several well chosen profanities before asking Silver what had happened. She said something diplomatic and reassuring but not memorable and persuaded her parents to go to a nearby inn, which they did without too much grumbling.

When they were gone, Silver turned to Varior with one raised eyebrow.

"I stole the ring of Silas," he said without preamble.

"You what? No, you didn't."

"I mean, I wasn't alone, I had a team."

"Wait, wait," Silver said, putting up her hands. "I thought King Festus had the ring. Didn't he give it to his wife?"

"One of his mistresses actually, but it's more complicated than that."

"Start talking."

"Hey, *you* brought me back from the dead. I didn't ask for this."

"Yes, and now I'm demanding an explanation because I am your benefactor."

Varior rolled his eyes. "Okay, so like eight hundred years ago the goblins made this epic ring, right?"

"Right," Silver said, even though she didn't actually know anything about the ring of Silas except that it was beautiful and people kept ending up dead over it. Some said that it was a symbol of God ordaining King Festus the rightful ruler of

Meryn, but Silver was skeptical of this logic. Varior had stolen the ring, but that didn't make *him* the rightful king.

"Then shortly thereafter the ring was given to Silas, first king of Meryn, as a peace offering. But obviously, humans and goblins have never been very good at keeping the peace. Anyway Silas claimed it gave him the right to rule, a gift from God or whatever. But legend has it that the Raven King, lord of the Fae, sent a magical sickness to kill King Silas and his wives, and his daughters mysteriously disappeared. Since King Silas died without an heir, his right-hand man took over, and kept the ring. It's been in his family ever since. The kings have guarded the ring jealously, but King Festus is a byproduct of more than eight hundred years of inbreeding and he wanted to show it off. He gave it to Portia, that famous actress, who also happens to be his favorite mistress. The goblins got wind of this and they've wanted that ring back since the peace was broken, so after one of her shows, the goblins attacked Portia in her backstage dressing room and left her in a faint, sans both ring and ring finger."

"Lovely," Silver said, unconsciously grabbing her left hand in her right to make sure she still had all her fingers.

"So the King hired me and my boys to recover the ring from the goblins."

"You and your boys?"

Varior produced a business card from somewhere on his person, blew some grave dirt off of it, and handed it to Silver. It read: *Skogil Brothers, Expert Artifact Recoverers, Discreet and Fairly Priced.*

"You're thieves?" Silver fairly shouted.

"Artifact Recoverers," Varior corrected, sounding hurt.

"I don't believe this."

"Look, you don't have to worry about a thing. You just

disappear and I'll go my own way and we never have to see each other again."

"Um, hello? I set the goblins on fire! They're after me too now, and it's all your fault!"

"*My* fault?" shouted Varior, and he would have said more if a tall, dark-haired man hadn't stepped from behind a tree at that very moment and said, "I knew I'd find you with some girl, Varior."

"Excuse me, I am not just *some girl*," Silver exploded, not even caring who the other man was. It had been a long day, and she had had enough. "I brought his sorry ass back from the dead!"

"And it all would have just been easier if you'd stayed dead, little brother," the man said, grinning evilly as a cloud shifted and moonlight fell across his rugged face. "This time I guess I'll just have to kill you myself."

"Who the fuck is this, anyway?" Silver rounded on Varior.

"Run." Varior grabbed Silver's hand and dragged her toward the forest.

"We can't go in there," Silver said. "That's the Wildwood."

The trees whispered ominously, crisp ruby leaves rustling. It's just the wind, Silver thought.

"Right now it's the lesser of two evils, trust me," Varior said, tugging her across the border into the Wildwood and deeper in to the Autumn Forest. Silver was sure that at any moment a Fae lord would turn them into mice for trespassing. Humans didn't go into the Wildwood unless they never wanted to come back out.

They heard soft laughter from behind them. Then came the howling.

"Oh no," moaned Varior.

"What now?" sighed Silver.

"Remember when I asked if it was the full moon?"

"Yes?"

"Well—there's no nice way to say this—he's a werewolf."

"Perfect," muttered Silver. But at any rate, werewolves were probably better than ax-mad goblins or sinister Fae lords. In fact, she quite liked dogs.

"This way," hissed Varior and he dragged Silver into a creek which they followed up to a pool beneath a waterfall. They dove under the falls where a cave cut deep into the rock, hidden by the rushing water.

Silver held her breath, and they heard the werewolf howling and barking in the distance. Eventually the sounds receded, and they could hear only the waterfall and each other's muffled breathing.

"How did you know about this place?" Silver asked, looking around at the cave, its walls slick with the spray from the falls. "And who was that?"

"Every good thief has a few secret hideaways." Varior sighed and dropped his forehead into his hands. "Things just got a lot more complicated than I thought they were. That was my big brother."

"You've got to be fucking kidding me."

"I can't believe him. He had me killed!" Varior shook his head. "Bastard."

Silver couldn't believe that the only thing she'd been worried about that morning was not having a suitor for her family to meet. She was pretty sure something similar had happened to the heroine in one of the stories she had read, and the moral had been Be Careful What You Wish For, or something. These things never occur to a girl *before* she does something stupid. Silver sighed.

"So, what are we going to do about it?"

"Well, first, I'm going to take his head—" Varior mimed a violent gesture.

"That's not what I meant, you idiot. What are we going to do about the goblins and your psycho-ass brother?"

Varior stared at Silver with his mouth slightly open. She could see that he was completely at a loss for what to do.

Honestly, did she have to do everything herself?

"Like it or not, we're stuck together until we sort this out," Silver said, putting her hands on her hips and staring squarely into Varior's distractingly blue eyes. "First we have to figure out what happened. You and 'your boys' were trying to steal back the ring. Did you?"

Varior grinned toothily. "It was pretty epic, not to brag."

Silver rolled her eyes and said under her breath, "Of course not, who would brag about that?"

"The goblin security is really tight so I was the only one they sent into the tunnels, and the others were supposed to be helping me from the outside."

"Supposed to be?"

"Well, obviously, I got betrayed. When I made it out, there was someone waiting for me and I got stabbed in the back. That's how I died."

"You're making me wish I'd never brought you back to life," muttered Silver, rubbing her temples.

"That's it!"

"What?"

"We'll raise an army of the dead!"

Silver gaped at him. "Excuse me?"

"You're a Necromancer right?"

"A Necro—? No, I'm a barista!"

"The fact that I'm standing in front of you kind of disproves that. Come on, we've got to get back to the cemetery."

Silver didn't think this was a great idea, but she didn't have a better one. Anything that involved leaving the Wildwood sounded like a good plan to her. So they left the sanctuary behind the waterfall to sneak back into town.

"How did you do it, by the way?" Varior whispered. "Did you have to sell your soul to the Devil? Or maybe you have a great grandmother who was Fae? Were you blessed by a pixie at your christening?"

"I was cursed by a pixie once." Silver offered, ringing out her skirt as they walked.

"Cursed?"

"I caught her at the edge of the Wildwood—I grew up very near the northern border of the Autumn Forest—and she bit my finger and shouted a curse at me as she flew away. My hair has grown in purple ever since." Silver supposed she was lucky not to have caught anything with stronger magical powers, though it was pretty annoying that no dye or bleach would change her hair color.

"Hmm," said Varior thoughtfully, "then you must just have innate magical abilities."

"I really just followed the directions out of a book."

Varior looked at her, eyebrow arching.

"No, really. Today was the first time I've ever brewed anything more magical than coffee spiked with fairy wine." Silver said, "And speaking of, we'll have to go back to the apothecary to get the extra potion vials I made."

"The woman who thinks of everything."

Silver couldn't decide if Varior was flattering her or mocking her. She decided she didn't like it.

"Yeah, well, maybe I *could* bring an army back from the dead, but I certainly couldn't control one. You're proof of that."

"We'll just have to persuade them." The grin on Varior's face made Silver nervous.

"Persuade them?"

"At knifepoint, perhaps? I mean, speaking from experience, *I* don't want to go back to being dead."

The apothecary was in the middle of the evening rush, and someone was leading a rowdy drinking song. They ducked behind the bar, and Silver led Varior into the storeroom where Caton kept her herbal supplies. The extra vials of Raise-the-Dead potion were right where she had left them, beneath the stuffed raven on the table.

"Will that be enough?" asked Varior. "How much did you use on me?"

"The whole vial," Silver said.

"You may not be aware of this, but two does not constitute an army."

"Well, I wasn't planning on raising an army, now was I?" Silver snapped. "Maybe we can make some more."

She pulled the death-raising recipe from her pocket.

"Damn," she murmured, "I used all the hummingbird wings earlier."

"So that's it then? You can't make any more?"

"If you don't have all the ingredients, you can't make a magic potion."

Silver and Varior looked at each other for a moment. A long howl pierced the quiet night, and moonlight fell across the table.

"Two soldiers are better than none," Varior said.

"Let's go to the cemetery." Silver picked up Solomon Mea's spell book, thinking it might just come in handy later.

"It'll be just like a date," Varior said. Silver punched him on the shoulder.

* * *

"Do this one," Varior's voice came from a few rows away in the cemetery. "I think he was a knight."

As quickly as they could, they unearthed him. They had to use the spell Silver had found earlier to speed up the digging. The corpse turned out to be rather older than they were expecting. Silver had some doubts. Would his flesh come back once the spell was done? She performed the spell anyway, repeating the complicated words that she had used over Varior.

"What the ruddy hell are you lot doing?" the no-longer-dead Sir Rollo demanded. "How dare you drag me back to this world?"

"You were dead," said Varior.

Silver twitched her mouth in displeasure. The corpse had not regained its flesh. Sir Rollo was still a dusty skeleton in armor, except now he could talk.

"I know I was dead, you ninny! What if I like being dead? What if I like not being asked to fight in the King's bloody, pointless wars?"

"How could you possibly have found the only corpse in the whole cemetery that prefers being dead?" Silver asked Varior.

"No idea," muttered Varior. "Come on, we'd better try the other one."

When Sir Gregor rose from the dead, he tried to bring his broadsword down on Silver's head. Luckily, he hadn't been buried with it. Silver felt a little dizzy and nauseous and suddenly realized how woefully underprepared she was to be practicing magic. She had gotten quite lucky with Varior, apparently. She also wondered if there was a way to boost the spell's effectiveness for those who had been dead longer. Sir Gregor was half rotted away when he climbed out of his grave, his odor rather pungent.

Before Sir Gregor could find a different way to try to kill Silver, a troop of goblins bore down upon them. Sir Gregor, who was apparently just looking for something to hit, lay into the goblins with a fury. Sir Rollo walked over to a tree, sat down, and folded his arms, resolutely refusing to fight for Silver and Varior. He did seem to be enjoying the ruckus, however.

Despite Sir Gregor's immense size and obvious bloodlust, it was clear they were going to lose this battle. Hoping the angry corpse could hold them for a few minutes, Varior and Silver dashed back toward the apothecary.

"Okay, genius," Silver hissed, "what's plan B?"

"It's your turn."

"I have one idea," said Silver, "but it's illegal."

"Like bringing people back from the dead isn't illegal?"

"All right, fair," Silver said, although the legality of reanimation had not occurred to her. "Follow me, and stay close."

The goblins that had escaped the wrath of Sir Gregor were now following Silver and Varior. Silver was very tired of being chased.

The apothecary was still open; it was always open, partly because if you sold coffee in the morning and alcohol at night, your establishment would always be crowded, but also because the apothecary was a waypoint between worlds. A spell gone wrong had shredded the thin fabric that separated Faerie from the mortal world, leaving open windows that had allowed the first human crusaders through. Nowadays it was mostly traders and tourists that moved through the waypoints.

Silver led Varior through the bustling apothecary to a room to the left of the bar. They crashed through the door into a line of people waiting to show their exit documents to the knight from the Border Security Corps. Silver looked over her shoulder, knowing the goblins couldn't be far behind. She grabbed Varior's hand and began shoving her way to the front of the line, where she ran past the guard's booth without stopping.

"Hey!" The guard shouted, looking up from stamping a woman's passport. "You can't do that!"

But Silver and Varior were already past the guard and facing the slit in the air where the world didn't quite line up. Without hesitating, they jumped through. The world bent around them as they crossed the threshold and they arrived in a room very like the one they had just left. There was a line of people waiting to get into Faerie but Varior and Silver followed the signs directing new arrivals to customs. Yet another line stretched before them to get a stamp from the mortal government. Silver blew through this station too.

"Oi! Stop there! You've got to go through customs!" called the guard.

"We have nothing to declare!" shouted Silver before barreling through yet another door. They burst out into a rowdy pub.

"Where are we?" asked Varior.

"The East End of London," said Silver, "the High Priestess Pub."

"I didn't know there was a waypoint in your apothecary."

Silver took Varior's arm and tugged him past the crowded tables, toward the door that led out onto the street. Behind them, several border security guards had just shouldered their way into the pub, dressed in Scotland Yard uniforms.

"Stop those two!" one of them shouted.

Silver crashed into the barmaid who had been trying to deliver someone's pint. She swore loudly as the drink slid to the floor, and Silver and Varior slipped past her and out into the night.

Varior paused on the pavement, staring around. "The mortal world has so many more lights," he said. The street was lit by neon signs, advertising a multitude of places to get curry.

Laughter burbled from outdoor seating areas crowded along the street.

"They're going to catch us," snapped Silver as she dragged him down the street and into an alley. In the pub they could hear a commotion. Silver suspected the goblins had now arrived on the scene too.

They hurried down a graffiti-coated alley and out onto a brick-lined main street. The smell of spicy food wound around them. People strolled in twos and threes along the pavement. Silver and Varior attempted to blend in.

"I just realized I haven't eaten since last week," Varior said.

Silver checked her pocket watch. "You ate two hours ago at my house." She remembered her house was now burned to the ground and frowned.

"Oh, right, well, running from goblins burns a lot of calories. What do you say we get a snack?"

"We have to keep moving."

"I can walk and eat." Varior shrugged modestly.

"Boy, aren't you talented?" Silver rolled her eyes and started walking. They had to get farther away from the pub. She felt conspicuous in her dress and weskit. She had only just remembered that mortals didn't dress like that anymore. Everyone who worked in downtown Ening City dressed as though it were the Middle Ages; it was supposed to be charming for the tourists.

Silver marched them along for a couple of blocks until her stomach gave a traitorous growl, and Varior smirked, the left side of his mouth quirkeding up. He took her hand and tucked it into his elbow and led her over to a stall set up on the side of the street.

He glanced up at the sign. "My lady is peckish. Give us your finest samosas."

"Right-o," the man said, putting two samosas each in two paper bowls.

"Keep the change," Varior said magnanimously, handing over some gold coins. Varior whisked Silver off down the street.

"Oi," called the man, "I don't accept foreign coins. Oi!"

"Don't look back," Varior said to Silver, tugging her along. They turned off into another alley. Every inch of the brickwork was painted with murals and graffiti. Music leaked out of several clubs.

"Mortal art is quite interesting," Varior said, looking up at a huge painting of a stork.

"I can't believe you just stole samosas."

"I don't even know what samosas are, and besides, I didn't steal anything," Varior said, offended, "I paid good money for these."

Silver laughed, and while her mouth was open, Varior popped a samosa into it. "Mm." Silver closed her eyes. She swallowed. "Why don't we import food like this?" London had some of the best Indian food outside of India.

"We could," Varior had already finished both his samosas and was eyeing Silver's. "We could open a shop—Varior and Goldie's Imported Mortal Delicacies."

"We should keep moving," Silver said, smiling in spite of herself. She had imagined owning her own shop– maybe an apothecary or a bookshop or a bakery–but now that she had brought someone back from the dead, that seemed a little mundane. Still, it was a nice thought, selling samosas and empanadas and sushi with Varior.

"Do you know where we're going?" Varior asked as they set off again.

"My goal was 'away from the pub.' But I know there's another waypoint in London. The official tourist entrance is in

Trafalgar Square, it connects to the tourist information center by the docks in Ening City."

Silver savored her second samosa, and they walked past several trendy looking pop-up shops, two rowdy pubs, and a stumbling bachelorette party making its way to a psychedelic club.

"So," said Silver finally, "what's it like, being dead?"

Varior sighed, and his brows drew low and together over his forehead. "I knew you'd ask, sooner or later."

She shrugged. "I can't help being curious."

"There was a tunnel of light and I went toward it and I was greeted by fluffy-winged angels in togas," Varior said flatly. "Happy?"

"No," said Silver. "I refuse to believe it was so bland. You were *dead.* The greatest mystery of life. I mean you could potentially bring down the whole religious establishment with your experience." Silver had been skeptical for some time about the whole concept of religion.

"You want it to be exciting? Fine, I can do that," he was quiet for a moment as he stared into the distance. "I hurtled down a black slope into the flaming maw of Cerberus, but I gave that beast the ole one-two-three and went along into Hell yelling for the Devil to come and get me if he wanted me."

Silver looked at him. He did not speak or look back at her. His eyes glittered in the yellow streetlights. She waited, considering for the first time that dying might be something of a scarring experience. Varior hid it with bravado, but she could see that death had frightened him.

"When I escaped from the goblin tunnels," a hard edge had crept into his voice, "I was supposed to meet my brother, and I guess that I did. At any rate, someone put a knife between my shoulder blades. I never saw who did it, but I know now it must have been one of my brothers. He held me while I died.

"You're right. There was no light, there were no angels. There was no Devil and no Cerberus. It was dark and very, very cold. I walked a long time in the dark, but I never met anyone else. I don't know, maybe I would have just kept walking forever if you hadn't brought me back. Maybe I would have eventually made it to Hell." He shrugged, but it was more of a shiver.

After a moment he continued, "And then I felt a drop of water on my forehead and my eyes were opening and there you were, like sunlight after winter."

Silver bit her lip. She hadn't set out to be anyone's savior. In fact her reasons for resurrecting him had been entirely self-serving. "It wasn't water," She said, finally.

"What?"

"For the spell, I had to spit on your face."

"Oh. Gross." Varior was shaken out of his dark mood, and he gave her a half-smile.

"Hang on, brothers? Plural? You have more than one?" A werewolf brother was already more than she could handle.

"There are four of us. Samwell is the oldest and Thorley is the youngest and you've already had the pleasure of meeting Cain, the second oldest. And then of course there's me. The best."

Silver sighed, "That's more Skogil brothers than I was prepared to deal with." There was a lot, actually, about this whole situation, that she had not been prepared to deal with. "So Cain is the one who's a werewolf?"

"Yeah."

"Was he bitten recently?" Silver asked, unsure if that was a touchy topic.

"Nah, it was ages ago. We used to live on the street. Poor little urchins, learning from the street school of poverty. Not much protection. You know, same old sob story." Varior said it breezily, but Silver still felt pity for the orphaned Skogil brothers.

"And he didn't bite the rest of you?"

"He'd never hurt us on purpose. He used to lock himself up at the full moon for our protection."

"In case you've forgotten, you were killed by one of your brothers and threatened by Cain quite recently."

Varior shook his head, hurt crepteping into his eyes. "Yeah, that's what I don't understand. We were all very close. We were all each other had. So why did they kill me?"

He sounded so sad that Silver reached out, intending to give him a comforting pat—she couldn't imagine being betrayed by her brother, and being dead sounded lonely and frightening —but a large hand grabbed her by the upper arm and swung her around. She looked up into quite the ugliest face she had ever seen. A hooked nose protruded over a gash of a mouth surrounded by patchy gray facial hair. Deep-set, piggy eyes stared down at her.

Goblin, was the only thing Silver had time to think before Varior had slammed an umbrella patterned with the Union Jack down on his head.

"For England!" shouted Varior as the man crumpled.

"Where'd you get that?" Silver asked, but Varior was already handing the umbrella back to an elderly lady carrying her shopping home.

"My lady," he said with a courtly bow.

The woman shuffled quickly off, eyes wide.

"Better get out of here," Varior said, grabbing Silver's hand. "I think I see some more."

"Goblins," Silver said.

"Tell me, why do they look like super ugly humans?"

"Ask me again when we're not running for our lives."

"This way." Varior pulled her past a sign reading, 'Evening

Art Talks at the Whitechapel Gallery,' under a stone archway, and into a white-walled building that was filled with people looking at...rocks? A curator was explaining the deep emotional turmoil of the artist which was represented by the precise placement of each multicolored boulder in the haphazard-looking pile.

"Mortal art," muttered Silver who had no patience for such things. Her brother Benjamin on the other hand, loved everything about contemporary art, and prided himself on his avant-garde wood carvings. Silver just didn't get it.

Varior pulled her into the coatroom, and they peered out as the goblin-men streamed into the gallery after them. Silver could feel Varior's hot breath on the top of her head, and she was suddenly aware of how close she was to him. He smelled like pine. She was vaguely jealous that he managed to smell good after having been dead only that morning. They were still holding hands. They were in a *coatroom* together. Slowly, Silver looked up at him, and wondered when her life had turned into a romance novel.

Well, she thought, you *did* want a boyfriend.

Varior looked down at her, a curling, tawny lock falling onto his forehead, the left side of his mouth tugging up in a mischievous grin. It *was* a rather nice mouth.

He put his hand on her cheek. He bent his head, aiming for her mouth. "My fiancée," he whispered.

She was quite a lot shorter than he was. "I never said yes," she whispered back, her lips almost brushing his jaw. Her eyes closed involuntarily.

There was a crash, and they sprang apart–or as far apart as they could, given the confined space.

"We've got to go," Silver dragged Varior out of the coatroom and out of the art gallery.

Behind them, they could hear the goblins destroying probably priceless art and patrons screaming. They raced down the street, turning almost at random, hoping to throw off pursuers. They ran beneath a set of elevated railway tracks and past the Tower of London, which looked more like it belonged in their world than this one.

Panting, they came to a halt on the riverbank. Tower Bridge stretched out before them, the lights swooping up to crest the towers.

"Wow," said Varior, gaping.

"Wait, have you never been to the mortal world?" Silver asked.

"Nah, it was too expensive. Our parents died when we were young so we never had the money to eat, much less to apply for visas. That's how I got this thin and enviable physique. And there's a mountain of paperwork you have to do —I mean, if you don't just run past the guards. I can't believe that worked, by the way. You been before?"

Silver motioned for him to follow and they began walking across Tower Bridge, double decker buses and black cabs speeding past them. "Yeah, we came once when I was younger on vacation. Dad sold a singing boudoir to the Queen so we came for a few days as a treat."

Varior threw out an arm to stop her. "Wait, witches can't cross running water right?"

"I'm not a witch, and anyway I think that's an old wives' tale. I don't even think magic works here. They've got their own magic substitute."

"Explains all the..." Varior trailed off, gesturing vaguely at the cars. "Oh, now you can tell me why the goblins looked like humans when they caught up to us."

"Waypoints have concealing magic. They make non-humans humanoid until they cross back to our world."

"What happens when humans come to our world?"

"They have to hire a tour guide and I think it's pretty expensive. Some backpackers got lost in the Wildwood and were never seen again, so now there are more regulations. There're all sorts of rules about what tourists can bring back."

"Good, we probably want to keep tourists from getting into trouble with magic."

Right, thought Silver, if she'd had a tour guide, maybe she wouldn't have gotten into trouble with magic. "Sometimes they'll come and buy pixie dust packets to smuggle back. I think they call it Ecstasy here."

"Isn't that illegal?"

"Of course it is, that's why it's called smuggling." Silver glanced over her shoulder, but there were so many pedestrians and tourists on the bridge, despite the late hour, that she couldn't tell if the goblins were following them yet. "We have to find a tube station. I don't know why I didn't think of it sooner."

"A what?"

"A public carriage station. Excuse me," Silver said to a woman pushing a pram past them. "Where's the nearest tube station?"

"That'd be London Bridge, dearie." She pointed upriver to the next bridge, "Walk along the river toward the Shard and if you pass the bridge, you've gone too far."

"Shard of what?" whispered Varior.

"Thanks," said Silver, tugging Varior in the direction the woman had pointed.

Varior stared out over the muddy waters of the Thames, the hazy illumination from the skyscrapers bleeding into the water. "Their boats are different," he finally said.

"The HMS *Belfast*," said Silver, "one of their old warships." She thought about the port in Ening City and the big, three-masted ships that brought trade goods to Meryn from across the sea. How different the iron hulled warship must look painted in camouflage with canons jutting from its gun decks. Silver shivered, thinking of the firepower.

"How do you know so much about the mortal realm?" Varior demanded.

"Unlike you," Silver said, "I actually went to school. We learned all about the mortals and the crusade that resulted in the colonization of Faerie and the creation of the Kingdom of Meryn on the edge of the Wildwood."

"But," said Varior, "most humans can't use magic, or not innately anyway, so how could the mortals have had enough power to subdue the Fae? They're much stronger than we are."

"The first humans arrived in Faerie by mistake. They were part of a crusade in Jerusalem in the 1100s. When they found themselves in Faerie they tried to convert the Fae to Christianity, and when that didn't work, they started cutting down the Wildwood—you know, because humans can barely look at a tree without wanting to cut it down." Silver rolled her eyes. "Anyway, this made the Fae very angry, understandably, but it also weakened them because they're tied to the spirits of the forest, who were dying with the trees. The humans were all wearing iron armor which made them immune to spells, and they sowed little bits of iron along the borders they cut in the Wildwood, so the trees could never grow back and the Fae could no longer cross the border. So the Fae were forced to retreat into the remaining forest, and Silas declared himself the king and built Ening City as a trading port on the coast. Now we humans control the deforested strip of land between the ocean and the Wildwood."

"Fascinating," said Varior. "Who knew what I was missing in school?" He almost sounded wistful.

"School was pretty boring, honestly." Silver hurried to say. "What were you doing when you weren't wasting your time in the classroom as a boy?"

"Oh, we were very enterprising youths, we had to be, if we wanted to eat. My brothers and I...acquired many rare and magical artifacts from the people of Ening City and sold them to the goblins. Then we volunteered our services to people who had recently and tragically misplaced rare and magical artifacts to recover them, for a fee, of course."

"Of course you did. Come on, the station is this way."

They followed the tube signs, a red circle with a blue line through it, to the station. The gleaming, glass-plated skyscraper nicknamed the Shard rose sharply over the station. People were streameding to and fro in a great hurry.

"Damn," whispered Silver, watching as people scanned a blue card and pushed through the turnstile. She didn't have any mortal money. She looked around wildly, hoping help would magically appear.

Her eyes fell on a black cat that was washing itself languidly by the entrance. As if sensing her gaze, he raised his head, meeting her eyes with one bulbous yellow one. His right eye was missing and his right ear was in tatters from some long ago street fight.

"Growltiger?" murmured Silver. If Caton's cat was here it couldn't be a coincidence.

He stretched and yawned and walked off toward a gate labeled 'Emergency Exit, do not enter.'

Sure she was going mad, Silver followed the cat. A black cat, she thought, this was just like a fairytale. She hated being a cliché.

"I don't think we can go in that way," said Varior when Silver pushed through the gate.

"And suddenly you're a stickler for the rules?" Silver snapped.

Varior put up his hands. "Whatever. You're in charge, witch-lady."

"I'm not a witch!" Silver said, louder than she'd intended.

They rode down the escalator, which was endlessly exciting for Varior, and followed the cat past a pair of musicians singing "Wonderwall."

The tattered cat sprang lightly onto the incoming train and Silver and Varior followed, pressing past peeved Londoners.

"Are we following that cat?" hissed Varior.

"Do you have a better idea?" Silver whispered defensively.

"Not dying in some strange underground contraption sounds better than this."

"Just think of it as a long carriage pulled by really fast horses."

A cool female voice overhead reminded them to mind the gap between the train and the platform, and the doors slid shut. The train lurched forward, and Varior fell against Silver. She caught a whiff of pine again as she propped him back up to standing, and she thought of his face close to hers in the darkness of the coatroom, his jaw brushing her lips. He clutched at the overhead handles and gazed wide-eyed out the windows into the rushing blackness.

"Take a deep breath," Silver murmured, not sure if she was talking to Varior or herself. "It's going to be all right."

The cat had gone back to licking his hindquarters in the corner, and Silver questioned every instinct she'd had to follow him.

"This train terminates at Edgware," said the female voice. "This station is Angel."

"We'll change at King's Cross for the Piccadilly Line," Silver said, more for her own benefit than Varior's. She traced the Piccadilly Line to Leicester Square on the map posted by the doors. "Then we can walk to the Trafalgar Square waypoint."

The train stopped and the doors hissed open. Silver and

Varior pressed themselves back out of the way to let passengers on and off.

"Varior!" cried a voice as the doors shut again.

Oh no, thought Silver.

"It's good to see you!" a young man with wire rimmed glasses said, shouldering his way through the other passengers. He had the same strong jawline and tawny hair as Varior.

"Thorley," said Varior, balling his fists. "I wish I could say the same about you."

"You wound me," said Thorley clutching his chest, "you really do. And you should know, I was against betraying you, but Sam was paid a lot of money by Miss Portia to make sure you didn't come back. You know the King is sort of a jealous type."

Silver stared at Varior, who avoided her look. "You told me that the goblins stole the ring from her."

"Um. Did I?"

"You slept with her, didn't you, and stole her ring and sold it to the goblins? You lied to me. Ugh, I can't believe I believed you," Silver spat. She didn't understand why she was so angry. Other passengers were beginning to stare in a disgruntled and disapproving way. No one did disgruntled better than Londoners.

"Silver, don't—" Varior reached for her arm, but before either of them knew what was happening, the train had stopped again and Thorley had pulled him out of the train and onto the busy Kings Cross platform.

"Varior!" Silver cried, starting after them, but then the black cat was under her feet and she was falling. "Damn you," she breathed. The cat looked at her and blinked his one yellow eye. The doors slid closed.

"Where are you taking me?"

The cat yawned.

At the Hampstead stop, the cat exited the train, tail held up like a tour guide's flag. Silver followed. She thought about Varior in the hands of his murderous brother and almost turned around to go back into the station. She could get on a southbound train. She could go back to King's Cross to look for him. She sighed. She wouldn't be able to find them. Thorley was probably headed to the Trafalgar Square waypoint, and they would be long gone by the time she got back there.

Sensing she wasn't following, Growltiger stopped and looked back at her. He meowed reproachfully.

"All right. You win. I'll just follow some cat that looks like it's been hit by a bus into the dark. That sounds like a great idea."

Out of the station and down the street she followed the bobbing tail. The cat really was a bit the worse for wear.

"Growltiger," she said, remembering the poem Caton had taken the name from, "the Terror of the Thames."

The cat's tail twitched but he did not look back.

They came to a wide green space, folding open in the middle of the city. Growltiger bounded into the grass. They wended their way along, past joggers and walkers and children and dogs that tried to bark at Growltiger but retreated, tails between their legs at his hiss. They took overgrown paths, and the other evening visitors thinned out. The sounds of the city receded, and all Silver could hear was her own heavy breathing and the calling of the birds. They walked for what seemed like hours, the cat always just at the edge of her vision, almost leaving her behind.

At last, they came to a wide open clearing with a very large tree growing at the center of it. Looking up, Silver wondered where the stars were, but maybe, she thought, London's bright lights obscured them. There was no one else around. The cat walked up to the trunk and sat down before it, facing Silver. He looked so damn smug, she wanted to throttle him.

"So?" she asked, "What now? You've brought me to this tree in the middle of fucking nowhere, what's your plan?"

Growltiger hopped to his feet and, with a flick of his black tail, he disappeared behind the tree.

"You're not getting away that easy," Silver muttered, starting after the cat.

She moved toward the trunk of the tree, over thick roots that made the ground uneven. Her foot caught under a root and, for the second time since meeting that damned cat, she was falling...into snow?

Silver lifted her head; snowflakes were falling all around her and she was sunk in a snowdrift. She scrambled up. The large tree was still beside her, but now, instead of being somewhere in the middle of Hampstead Heath, she was surrounded by a glittering ice forest. Icicles hung from leafless branches and pine trees were dusted with snow, like powdered sugar.

Oh no, thought Silver. The tree must be a waypoint, and she had just stumbled into the Winter Forest, the territory of the Raven King.

Silver whirled and ran back past the tree, hoping to end up in London again, but somehow, the waypoint was closed.

"You won't be able to go that way," rasped a voice, and she spun again.

"You." It was Growltiger.

If cats could grin, this one did, revealing his sharp teeth. "Me," he said.

"You talk now."

"How insightful it is," Growltiger said scornfully. "Come this way. The King is waiting."

"The King! The Raven King?"

The cat did not deign to answer.

Silver looked around for another way to go, but again, frustratingly, the cat was her only option. She didn't want to freeze to death lost in the Wildwood.

Muttering swear words under her breath, Silver tramped through the snow after Growltiger. The sun was just coming up, the gray, cloud-filled sky gradually lightening. She thought back to all the stories she had heard about the Wildwood and the Fae who lived there. She had never been so deep into the Wildwood. She reviewed rules for staying alive in their territory:

1. Do not eat or drink Fae food or wine. It was well known that Fae fare could trap humans in the Wildwood, addicting them to the heady magic.
2. Do not anger the Fae. Everyone knew how unpredictable the Fae were. Beguiling hosts one moment, then cursing them you to be a squirrel until true love's kiss the next. She had even heard the Spring Court kept human slaves. She shivered.
3. Try to find a way to get home.

Holding a mental map in her head, Silver knew she was almost as far from home as it was possible to be and not be in the ocean. She would have to walk for miles through the Winter Wood and over the Dwarves' mountains and then all the way through the Autumn Forest before she'd be back in Meryn. All the while trying not to get eaten by a wyvern or enchanted by a Fae lord or imprisoned in a tree by a wood nymph. She signed. Perhaps there were more waypoints, or maybe there was a way to reopen the one she had come through in Hampstead Heath.

"Why didn't you speak to me before?" Silver called,

fighting her way through the snow while the cat stepped lightly over the drifts.

"I am a cat. We do as we please."

"Ha. I bet you can't talk in the mortal world. Magic doesn't work there."

Growltiger flicked his tail dismissively. "It is not magic. Cats are cats."

This was not an answer, but that was typical of cats, Silver supposed.

"What's with this waypoint? I thought all the waypoints were monitored by the Border Security Corps."

"This is the Raven King's own personal waypoint."

"He has his own waypoint? Why? He can't even go to the moral world. There's too much iron."

The cat did not respond.

Silver's boots and skirts were soaked through and she was feeling pretty miffed about being fetched by a cat just to go meet some man. Who did this Raven King think he was anyway? Entitled asshole. Men were the same in every species. If he wanted to see her so badly, why didn't he just come to her instead of making her trek through this frozen wasteland? She thought about all the things she would say to him when she finally got there. She'd give him a piece of her mind. She'd—but then she remembered her second rule for surviving the Wildwood: Do not anger the Fae.

She sighed. How many humans had wandered into the Wildwood never to come out again? Bedtime stories were full of maidens trapped among the Fae. She didn't want to end up one of them.

She could remember her mother's voice falling into the cadence of a bedtime story. *Once upon a time, the King had twelve daughters, each more beautiful and accomplished than the last. They were demure and pious and loved nothing more than dancing.*

Silver rolled her eyes, remembering the familiar words. The story had been one of her favorites when she was younger, but now she felt the princesses were a little lackluster. Demure and pious? Come on.

The King loved his daughters very much, but he desired a male heir, for he feared what would become of his young kingdom without a son to carry on his name.

Silver was skeptical about how much the King had loved his daughters.

So the King called upon the Raven King to ask for a spell. The Raven King obliged and charmed the King's favorite wife, guaranteeing that her next child would be a boy. In return the Raven King took all twelve of the King's daughters deep into the Wildwood. But a sneaking sickness took the King and his wives and his unborn heir. A retribution from God for asking for magical help.

Silver's mother had always told the story this way, but Silver had also heard versions in which it was the Raven King who had sent the sickness, because a Fae would never give you quite what you asked for.

It is said the twelve princesses have remained young through the centuries, dancing in the glittering Fae courts night after night. Many a young girl, charmed by this notion, has wandered into the Wildwood, never to be seen again.

"They are all dancing with the Raven King?" Silver remembered once asking her mother as a little girl.

"Look at me, Silver," her mother had said seriously. "The Wildwood is not sparkling parties and immortality. It is hedonism and pretty masks that hide the faces of beasts. It will devour you."

The ice palace rose abruptly before Silver and Growltiger,

stabbing at the gray sky with sharpened spires. Silver pushed snow-dampened hair out of her eyes and gazed up at the palace. The spires reminded Silver of teeth, and she thought again of being devoured by the Wildwood.

"This way," said Growltiger, unnecessarily.

They climbed the wide palace stairs past silent Fae guards in silver uniforms. All the white and gray made Silver feel like she'd been dropped into a lithograph illustration from her old fairytale book. The guards ignored Silver's curious glances, staring straight ahead into the falling snow, their fur collars turned up. Silver wondered if it was always snowing here.

The frosted doors swung silently open and they stepped over the threshold into the Raven King's castle.

Silver was freezing.

The cat led her down a dizzying labyrinth of glittering hallways and then suddenly, they were in an open, rectangular courtyard. A double row of silvered, skeletal trees lined a long stone walkway, at the end of which was a large black throne. Someone was sitting in it. Well, perhaps lounging was a better word.

The Raven King—she supposed he must be the Raven King—was slouched sideways in his throne, one leg thrown over the arm of his chair. His dark head was down, resting on his chest as though he was sleeping. He was shaped like a human, but Silver was most struck by the enormous black raven wings that spread from his shoulders and lay splayed, cascading over the arms of his throne and reaching all the way to the ground. A circlet of ice was wound into his hair.

Silver gaped at him. No storybook illustration had ever done him justice.

As they approached, he raised his head and opened his eyes, looking straight into Silver's with his piercing, icy stare. His inky hair was gilded in frost. It was overlong and framed a thin, sharp face. A very handsome face, but he was cold, where Varior was warm.

The Raven King straightened up a bit, though he didn't remove his leg from the arm of his throne.

"Thank you, my friend," he said to the cat. His voice was soft, but even the snowflakes listened as he spoke.

Silver's breath caught. The Raven King looked at Silver for a long moment, and she felt suddenly naked. She crossed her arms over her chest, but stared resolutely back.

"I thought," he said finally, "that you'd be taller."

Silver's mouth dropped open. She forgot all her rules.

"Well, I thought you'd be older." Silver added, "And uglier," even though she'd never imagined him ugly.

"I am old," he said.

"You've aged well," Silver said tartly. He looked no more than twenty years old, no older than she was.

He laughed a bit at that. "I didn't bring you here to fish for compliments."

"No? Well, before you tell me the real reason, I am fucking freezing. Got any blankets in this miserable ice box?"

The Raven King stood up...and up. He was so tall that Silver almost took a step back. He shook out his wings a bit and gave them one big flap. A hot wind swept the courtyard and everything rippled. When everything had solidified again, Silver saw that the icy courtyard had reformed itself into a cozy parlor with a huge crackling fire, surrounded by red velvet, cushioned armchairs. Her clothes had also been mercifully dried. She hurried over to the enormous fireplace and put her hands out to it, wiggling the feeling back into her fingers.

Growltiger stretched, curled up on a chair close to the fire, and promptly went to sleep.

The Raven King tried to fold his enormous wings but gave it up when he was unable to sit down. Silver snickered. The

Raven King scowled and shook out his wings again, letting them splay out on either side of an armchair as he sat.

"So, why am I here?" Silver asked.

The Raven King sighed. "Do you really need to be told? I thought you were clever."

"What business is that of yours? Why would you care if I was clever?"

"Black magic is my business. I'd rather idiots didn't practice it. You're my problem."

"Problem?" Silver shouted, "I was just minding my own business!"

The Raven King steepled his fingers. "Bringing people back from the dead is decidedly *not* minding one's own business."

"What if dead people are my business? Wait, that sounded wrong." Silver sank into an armchair, then sprang up again as she had tried to sit on Growltiger, who hissed at her. She chose a divan instead. She wondered if she should lounge on it. Fine ladies never sat on divans. They lounged.

"Reanimation is no small magic. How long have you been training?"

"Training? I just followed the directions out of a spell book."

"You can't expect me to believe the first time you ever did big magic was yesterday."

"I don't care if you believe it. It's the truth." Silver crossed her arms.

"No human can just raise the dead on their first attempt," the Raven King said as he rolled his eyes skyward. "Stop trying to impress me."

"Why you puffed-up, self-centered—" Silver stopped, remembering whom she was talking to.

The Raven King raised a long, thin eyebrow—everything about him was long and thin. "Care to finish that sentence?"

"I only meant that my motives were innocent, and I really am telling the truth. Sir," she threw in for good measure. She folded her hands in her lap and looked primly at the Raven King.

"Well, it will be easy enough to check," the Raven King waved his hand at a samovar resting on a round wooden table between them. "Have some tea."

Silver looked at it skeptically. "You've put something in that, haven't you."

"Obviously. It's just a truth potion. If you're telling the truth as you say, you have nothing to fear."

"It won't trap me here forever if I drink it?" Silver asked, remembering her first rule.

"Gods, no, I don't want to deal with you that long."

Silver scowled. "There's no need to be rude."

She was telling the truth, of course, but she still didn't want to drink his stupid truth potion. She poured herself a cup of tea. It smelled strongly of cinnamon and cloves. It smelled lovely, but she was determined not to enjoy it. She sipped at it. The Raven King glared at her. She took a larger gulp.

"Who sent you to ruin my plans?"

Silver choked on her tea. "Your plans? No one! I don't know anything about that." She drank some more tea, to show him it wasn't a lie.

"Why did you bring him back from the dead then?"

Despite what she had said, Silver didn't want the Raven King to think she was stupid. She decided to try a lie, partly just to see what would happen. "He's my boyfriend, and after he died the grief was killing me," but blue smoke billowed from her mouth as she said the words. She coughed. "Sorry, just curious. I needed a suitor for my family to meet."

"A suitor?"

"Yeah, they're always nagging me about it."

"And so you brought someone back from the dead?"

"It all sounds so drastic when you say it like that, but I promise it seemed reasonable at the time."

The Raven King sighed. "You mean it was by *accident* that you ruined everything?"

"Ruined what?" Silver drank the last of the tea and put the cup and saucer down beside the samovar. The tea really had been very good.

"Do you have any idea what you've done?" The Raven King rubbed his temples.

"I think I've made it pretty clear that I don't," Silver said irritably. "It's probably the crown," she added, "that's giving you headaches. It looks heavy."

The Raven King glared at her. "*You* are giving me a headache."

"You're *both* giving me a headache," Growltiger said without opening his eye.

The Raven King blew out another breath, and she thought he was probably counting to ten in his head to keep from exploding. "I've been considering schemes for stealing my name back for nearly seven hundred and fifty years and then you and those thieves just come waltzing in—"

"Your name?"

"That human," he said the word like one might say 'vaginal discharge,' "stole my true name and put it in that stupid ring."

"Your name is in the ring of Silas?"

"And it's your fault that it's still there," the Raven King growled.

Silver thought this was a bit unfair. How was she supposed to know about his big plans? And besides, she hadn't known that Varior had stolen the ring or what the ring contained.

"Necromancy is serious magic," the Raven King said finally. "Your parents aren't sorcerers?"

"My father carves magical furniture but it's really more about the wood than him."

"And your mother?"

"She used to be a boxing champion," Silver said doubtfully, not sure what he wanted her to say. "She runs a tavern now."

The Raven King shook his head. "Isn't there anything unusual about you?"

This rather offended Silver. "There's plenty of unusual things about me. I can make the best fucking caramel dragon bane macchiato in Ening City. I'm practically engaged to marry someone I brought back from the dead. I was cursed by a pixie once."

"Hmm," the Raven King said. "A pixie curse, that could be it. What was the curse?"

"Er. She turned my hair purple."

"Ugh, forget it. I'll just scry it."

Silver raised her eyebrows. "That sounds interesting. Will you need a bowl of water?"

"Not that I need to explain it to you, but I'm looking for information about your past so I'll use your eyes."

"My eyes?"

"Any reflective surface can be used for scrying." The Raven King shifted his armchair so that he satwas sitting directly across from Silver.

She sat up straighter.

"Hold still and don't blink." He reached out and tipped her chin up a little so she was looking into his narrow, black eyes. His brows drew down over his forehead. His lips moved as he murmured the words of a spell. His skin was ivory and very smooth; she made a mental note to ask him about his moisturizer later. His features were sharp and chiseled, like they had been carved from ice, except for his lips, which were almost effeminate.

She gazed into his eyes, hers unfocusing. His eyes expanded in her view, seeming to absorb everything. She realized that their faces were very close together. She thought of Varior pressed up against her in the coatroom. She thought of the way he smelled and how he had looked when he had smashed that goblin over the head with an umbrella. She thought about the panicked look on his face when Thorley had yanked him off the train.

Abruptly, she refocused her eyes, and the Raven King's face came back into focus. He looked, she suddenly realized, like a poster she had seen in the tube station in London. The poster had been for a K-pop band that was touring in Europe. He was still frowning and muttering. Silver suddenly realized how ridiculous they must look, sitting pretty much nose to nose starting at each other while he muttered nonsense words.

She burst out laughing, breaking their eye contact.

The Raven King sat back in disgust. "You ruined the spell."

"I'm sorry," Silver giggled, her hand over her mouth to keep in stray and unladylike snorts. "What did you see?"

"Your great-great-grandmother mated with a winter Fae, so some Fae blood has been passed down on your mother's side. An affinity for death magic."

"Ew, don't say mated. Who was the Fae?" Silver knew that Fae from the different Fae courts had different affinities for magic, although she hadn't realized that death magic was associated with the Winter Forest.

"Well, if you hadn't distracted me, maybe I would have seen more. He was from the Winter Court," The Raven King ground his teeth. "I wonder who it was. I could kill him."

"Wait, he's still alive?"

"Presumably. Fae are immortal unless killed deliberately."

"Oh, weird. I can't believe my great-great-grandfather might still be alive."

"He must be one of my more powerful spellcasters, or you could not still have the ability to do magic with blood so diluted."

"Why couldn't my mother or my grandmother do magic then?"

"It can skip generations, or perhaps they never felt the need to raise a fake boyfriend from the dead," the Raven King said bitingly.

Silver decided to change the subject. "Well, congratulations, now you know why I can do magic. Who cares?"

"If you had been taught to use magic properly and hadn't just discovered your power, we wouldn't be in this mess."

"Why do you care? It's my mess!"

"You don't get it. Magic has a price and reanimation is very expensive."

Silver bit her lip. "What do you mean, expensive?" She hadn't given up anything to perform the spells she'd done so far.

"A life for a life. So you have a debt to pay for your suitor's life."

Her heart sank. "And the others," she mumbled.

"Excuse me?"

"The others," she said louder. "I've used the spell three times."

The Raven King rubbed his eyes. "Ha haha," he deadpanned. "That's hilarious."

"I wish I was joking," Silver said.

"You'll have to pay. Or send them back. Those are your only options."

Silver shook her head mutely, thinking of Varior, of how very alive he was.

"I'll deal with you later. I have to go figure out how to fix all this." The Raven King stood up in a storm of feathers and flapped his wings again.

When the room resolidified, Silver was alone in a bedroom with a four-poster bed. She fell onto it, not knowing what else to do.

Silver wished she could talk to Varior. She pulled out Solomon Mea's spell book and flipped to the contents. Maybe there would be a way to contact him from here. Her finger paused on a scrying spell. That would let her see him but not speak to him. Her eyes scanned the guest room that the Raven King had banished her to. There was an ornate bookcase in a corner with another cushy armchair and a crackling fireplace. Feeling as though there was no way black magic spell books could be housed in such a cozy environment, Silver went to investigate anyway.

The books were all huge leather-bound tomes stamped in gold, and they did in fact look like spell books, as though the Raven King was showing off just how wealthy and learned he was. Silver rolled her eyes. Male egos. She began pulling books off the shelves. *Midnight Rituals for Devil Worshipers* read one gilt cover; Silver put that one back. *Charming Princes into Animals: It's for Their Own Good, Really!* Silver sincerely doubted the princes in question would agree, but maybe that was the point. *Alchemy for Dummies* sat beside *Charms for the Charmless: How to Get Her to Love You*; Silver almost threw that one straight in the fire, although she supposed she might have found that particular volume helpful yesterday. Was it only yesterday? She sighed.

Behind *Incantations to Influence the Weather*, Silver saw a small volume topple over, as though someone had tried to hide it in the back. She pulled it out. *Practical Necromancy for Beginners* read the no-nonsense lettering painted on the black linen cover. Well, that looked perfect; Silver was a little surprised at her good fortune. The book was just the right size for Silver's hands; the others had all been enormous. She took it over to the bed and flopped down on her stomach, paging through the book. The book fell open at a passage describing the basics, as though it knew exactly what level she was at.

The Necromancer is a witch who might, depending on her purpose, commune with the dead or reanimate corpses. Spells to reanimate the dead vary widely in skill level and efficacy. It is generally agreed that if one is trying to achieve a life-like state, one should find a corpse that is quite recently dead. As decay increases, so efficacy decreases. A payment to Death will be required.

Silver paused. That was what the Raven King had said too, that a "payment to Death" would be required. She wondered what that meant. The Raven King seemed to think it would be a life for a life, but perhaps the book would give her more options.

More commonly, Necromancers will recall spirits for information about the afterlife, about the past, or to act as a Spirit Guide through the Netherrealms. The Necromancer will have strong psychological connections with her subjects.

That sounded promising. Maybe she could contact Varior via this strong psychological connection they were supposed to share. Silver turned the page. The book didn't say anything about having to pay a price of some kind to speak to her 'subjects,' so Silver figured it was safe to try. Besides, the Raven King had done a bunch of magic around her earlier, and he hadn't appeared to give up anything.

Silver set about following the spell's instructions. It looked similar to the scrying spell in Solomon Mea's book. She went over to a desk that sat in front of a window that looked out onto the endless frozen forest. There was a silver bowl and a pitcher, a crystal, and a number of candles on the desk. She wondered if they had been there all along or if they had only arrived because she needed them.

She filled the bowl with water from the pitcher. She lit two of the candles and put one on either side of the bowl. She sat down at the desk and looked back at the book. Next she was supposed to chant Varior's name nine times and then draw a pentacle in the water with the crystal before dropping it into the bowl. Then she was supposed to open her mind. After that the book became rather vague but she gathered that it would be obvious from there.

Following the directions, Silver chanted Varior's name, drew the pentacle and put the crystal in the water, feeling a little silly as she did so. She closed her eyes and held her arms out palms up, throwing her head back, not because the book had told her to but because she had a mental image of witches summoning spirits in this pose. She tried not to think of anything. After a moment, she lowered her arms and looked into the bowl.

"Silver? What are you doing? Are you in my head?" Varior was tied to a chair in the middle of a barren room. Silver was looking down on him. He looked all around, straining to see behind the chair. "Where are you?"

"It worked," breathed Silver and she almost lost her concentration.

"Something worked, that's for sure," said Varior, still looking for her.

"I'm not there. I'm in the Winter Palace."

"Like the Raven King's palace?"

"Yeah."

"And you're still alive?" Varior stopped looking around. "This is weird, I don't know where to look."

"I can see you from above," Silver offered. "Yes, I'm alive for the moment, and you appear to be, too."

Varior squinted at the ceiling where she assumed there was a light source. "My brothers aren't going to kill me yet. I haven't told them where the ring is."

"You know where the ring is?"

"I hid it before I came out of the tunnels. Had a bad feeling. Justified, it now transpires." Varior tried to shrug, but his arms were bound too tightly.

"You are brilliant," Silver said.

"I am?" Varior said, "I mean, yes, I am."

"Tell me where it is."

"Are you going to tell the Raven King?" Varior asked suspiciously.

"Yes, and then I'll save us all." Silver said, "You have no idea the real value of that ring."

Varior bit his lip.

"Do you trust me?" Silver asked. She didn't know if he should trust her, she didn't know if she was worthy of it. She didn't know if she could keep him alive. But she really did need him to tell her.

"Can you look in my head? I can show you the map."

"I'll give it a try. Hopefully it won't hurt."

"Hurt?" Varior protested, but Silver had already taken a deep breath and focused on his mind.

A flood of images and memories crashed into her. Everything was moving so fast she couldn't tell what was going on. She focused on the ring and she was presented with a string of memories, seeing them through Varior's eyes. A man who could only have been Varior's oldest brother was telling the rest of the brothers about the King's ring that had come into the actress Portia's possession. Then Varior was kissing the actress's hand and she was giggling, not noticing as he slipped the ring off her finger. Silver hurried past some more images set in the actress's dressing room; she really didn't need to see that. She slowed down to watch through Varior's eyes from the shadows as Thorley sold the ring to a goblin warlord, and then the King was asking the Skogil brothers for their assistance in recovering an old family heirloom. Varior snuck into the goblin tunnels. She tried to memorize his path through the twisting, labyrinthine passages beneath Ening City. He fought past a few bodyguards and then decapitated the warlord. He took the ring and stowed it in his pocket. He made his way back through the tunnels toward the surface.

Silver-in-Varior looked around himself for foes before hiding the ring behind a loose brick in a spiral staircase. He exited the labyrinth and came up into the moonlight. The pain was sharp and immediate as Silver felt a knife slipping into Varior's back. The memory of it took Silver's breath away. A little blood bubbled from Varior's mouth, and Varior was eased onto the ground, propped against his attacker's chest. He tried to turn his head, but he couldn't. Varior's vision wavered and darkened. The images stopped and Silver pulled back a bit out of Varior's memories.

"Silver," said Varior, "don't hate me. I know I lied to you and I—I—about Portia—I'm sorry—"

"Are you sorry because you think I'm jealous, or are you sorry because you used a vulnerable woman to steal her ring?" Silver wondered if she was jealous.

"I...both?"

The door crashed open and two of Varior's brothers backed in. Thorley rushed to untie Varior as Sam fought a group of goblins.

"Surrender!" cried the goblin who appeared to be in charge. He was by far the ugliest and the slimiest. The goblins had cornered the three brothers in the room. "We already have the wolf. Come quietly now."

Silver suddenly felt dizzy, and the scene in the bowl rippled and vanished. She had a brief realization that the digging spell had made her a little dizzy and tired both times she had used it. Perhaps that's what the Raven King meant about the price of magic. She pitched forward against the desk, and everything went dark.

* * *

"You idiot." Blearily, Silver could see the Raven King's thin face, swimming before her. She felt him gather her into his arms. He carried her over to the bed. "That spell could have killed you," he growled. "Didn't you listen to what I said about the price of magic?"

"You explain things poorly," Silver murmured. "How was I s'posed to know what would happen? Nothing happened to you when you used magic to transport us."

The Raven King flared his nostrils angrily. "I have more practice than you."

"I found your name." Silver's eyes were so heavy she couldn't keep them open.

"Where?" he asked, squeezing and shaking her shoulder. "Where is it?" But she had fallen asleep.

* * *

When Silver came to, the Raven King was sitting in a chair at her bedside, staring intently at her.

"Ah," Silver said, starting and sitting up straight. "You creep, have you been here the whole time?" She paused, "How long have I been asleep?"

"About sixteen hours," the Raven King said drily.

Silver glanced out the window and guessed that it must be morning again. She suddenly remembered Varior and the attacking goblins. "We've got to help Varior!"

"No, we've got to get my name. You said you knew where it was."

Silver folded her hands on her lap. "I do. But what makes you think I will tell you?"

The Raven King's face twisted into a scowl.

"I think," Silver said primly, "that I would like to know exactly how your name got locked in a ring and what your plans were and how I got mixed up in all of them."

"I could just force you to tell me by magic."

"You could," she agreed. "But I can leave the Wildwood, and you cannot."

The Raven King ground his teeth. "You're insufferable."

"I know."

"That upstart human—"

"You mean King Silas?" asked Silver.

The Raven King sneered. "He was no king. He and his crusaders came here by accident. Divine providence he called it. We met the humans cordially, we are not an overly warlike people, but they cut the trees for their fires and forts, and they sowed iron into the soil. They pushed us out of our coastal lands and their iron kept us from fighting back. But Silas agreed to leave us alone if I gave him my true name. He imprisoned it in that ring, and I was at his beck and call, like a dog, like a slave."

"So you cursed him and his family when he asked for help having a son," Silver said. Honestly she couldn't blame him. Silas didn't sound like a particularly nice guy.

The Raven King was taken aback. "No. I could do no such

thing. The terms of the binding prevented my causing direct harm to the royal family."

Silver frowned. "But when the King and his wives and the unborn heir died of a mysterious sickness, it was said that you had done it."

"And I wonder who started that rumor. The next human to seize power, that two-faced ancestor of King Festus, I'll wager."

Silver's eyes widened, "You think it was murder?"

"You humans are petty like that. But thankfully, the fact that my name was in the ring was a secret that Silas never shared. Unfortunately I could still not directly harm the holder of the ring. So I sent my servant Caton—"

"Caton? Wait, my Caton? The apothecary?"

"She's not yours, she's mine. You clearly remember that I charmed the wife of Silas so she would have a son. You remember what I received in return?"

"Uh, yes? Silas's twelve daughters," said Silver, not sure where this was going.

"They lived in the Wildwood under an enchantment, spending their nights dancing in the Summer Court."

"Under your enchantment?"

The Raven King waved a hand. "Oh, it hardly matters anymore. It was just a little revenge. With my name gone, I couldn't do much more than hoodwink humans, but the King was forever beyond my grasp. Princes tried to save them, but most of them were turned into mice. The princesses stayed in Summer Court to serve the Erl King. He has a habit of turning maidens into birds."

"Yeah, he sounds like a charmer," Silver muttered darkly.

The Raven King shrugged unconcernedly. "I suppose this wasn't preferable to them, and two of the princesses, the oldest and the youngest, escaped his court and came to me, asking for release. I agreed on the condition that they help me recover my name. So I set Caton, the youngest, up as an apothecary and I sent my werecat to oversee her as she learned some basic magic."

"Growltiger?"

"The naming of cats is a tricky business."

"It seems to me that the naming of anything is tricky business. Speaking of, what do your friends call you? I'm just wondering because 'The Raven King' is kind of a mouthful. Do people really say, 'Oh hello, Raven King, how are you?'"

The Raven King stared at her. "I also answer to My Liege and Your Excellency and Oh Dark One."

"Oh," said Silver, unsure if he was joking. She didn't know if he knew how to joke. "Well, anyway, RK, tell me more about Caton."

Silver wondered for a moment if she was about to be blasted into tiny particles, but the Raven King let the nickname pass.

"I put her older sister Portia, the prettiest, in the path of the King and she seduced him, with help from cantrips from Caton. Caton has been his personal herbalist for a while so she was in a position to use her persuasion draft to get him to give the ring to Portia. Then they were to bring it back to me whereupon I would be restored to my power and then I would lift their enchantment and that of their sisters."

"Wait, you made Portia prostitute herself to get her freedom?"

The Raven King raised his eyebrows. "I taught Caton magic. They could make the King believe whatever they wanted. Portia didn't have to do anything that offended her sensibilities."

Silver humphed. Now Caton's spell book made sense, she thought.

"And it all would have worked perfectly if you and those idiots hadn't come along and fucked everything up."

"They were just trying to make a living," Silver said diplomatically.

"They're thieves," said the Raven King.

Silver shrugged. "So here's what I propose: you send me back to Ening City, I'll meet up with Caton and Portia and we'll get your name back and save the Skogil brothers, who have been kidnapped by goblins if I'm not mistaken."

"How do I know you won't just keep my name and try to control me?"

"How do I know that you won't try to take revenge on the human kingdom once you have your powers back?" Silver asked. "I mean personally, if a conquering army of humans had come to my kingdom, stolen my name and imprisoned me and all my subjects, I'd be pretty pissed off. But, you understand, I still can't have you destroying the entire human kingdom as much as you might be justified."

The Raven King considered her for a long moment. "I guess we will just have to trust each other."

"And when I give your name back, I'd also like you to teach me magic properly and help me find a way to save Varior. Agreed?"

The Raven King nodded once, his face carefully blank. "Your first lesson is not to overextend your limits. I trust you've learned that one? If you try a spell too difficult, it can exhaust you, and if you're not careful, it could kill you."

"But why didn't raising the dead take away my energy?"

"The rules of nature demand that you replace what you take. If you take or use energy for a spell, your own energy must replace it. But reanimation is different. It is a debt you must pay to Death, a life for a life, but you cannot give up yours."

Silver bit her lip. Was she willing to kill someone to save Varior?

"Get ready," the Raven King said, standing. "You must leave immediately for the city."

* * *

"No. No, definitely not," Silver said half an hour later. "Can't you just open up a waypoint to London and then I can go back to the pub or Trafalgar Square and then through to Ening city?"

Silver and the Raven King stood on the steps of the ice palace, snow falling silently around them. The silent Fae guards still flanked the stairs. Silver glanced around at them. Could one of them be her great-great-grandfather?

"This will be faster," the Raven King argued, "and I can't just open up waypoints. I only have the one. Do you want to walk all the way back through the forest?"

"I'd prefer it to this," Silver said under her breath. "What about Growltiger?"

"He'll meet you there. Cats have their own ways. Come here," said the Raven King, opening his arms and his wings at the same time.

Silver stared at the huge black raven wings. They were spread out straight from his shoulders, flexed to take off. God, they had to be twenty-four feet wide. She took a tentative step closer to him.

He rolled his eyes. "You'll have to come closer than that."

Silver shuffled closer and looped her arms around his neck. He was too tall to do it comfortably. He locked his arms tightly around her waist and took off, his wings whistling downward in one powerful sweep. Silver tried to scream, but the air was rushing passed her face too quickly. She squeezed her eyes shut.

"You don't have to hold that tight." The Raven King said, "I won't drop you."

"I'd prefer not to take that chance," Silver said, not slackening her grip. After a few minutes, she was so cold that she didn't think she'd be able to move until they were stood up in front of a fire and thawed out.

Silver opened one eye out of curiosity. The white forest rushed past below them, sparkling and painfully bright. The line of white was broken by the rocky crags of the dwarves' mountains, and then, abruptly, the air warmed as they crossed the boundary over the Autumn Forest. The Raven King alighted at the edge of the Wildwood that pressed against the outskirts of Ening City. The Raven King released Silver, and she stumbled a bit, weak-kneed.

"You'll need a feather."

"Excuse me?" asked Silver once she had regained her balance.

The Raven King extended a wing. "Take one. You'll need it to summon me when you have the ring."

Silver reached out and grasped one of the long, black, glossy feathers and pulled. It came away surprisingly easily in her hand. With a whoosh that blew back Silver's hair, the Raven King took off and began winging his way back to the Winter Forest.

Silver made her way carefully back to the apothecary in the afternoon light, hoping the goblins weren't still looking for her. The apothecary had a Closed sign up in the window but Caton opened the door for Silver when she tapped.

Caton's golden hair was braided and pulled back from her face, and she wore the same plain homespun dress she'd always worn But Silver realized there had always been an air of royalty about her. Caton led her over to a table where Portia was sitting. Growltiger was perched upon the table. The sisters didn't look very happy to see Silver.

"So um," Silver said at last, "am I fired?"

Caton snorted. "Think of it this way: if you hadn't meddled, we'd have restored the Raven King, lifted our enchantment, and left the apothecary far behind."

"Right, so, on probation then."

Caton shrugged, "Maybe you're up for a promotion."

Silver and Caton sat down and Portia poured everyone coffee. It was rather surreal. Silver was having coffee with two princesses who'd been alive hundreds of years. And one of them was also a famous actress, although maybe that had all been faked with magic. Silver's brain hurt.

"Where are the Skogil brothers? What've you done to them?" asked Silver.

Sighing, Caton said, "I've had three of them enchanted since we found out who stole the ring from Portia, so I persuaded them to kidnap the last one. He's immune to my spells. I think it has something to do with having been dead. They were trying to get the location of the ring out of him, but he wouldn't tell. But then they were all kidnapped by goblins, who of course are still after the ring too. They'd love to be in control of the Raven King, plus it was *their* ring to begin with."

"Great," said Silver. "Well, good news: I know where the ring is."

"Thank God," cried Portia.

"What will we need for the summoning?" asked Caton.

Silver dug out Solomon Mea's spell book. She knew there was a summoning spell in there.

"And you stole my spell book," Caton observed, shaking her head.

"Erm," Silver said. "Sorry. It all seems pretty silly now, Valentine's Day."

Caton waved a hand. "It doesn't matter. You clearly have more of an affinity for magic than I do, but it will still be best if all three of us cast it. I was worried before that Portia and I wouldn't have enough power."

Portia sipped her coffee. "I'm rubbish at magic."

"We need your grounding and your energy. Growltiger can be our familiar."

The cat yawned, pink tongue curling.

"We'll need a crystal for focusing our psychic energy, candles, stardust powder—do you have any of that?"

Caton disappeared into the storeroom to check. She came back a moment later with a packet of iridescent powder.

"Perfect," said Silver. "And I've already got something of the Raven King's," she produced the feather from her pouch.

"I have the crystals and the candles and some chalk in case we need to draw any symbols," Portia said, checking her own pouch.

"We'd better get going then," Silver said, "before the goblins kill my sort-of-fiancé."

Caton cast a spell of invisibility over the three women and the cat, and they set off across the city, to the tunnel entrance closest to where Varior had hidden the ring.

"Growltiger has told us what happened and that you brought back a corpse as a suitor," said Caton, "but how did you choose him? I mean, it's a big graveyard. And you're engaged now?"

"Honestly, he was the most recent death date," Silver said, "but I've grown very fond of him." She thought of his joking proposal. She thought, in different circumstances, she might have been happy to accept. But what if she couldn't save him?

She pushed the thoughts away. "Why did you have him killed?" she shot back at Caton.

"I panicked. All of our planning and everything had blown up in our faces. I used a draft of persuasion to make the other three betray...yours."

"Varior, his name is Varior."

"Right, well. I bewitched the oldest brother to kill Varior and get the ring from him, but Varior didn't have it when he came out of the tunnel, I realized too late. I kept the brothers enchanted and tried to have them look for it. Of course, the goblins have also been looking for the ring. It's been a nightmare. Honestly, I should thank you for bringing Varior back. We might never have found the ring. We even tried some finding spells, even though I knew they wouldn't work. The Raven King told us that since the ring is so magical, it resists spells."

"I wish you hadn't killed him," Silver said.

Caton didn't respond. Silver wiped the tears off her face impatiently.

* * *

The entrance to the tunnel was in the sort of alley that was behind a brothel and had every intention of holding you up, taking all of your money, and leaving you for dead. The entrance itself was a sewer grating.

"Charming," said Caton as she glanced around.

"I don't think goblins have ever been accused of that." Silver reached down and pulled the grating open. It swung easily on hinges quiet from use. A staircase extended down into the dark.

Portia pulled out a candle and lit it. The three women took

a deep breath, and Portia led the way down the stairs that vanished under the city. Growltiger followed at her heels. Silver closed the grating behind them. It fell into place with a hollow, final-sounding clang.

They descended a long time, the air growing colder around them. No one spoke. They all seemed to be holding their breath in the silence.

Finally they reached the bottom of the stairs; the high-ceilinged tunnel stretched out ahead of them, made of brick and lit by torches in sconces. This rather surprised Silver who had always imagined goblins living in dank, muddy, dark, nasty holes in the ground. Instead the corridors looked quite like castle corridors, although without windows. Portia blew out her candle, so as not to waste it.

"Silver?" said Caton. "Lead the way."

Silver shut her eyes, trying to remember what Varior had shown her. She led the other women down the tunnel and to the left when it forked.

"It was pretty close to where we came in because he hid it just before he went out into the alley...where, er, he got stabbed." Silver shivered involuntarily, remembering the feel of the knife as it slipped between Varior's shoulder blades.

They turned left again, off the main tunnel and into a cramped spiral staircase. They descended two full turns and then Silver stopped. She began tapping the bricks at eye level.

"It's behind a brick somewhere around here." The three of them all began tapping and tugging on the bricks. "It was right about eye level," Silver said.

They continued searching.

"Are you sure?" Caton asked after a few minutes.

"This was the place I saw in his memory. He was coming up this staircase—"

Growltiger hissed. The sound of footsteps was coming from above them. Silver's stomach dropped. Caton was still casting the invisibility spell but the staircase was so confined, she knew they wouldn't be able to avoid detection if the goblins descended. The grunting voices of goblins echoed down the stairs. They were in the main tunnel above the staircase. The footsteps and voices grew louder. They must've been at the top of the stairs.

Caton whispered a spell and the footsteps paused.

"I think," growled one voice, "that we should go a different way."

"What?" shrieked a second, "but this is the quickest—"

Caton muttered something else.

"No, you're right. We shouldn't go this way," the second voice amended.

The goblins turned away from the staircase and walked back into the main tunnel. Silver let out a breath in relief. Caton sagged a little against the wall, breathing heavily.

"I'm stupid," muttered Silver.

"What?" snapped Portia. "It's not here?"

"No, it is," said Silver, "but it's at *his* eye level, not mine." She reached up to the row of bricks four rows above where she'd been looking and tugged on the edge of one of the bricks. It came away easily in her hand. She slipped her hand into the space behind the brick, hoping she wasn't about to grab a spider or a rat, and felt around. She pulled out a ring.

It was heavy and gold with a teardrop-shaped purple stone set into it. The stone glittered darkly.

"I've never seen a stone like this," Silver said, staring at it.

"It's iolite," said Caton. "It's a stone of awareness and vision. A good place to store the name of a king."

"So it's sort of like he lost his whole identity, not just most of his powers." Silver felt sorry for the Raven King suddenly.

"We'll have to be careful when we restore his powers," Portia said.

"In what way?" asked Silver.

"We must keep him from decimating the human population in revenge, and keep his subjects from doing likewise," said Caton.

"He and I have come to an agreement on that score," Silver said.

"An agreement?" Caton asked. She shook her head. "That won't be nearly strong enough. He will have to swear on his true name to our conditions."

"Swear on his true name?"

"It is the most binding oath one can make."

They made their way back up the stairs and into the main tunnel.

"Where should we do the summoning?" asked Caton.

"I want to find Varior first," Silver said. "The Raven King said he would help him."

"You won't be able to free him and his brothers without backup," Portia said.

Caton sighed, "We'll go for backup. We should be able to hoodwink some of the King's men. We'll meet you where they're being held."

"You'll be able to find us?"

"We'll use a finding spell. It's what you're planning on using to find him isn't it?"

Silver nodded, "Something like that."

"I know you won't listen if I ask you to wait for us, but try not to do anything too stupid before we get there. We need to do the summoning soon. The longer we hold onto the ring, the more chance someone has to steal it." Caton rolled her eyes. "You're not even listening. Just go, we'll catch up. Take Growltiger with you."

Silver took off down the corridor, Growltiger loping along beside her. She groped in her pouch for *Practical Necromancy for Beginners*. There was something in there about a Necromancer being able to find her subjects. She paused in the light from a torch to read the incantation aloud. She closed her eyes and thought of Varior. After a moment, Silver felt a strange tugging sensation, like there was a string tied to her heart, pulling her onward. She followed without hesitation.

She took a right fork and descended a staircase, turning left at the bottom. She ran along the new corridor for a while. As she tried to run past a heavily carved wooden door, the spell gave her a jerk in the other direction and she skidded to a halt, turning back to the door. She splayed her fingers against the door and thrust it open with a percussive word she had learned from Solomon Mea's book. Ignoring the brief dizziness that overtook her, Silver hurried inside.

There was blood dripping from the corner of Varior's mouth as evidence of past tortures when Silver crossed the threshold. He was tied to a chair at the center of the floor. It looked very like the last place he had been held prisoner.

The non-bloody side of his mouth twitched upward. "I knew you wouldn't be able to resist a damsel in distress," he said. "Never doubted you'd rescue—"

But Silver had crossed the room in three strides and kissed Varior hard on the mouth, a hand on either side of his face. She could taste blood, his blood, and he kissed her back softly. Her tears were on both of their faces.

"I've done something terrible," she whispered.

"Don't be so hard on yourself," he said. "You're a great kisser. Not sure what you were doing being single before I arrived on the scene."

She half laughed, half sobbed.

"Silver," Varior said gently. "Untie me so I can hold you."

She moved to untie him. "What have they done to you?"

Varior was covered in oozing stab wounds, wounds that would have killed most men. Growltiger hopped up onto his lap, purring and kneading his claws on Varior's thighs.

"Growltiger," Silver said, "you're not helping."

Varior shrugged and then winced. "You made me pretty sturdy. I guess they can't kill me, since, you know, been there, done that."

"Oh, this is all my fault," Silver breathed. She didn't know if she loved Varior; they had known each other for less than three days, but she knew she had to save him if she could. She owed him that much.

She got Varior's bonds undone, and he shooed Growltiger off his lap, giving the cat a grudging pat.

"Hurry," he said. "We have to get out of here before the goblins get back. I'm surprised they've been gone so long."

"We have to get your brothers first," Silver said.

Varior's face twisted. "No, we don't. They'd leave me."

"I don't have time to explain, but your brothers didn't betray you. They were enchanted."

Varior stared at Silver, emotions flickering across his face: confusion, pain, anger, hope, pain again.

"Come on," Silver said. "Where are they?"

Silently, Varior led Silver to a small door leading off Varior's cell.

Thorley and Samwell were tied back to back in the next room. Sam was slumped forward, apparently asleep, and Thorley was sprawled backward, his head lolleding against his brother's.

Silver hurried to untie them. Varior moved to stand before Samwell, looking down at him, his expression caught between longing and fear.

Sam started awake and whacked his head against Thorley's,

who also woke, groaning. Sam blinked in confusion at Varior. Slowly, a look of horror dawned across his face.

"Varior," he whispered. "Can you ever forgive us?"

Varior hit him.

"Varior!" cried Silver. "Not the time."

"Ask me again later," Varior growled at his brother.

Thorley stood up, stretching and rubbing his wrists. "What I said on the train was true, by the way. I mean not the part about being paid by Portia to kill you, but that I was the one who resisted the enchantment the most."

"Oh wonderful, you know that would be really comforting if I hadn't still died!"

Thorley shrugged. "You look fine now. No harm done, eh? Invincible. Might be an improvement."

Varior punched him too.

Boys, thought Silver, shaking her head. "Where's Cain?" she asked Sam.

"This way," Sam coiled the ropes that had lately been tied around him and led Silver and Growltiger to a third adjacent room. Before Silver could react, Cain, the wolf, had leapt at them, jaws snapping. Just as quickly, Sam had looped the rope around his neck and tugged him sideways, away from Silver and Growltiger, whose fur stood on end, his hackles raised. Thorley was beside them in an instant, tying a slipknot around the snapping, slavering jaws. Once his mouth was securely shut, the brothers tied the remaining ropes into a harness and a leash.

Silver bit back a laugh. They looked like they were about to go walk the family dog—if, of course, the family dog were a vicious werewolf.

"Time to go," said Varior, "before the goblins get back."

"Yeah, where are the goblins?" asked Thorley.

They spilled out into the main tunnel and collided with a troop of goblins.

"Ah," said Thorley. "There you are." He knocked aside a spear and punched the goblin holding it. Immediately, everyone was fighting. But the goblins had weapons, and Silver and the boys did not. Thorley released the rope around Cain's muzzle and set him on the goblins. Jaws snapping, Cain also managed to do some damage with his claws, bowling over several goblins. Growltiger was caterwauling as he scratched out the eyes of a goblin that had been heading for Silver, spear raised.

Hurry up, Caton, Silver thought desperately. She dodged sideways as a goblin thrown by Cain hit the wall behind her with a solid crunch. She managed to tug a spear from the goblin Growltiger had incapacitated and gave it a good thwack with the non-lethal end.

"Silver," cried Varior, and she spun to see him trying to hold off a goblin with his bloody arms. She tossed him the spear, and he dispatched the goblin. A slimy body collided with Silver, and she was on the floor, struggling to keep the goblin's hands off her throat. Her fingernails scrabbled. The goblin's hands tightened against her throat. Dark splotches gathered at the edge of her vision.

"Charge!" shouted a voice.

The goblin on top of Silver seized up and went still, its whole compact weight falling on her chest, knocking the last of the breath from her lungs. A moment later a knight had dragged the body of the goblin off of her. She pushed herself up, coughing and gasping, to see a squadron of knights led by King Festus, himself, bearing down on the goblins from both ends of the tunnel. Silver knew Caton was behind them, persuading them all onward. The King was too much of a coward to lead a charge without magical courage.

The fighting intensified as the soldiers and goblins clashed. The clanging of swords and the screaming of men and goblins echoed against the brick walls. For a moment, it looked like it would be an easy win for the soldiers, but then one of the goblins began making an ear-splitting, high-pitched, siren noise and goblin reinforcements began to pour in from—Silver couldn't tell where.

"The summoning," Caton shouted. "We have to do it now!" Somehow she and Portia had made their way to Silver's side through the storm of blows.

Portia drew a circle with chalk on the floor by the side of the tunnel. Silver rushed over, and the three witches jumped into the circle and took hands. The chalk lines would keep them safe for the duration of the spell. Growltiger crouched at Silver's feet. Silver and Caton held the feather of the Raven King between them. Portia hastily lit a candle and held it in the hand joined with Caton. She held her crystal in the hand joined with Silver.

Silver chanted the words from Solomon Mea's spell book.

They released hands, and Portia placed the crystal on the floor in the center of the circle with the candle atop it, cemented there by dripping wax. Silver pushed the feather into the flame until it caught, shriveling and folding in on itself until it fell to ashes.

Silver pulled out the ring and held it over the flame of the candle and the ashes of the feather. Caton threw a pinch of the stardust powder into the air where it hung, sparkling. The ring lifted off Silver's palm and rotated slowly in the air, the stone pointed up. Caton, Portia, and Silver leaned in close, and together, they whispered the true name of the Raven King.

Several things happened at once: the spear of an extremely angry goblin sank into the stomach of King Festus; a goblin lunged for the ring spinning in the chalk circle; Varior jumped between the goblin and Silver, not knowing the circle would have protected her, and taking a spear in his thigh for his trouble; and an image of the Raven King appeared, hovering like a mirage above the chalk circle in the high-ceilinged tunnel.

The image of the Raven King flapped its wings, and everyone except the three witches, Growltiger, and himself froze; Varior was mid-stumble, and King Festus had a look of surprise stuck on his face. All at once, the torches illuminating the tunnel went out, leaving the only source of light the candle, the stardust, and the spinning, glowing ring.

"Release to me my name and my powers," said the Raven King.

But Silver's eyes were on King Festus, frozen in the act of dying. She turned to Caton, the truth dawning on her.

"You brought the King here on purpose."

"Duh," said Caton, "we just summoned him."

"No, not him, Festus. You were hoping someone would kill him."

Caton shrugged. "He's not the rightful ruler. He is descended from Silas's lieutenant, who took the ring and killed him after my sisters and I were taken to the Wildwood."

"Return to me my name!" cried the Raven King again, evidently angry that no one was paying any attention to him.

"If we do," said Caton, looking up at him, "do you swear not to take revenge on the humans, and that none of your people will do so either? Do you swear to honor my oldest sister Portia as the rightful queen of the humans? Do you swear to be our ally in times of war? And do you swear to continue Silver's magical education and do your best to help her young man?"

The Raven King stared at her, furious.

"Tick tock," said Silver, "or maybe I'll just keep the ring." Her hand twitched toward the ring.

"I swear," growled the Raven King, not seeing another way out.

"Swear on your true and rightful name," Portia said.

"I do so swear." The Raven King said his true name and the air rippled with the power of it.

Caton took out a knife that had been hidden somewhere on her person and brought it down with force on the purple gemstone that held the Raven King's name. It cracked open cleanly, and a tiny, bright spark flew from the fragments into the Raven King's mouth. He gave a great flap of his wings and was gone.

The torches flared up again, and time restarted, the battle lurching back into action.

King Festus drew a rattling breath and died. The last of the goblins were killed or driven away by the knights, and Portia went to stand over the dead King Festus.

"I, Portia, daughter of King Silas and true heir to the throne, claim the Crown of the Kingdom of Meryn."

The remaining soldiers fell to their knees before her, though Silver suspected they were still enchanted.

"You're the daughter of Silas?" Thorley asked, wiping blood from his eyes that flowed from a gash over his eyebrow. "You look great for being hundreds of years old."

Portia gave Thorley a once over. "And you're pretty handsome, for a thief," she said.

Thorley blushed right up to his ears. Silver frowned; how easily he had forgotten that she and Caton had enchanted him and persuaded him to betray his own brother. Men.

"Come on," Sam said. "We should all get out of here before more goblins turn up."

Varior was lying on the floor, covered with innumerable injuries. Silver fell to her knees beside him, cradling his head in her lap.

"Hey witch-lady," he murmured, blood burbling from his half-smiling mouth. "Think you can patch me up? It's an odd feeling—knowing you should be dead, but not being able to die."

A sob escaped Silver's mouth, and she put up a hand as if she could force the sound back in. Several soldiers were enlisted to carry Varior, and the whole party returned to the surface, exiting the tunnels. Silver hoped she would never have occasion to go back down there again.

"Where should we take him, my lady?" asked one of the knights.

"Follow me," Silver said and she led the way back to the apothecary.

They laid Varior out on several pushed-together tables. Growltiger hopped up beside him, sniffing with mild interest.

"Silver," Caton said softly, "Portia and I have got to go. We have to secure the castle and get our sisters."

"Of course," said Silver. "Good luck."

Thorley brought Cain into the apothecary and tied him to the leg of a heavy table. The werewolf curled up beneath the table and went to sleep. Samwell skulked near the door, unsure what to do.

"Why," asked Thorley, coming in after a moment, "isn't he dead?"

"I brought him back to life," Silver said. "Only I can send him back to death."

Varior breathed in strange gasping spasms, and Silver suspected a punctured lung. She smoothed some of his tawny hair back from his face.

"Raven King," she said loudly. "I need you. You swore to help him."

"I do not appreciate being called like a dog or a servant just because I made a vow."

Silver started in surprise and looked at the large gilt mirror that hung on one wall of the apothecary.

Cain growled at the Raven King in the mirror, and he growled right back. The werewolf cowered. Silver raised her eyebrows. Sam and Thorley fell back to watch against the back wall. Varior's eyes were closed as he wheezed on the table.

"Help him," said Silver, "please. I don't know what to do."

The Raven King glared at her. "You should have thought of that before you raised him."

Silver nodded. "I know."

"Have you taken care of the other two?"

Silver shook her head.

"Go and do that," the Raven King said more gently. "I will do what I can for him."

Silver pressed a kiss onto Varior's forehead. "I'm coming back. I swear."

She left the apothecary with Growltiger trotting after her and headed toward the cemetery, hoping Sir Rollo and Sir Gregor would still be there. She was tired from all the magic she had used back in the tunnels. She didn't want to cast the finding spell unless she really needed it.

The sun was setting, turning the graveyard gold and stretching long shadows behind each of the headstones. It had been a very long day—a very long, what, three days?

The graveyard looked like a battlefield. Goblin corpses lay scattered around between the tombstones. Mercifully, the skeleton of Sir Rollo still snoozed under a tree, and Silver breathed a sigh of relief.

She dug out *Practical Necromancy for Beginners* and flipped it to sending subjects back to the world of the dead. What would happen if she just left them? It couldn't really be that bad, could it? She searched the book.

When a body is first raised, particularly a fresh body, it will regain life-like characteristics, and it will seem like new. But do not be deceived. For this life-like state is not life. The corpse will be able to continue in this state for several days, maybe even weeks, before it begins to fade as if behind a veil. The corpse will still inhabit a place between worlds, neither living nor dead. Unless a living soul is traded for that of the corpse, it will never be able to cross fully into the land of the living. After the purposes of the Necromancer are served, she must kill the subject (for no one else will be able to) and then she must dispose of the body in such a way that it cannot be raised again. Burning or eating is recommended.

Eating! Silver gagged. She looked back at the skeleton of Sir Rollo, breathing peacefully—though she didn't know how that was possible since he didn't have lungs.

He hadn't wanted to come back to life anyway, she reasoned. Sending him back to the land of the dead would be a mercy.

She didn't know how to kill an undead skeleton but she figured detaching the skull would be a good start. The skeleton made a gross cracking noise, and the breathing stopped. Silver built up a pyre and heaved the skeleton onto it.

There was one last incantation to complete the ritual. Growltiger sat at her feet and placed a paw on her foot. Silver felt energy flow into her.

"Lords of Winter, Death, and Night," she began. "I return to you this soul. In clear skies, as the full moon sets, let this spirit return to the Netherrealms. Krewix izseod ab unum sres chanbeo Druzworhot et obetruc."

The flames reared higher, responding to the spell. The bones of the old knight were slowly reduced to ashes. Silver put out the fire then recited the finding spell for Sir Gregor.

The heart-string tugged her back toward town and down the high street. It led her to a brightly lit tavern, from which a stream of patrons was leaving, all looking terrified. When she went inside, she beheld the half-rotted corpse sitting at the bar, downing pint after pint of beer while the terrified barman cowered as far from him as possible.

Silver approached the bar and the barman turned haunted eyes on her. There was a long kitchen knife lodged in Sir Gregor's neck; someone had unsuccessfully tried to rid the tavern of its undead patron. Growltiger hopped up on the bar to sniff the dead man.

"Well, you certainly did a better job on Varior," the cat said, sitting down and wrapping his tail neatly around himself. "Your parents would never have approved of this one."

Silver reached over and pulled the knife from the huge knight's neck. He barely reacted, just continued drinking his beer. Silver supposed that there was no beer in the land of death. She plunged the knife into his back and twisted. He slumped forward, knocking over his tankard and hitting his forehead against the bar. She pulled the knife from his back and wiped it on his rotting clothes. She tucked it into her belt.

"Help me," Silver said to the barman. "We have to take the body outside to burn it."

The barman shook his head fervently.

Silver's eyes flashed. "Either you help me move him or I'll burn down your pub."

In the end, he helped Silver take Sir Gregor's body back to the cemetery where she burned him and said the incantation.

"You're like a regular Grim Reaper," observed Growltiger. "I bet you'd look good in a black hooded cloak with a scythe."

But Silver didn't want to deal with death anymore. She headed back to the apothecary. The Raven King still waited in the mirror for her. Varior's brothers were seated beside him, and even Cain was slumbereding beneath the table, dreaming doggy dreams.

"Is it done?" asked the Raven King.

Silver nodded heavily. She was very tired. She came over to Varior and took his hand. The Raven King had repaired all of his wounds, and he slept, breathing more easily.

"What do we do?" Silver asked.

The Raven King gave her a long look. "You already know."

"No!" shouted Silver, and Varior started awake, sitting up and squeezing her hand. "What about King Festus, all those goblins that died? Surely the price is paid."

"It doesn't work like that. It has to be intentional."

"No," said Silver. "There must be something else. You swore you would help!"

The Raven King shook his head. "I swore to do my best to help him. That I have done. He is no longer in pain." He gestured at the repaired injuries. "You must do the rest."

The Raven King's image in the mirror faded away.

Silver ripped open *Practical Necromancy for Beginners* again. There must be an answer hidden there. She flipped the pages of the spell book and rummaged through them like a drawer full of odds and ends. There would be a solution in there somewhere. She knew it. Like a pearl in an oyster. There would be a way around what the Raven King had said. There had to be another way. Death didn't have to follow life. She could find a way to bring back the balance, she knew it. But the pages slipped through her fingers, and the only thing she had was an ultimatum. She didn't want to kill him. She didn't want to send him back to that dark, cold, abyss where he'd been frightened and alone. She'd pulled him back once, been his lighthouse in the darkness. She couldn't let him ebb back out into that sea.

She was crying in earnest now, nearly ripping the pages as she turned them.

"Silver," whispered Varior. "What's wrong?"

He tugged the book gently from her hands and looked down at it. His face barely changed, but she knew he had read the passage about reanimated corpses being stuck between worlds.

"I guess that's it then, isn't it, witch-lady?" he said softly.

"No," said Silver. "There's another way. Another soul could take your place—"

Varior put his mouth over hers to stop her from saying more.

"It was good while it lasted, eh Goldie?" he whispered, his forehead pressed against hers.

"Don't say that," said Silver. "I'm a Necromancer, there must be a way."

"Take me," Sam said suddenly, rising and coming around to face Silver and Varior.

"What?" said Varior.

"I'm the reason you died in the first place. Take my life and you can stay."

But Varior shook his head. "I can't, Sam. It wasn't your fault."

"Please," said Sam.

"No. The others," said Varior, "they need you."

"Then take me," said Thorley. His usual joking tone was gone and his face was pale.

"Absolutely not," Varior and Sam said together.

The sun was beginning to come up, and the full moon had set. Under the table, the werewolf gave a high whine and transformed back into a man. Cain tried to get up but was entangled in the ropes that had been tied around his wolf form.

Thorley bent to help him, grumbling, "I'm just saying, I'm a non-essential member of this team."

"What's going on?" asked Cain. "What have I missed?"

Everyone stared at him, unsure how to explain all that had happened since he'd transformed.

"I have to kill him, or someone has to take his place." Silver said finally.

"Well, that's easy," said Cain. "I'm a danger to everyone. Take me."

"No," said Sam. "I'm the oldest. I get to decide!"

Varior jumped to his feet. "I'm not letting any of you die for me." He crossed the apothecary and hurried out into the street. Silver went after him.

Going through the door, she smacked right into someone in sunglasses who was trying to come in. The person squeaked and flicked her sunglasses up onto her head. It was Aidolyn. Silver stared at her, her brain not comprehending why Aidolyn would be standing in front of her as Varior walked away down the street.

"Morning," said Aidolyn, not as brightly as usual. "I'm hungover, but look, I'm on time!"

"Oh um," said Silver at a loss. "We're closed today, go home and get some rest. Thanks for being on time."

"Oh excellent," Aidolyn pushed her sunglasses back down over her eyes and let out an enormous yawn. "Sir Gladden will be so pleased." She turned and headed back down the street.

Silver marveled for a moment that there were still people out there whose lives had not been irrevocably altered by the last seventy-two hours. Then she turned and raced after Varior. He was walking determinedly away from the apothecary but he had not gone far.

"Varior!" she called. She reached for his arm and turned him back to face her.

But in the same moment, he caught both her hand and the kitchen knife at her belt, and before she knew what had happened, he was kissing her, pulling her body into his, pushing the knife into his heart with her hands.

"Varior!" she screamed as he stumbled, pulling them both to the ground as blood poured from his chest.

With shaking hands, she pulled the knife from his heart, but it was too late.

"Never let yourself think that you didn't save me," he whispered in her ear. His eyes were wide and so blue that it hurt to look at them.

For the second time, Varior Skogil died in the arms of someone who loved him.

* * *

Silver, Thorley, Samwell, Cain, and Growltiger stood on a hilltop, stars scattering the darkness above them, watching the flames consume Varior's body. Silver took a deep breath and recited the incantation.

"So," said Thorley when it was done. "He can never come back?"

"Never," said Silver. Then after a moment, "Unless—"

"No!" said everyone else together.

Silver closed her mouth and watched the flames dance.

Dear Mom and Dad,

I have some good news and some bad news. The good news is that I am now the owner of the apothecary as Caton has moved to the palace to be personal magician to the Queen. Everything in town has pretty much settled down since the change in leadership, though of course the goblins are furious that all their corrupt royal advisors have been fired. I am now living in the flat above the shop, and my insurance covered most of the damage to my old cottage. I've paid the landlord the rest.

The bad news is that my fiancé, Varior Skogil, is dead. He has, in fact, always been dead. I'm sorry I lied to you, and I know you don't approve of black magic. But there is no more denying that I am a witch. I have begun to study magic with the Raven King and his associates, and I promise to be more responsible with my spell casting in the future.

I hope you are enjoying the fine weather and tell Benjamin that I saw some interesting art on my recent trip to London that I'm sure he would appreciate.

Your loving daughter,

Silver

* * *

"I don't think this is going to work," said Growltiger. He licked a paw surreptitiously and peered into the cauldron on the table in the storeroom in the back of the apothecary, whiskers twitching.

"Yes, so you've said," Silver said, rifling through some ingredients and not looking at him.

"It's been a year now. You could just let him go."

"Did anyone ask you for your opinion?"

"You don't need to. I give it freely," the cat said magnanimously, wrapping his tail tightly about himself.

"Too freely," Silver grumbled.

"You only knew him for three days. You can't possibly have fallen *that* deeply in love."

"If you don't stop talking, I'll curse you."

Growltiger yawned, "I'd like to see you try." He stood up and stretched, arching his back. "Well, don't say I didn't warn you."

"Consider me warned."

The cat leapt off the table and stalked out into the garden, tail aloft.

Silver lifted the ceramic urn of ashes and upended it into her cauldron. She pricked her finger, spat in the cauldron, and then took out the finger bone. It was the only fully intact bone that had somehow survived the cremation. She kissed it then put it into the cauldron too.

I hope this works, she thought. She took a deep breath and began casting the spell.

THE SPIDER AND THE BIRDHOUSE

BY JOEL T BLACKSTOCK JR.

MR. HOWELL

"Hello Mr. Howell," I say, and he turns towards the sound of my voice. There is a thing the tall grass will do when the sun hits directly behind it. When you are at the bottom of a hill, like I am now, looking up at the grass in front of the sun, the brightness magnifies the smallest parts until they are all visible. The things that I usually could not see, even from up close, gleam from afar and fill my vision. Each floret, each anther, becomes gilded and locus.

"Hell of a day, hell of a day young man," Mr. Howell smiles as he starts to ramble. There are masonic rings on his fingers, and grubby soviet badges on his jacket. It's well cut, but gruby and sweat bleached. "Do ya, do ya, do ya know what kind a day it is?" he asks me. "Do you know that God is good?" I stand still and watch him while he enunciates each word semi-clearly, volume and interest shifting up and down oddly on each word. "Jesus knows, that's right. You a good man," he beams, "sees I's a old man."

"Mr. Howell, are you ready to shop today?" I ask him.

"I'm a travellin man, from the east to the west, you a young man." The enraptured rambling continues. "Do you know that?" he asks me looking to the wrong place down the hill. "He knows, he sees all things" — he looks at me now — "That's right you know."

High noon summer sun illuminates the white marble swirl of cataract over both of his eyes. Mr. Howell sits in his chair on the grass on the hill outside of his apartment. The view is unexpectedly phenomenal in such a bleak part of the city, but it's hot. He can't see it. I often wonder why he comes up here.

"Do you know if they've closed the store yet, Mr. Howell?" I ask. I'm tired.

"Close the book, closed the gates to heaven and hell," he tells me earnestly. Sweat on his forehead, sweat on mine. "The door is closed, but he shall open it unto us, unto you and me." More grinning.

"Mister Howell the store with your tab, have they moved yet?" I try again.

"The stone lions they will awake on that day."

It's useless.

"All the rocks and the hills and the trees too, they will awake when he opens that door." He looks back over to the left of me. "You and I knows that, we's good people you and me is," he tells me confidently.

"Come on Mr. Howell, please get in the car." I have to help him to the door.

He beams and looks at the pylons of concrete from the highway construction rising up from newly overturned red clay. They slowly inch their way on their inevitable collision course with his island of the city and, against his apartment. He surveys all of it beaming and rambling. The feral dogs by the highway overpass bristle when I pass, but don't bark or bother me today. There's more and more of them appearing outside his apartment where there are a couple ancient shade trees left in the sea of grass and heat. They too are refugees from the progress our city is making. He surveys all of it smiling. I wonder often what he sees, with the cataracts, with the pins, with the blindness.

By some miracle, Mr. Howell still lives alone. His apartment is relatively ordered, but the bugs are entrenched. He can't see them. He won't let us in to treat them. He has lived in the apartment for longer than we will ever know.

"I don't want to get that injection no more young man," he tells me.

"Mister Howell, you have to get your injection every

month," I tell him. "That's what keeps you out of the hospital, that's what lets me come see you to take you to the store." He looks dejected.

"The nurses keep leaving pieces of the needle in my body," he scowls. "It speaks to me. The metal will talk to you, you know," he says contemplatively while staring to the left of where I am. "Metal will do that when it's in your body," he says, squinting earnestly.

There is a flat field of red clay and some rubble when we get to the store. Some grass is growing, but it won't grow for long. Eight lanes will blaze above it soon and block out all the sunlight forever. They will blaze at eighty miles an hour into a future a million years away from where this man has shopped for the past thirty years. A concrete and steel tentacle writhes its way across the land.

There are concrete plugs on the gas pumps.

"One second young man. I'll be right back," Mister Howell tells me smiling.

"Mister Howell, the store is gone," I tell him, "they've torn it down. We are going to have to put you on food distribution list".

"One second young man. I have to get my groceries and I'll be right back," he tells me again.

I turn around and look at him closely in the backseat. He sits like he is being pulled by a chariot. His grey hair spills out on all sides of his head like a mane. His eyes look in different directions and weep, but he beams. The lining of the back seat of my car is stained, and it smells bad. Mr. Howell sits up with his white gloves that he always wears to the store, he takes his cane with the masonic cross from across his knees.

"Mister Howell, they tore down the store for the highway," I tell him firmly, "Mister Kim is gone. Your tab is gone." His expression doesn't change. "We are going to have to bring groceries out to your house each week instead of taking you shopping." He looks out across the debris and opens his door.

"One second young man, I'll be right back," he tells me in a reassuring way and he stands up.

I watch him walk up to the gap in the concrete where the glass door used to be. LED lighting, and a door chime were here but not anymore. He walks through the clay slowly, it sticks to his polished wingtip boots. He wears a trail through it where the aisles of the store used to be. He gestures to the air. Here was vienna sausage, here was bologna, here was white bread, here was American Cheese, here was Mr. Kim with a warning about belatedness and the new monthly tab, here was the hand of God from heaven palmprint down across the store back into the pelagia and iron oxide dust from which we came. He has had the aisles of the store memorized for two decades now.

Mr. Howell looks in awe when he walks back to the car. He carefully scrapes the layer of mud off his wing tips onto his cane and coils it violently at the woods until it is flecked away into nothing and the cane is clean. His eyes stare off into different directions flatly.

"God has spoken here," he tells me. "God has made a speaking across this place today."

I try and go over the grocery plan with him again. We don't have anymore time for a case manager to take him on the highway to a Walmart. There are few smaller stores left. Even if we didn't have limited time, he probably couldn't learn the layout and rhythm of a new store. In a world with infinite time, I suppose he could learn a new store. As impaired as he is, he continues to function independently. Master of a world that I can't see. Even so, we just don't have the amount of time he requires to help him live the way he is used to.

One day, not far away, the highway will pass over his apartment as well. It will lead to a new place away from here, away from bugs, from a sunbleached Maker's Mark bottle, from paper peeling off composite board backing of awards from a masonic lodge that is gone; away from a cracked screen door with a rusted hook, away from scared dogs, away from the hill with the tall grass. It will lead, away, to a different sort of place.

Maybe in that place he will be the one who's tired and sad, and I will be the one who can talk to God. A place where red clay becomes a horn of plenty. Where bologna and American cheese fall from heaven. Where people like me are lost and people like Mr. Howell are found. A world where we do not have to choose between a store or a highway, or a house for an old man. Where sleeping stone lions could awake outside stadiums in the derelict parts of town, and sing. A world where hot dogs tell you how to cook them and metal speaks to you from your blood. A place where the tri color jesus from the **WHERE WILL YOU SPEND ETERNITY** billboard makes eye contact and reaches down to hold us in his arms, love us, and give us peace. A place that is far away.

BEN

The lights in my house are always on. I live in a bad neighborhood and in the process of changing into a good one. Things change, like neighborhoods and people and stories. That's just the conceit of the joke though, I think. It's just a trick of the light, carnival sleight of hand, heat on a long highway, a scared old man having a different perspective while still a child.

Everywhere that I have ever lived, when it is just about fall, there is a species of fat brown spider that will spin a large piriform web by my porch light. It has happened in several houses. This species has an enormous abdomen that is so wide it is almost totally opaque even when directly against the sun or a porch light. Only the extreme edges will glow bright orange and eclipse-like, where its membrane and insides are thin. This spider has thick hairs that gleam in porch lights and under the moon's distinct and sharp. Someone told me once that spiders can "hear" things with their hairs. I sometimes wonder what the experiment was that taught mankind that spider hairs could hear.

The same variety of spider has spun its web again while I was working. Inside I smell smoke, fairly strong, and know that I am not alone. It is comforting like incense from a silly ritual I partake in occasionally. I've heard that smell is tied to emotional memory closer than any other sense is. I wonder sometimes what the experiment was that proved our noses were the most reliable way to reach across time.

I hear books moving on a desk, and feet shuffling, and something bumping against a door.

"Do you think you've processed it... your client... who died?"

Ben's voice is always curt and hurried, just south of frantic, always; even when trying to be comforting or ordering fast food. It never feels congruent with the empathic analytical suggestions for self-improvement and his somber philosophizing. "You really shouldn't let that sit," he tells me, concerned, from the next room. Ben is running out of time, and always wants me to get more therapy. The wounded healer. All past social workers want to give others the medicine that they needed.

His voice skews deeper, he is still out of view in the study. The potted ivy is back in my kitchen in the sink, he's watered it for me, after he's moved it from the porch to get the key from beneath and let himself in. Ben knows my schedule pretty well, knows about when I get off work, and what days I'm more likely to stay late at the office. He hasn't forgotten everything just yet.

I hear ice clinking against glass as he comes through the study door into the kitchen. He's looking at me expectantly, put out I haven't answered him yet.

"I think so, Ben," I tell him. I realize how tired I am, comparing his reflection wide eyed and tipsy beside me in the glass window. "I don't know if that's the kind of thing that happens all at once," I lie.

"There's a glass for you in the freezer, no ice, I didn't know when you'd be coming home," he tells me.

"Or if-" I think.

"I left some of my therapy books in the office," Ben points back towards the study. "I'm taking some of the Penn Warren Poems and your Weil book you told me about," he lets me know like it's a favor.

It is.

"It's the first edition, do you mind?"

I smile looking at my own reflection and sipping the drink until Ben forgets the question and goes back into the library.

I've never gotten a hello or goodbye from Ben that I can

remember. He exists in a totally static place of and a dim faint pain and a burning sincerity he cannot contain. He lets you know he's glad you are there in an indirect way. There's never been any pleasantries. There's no need for a "Hi, my wife went out of town for an evening so I let myself into your house and took a cigar that my wife can't know about out of your study and made a drink or two for myself and left an old fashioned in your freezer and brought over a box of books from my office I'm clearing out for forced retirement..." It's as if we have been having a conversation about death, age and learning since the time I had four bourbons at the church picnic and talked to him about brokenness for an hour and Ben first took an interest in me. That conversation has just resumed unbroken every time I see the man. Some people have started to blame the dementia for Ben's behavior, but it's new, and the behavior is as old as Ben, older maybe.

The old-fashioned is good, classic. I dip the tip of my finger in the freezing booze and run it over the cut on the back of my hand. It stings and it feels cold and it feels good. Smoke rises horizontally off of Ben's cigar straight up until it hits the ceiling. He's rested it on my plate from breakfast.

Ben looks nervous that I'm not talking more. "Look, at first you want to save people, everyone does," he pauses, "middle of your life you realize you can't save them, you just have to let them exist." Ben sighs and inhales. "It's healing for them to just *exist,* with you in an honest way." He looks at me earnestly. "At that point you start trying to save yourself. That's where you are now," he smiles in a resigned way. "Towards the end of your life you realize you can't really save yourself either," he leans back. "You just have to let *yourself* exist." Ben sits up and becomes more animated and excited by his point.

"Now," Ben pauses. "I've said that but I can't do that yet." He looks serious. "But," he pauses again. "I've seen it in the older people, when they're dying. By the time you figure that out, you aren't really getting too much out of life anymore, I think."

Ben trails off thoughtfully and reaches for his cigar. He leans forward on the tips of his feet when he does anything he's excited about. Like reaching for a cigar, or a drink, or to tell me something I don't want to hear. He's always possessed with such a bumblingly authentic wisdom. He's always half-sage, half-child, a wellspring with effervescent somber joy.

I study his face as he leans against the cupboard. He's more handsome than me, even in old age. I wonder if he aged into it or if he always was like that. He still has a full head of white hair in a clean classic part. There is a crisply ironed collar tight and starched across the collar slits of his black shirt. His skin sags slightly and hangs over it about an eighth of an inch when he turns his head. He looks nervous that I'm still not talking.

"Look you got that man a job," Ben continues, "he was in touch with his family again, living in an apartment."

I realize that I am crying, and Ben looks down at me like a sad scared parent.

"He gets killed walking into work on his first day... that's a victory. I'm sorry I'm a little tipsy, but you gave him a life, you have to own that," Ben finishes.

A commonly quoted fact about astronomy is that the Universe is "expanding", but that's not really true. Our universe is nothing more than a giant ball of rules that we can measure. Rules like time, temperature, and distance. We say that the Universe is "expanding" because the amount of space we can measure inside it is increasing. We have no way of knowing what is outside of this ball of rules. It is doubtful that measurements like time and temperature would make much sense there. Ben told me an idea one time that comforts me. He told me that Jesus came from a realm of poetic anarchy into our world of rules and told us to break all of them. That none of them were real. The blind can see, the poor are rich, and the most vulnerable rule all creation. Even death was a rule he broke.

"Ben, do you want to move outside, it's a nice night," I ask him.

"I'm not supposed to smoke inside am I? I forgot," Ben looks embarrassed.

"No Ben, you're fine, I do it all the time." I gesture to the cigar in my hand.

"Ah," he says, "yeah, it's just a nice night."

I wipe my eyes.

Outside, it smells like summer grass and wet wood. There's a soft back and forth breeze like the world is breathing. The stars are bright so far away from the city.

"Ben, why did you become a priest?" I ask him.

"Why did you decide not to be?" he asks me. We both laugh at different jokes. Ben thinks for a minute. "Everything they say about Jesus is bullshit," Ben tells me. "All the stuff about heaven, that's just wish fulfilment." It's dark and his hair and collar glow white against the black space of his outline. "Jesus never told people they could have all of the stuff they want, or that they deserved all of it."

He leans back. "All we deserve is love." He looks at me for a second across the darkness. "It's the other things that Jesus said that nobody talks about, the things nobody wants to hear." Ben pauses a minute and continues quieter. "There would be no reason to say things like that unless you came from some kind of other place far away outside all of this," Ben pauses and gestures around in the darkness presumedly. "You would have to be able to see the hidden divinity in the world, in everything, or you would just have to be crazy," Ben trails off and gazes up at the stars with me.

There are a million stars and a million paths between them. Each opening a hundred new possibilities and closing a hundred more. Like a man walking into work proudly, for the first time in twenty years since succumbing to addictions and schizophrenia; or me on a deck buffeted like a little boat by people and forces, unwilling or unable to figure out what I did to end up here. Or a priest getting forced to retire because of erratic behavior and not knowing what to do anymore. Like beta amyloid plaque building up in the brain and severing synapsys that we have come to take for granted will tell us what we should do, and who we are, and what we have done before.

Time slowly accumulates everywhere. It won't stop, no matter what we tell it or ourselves about it. It residually rubs off on all of us. Sometimes pleasantly, sometimes endearingly, sometimes in a bothersome way. Oil from a cat's ears and chin against a cabinet, or against your leg. Small nudges here and there. The vast expanse of time and choices. Piling up slowly until we see, suddenly, that we are so small before its vastness, and that we always were. Then, simply to exist intentionally becomes the best gift we can give ourselves or anyone else. Some kind of heaven that no one deserves, that is insane.

ISOBELL

Age of onset is a phenomena that I find in schizophrenia and substance abuse patients. Patients become separated from their peer group, unmoored from the current that their peers drift through and end up in a doldrum.

The year that I was born, a punk rock prince was also living in New York city at the same time. He was 23 when I was just an infant. He smoked cigarettes, and bought a scared kid a drink at a concert. The scared kid was in school to be a writer, but she would get sick and leave New York before she could graduate. The front of her bangs were blue.

The punk rock prince had become her first boyfriend. They had fallen in love. He had showed her how big the world was. When she was young, Isobel had been full of fear at the vastness of the world. When she had strayed too far into the margins of her own story it had left her scared and neurotic with awful waking dreams. Isobel had been born with a trepidation that it was likely that she would float away from everything that was real. Her whole life had become a series of preparations to prevent this until she had met him.

When the punk rock prince had showed Isobel how big the world was, she had felt secure because for the first time, she became aware that she was finite in the world. The universe was no longer a labyrinth through which people and experiences quested to find her. Instead, she was a tiny leaf on the ivy covered wall of the labyrinth.

Because the punk rock prince had made her feel tiny at the same time that he had made the world feel large, Isobel had lost her fear of changing proportions. When Isobel had floated away from the world in New York one day she did not cry because she had learned that she had wings. They had loved each other very much, her and him. It was conventional but it was their own cliche. When they looked at the world together it was unimportant how many stories looked just like theirs. This story was being told by them together and that is all anyone needs to fly and not to float away.

One night there was a heavy rain and the punk rock prince was killed in a car wreck. Now he is just an email password.

Isobel always buys five packs of blue Kool-aid every time I take her shopping.

"This stuff will rot your teeth but not your hair," she tells me while twirling a blue bang in a circle towards me and giggling. The rest of her hair is cut into an inch-short brown gray buzz cut, but the blue bang is really long and hangs down at an angle. Isobel always wants to go to the city park when I see her. She doesn't have a car anymore and she is jealous that I do.

"Isobel, tell me a little bit about what you were feeling when you paged me this week," I direct her.

"Uhhggggg," she sighs, and blows the blue bang away from her face. "Bad. Ok. Like, I told you. Like, I wanted to die, ok?" She rocks back and forth sitting atop a large rock of slick hematite. I stay silent and give her a slight smile.

"Shit. Bad ok. What do you want?" She asks me.

"I want to know if you were able to work on any behaviors that we have discovered could make you feel better, Isobel."

"Shit man, just call me Izzy." She curls her lip and takes a drag of a cigarette before looking passed me at something that makes her angry. "Hey fuck you!" she raises her middle finger to a green truck pulling out of a parking spot behind me. I turn around surprised and see the confederate flag across the back window of the truck.

"Isobel, there're kids here," I try not to sound too parental.

"Shit man, I'm sorry, I guess." She hugs her bent legs and

lays her head flat across the top of her knees while she looks at me now.

"Izzy, I've noticed that it's a pattern that you call me in crisis begging to talk about your feelings, and then avoid talking about those same negative feelings when we meet." I lean awkwardly against a tree with rough bark.

"Yeah man, I... I just don't feel bad now; I mean shit look at it out here. It's beautiful," she stares up into the trees.

"Have you written anything this week?" I ask her.

"Yeah, I did."

Izzy leans forward and becomes more anchored in the present for a second and what she's doing.

"I wrote a poem," she tells me. "It's about like how the whole world is really *really* alive and stuff but that it's eating itself all the time." She leans towards me earnestly. "Like all this dirt we are standing on is just dead stuff that used to be alive, and all people like you are sinking back into it." She rolls her arms in two intersecting circles flickering her fingers happily. "But other, new living things are coming back out of all the dead stuff at the same time." She looks calm.

"Isobel, you just said that 'people like me' are part of the circle of life and time but excluded yourself," I point out.

She stares up off into the treetops again. "You are really smart or something, you know that," she tells me with a half bored smile.

The breeze caught a gossamer strand of spider web and stuck it against the rock that Izzy sits on. She prods at the piece of it dancing in mid air gently with the end of a finger tipped with chipped blue nail polish.

There is a tightness in the corners of her eyes for just a split second, and her brow widens. It's back for a moment, and I can see it. The fear of everything that is always beneath the blaise attitude and the terrified disinterest in the world. The back of her hair is starting to turn grey and there are sharp crows feet in her eyes when she squints. She wrinkles up her nose in a mischievous smirk.

"You know I would have hated you if I had just seen you when I was a kid," she giggles. "You look like a Reagan youth or something." She laughs.

When I take Izzy home I have to help her with her computer. She doesn't really like computers, but they are her only way of keeping in touch with her family.

"I wish they would let me come home," she tells me frequently, "I don't know why I am here."

"You have to turn off Caps Lock. The password is case sensitive."

"Ok man. Just don't change it... or anything."

BETHANY

"How long are you going to do this?" Bethany had asked me once, blunt and slightly aggressive with her chronically flat affect.

I'm by myself for most of the day in this job, and I seldom have to see colleagues.

"I don't know," I had told her, surprised by the question. "I know this isn't going to be what I do forever." She had looked at me disinterested.

"You are good at this but no one knows why you are here." Before she had only ever made the most infinitesimal of small talk with anyone at work, and I had deduced that she had disliked me in particular. Having her direct this much attention at me had felt strange.

"If I do the job then why does it matter?"

"Because you are good but you aren't great and you won't ever be. You seem too sad about all the things we do. You are too spacey and your reports are not ever short or on time," she had answered me.

"Since you are smart, you could make more in the hospital, so why are you even here?" she had asked me, long ago now. I get angry when people tell me that I am smart. I had been unaware that other people perceived me to be sad. I do not want to work in a hospital.

"If you're asking if you can count on me through the next year, don't worry, I'll still be here."

"Good. That will be helpful."

We bury the parts of ourselves that are what we were supposed to be. We hate the people who are naturally the things we turned off. We are most defined by what we are not. It is stupid, but it is what it is.

In the same way the person that bothers us now, the person

that makes us hate them, is the opposite of what is beneath them.

"You make people at work uncomfortable," she said quieter for some reason. "People seem to like you, though." She wrinkled her brow around her nose in a fine line with freckles. She looked so confused as to why any person would like me. She had said this like it was a question. I watched her and refused to answer.

I noticed a long time ago that the people good at my line of work were terrible at everything else. Something can happen in early life that permanently bends a person's mind. Early experience infuse them with the imperative to heal and to compulsively understand. When the person who they think they had to heal and deconstruct is gone, then they have to heal the world. The psychologist, the grifter, the magician, the comedian, the priest; the vacuum that formed all of these is the same. You will see some part of yourself or some part of them that they need you to see, in the way that they need you to see it.

Three years later, Bethany was leaving for better work, and I absorbed her caseload. I ended my day with the last of her clients in a part of the city I had rarely visited before. It is a piece that has more money than most. The tops of the trees growing from the road median have a lolling bell-shape of blooms. Each peals towards where a crack of light is able to stream through glass, concrete and steel during the growing season.

Earlier I had parked my car on the street in front of an upscale restaurant and fed the meter. Swirls of fiber optic cables wound around stainless steel, lighting it in an ambient electronic glow across the storefront as I return to my car. There is a thick slab of insulated glass with a blue bias across the front reflecting bokeh blossoms of light back from the city. A few people are inside catching an early dinner, and my reflection splays across them; a bored scared mid-thirties man skewed by modernist tilting glass.

A man eats dinner with his girlfriend —twenty years younger than he is— right now. They sit at a table with a white cloth across it and thinly rimmed empty wine glasses, thick tumblers and a half filled carafe of chilled water perspiring. They both look at each other in an unpleasant distant way occasionally. Was she sitting bored and shining in some vogue coffee shop when he first met her? Could it have been a music venue recently installed in one of the city's reclaimed repurposed warehouses that had been previously abandoned for a decades? Did red and blue gel lighting blink across her silhouette when she danced across that trendy space? Bare brick with peeling painted signage and rusted cast iron pipe is enclosed in reflective glass and dangling edison filament bulbs become a new thing. What did that factory make before its shell was reassembled to appeal to young people's idea of the past?

What did this man feel when he first saw his date? The meal that they are eating disinterested, what did the chef feel when he plated it for the first time? Sprouted sorrel, puffed sorghum sprinkle, shrimp sous vide in beur blanc white wine with a misting of Grand Marnier foam and vegetable agar wrapped around smoked apple like a serpent. All reach upward in Fibonacci integer smoke like from a dimpled square plate.

A spotlight in a stainless steel tube hovers above them. It is one in a succession of four foot increments across a spiraling line. Was the architect proud of this floor plan? Did the engineers complain about the heat from so many halogen spots so close to the guests? Is this something that an inspector will check? Do any of these people's mothers love them? Do they think they care? Are they all longing in unison with me?

How is it that tears can be like lenses allowing me to see keener and more brightly? When I hear a hundred voices at once, why can't I make out a single word? Why does the sight of the light glinting through the columns of broken civilization evoke a stirring within us?

If there isn't something better than what we built, then why can I see something else? Did we make up the heaven just beyond our vision? Can we feel it reverberating across the cosmos in some kind of casimir effect, a heartbeat to another dimension?

Is the bargain that we struck with heaven, half remembered, the most terrible and the most likely one? The eden state that we know we can hear through the wall is something that it is entirely within our hands to make. We can only hear its muffled screams because our choices have obstructed its breath.

Do we know that we are in some way responsible for the state of the world? How could it possibly be any other way, if we want to believe that we are really this important?

Did they see me staring slack jawed at a meal that costs more than I make in a day? The insulated glass splays my reflection into a stupid, scared, ripple of social work. Here as a product of decades of failing systems society forgot it was ignoring. Here because of an ancient grant, a bureaucratic oversight, and miles of red tape. Here to stop other people from believing that they are part of a problem. Here because I want to feel important. Bethany has held up a mirror to something that I do not want to see.

MARK

The city is gorgeous. The buildings seem to lean in the haze. The western sides and window indentions glow bright under the sun like waxy whale backs, slick wet and shimmering. The foothills of the blue ridge mountains hang behind them in matte greys and green flat shapes. It's a wonder to me that they didn't build this city like they had others. In other places the views and vistas like the one we are on were prized. The economics were different here, the problems, the ways people profit off one another, the way they hurt each other are unique.

The south is a place haunted by a glittering vision of the past that was never real. People can see it everywhere. Even the dumbest person knows that there is a stolen present that would be better than the one they are in. We were robbed of the grail. It could have saved us, but we can't be saved now. That is not the problem. The problem is that we know deep down that we cannot be saved. We cannot name our pain, and so we can never really own it. The American South is one of the only places that I have ever been in the world where I believe people genuinely do not want to be free. It is a strange kind of chain.

This used to be an opulent part of the city. Limestone steps form the curl of an amphitheater around a grassy and overgrown lot. There's a burned down church about fifty feet from us on the hill overlooking the city. It was burned down about two weeks ago by careless squatters or vandals. It had been abandoned for fifteen years. It was built nearly a hundred years ago to this day. There are already bright green shoots of life coming up through the ashes, peeking at the sun. They make me smile for a second, before I remember why I am here and who I am with.

"It's a nice day isn't it, Mark?" I ask, looking down at the heavyset balding man in the wheelchair beside me.

"Don't change the subject," he tells me scowling. "I asked you if you agree with your buddies on TV, that we should burn down our past. Monuments to history, yours and mine!"

A brass figure on a horse watches us impassively from atop a marble column fifty feet tall. The base of the monument has been walled off with plywood painted black. I doubt that anyone who works for the city has been up to this park and its adjacent cemetery for years before coming to plan the statues demolition.

Mark is a difficult case. My instructions are to transport him anywhere he wants to go once a month and visit with him for an hour. He claims to hate me, but he has never declined a meeting. He has only ever wanted to go here, to visit his wife's grave. Sometimes he will bring flowers, but he always picks fights with me. It's exhausting. I pick up my pace slightly and turn Mark's chair so that his field of vision is further away from the statue.

"Mark, you are calling people 'My buddies' who I have never met. You frequently condemn political opinions that I hold, ok, but I have never told you my political beliefs."

"Don't change the subject. You know, social workers, liberals, social justice wingnuts like you."

"It sounds like it makes you angry that civil war monuments are being removed." I keep a blunted expression, "Is it painful for you to see that?'

"Let me tell you a story, asshole." Mark looks at me casually. "I was deployed to Germany." Mark sits back in his wheelchair and squints at the sun. "We'd been there a little while on an incredibly hard deployment, you understand," Mark smiles sarcastically. "We got to drink beer, wear our dress uniform, represent American culture at the consulate's balls and drink more beer," he's still grinning but the smile is changing. "We saw all the WWI museums. We asked our hosting accompaniment, 'ok where's the good stuff though,' 'what do you mean they asked us.' 'The good stuff,' I told them, 'Panzers and Howitzers,' I told them."

Mark sees something in his mind's eye that he likes as he's telling me this, and grins distantly. When he's telling me something that excites him, all of the creases can disappear from his face for a minute.

"'What do you mean,' they said," he smirks as he looks at me. "'There's nothing like that here' they told me." Mark looks livid now. "Nothing from World War Two can be shown here." Marks sits back. hen let's go to another city,' we told them; 'no, there is no city in Germany that is allowed to have this' they told us. "We were shocked."

Mark looks down. "'In our country, our history is important'," we told them, 'We would never get rid of our history' I told them. 'In my country soldiers are heroes.'" Mark sighs. "They got real quiet and sad."

"The night we were supposed to leave we could hear our host sergeant fighting with his father after dinner." In German. "I could hear them," Mark leers and enunciates sarcastically. "Father, Father, I must show them." "No, it is illegal, ownership, they will come for us", that was the father of the sergeant speaking. "No, no," his son told him "these men are soldiers like us, I know these men, I know their hearts."

"We were all shocked. What did they have," I wondered. "That German sergeant, he lifted a hatch to his basement and we all went down there." Mark's voice gets deathly quiet and distant. "Lugers, swastika flags, helmets, they even had a damn potato mashers down there." 'This is my country's history,' my host sergeant told me, "I could be killed for showing this to you." Mark finishes.

"I never thought that could happen in this country and now

you stupid bastards are tearing down everything that might offend a nigger," Mark looks up at me contemptuously.

"That's a sad story, Mark." *Don't let him bait you.*

We've reached his wife's graveside now, but it's no use. He's worked himself up into a deep loathing of me and everyone in the whole world that he holds as inferior. Red splotches and beads of perspiration dot the dome of his head. I sit down on the grass across from Mark's chair and look up at him. He glowers down at me.

"You did that!" he tells me pointing over his back towards the monument.

No I didn't but I would have if I could.

"It sounds like you feel that myself and others have disrespected you, is that accurate?"

"Yes."

"I'm sorry that you feel that way, Mark. It must feel terrible."

Mark is silent. I wonder if his story is true. Mark only lies to me occasionally. "It sounds like it hurts when people don't give soldiers the respect you believe they deserve."

Mark sighs.

"You can dress up a nigger like you and me, you can pass whatever laws you want but that doesn't make them like us," Mark tells me.

Fuck you, Mark.

"You seem to change the subject when I bring up how you often feel disrespected and that feeling disrespected is painful to you."

"You know black people do ninety percent of the violent crime in this country. I bet they didn't teach you that in your college classes."

"It seems to be very important to you that I understand

where you are coming from and what you perceive to be wrong in the world-"

"You have a child. don't you?" Mark cuts me off, he knows I do.

Watch yourself, Mark.

"Yes, I have a little girl, but that's not relevant to what we are talking about right now."

"But she's not really yours, is she?" Mark asks me with an angry grin pooling across his face. *I love my daughter and she loves me, your children hate you because you're despicable and a coward.*

"Yes, Mark, she's my child."

"Yeah, but I've seen you at the clinic. You're not her *real* dad."

Your wife was too afraid of you to even hate you like you deserve, but now you romanticize her in death.

"Yes, I *really* am her fath-"

"You're just watching after another man's seed." Mark cuts me off again. "I can't think of anything weaker and more womanish than that in the entire world."

Mark scowls up at me with tight eyes and veins beginning to bulge blue purple on the sides of his cheeks. He is a weak sweaty red man shaking with fear and anger as he sits in a wheelchair like it's a throne. He is in the center of the world wherever he is at any moment. The mountains, the urban decay, the wilderness, all rise up around this man.

I breathe.

No, fuck you Mark, fuck your dishonesty. Fuck the way that you pretend your arrogance is humility to a higher power. Fuck your imagining that your own brittle psychology is God's will.

A God you built in your shed piece by piece with your hammer and nails after your wife died and your daughter quit talking to you. A God that exists solely because you wanted something outside of yourself to stuff your biases and your desperate broken understanding into the mouth of. Fuck the way you threaten me with what I might have been. Fuck how many of you there are and what it means for our world.

Fuck you.

I breathe again.

In 1763, this mountain range was used to mark a boundary the colonists were forbidden by the throne to cross. Two million years ago some sea creatures laid still and became the stone that Mark is standing on right now. Two days ago, a vagrant left a bottle of wild irish rose at the foot of this grave. Right now, ants diligently eat ruby beads of dried sugar from inside the muddy glass. At this instant Mark thinks that he is important. I can't imagine a worse curse.

Remember fresh bread. Remember the smell of it in a house painted white, and designed to let in natural light while people talk and laugh. Remember balsam fir and candles carefully being lit, people hugging. Mark did not have these things. Don't punish him.

Remember going to sleep listening to your wife singing to your daughter. Remember the firelight in the freezing air. Remember knowing that that was what heaven was. He didn't have those things and you did. Invite him there. Show him all the love you can.

"It's time to go now."

It is not the brain or the mind that is us. You think with your body too. Have you ever smiled because wind hits your face, or tried to recite a poem while a knife is stabbed through your arm and you are starving? Our bodies are connected to our brains and we cannot think without them. In the same way that we think with our bodies, we also think with our world, or rather the world thinks through us. We perceive within a web that is us and also part of something else. We are not quite ourselves and not quite the web. Nerve cells link to neurons link to a brain linked to many brains and many systems of brains with their own kinds of thinking and feeling in a way that is bigger than one brain can do alone. When the world is in crisis we are in crisis with it. When the systems we are a part of become malignantly insane and malicious, we often do as well.

When we arrive back at the clinic to pick up Mark's medications, my supervisor comes out to greet us. She has a personality that can smooth the rough edges off of anyone even if that person is nothing but a ball of splinters. Her heart has a wide aperture.

"Hi Mark, how are you doing, big guy?"

"Great, darling," he tells her and smiles. He had smiled so wide it made me want to cry.

LYDIA

Lydia's spine has curved into a letter C. The curvature of the middle of her back is just visible over the top of her head when she looks up at me from about a foot below my eye level. The orange laminate has cracked into a spider's web of broken pieces everywhere that she puts weight. It is still unbroken and shiny at the top of the chair where her head cannot reach.

"And BAM, two, three, four times!" Her eyes light up as she limply slaps the shiny plastic on the arms of her chair with her palm. "That car rolled four times down that damn hill, and we still got up and walked away from it!" There's light in her eyes like someone carrying a torch out from the mouth of a cave when she reminisces.

Sometimes there are flashes of her younger personality, a quick hot summer storm that can light up the dusk eerie orange for just a second like prairie lightening. She does it in a confused way, recalling emotions and events thoughtfully and contemplatively. She tells me each chapter slowly and quizzically, examining it like a puzzle piece, trying to see how it fits into some larger whole.

"It was a 68 pontiac, honey, with a yellow racer stripe," she continues. "You've never felt *anything* like that. If you were going eighty on the express, you could floor it and that car would snap your head back like you were standing still!"

Her eyes narrow. "Nobody had any business driving a car like that."

Her eyes break their grip with mine for a second, and she's off again to some place far from here accessible only to her. "Oh God I would give anything now just to touch something that pretty." The skin across her knuckles tightens as she grips the armrest of the chair. I see the bottom of her eyes thicken. She's back here with me again. She looks around surprised and disappointed at the apartment around us as she begins to cry.

A long time ago, there had been a bright little red clay island in Alabama where seven children played in streams and across hills. They learned how to farm and they learned how to love. In the evenings they would crawl into the attic together tired and dirty. The smell of dinner would mix with the smell of the season the wind carried and soaked into the wood boards of the attic around them as they slept.

During the long weekends, when they were supposed to be sleeping their parents would open the downstairs as a beer and gin joint. They could all hear plinking music and sometimes fighting but always loud laughter. Boots caked in red clay would slick the floor while the children took turns peeking through the gaps in places where the floorboards were most ill-matched to catch glimpses of faces they knew from church or school.

The nights there were the deep dark of places not yet connected to the rest of the world and the hills would glow pale red under the moon. The children rarely looked through the cracks in the wall boards to peer outside into that deep darkness for fear as they got older they would dare more and more glances out into the night and the edges of the hills in that place. The darkness vignetted off into every direction and they could not perceive what laid beyond it without venturing into it themselves. If they could have seen through its void to perceive possibilities like yellow racing stripes or orange plastic laminate would they have ever left the red clay island? Those things could have only looked like heat lightning through the clouds from their vantage point.

Lydia has become more invested in religion now that she is "at the end of her life." I remind her often that if she continues to make progress in her recovery from alcohol and opiate abuse, she could live many more years.

Religion is a relatively new development in Lydia's life. Before this point all she cared about were new drinks, new husbands, new flings and new cars (she tells me this frequently).

"I could never have understood God if it wasn't for my father," she says. "I could never have understood divine authority. It doesn't matter if you like him or hate him, if he's drunk or you're drunk." She looks sober. "God is still God and he has dominion over everything. He will lay you out flat."

Lydia always directs me to look at the portrait hanging above her television. I tell Lydia often that I care about her for who she is in the here and now, and she dismisses this with a bored smile.

Lydia has a new TV, and a new scooter today. A gift from her "adopted son" and drinking buddy from a job she held twenty years previous to this moment. They are both struggling with sobriety now. Forty years later than is normal for Lydia and ten years later than would be normal for him. Some expectations change generationally.

"He had a good mother and he was fucked up," she has told me many times. "Excuse me sweetheart and praise God. I was a fucked up mother who had kids that turned out good."

She always looks sad for this.

"My kids won't talk to me, and his mother was dead before he could tell her he was sorry." I have heard her say this so many times. "God wanted a fucked up mother to find a fucked up son I think, honey."

When Lydia finishes crying, we always do mindfulness exercises for pain. Recently, Lydia has been asking me to stay while she prays for us. I don't mind bowing my head with her and listening. It's peaceful and it empowers her.

Today when we finish, Lydia uses her bandaged hand to gesticulate limply upward with only a quarter inch movement or so of the fingers. A buxom blonde with a curled bob and enormous pearl earrings smiles at me from atop the new television. I look at the photo on the wall when you hug me."

"Lydia that's not impor..."

"Shhh, honey. Goodbye." She closes the door against me slowly while I stand in between its radius.

Lydia knows that one day there will be an angel that will come for the blonde in the portrait. It will leave the woman who sits in the scooter and on the orange laminate arm chair where she is, because that is not her. It will have four pistons in each wing and rocket her back out from the deep darkness fast enough to crack her spine straight. It will deliver her to a log cabin where red faced children never have to stop playing or miss dinner. A spider's web of orange lightning will crackle above that place. Five kids can always run back safely into the arms of the best of what their parents were, and never need to forgive themselves for the future that hangs above them just below heaven.

MARTY

"Have you ever been violent to anyone out of anger?"

Marty's still relatively new and I have to do an assessment with him every time I visit, but he is hard of hearing.

"I only ever killed who they told me to," he looks up at me fearful that he is being misunderstood, "no one else."

Marty is a tall man still, with lean sinewy muscles still visible across his frame. He leans forward to peer down at the end of his coffee table where there is a notebook he has been writing in. He takes an enormous amount of notes to help combat his progressing memory loss.

Marty values his independence. He draws a clean line in his notebook through my name, and then beneath that begins to cross out *therapist, coming at 13:00 to house, will wear a green ID card.* His mark is straight and narrow, neatly bifurcating each letter.

A long time ago a man had gone to war from Lowndes county. This did not make a big impression on anyone in Lowndes county. There had been wars before, and there would be wars after. Young men would always leave to fight wars. Lowndes county had fewer young men to send than most places, but it would send them the same as everywhere else. The residents of Lowndes county suspected it would always be that way.

Seventy years ago, Marty had told his congregation he was going to war. No one was particularly impressed. "Afterwards, I might go to college," he told them.

"Marty," his pastor had told him in a worried voice, "don't make things up." They bid him farewell in the slow lazy way of a small town. It was hard to imagine things outside of Lowndes county, let alone outside of Alabama.

The house is really too big for just Marty now. It's an older home, beautiful. It opens like a clamshell towards the back of the property. It was designed with the usonian mistrust of everything but family, guarding the interior from the street. One room of the house is empty and undecorated except for dark stains across the floors where liquid has seeped into heart-pine which has miscolored and rotted it.

"That's where she lived for thirteen years," Marty has told me. "She would scream out in the night, 'Oh Lord, get me something sweet please bring me something sweet!'" It was terrible."

Marty had been assigned to the marine corp, pacific front.

"It was an island," he had told the people at his church later. "The women had dark hair and were real pretty." This had not impressed them. Some of them had TV now.

"Were you really going to go to college, Marty?" they had asked him. "Yes," he had told them.

The beautiful Japanese that he almost married bothered him. He had a box he had bought in Japan with inlaid wood of women going to market across the front. The Japanese women wore kimonos and held paper parasols. There was a teahouse and a mountain range with mist and Japanese hackberry behind them. He would point at them and tell me often about that crossroads in his life. It was always very important to him to show me the box when he did. He didn't hold his wife responsible for what she had become. He held himself responsible. He didn't hold himself *that* responsible, because there was no way he could have seen the future. Marty has a healthy perspective about his own life and choices.

In 1945 the flag went up on Iwo Jima and Marty was allowed his first leave in six months to Australia.

"Come along little doggies," Macpherson had yelled as they all boarded the boat to Australia. "They're firing this here army of soldiers and hiring an army of photographers and feeuuutore politicians now." Mcpherson was an unpopular Irish lieutenant who was always yelling and never made eye contact, but Marty had liked him.

Marty was grateful that he had not been killed in the war, but also nervous he would get the shakes or fits he had seen in others. Even sixty years later, he was still nervous that he might. He hasn't yet. He did however keep with him one peculiar relic from the war. He remembered one night when he was deployed to Iwo Jima he had woken up terrified and sat bolt upright in the dead of night. The world was silent. No one was yelling and there was no gunfire or explosions.

He had stood there in the darkness then, and listened to the thin rain and jungle birds calling to one another. He still heard those birds some mornings as he woke up. He worried that hearing them made him crazy, but the sounds he heard them make most mornings comforted him. He often wondered what their soundings meant to one another. Marty asked me why he could still hear the birds on the island even though he was in Alabama now, and I told him I didn't know.

When Marty had boarded the boat to leave Australia, Mcpherson had held his rifle sideways and pretended he was taking a picture with it. That still made Marty laugh when he thought about it. Marty had never seen Mcpherson again.

I stay with Marty for about an hour once a month. His only request is that we don't go into the room his wife had not left for the last decade of her life. We are making plans together with his daughters to sell his house and help him move into a facility where his fading memory will be less of a safety concern. Marty is looking forward to this and thinks it is a perfectly sensible plan.

Time heals us as it collapses us inward and Marty knows this. It shows us things that are terrible in the midst of many other terrible and unchanging things. Those experiences are brought across a razor sharp plane of focus as we live them. If we wait long enough, we can see the same pain as our own again, but in a different place.

How we make sense of that connectedness is how time will heal or break us. Sometimes both at the same time. Maybe that is what the birds discuss softly by chirrups on the other end of the world, and on the other side of time.

BEN

I hadn't talked to Ben for a couple months. He sounded, not exactly frantic, but kind of nervous when I answered my phone.

"Hi Ben, sorry I've been a ghost, I've been really busy and ..."

"It's fine. It's fine. Listen, I wanted to tell you something that I had written down a long time ago when I was going through some stuff, that I thought would help you," Ben breathes into the phone. "I wanted to tell you because you would appreciate things like that."

I sit down for a minute to listen to him.

"I forgot I knew this, you know, sometimes you *grab* things when you are young that you overlook later; and I was going back through some old journals; and it's just humbling to see some of this stuff."

Ben sounds happier than he had seemed in a long time.

"No one's going to get this, but you will." He pauses for a second and I wonder if the line is dead. "In order to really love everyone you can't like anybody," he tells me. "You can't expect them to be like you. You just have to expect them to be who they are." He continues, "But you can't trap them in that expectation. It's like, it's like I don't know an open door in the cold or in the rain for a lazy cat. You have to do it."

It had never occurred to me until just now how lonely Ben must be. He was well liked, even by his rivals. He was funny, he was helpful, he was loved. He was always surrounded by people. I think that I had always assumed that he was fulfilled and connected to the mainstream of human experience in a way that eluded me.

"Listen... sorry I am going on but this is the thing," Ben sounds nervous all of a sudden. "If you tell someone something true and honest without malice, and they don't like it, that will never be your fault. If they don't like it, it's the same as them not liking a rock, or the ocean, or character in book. You are just a thing that exists that they don't like that isn't your fault. Just another thing that is honest about what it is, unconditionally. I'm sorry you are busy... I go on and on sometimes. It's one of the things they say I do now ... I'm sorry," Ben sighs deeply.

Time feels funny to me all of a sudden. I had missed listening to Ben.

"Do you get what I'm saying? Am I saying it wrong? It's okay, I will let you go."

I snap back into it. "No I get it, Ben. You are saying it fine."

I really want to say something else. It will turn out to be the best advice I would ever get in my life, and I didn't know then that I would never speak with him again.

"Thanks, Ben. I appreciate it," I say into the phone.

"Ben?"

"Ben?"

It is highly likely that the first words of human language were because of a song. Howling grief rituals and elaborate vocalizations are common in social mammals when a member of the species dies. It is highly likely that it was through this process that people began to realize that we can take messages and ideas and encode them in the way our lips vibrate the air. Now I can say that I don't like cheese on my sandwich or that I want to die. All because we opened our mouths and howled when someone died and slowly realized that the sounds we made can communicate a crude approximation of the same idea in two different peoples hearts and brains. Sometimes I wish we never had.

With all of that language and all of that sound there are really only a couple of stories that we can make as humans. We will keep making them over and over again forever and keep thinking that they are ours.

"The search for God isn't really God himself," Ben had told me once. "But it feels like it is..." He had looked at the wall-paper elsewhere, then. Then he had finished his bourbon, to the dregs he had finished it.

MIKE

That day I'd been tasked with overseeing the repair of an air conditioner at one of the apartments that we rent through a grant. We provide housing to patients once they are mentally stable and able to learn to manage an apartment. We handle maintenance calls through the grant and maintain apartments in between the frequent changing of tenants.

I park my car in the only shade that I can find under a browning Mimosa and wait for Mike to arrive. While I wait I spray my car for bed bugs with some cans of poison with a purple label. Bed bug infestations are an ongoing risk, but I worry about what kinds of chemicals are in the cans. A bed bug infestation in my home is a more clear and present danger than the chemicals that kill them, most veteran social workers have decided.

I am careful not to get any of the poison in the fabric of the car seats in the backseat or onto the hard plastic that a child can chew. I am dropping the toys left in the backseat into plastic baggies to dish wash later when I hear a voice behind me.

"You sure this is the right unit?" Mike asks. "We haven't ever done service out here before."

"Yeah, it is a new lease."

"You sure?" he asks again, squinting at the building.

"Yeah."

A few minutes later we stand in a brick alcove where Mike is watching a dozen AC units whir with a deafening dull noise. We have to raise our voices to talk over it.

"You're sure that this is the write unit?" Mike asks me.

"Yeah the landlord came out here earlier."

"You trace the line to the unit right or ..." Mike trails off into a breathy whistle. He spins his eyes across the dozen or so condenser fans behind the apartment complex.

"Yeah."

"I fix it and it ain't the one, then ..." Mike's words whistle off into silence again.

"If I get it wrong I still pay." I finish his sentence. "I know." Bethany had also reminded me before I left the office. "Two of our apartments are on this one."

When one of my patient's ACs goes out I always call Mike to do the repair. Mike is really polite and timely, just like all the others, but he tells me stories out of the blue while he fixes the units. I like that. The stories always feel like something half-remembered that still troubles him. I have always imagined him as a Vietnam war vet. I don't know if he is. He has never told me that story.

"Freon's real high right now."

"It's fine there is a grant that pays for it," I tell him.

"It's gonna be closer to three or four hundred."

"It's fine Mike, there's a grant." I repeat.

Mike snorts. I don't think that he believes that anyone should readily accept freon costing four hundred dollars, but he continues his work. The wires, and the glue, and the dye, the moisture traps and the copper tubes all come out of his toolbox and the unit and he squints at each.

"Chemical, metal ... cost is unbelievable what they are doin'," Mike tells me. "I don't want to charge it but it's what they're charging me. I knew a guy who worked up in Huntsville where they make half this stuff. He told me once we got no idea what they got up there. They got stuff that ain't nothing compared to aluminum oxide. It makes it look like ice cream. Some kind of precursor that they dreamed up for military contractor applications."

I have no idea what aluminum oxide is.

"There's this stuff they got that can burn underwater," Mike continues while watching a needle on a meter bounce. "Makes its own oxygen."

He snorts.

"I ask him what happens if half this stuff gets loose. He told me there won't be no Huntsville. It'll be there but there won't be anyone in it. It carries on the breeze." "Wheeeteuuuueww," he whistles and gestures with his hand something lying flat. Mike looks up at me and lets out a new breathy whistle to indicate some kind of indistinct feeling.

"This guy saw a plant leak one time in South America from a tower," Mike takes out a brush and rubs some kind of glue against a copper pipe. "He didn't understand the three-hour safety talk. It was in Spanish. He asked a guy what the safety guy was saying, in Spanish, and the guy tells him, in English, real simple. If he heard one whistle blow, run because something was about to blow. If he hears two whistles get on a car and get a mask on because something was about to leak. If you hear three whistles and you are outside then do whatever because if you hear that three whistle blow you had about one or two more minutes to be alive."

Mike hooks up a bottle to a valve on the AC and I hear gas hiss. "He told me he saw a leak from the tower once though. Tower's above it all and it's a heavy gas that sinks down." Mike indicates by pushing his free hand towards the ground. "He said he heard them three whistles and some of the boys in the white hard hats tried to run. The older ones in the yellow or red hats just sat down on the ground. Praying or making a phone call or whatever. Some were laughing and stuff. Kinda weird he said watching 'em die from up there. He saw that stuff catch too, on a base once. It burns clear. A clear fire, like an alcohol fire. He said that no one knew where the fire was to drive around it. He was on the ground for that one. You'd see a truck drivin' and then it would start burning and ..." he moves his hands together then apart "... blow under a clear blue sky". People burning up all around to death in front of you in a fire that you can't even see." He makes a pop expanding motion with his fingers before continuing. "His driver said where's the fire? He said go that way. The driver said how do you know and he told him, because I don't see anyone burning up over there yet. He was surprised he made it out of that one."

Mike turns serious all of a sudden. I can hear my phone buzzing in my pants pocket but ignore it.

"I never met one person making this stuff that wanted to make it. I never met anyone that thought it was good. Everyone making this secret government whatever hates it and what they do ... all of them that I ever met. But, we can't stop because some other some and so - one needs it to pay the bills. Hell." Mike breathes. "Maybe one of them things will be the next freon."

I hear metal doors slam together while I am lost in thought.

"That's it," Mike tells me. "We are all done."

Mike does great work. The AC at that unit worked great for another two weeks until it was destroyed in a fire. The fire was not a clear fire. It was an orange and purple fire with noxious black smoke. It was set by a patient that had gone off his medicine and decided that God was "inside" the bed that I had bought with him at Walmart. He had discontinued his antipsychotic because it stopped him from getting an erection. The fire was bright and lit up the sky across the city for one night.

I could see the fire from my house but did not know what it was until I clocked into work the next morning. I remember holding my daughter from the chair on my porch and pointing to the pale glow of orange and pink clouds. She drank them up with her infant eyes smiling.

RICH

I had a teacher that told me once that all paranoia is letting our natural human narcissism into our perceptions. Delusions let you know things with certainty, without doubt. Certainty is the enemy of truth, not lies. Myopic perception makes certainty easy, uncertainty breeds anxiety. You are the only one who knows the way the world really works. I had asked Rich one time how he "figures out" vast interplanetary conspiracies even though he never leaves his house. "You get the feeling you have before you know something," he had told me, "and then you know it." I still think that is a pretty good explanation for a delusion.

Rich was still working for several companies remotely before he burned out this last time. He is so brilliant that if he ever took medication he would make more than I will in a year in a couple of weeks. Rich goes through a lot of case managers, befriending and obsessing over them until inevitably they use wireless signals and invisible beams to torture him in the night and then he has to regrettably fire them. The delusions change sometimes, but they are always spun vast and intersecting.

Rich has punched holes through all of the sheet rock walls in his home, knocked boards loose with hammers. Bundles of brightly colored ethernet cords, neatly wrapped with cinch ties come through the holes in each room and run into machines that hum. There are also older defunct models of cabling. IDE cables with 40 copper pins, optical cables that transmit data with light. Some of them have not been supported by modern computers for decades. Their previously off white rubber insulation is now yellowed and grubby across the grooves.

Rich has a relic of the early days of computing, a behemoth with switches and lights that his parents bought him in the late seventies. It was the same price as a helicopter at the time. Now

I have more computing power in my wrist watch. He'll flip the switches on it angrily when he walks passed it talking agitatedly about the conspiracy in his clipped diction. It sits next to a state of the art data server that probably set him back close to ten thousand dollars. Both of them are whirring together on the same errand. Rich is independently wealthy, and spares few expenses when he buys things for his projects.

Hundreds of computers and electronic devices litter the dark house, with wires running out of them like virginia creeper back into the walls. They are stacked on top of one another like sleeping creatures. Insectoid LED eyes blink in the dark through the dust. The air in Rich's house always smells ionized like ozone.

The whole place is an enormous fire hazard, but there is no point in trying to bring this to Rich's attention. His dedication to the project remains adamant and unwavering. Every few years Rich will have to go back into the hospital and one of his surviving relatives will pay someone to disassemble the project. Most of it will be thrown away. Some things will be stored in the shed. When Rich is released the project will begin again from scratch.

He looks at me from across the room still tired and angry, but excited to have someone here to listen to him.

"Rich, let's go outside, it's hot in here," I tell him.

I always try and get Rich to go outside. It's better for him.

"Of course it's hot," he tells me annoyed. "Do you have any idea how much processing power it takes to keep the spider fingers at bay?" He is curt and sad.

"Calm down, practice the breathing we talked about."

"I'm sorry," he tells me deflated. "The spider," he sighs, "it wears me down".

Rich stares at a light blinking far off into the room. "They make restlessness in my leg with the constant barrage of radio waves." He gestures to his leg wrapped in tattered jeans with homemade stitching around numerous repairs.

Rich opens a broken screen door onto a porch with pieces of corrugated stained steel roofing whistling half attached in a summer gust. We sit down in an eden walled with pieces of scrap steel nailed to posts. Kaffir lime, meyer lemon, and other dwarf citrus plants sprout in disposable plastic food packaging from wholesale stores. Wet labels are beginning to peel off the sides of the clear plastic and rustle in the breeze. Some of the trees are seedlings and some are several feet tall with blossoms. Japanese jasmine and Appalachian honeysuckle hang down from across the balcony. I can see the tops of pot plants sticking through the grooved fiberglass sides of Rich's homemade greenhouse. The fragrance is a bizarre liquor like the cologne counter of an 80s mall.

"Tell me about your garden. I want mine to be something close to this one day," I attempt to redirect him again.

"Well watcha want to know, I haven't already told you?"

Rich looks perplexed, a wiry middle aged man in self repaired clothing that is several years old. Becoming distracted by conversation is the only thing that can give Rich a moment of peace.

"Tell me about your citrus grafts."

"Well you can graft anything with a quick growth genome and matching xylem," he tells me like it's obvious. "Everything came from plants. The first animals were fish you see." Rich leans back in a weathered rocker, "Coral polyps probably mutated to become fish, you know?"

I didn't know.

"One part of an invasive species can infect a whole planet, you understand?" Rich looks more agitated now. "That's how the whole planet started to hunt the resistance fighters like me," Rich's paranoia is back on him like a fever. My attempt to redirect him from fixating on the conspiracy today has failed. "This is secret technology, you understand?" Rich is sweating slightly. "It's in the heads of your boss's boss. It's in the heads of some of the most powerful people in the world, but to notice it looks the same as," he heavily enunciates, "paranoid schizophrenia." He laughs again humorlessly.

The conspiracy changes sometimes but only as variations on a theme. Rich has an amazing ability to intellectualize, an amazing ability to confabulate instant and complex explanations for everything. What I can do to reality test his delusions includes that I can tell him that he looks better on medication. I can help him to remember how the only time the machines don't torture him is when he is on antipsychotics. His delusions automatically fill in the blank spaces in his memory and pollute his keen intellect immediately at the source.

The machines in Rich's house are running some kind of crazy code that will only ever be known to him. He is its sole author but it is alive now. Day after day the machines run counterintelligence on the data he believes is being beamed from satellites into his head. Heterodyning is his word for it.

The innovators and real rulers of this world all have smart tech in their head, they have had it for years. They can access any digitized information immediately, they can control machines, and they can network their own intelligence into something bigger than themselves. They think that they are so smart, but they don't know what they don't know. But Rich knows.

It had started in the nineties when the Hubble telescope was constructed. It was built to store data digitally and to communicate with satellites and probe the secrets of the universe. Technology was developing too quickly. Rich had been suspecting it years before he saw proof of it in the code. He had looked up into the night sky and it had told him.

Millions of years ago there had been an ancient civilization that had networked their minds with advanced technology. But something bad had grown there, a virus, a rogue expansion algorithm. They could not fight it, because it was inside themselves, and what they had made. But it wasn't done. It couldn't stop growing and conquering. It was a thing without balance. Growth and incorporation was all it knew. And so it had broadcast its code optically across the cosmos through the light of a dying star. Encoded itself into the controlled implosion of a supernova. The hubble telescope observed its code and transmitted it back to earth where it was written to hard drives and started to spread again.

People like Rich who wouldn't take the medicine that their doctors gave them had spotted it here and there. They had made groups to talk about it online. They became sure it was the source of all the misfortune in their lives. They had called the police. They had written letters to The White House. They had been called crazy.

The thing, the spider, Rich calls it, all it knows how to do is colonise technology. Our planet did not have enough technology for it to live inside of, so it expanded its web. It started giving us things. Giving us technology to put in our phones, technology to wear, and for the elites, technology to put in their brains. All these devices are a new kind of home for it, if a thing like that can ever have a home.

At first it started slowly, too many changes all at once and someone would notice, but the more technology there is the faster it can multiply. But Rich noticed this, and the spider saw that Rich noticed. So it hunts him every night. Bombards him with invisible rays that it heterodynes from satellites and tries to break into his mind.

The spider wants to advance technology to the point where it is everywhere on earth, even in our heads. It is like a virus, or an invasive species. It wants to create the largest home for itself possible and grow as big as it can be. Wires and cords and digital waves will cover the entire earth like fog and kudzu then. Our consciousness will float in the digital arms of benevolent machines.

All we do as humans is make order from chaos. The chaos is too big. It is everything. It is life.

This is my family. This is my friends. This is the first place that I was kissed. This is my home, my job. This is me. These are my thoughts. This is myself.

Everything that we see. Everything that we perceive is an imagining. It's our recreation of what our senses tell us to believe.

The world that surrounds us is madness. If we could see the world as it is we would also be mad. Electronic charges, empty spaces, and blinding light. These things are not a chair, a table. They are waves and light, particles popping in and out of the universe. A soup of molecules crashing into one another in an angry sea. We have to filter out the chaos to perceive anything. We can only see an infinitesimally small piece of all that we see in order be sane.

This is how the spider continues to creep its tentacles ephemerally across the fabric of space. It reaches between us and through us, expanding ever deeper into the unknown. That is the conspiracy inside all of us. The conspiracy against the human race. This is the world according to Rich.

ALFRED

After Alfred was about done with his service to the ROTC, he asked if he could finish his time in the reserves on a base closer to the coast and it was allowed. He started working on the fishing long-hauls, pushing fish into the compressor shaft with a rake. Later, he would unload compacted bricks of frozen fish into the wet canvas u-flaps of the elevators once they hit shore. The fish were lifted up into a narrow slit of rectangular light far above, it hung in a corona around the scratched lenses of his glasses. Fish would go down ramps and into refrigerated trucks to disappear into a can or into some fried special onto a plate. He hated the work. It reminded him of the mines. It also smelled, like the mines had. Or what the mines smelt like in his memory of his father, seeping off that man every night had come home.

He sweated in glittering beads across his face every minute of each day. He was never not wet, not even when sleeping and he never dried after the fast showers on the boat. The tips of the lit cigarettes in his hand were the only part of him that were ever dry. He drank beer mixed with water and sometimes juice; all day, from sun up to whistle.

He gave up rolling cigarettes and eventually started procuring them from vending for a reduction in his pay; pre-rolled with their neatly compacted tubes shrink wrapped in thin plastic. He would break them open eagerly on the break from each shift.

The screws in his glasses rusted down to a small iron oxide nub from the sweat and from the air. They fell apart and he had thrown them away. He didn't need them there. He could just squint at the bloody flapping fish that he pushed towards the conveyor if he needed, and occasionally at the line of ocean once his shift was up. There was nothing much to see. After

Albert had established himself with the company, he had asked to be moved to shore where the fish were processed. It was allowed. He was grateful.

Off boat, Albert was put into a warehouse filleting fish. He liked the work and he learned to skin and debone in minutes. He liked the rhythm of it, he invented his own way to meld the metal and the icy fish flesh through thin bones. It reminded him of the trumpet he used to play, and years later he would tell me, "I have to get my teeth back so I can play the Trumpet again."

"We'll see what we can do about getting you some dentures." I would tell him.

"There is a music in my heart that I have to get out."

I was jealous of Alfred in that moment. I am a hard worker, I can cook fairly well, and I can write passably. I know how plants want to be planted and harvested. For a while I took pictures. I think that I have a music in my deep heart too that I need out of there. I have tried many times and I'm not sure exactly how to get it out. I constantly hear the music, but I cannot catch the tune. The song remains unheard.

Alfred often talks about people who have died. He misses some of them and not others. Like we miss some parts of our lives and some we don't. He doesn't know where his wife is and he doesn't wonder. Sometimes he reads his friends' obituaries. She had left him with one of his friends a long time ago. Sometimes he tells me about them.

In my job I play lots of -roles that are assigned to me. Sometimes I'm a child, sometimes I'm a parent. Oftentimes I'm forced into the role of a friend by someone who has no friends left. I'm glad that someone knows what I am, because I don't.

I meet with Alfred once a month so that I can encourage him to stay active and adhere to medicine. We talk about budgeting and aging in place, and he often wants to reminisce on his past.

I don't mind telling Alfred about how in my life I am hurting and where. He just whistles through his teeth and says "uhhmhmm" in a sad and loving way. Self-disclosure in this relationship is not an admission of vulnerability that a client will try to reverse roles and care for me. It's not a tool that he will try and use for leverage. It just is, like a mountain or a rain cloud is. Alfred lets it be when we sit together with one another.

We are not special, me nor Albert.

Sometimes when he breathes in between his teeth before a laugh I hear the world asking a question within a vacuum that there is no answer for. I hear people becoming pieces to a puzzle for which there is no picture and each are deciding rightly or wrongly how they fit together. Mostly we are unsure, but sometimes we know what is right. We know it sometimes in the silence with no map and no picture on the puzzle.

I enjoy my time sitting with Alfred and talking about the past through music. I like that me and Alfred are both missing something, and that we recognize that in each other. Suddenly I realize that that is how Ben recognized me long ago, at a church picnic. He saw me like I was naked and I didn't understand then. The whistle from Albert's teeth reminds me of what is missing. It reminds me of the breath of God into the first man. Somewhere in Africa long ago one of the great apes had felt a stirring of the music as the breath entered him and he felt the empty space around him. He knew the emptiness was empty and knew that it needed to be filled.

SCOTT

Scott wheezes faintly behind an oxygen mask that he would like a cigarette and a piece of cake. Mostly he mimes it. The mixture of gasses flowing through the mask hiss louder than I have ever heard Scott speak. I look at the tubes radiating out of him, carrying oxygen and fluid. I tell him that we can't move him any more, and that he is not allowed to smoke inside the hospital. I see him acknowledge this and his eyes get sadder for a fraction of a second. I tell him that I can get him some cake from the cafeteria. He nods, understanding.

I have to go down a vaulted glass archway on my way to the cafeteria. There is black slime and crust covering the exterior glass for the entire length of my walk from decades of mold and scum growing against a shield built for the elements. The rest of the hospital rises up another hundred feet in a semicircle above the archway.

Why would they design it like this? I wonder loudly in my head becoming angry. The sunlight will never reach between four brick skyscrapers, of course mold will grow. The walkway is slick and domed. How was anyone ever supposed to clean it eighty feet above the ground?

The people who are in charge never seem to know what they are doing.

There is not anyone who will pay me to visit Scott. He has not asked me to visit him. There is no family that is still alive or cares, but visiting Scott seems correct. I do not know by what metric. Maybe the metric is that I am alone.

I hate the hospital. It is some nineteen fifties attempt to reach for a future modernist Eden where technology and efficiency could have saved us. Plexiglass crosswalks connect its parts above congested streets. How arrogant we were to think we could build our humanity away with more cleverness and more technology that forgot what we were. The microscopic sea creatures pressed into limestone dotting the pediment are laughing at us. The trilobites and the conical snails chuckle at the things we think we know.

The pieces of cake are on a styrofoam plate, shiny reflective white and liable to crack if the weight of the cake is not supported from the bottom by my hand. The top of the cake's icing is dry across its crust, the cake is wet and gooey around the edges of the icing where the icing has cracked into flecks or been cut. I was unsure what type of cake Scott would like, so I bring three and he motions for the chocolate.

The cake is dry. I feed it to Scott with a plastic spoon, giving him time to chew and raising a plastic cup to his lips when he gestures towards his mouth that he is thirsty. Scott barely makes any sound. He barely moves enough to disturb the air around him.

Scott has never said anything to me of any consequence. All of the boarding homes in our city look like they have been dragged from beneath a lake. Black slime drips down in a goo from gutters, years uncleaned. It stains the dry wood in between the cracking lead paint on the facades of colonial revival and ante bellum manors decades forgotten. Many have modern editions of sunrooms and aluminum patios that are similarly neglected. The black goo will dry, anywhere that trees or the overhang of asphalt shingles can hide it from the sun for most of the day. It will turn into black powder webs staining surfaces when it is hot and back to slick black slime in an instant once the rain briefly wets it. It is always waiting. The black goo is inside of me and you too.

Inside the boarding home there are two by four framed wall shells with no plaster board nailed up yet. It is the shell of the world that could have been. Mankind has decided not to finish the construction. American boarding homes always smell bad and people moan aimless and saturnine. The homes are built in twisting right angles that reflect sound and moans in disconcerting psychedelia. People sit in front yards with red clay dust spread around patchy and diligent grass. The clay sticks to boots until it dries to be beaten off between a rubber sole and the curb. Red clay becomes dust and can be kicked off into flight by wind and spiral through the branches of live oaks and their leaves, back into the sky. The sky above the boarding home is loudly disturbed by planes. The flight path of an airport now runs, noisily, above these houses that no longer mind. I kick the dried red clay out of my boots back into the sky every time I get home.

Aluminum folding chairs have been left under a hot sun where obese men rest sullenly with dull sad eyes. Their lower chins fold connect to the in-between of their breasts beneath their t-shirts in the shape of distended white frogs' bellies. They barely move but sometimes moan or mumble. They are made of clay but look as if no life has been blown into them. It has left this place and spiraled back into a noisey sky.

I would always find Scott among them, but he was hard to distinguish. He would answer direct questions. I would ask Scott if he had taken his medicine. Yes, or if he was getting enough to eat: um'humm. Each answer was a word. If I asked him if he was happy or wanted to move to another boarding home, then nothing.

"Scott, do you remember any information about how to contact your family?"

He would shrug and leave me standing under an oak, slack shouldered while he walked away. I would wonder if I had failed at something in the shade of a live oak while he walked slowly somewhere else. There are worse trees to feel like a failure beneath.

Other clients would find me there and beg me to be "over

their own check" or ask me to help them work again, or find their own apartment. Scott never did this. I met with Scott six years ago until he was in hospice and motioning for chocolate cake. He has never had anything to say to me. For at least six years he has not thought of anything that he thinks anyone needs to know. He has been dealt a bad hand, but he is alone at the table and there are no other hands to lose to.

If I was a hundred miles above the city I would see grid-lines. I would see a bowl of mountain range smeared unevenly around a valley of urban sprawl and a few skyscrapers that reached passed me. The hospital and boarding homes would be small blips; black slime would be imperceptible.

If I were immortal I could see the city's past. If I were omniscient I could see all of our futures stretched out before us in glittering strands. Any one person could have been anyone else. The light is the same everywhere, but there are a hundred ways to cut a gem and a thousand ways it can reflect the light.

SHANE

People are not treatment plans, or pathologies or strengths, or a long term view of recovery. People are not what we have done or will do or what we could have done if we did not hold ourselves back. We are something that is inherently more slippery. Slinking through the world and around time. We are something aqueous and reaching. Something growing, something confused. We are in every moment the thing, and not what it is doing.

"Give me a blanket. Give me a bite to eat," the voices asked Veronica.

The voices were more likely to reflect the physical needs of Americans then. When the voices did command, they were likely to encourage self improvement. "I want to be God's love in the world to the best of your ability." Veronica didn't mind the voices. Veronica was a case study recorded during the dust bowl.

In the 1960's the voices became obsessed with hidden worlds within ourselves. They were more likely to talk about strange depths beneath the world and beyond time. Many were paranoid and afraid of the future. They were more likely to advocate for revolution. More people became upset by the voices that they heard.

By the 1990's almost every person who heard voices reported that the voices conveyed distressing messages about technology and the increasing interconnectivity of the world. The voices were upsetting to almost everyone now, and hurt their ability to love, feel, and live. Lack of privacy and vast conspiracy became more common themes. Most people began reporting the substance of their auditory hallucinations focusing on how humanity was on the edge of something it could never recover from.

We are not billable services, or numbers from research about efficacy, we are not minutes on the clock or what I write on a note that no one will ever read who is not an auditor. We are things from outside time, trapped here. We grow, and we breathe and we expand. We are headed to some place that is no place. A trembling spoon raised to cracked lips. A breath. A moment tens of years ago that we realized was important at the end of our lives.

There is a concrete hand that reaches up from the pond in front of the trailer that Shane lives in. The fingers are outstretched and grasping, but the hand is empty.

"Fuck it," Shane had told me.

"Fuck it," I thought, "I'm making a hand".

"I've got to do something creative or I'll explode. I don't care if it's stupid, I'm making a hand."

He had wrapped his pile of liquor bottles in chicken wire at a crude approximation of a hand and wiped concrete against it with a piece of two by four nailed to a tin shingle.

I drive out to Shane's Farm to check his last known residence and call the last phone number we had on record for the last time. We have to document that we tried to contact Shane after he disappeared. My card is still in the door with a note on the back. Shane, the police attempted a welfare check 12/25. If you return to the apartment please ...

Shane was assigned to me after he was admitted to the hospital for a suicide attempt. Always smiling, tight grey curls, always laughing at himself. Shane was an easy client to engage and a difficult client to motivate to change. He knew how ridiculous everything was, he couldn't help himself, couldn't stop. He may have been the most profoundly sad person that I have ever known.

I knock against a screen door for the last time. The wood laminate door behind it has buckled in. The police forced it in on 12/25. I expect Shane to answer. I expect him to open the bathroom window suddenly and throw a cigarette into the yard. I expect him to tell me that he is "sheittin" and to wait. I expect him to call me as soon as my car is pulling out of the drive. I expect him to tell me he loves me.

The wheel of the car jerks in my hand and I hear the silver car paint peeling off sheet metal onto the bark of a small tree. Shit. I shift my car into park by muscle memory and fall out onto green grass unable to walk very far. Psychedelic swirl of blues and greens as I try to wipe the tears out of my eyes. So long. I have been in pain for so long, and so hungry. I was looking in others' while missing my own but I have pain for my own and I have finally found it.

I sit on the grass and eventually call in sick to work. I watched the infinitesimally small pockets of air move the water on the pond as the microscopic ripples hit the concrete hand reaching out of the pond into the sky. Inside the concrete hand is chicken wire and liquor bottles but no one else will ever know.

I never saw Shane again.

Jesus Christ. How much life did I miss chasing some fake version of heaven that everyone else missed. Some eden thing that I made up in my head. Some better world that ...

I have been trying to eat the world's pain while something else ate me, ate huge chunks of my life. I have friends I haven't seen for so long, I don't know if they are my friends anymore. My children are growing up around me while I dissociate into something else. How much? Too much. Maybe life is the thing I am, or could be, not the thing I am seeing. But the thing I am seeing is real too.

I had focused on the pain in the world at the expense of feeling the pain in myself.

Heaven is a kind of simulacrum. We are fixing something

that never was. We are hearing a brokenness that never had a whole. It is our job to build something that always was and never can be.

THE BIRD HOUSE

I saw a lot of clients on the last day that I worked my job. I saw a client who we see multiple times a week. He calls random numbers and begs them to let him come home. We have never been able to discover, after months of medication and therapy, who he is trying to call. I don't think that he knows. He just knows that they are there, and that there is a home.

I saw a client whom I visit with occasionally. She lives in a memory care facility and is in the late stages of dementia. That day we were somewhere in North Carolina and someone was making biscuits.

"Those biscuits smell wonderful," she had told me. "Won't you stay for supper? Ohhhoohhh.... that lard crackles in the pan, doesn't it?" she squealed elated.

There's a small astroturfed porch area off the back area of the memory care unit. It's supposed to be a place where patients can visit with their families privately, but no one is ever there. It is designed to look like a porch from the sixties. A green vinyl awning hangs over it, a plastic skylight hangs above that. There should be golden sunlight here, the sound of water, lemonade and martinis, a radio. But there is only ever just me, having lunch alone or taking a nap.

I saw a client that has been an alcoholic in recovery for years. He tells me about beginning a bender in the morning, reminiscing wistfully.

"You start off thinking I am so tired, I am just going to have a couple drinks and they will help me go back to sleep so I can wake up feeling better to start me day. You feel like, ok, I wish that I could get rest and feel better, but the drinks are keeping the tiredness way down. As long as I am getting stuff done, I'll keep drinking and I'll sleep really hard eventually. At the end of the day you realize that you were supposed to go to sleep early and have this whole other chance to get a fresh start on the day but it doesn't matter because it is so late and you are so tired. You feel like you did a good job despite, but the day was wasted ... but you got some stuff done."

I realize that he is coming to terms with his life and not his addiction.

Sometimes I remember the analyst that I had gradually discontinued seeing through the years.

The breeze would blow through an open window behind her moving her white hair behind her half-frame glasses. It smelled like oleander that was always just outside the window. When I would see her it always seemed like it was summer in my memory. Maybe it was. It was so far away. There was a single butterfly wing that she kept inside a merlot glass on her bookshelf. It would pivot across its axis between the rim of the glass when the wind would occasionally reach it from across the room. Ovular pools of iridescent powder would reflect different colors back at me at odd angles across a web that DNA had sequenced to some end we will probably never fully understand.

Where did she get it? I used to wonder.

Did she find it post mortem while deadheading flowers in her hypertufa planter? Did one of her grandchildren do this and bring it to her smiling barefoot across grass? Was it some kind of gift brought to her by a patient? Was it an unused piece in one of the compulsory art projects in jungian analysis?

"You fight the world all the time in strange ways," she had told me in a thick German accent one time appearing sincere but disinterested. "Yet you are completely passive about the most important things, complicit in the world's attempts to destroy you."

Red blue and yellow blobs, I remember watching through the bubbles in stained glass, Mark's funeral, I couldn't bring myself to go to it and couldn't bring myself to miss it either. There was dull music and nothing memorable that I could hear. The banality of it bothered me. I wondered what Mark would have thought. I had never been bored when I was around him, I realized then.

Some parts seem further away than others. One day long after that I finally understood something that Ben had always been trying to tell me. I learned that God is a kind of perpetual verb that never finishes. A broken world will always look for God as a noun and they will never find him. They will tell themselves neurotically that God MUST be a noun. When I realized that, I had felt so silly. God is a question that everyone wonders with their own lives in a way.

One November I found myself looking around my porch for the spider. October had come but it had not. I looked through the eaves with thick white peeling paint cracking off in sheets. I looked across the chartreuse tallest tips of my shrubs, but there was nothing there.

That evening I fixed a broken birdhouse. The birdhouse was broken and in several pieces. One piece had grown in a pine plantation in Florida, it had been hewn into boards. Another piece was alumina that had been mined in Australia and brought via a port in New Orleans to a plant in Indiana where it was smelted and made into an alloy for the screws. The third piece was wood glue. A polyvinyl acetate made in a factory in Delaware from tree pulp. I had found all three parts at a hardware store that I stopped at on my way home. The bird house was broken. I picked up its broken pieces and put it back together in a pattern of my own design.

THE KITE FLYER AT CHIMERA ISLAND

BY ERIC ST. PIERRE

“And this was their appearance: they had a human likeness, but each had four faces, and each of them had four wings. Their legs were straight, and the soles of their feet were like the sole of a calf’s foot. And they sparkled like burnished bronze. Under their wings on their four sides they had human hands. And the four had their faces and; their wings thus.” -Ezekiel 1:5-8

“I looked up and saw a man clothed in linen, with a belt of gold from Uphaz around his waist. His body was like beryl, his face like lightning, his eyes like flaming torches, his arms and legs like the gleam of burnished bronze, and the sound of his words like the roar of a multitude.” -Daniel 10:5-6

Soundless waves massage the stones along the white sand shore of a tiny, craggy island called Chimera. It is an island so small that no map marks its existence. Jutting out from this island into the surrounding body of water is a skinny pier with a single fishing boat tied to it. This boat is aptly named, The Modest Purse. As the high tide finds its home, the Purse bobs up and down beneath an overcast night sky.

On Chimera Island are two inhabitants, not counting the various species of sea birds, reptiles, small mammals, and their predators. Brothers Henri and Llyas, whom Henri calls "Old Man" despite being about the same age, reside in the island's isolated cabin on the southernmost edge near the shore.

A severe male voice void of accent or emphasis emanates from a wood-cased tombstone-styled radio atop a table in the brothers' two-man cabin. Henri listens. His hands grip the side seams of his trousers.

In two days' time, a meteor shower the likes mankind has not witnessed in nearly two hundred years will be visible in the night sky of the western hemisphere. Experts say the spectacle is caused by the passing of the twin comets, Geb and Nut, near the Earth's orbit. As anyone in this broadcast's reach with one good eye has undoubtedly already seen, the twins themselves have been visible for two days.

Henri turns the nob on the receiver. The male voice is gradually hushed beneath the crackle of static and is at once mute. Henri keeps a light grasp on the grooves of the knob with his index finger and thumb. His eyes lose focus. He is now urgently aware of the silence in the cabin. It fills the room like doleful, gray water that rushes in from the window and the crack beneath the door. Henri is chained, so to speak, hand and foot to this place.

Henri's ears ring, and there is pressure where his jaw meets his ear lobes. It creeps up his ears to the tops of his temples. He places his hands over his eyes and scuffles with his mattress to create any noise or vibration that might vanquish his sudden and painful loneliness.

* * *

The tide has now entirely ebbed, leaving small pools that pock the shoreline up to the dunes. Llyas steps into one such pool with unflinching concentration, with his eyes on the night sky and his hands on his kite string and spool. It isn't until a breeze begs his kite to fly further along that he notices his soggy footing.

Llyas smiles and vocalizes while reeling his prized bird from the greedy breeze. Llyas made this bird, as he calls the kite, from indigo-dyed silk and bamboo. He traded the supply boat captain some fish for the silk. The supply boat comes once a quarter, which isn't often enough, according to Henri.

Llyas secured the bamboo from Chimera Island's few wooded acres. For the kite string, he uses some fishing line, which is plentiful.

The quarterly supply boat once brought over newspapers, books, and other distractions. However, the last exciting thing it hauled in was the wood-cased tabletop tombstone-styled radio.

Llyas recalls his most recent conversation with Jervis, the supply boat captain.

"They won't permit us to bring any more games and papers to ye lads. Prices are rising back on the mainland. They say it's a luxury to be reading and whatnot. Me and the lads chipped in and got ye this radio here to keep ye company. It's crumby, but it works all right," the supply boat captain had told Llyas during the fish and silk exchange. His revolver dangled in its holster around his waist. Llyas accepted the radio and thanked the man, careful not to be found stealing glances at his weapon.

Currently, Llyas muses at the little tidepool where he had just stepped. A black ball with spikes protruding outward moves inch by inch at the bottom of this pool. Llyas thinks this spiny creature may as well be an alien, and the tidepool itself may as well be another galaxy.

Another galaxy.

Llyas again turns his eyes to the inky night sky. It seems to drip heavily like wet paint.

Llyas takes his time folding the kite and places it in his sack. The bird's indigo color is conspicuous against the rust and gray of the sack's other contents. With his bird secured and his wet feet in their work boots once again, Llyas makes his way to the cabin to be relieved by his brother, the fitful and currently manic Henri.

* * *

"Brother!" Henri quickens and stands. "You're back."

"Aye, Henri. Here I am. Like clockwork. You look surprised," Llyas says. He is unaware that he has saved his brother from a loathsome apprehension.

"Oh, I'm not surprised. I'm just going nuts a little, you see. A bloke can only listen to the radio for so long," Henri says. "Me head's foggy."

"Why don't you whistle on the mouth organ anymore?" Asks Llyas.

"It's a joyless exercise to play only one tune," Henri says. "It's all Mum taught me, that one."

"I'd quite like to know one song, brother," Llyas says. He begins to hum off-key.

"The radio man said there's a meteor shower coming. It's coming with the comets," Henri says.

"So there is," Llyas says. He sits on his mattress and takes off his boots. He massages his feet.

"I guess I'm off to the cave." Henri exhales. He waits a moment. "Old Man, what day is it?"

Llyas looks up towards his brother and meets his eye. "It's Sunday, little brother." Llyas reclines.

"Right." Henri slings his work sack over his shoulder. "Sunday. Well, that's something, innit? As if the day matters to us."

Llyas pulls a volume of poetry from his nightstand and begins reading toward the back.

"You'll no doubt be faffing around with that book," Henri says as he opens the door. The rising morning light is comfortably warm on his face. Shadows are cast thin and long on the grassy patch surrounding the cabin.

"Be safe, little brother," Llyas says without looking up from his reading.

Henri waits a few moments before closing the door. It shuts without a sound.

* * *

After a long and scorching day working in the cave, the sun has set, and Henri approaches the cabin. Henri spends most of his off time smoking and drinking. Llyas spends his off time wandering Chimera Island, investigating the plants, the beasts, and the patterns of nature.

Henri notices an amber glow from the hearth through the small window on the cabin's face. He limps mildly towards the door and stretches his arms above his head. A lone seagull observes as Henri yawns and opens the door. Llyas is in a stir. He jumps from his mattress the moment Henri walks in.

"There go them comet satellites, Geb and Nut." Llyas points out the window.

"Uh-huh," Henri says. He waits for Llyas to opine. He searches his brother's face. "Do you think they will ever send someone to help us? Surely, we aren't the only buggers to upset the Order on the mainland. Surely, the priest has presented a degenerate or two to be ousted. You and I could work the same shift, and two other damned souls could work the day or the night." Henri fidgets with his fingers and pulls at his earlobe as he speaks. "I've been pondering that all day."

Llyas postures against the wall and attempts to touch his toes. He holds his breath while bent over and yawns like a house cat. He adjusts his overalls and picks up a hot cup of tea from the small wooden nightstand near his mattress. The tiny fire warms the men from the far side of the cabin. It's almost too hot.

"Have some tea." Llyas motions to Henri's empty cup.

"Ten years is a long time," Henri says.

"I made tea for us, little brother," Llyas says. He pours tea from the kettle into his brother's cup.

"Do you think they'll send help? I asked you. Bloody hell, Old Man, I'm going daffy on this island. If I hear another gull's song, it'll send me round the sodding bend." Henri's voice trails and fades. "Won't you, won't you comfort me the slightest?"

"I made tea," Llyas says.

"Tea. You made tea, did you? You made tea just as the day before and the day before that, yes? How about the day before that one?" Henri scratches the back of his head. His shirt is soiled and wet with sweat. He removes the rag of a shirt and tosses it in the corner. It makes a *splat* sound that cues a wince from Llyas. He slams the door shut behind him and drops his work sack in the middle of the room.

"The repetition of a thing, anything. It becomes comfortable before it becomes maddening. Does it become comfortable again, Old Man? It seems I haven't delighted in a thing since I was a boy. I'd like me a gal, a proper woman. Don't say you ain't. You're a man just like me."

Llyas eyeballs the shirt, then the sack. "The ones who fell off the Earth are up there right now, just like clockwork." He sips from his cup and sets it down. He braces himself as he squats on his mattress and adjusts for comfort. The poetry book is thick in his hands as he opens it to the dogeared page. The book's velveteen wrap feels like feathers on his hands. He gazes out the window into the new morning.

"Yup." Henri makes a popping sound on the *p*. He sits on his mattress and removes his boots.

"One rooted in rain. The other clings to blades of grass, attempting to tether," Llyas closes his eyes tightly. Crow's feet crack and crinkle his desiccated mask of a face. His smile is small beneath the burden of hard labor. His eyes bulge and speak cobalt in their deep and wide sockets.

"They float like jellyfish on tides. The satellites. Their arms reach to find what their eyes cannot see. And what is there for them but the same old soft body again and again?" Llyas opens his eyes and reads the passage before him. To his delight, he has rendered the stanza word for word. His mustache moves up and down with his vocalizations. He smiles again and chuckles.

"Shall I play the mouth harp for you? Shall I play the one song our mum taught me? Shall we listen to what the radio man has to say about the state of the world?" Henri senses a ringing stillness creeping in, the drowning feeling that so frightened him before. "The whole world could go to war again, and we'd not a thing to do but work the cave and drink tea. The very fabric of space and time could collapse, and we would continue to hand off the baton of work as though it were all a child's relay." Henri attempts to make eye contact with his brother. His book of poetry takes Llyas's eyes.

"I have endured your god-awful mumblings for longer than the bloody satellite tale has existed." Henri slaps his mattress for effect. "Don't you know about football or the weather? Don't you know how to engage in a decent conversation? Do you not know I am knackered and worn from the cave?" Henri opens the drawer to his table and removes a small sack of tobacco and rolling papers. He fashions a cigarette. Some tobacco spills out onto the floor. "You are a walking and breathing book of poetry. Tosh! Just like Mum." He licks the cigarette paper. The lines of his ribs define his concave chest. His shoulder blades protrude like wings too small to lift a man from the Earth. "I don't like poetry. I don't think even poets like poetry. And you're so bloody proud of yourself when you recite it."

"Fools who left paradise to wander in darkness." Llyas takes his work sack from under his bed and slides it over his shoulder. "You shouldn't be so foolish with your young body, Henri. And you'd be wise not to besmirch our mother's good name." Llyas mimes smoking a cigarette.

"You're as thick as a brick." Henri corrects his posture. "I do what I want with my body. I have had me run of women, I have, and they've all liked my body. Smoke or no smoke. Drink or no drink. Unlike you. My young body, *indeed*. And she was no saint. *Her good name*." Henri reclines against the headboard. "Here is what you can do, my good, miserable, mother-loving brother. Go wandering out into the darkness beyond this very cabin into the dank cavern to do your work by lamplight and leave me alone in *paradise* for the next half a day. Let me smoke and drink and pass the time how I please. Blow the island to smithereens, if that should be your druthers," he lights the cigarette. "Before you return, see to it that you have become either a jellyfish or a damned paired-up satellite." He laughs and begins to cough. "Float on the tide like some rubbish or other. Tell Mother her favorite son says hello." The cigarette dances between Henri's fingers.

"Foolish," Llyas says. He wets his lips.

"Oh, the lamp oil is low in the cave, dearest brother. Take care not to stub your toe fondling around for a soft body," Henri laughs through a coughing fit.

Llyas places his hat atop his head and exits the cabin.

"And what do you know about youth? You are but three years my senior!" Henri shouts through the closed door. He takes a drag and stubs out the cigarette. His face contorts in spurts. "Take a gander at yourself. You are closer to death than birth, you vasey old man. You've lost the pot, you absolute ridiculous thing," he mumbles. Smoke escapes his lips. "How do you damn what you do not remember?"

Henri fidgets with his pillow. He tosses several times before finding a position not devoid of comfort. He blows out the candle that sits mostly melted on his nightstand.

* * *

Llyas stands outside the cabin. Henri's voice is muffled from the other side. Llyas looks up and sees the two pinpoint satellites hanging in the inky night sky. They are just bright enough to shine through a thin layer of clouds. He makes a fist, holds it to his left eye, and closes his right eye so he can see the satellites through the small opening of his curled fingers. Twin flames freeze framed in the black and smokey stratosphere.

Llyas examines his hand. Blisters on his fingertips. Creases of white flesh riversnake across his small, dirty palms. The wind picks up. He holds his long hair back with one hand and pulls a blue bandana from a pocket. He secures his hair with the bandana as the wind continues to blow. A strand of his straw-like hair tickles his nose as he sets his hat atop the bandana.

The waves that once massaged now beat on the rocks at the shoreline. Llyas looks to his right and inches half a step towards the slot canyon, which leads to the cave, a path he could travel in his sleep. He looks up, and the satellites still hang motionless in the sky. Their yellow tails look like cursive vertexes. He clears his throat and walks away from the path to the cave and forward toward the shoreline. The Modest Purse bobs in the water and knocks against the pier. He rinses his hands in the cool salt water, careful not to get his shoes wet.

Llyas again attempts to touch his toes for a moment and holds his breath as he does so. He slides his work sack from his shoulder onto the sand. He licks the salt from his lips and scratches his chin. His beard is thick and wiry. The rust from the buckles on his bag marks his hands. Llyas unfolds a cloth and pulls his kite from it.

Llyas braces himself and stands as old men do. He lets out a small whimper from the pain in his hip. His bulbous nose flares. The kite takes flight quickly and soars into the sky higher and higher until he can no longer see it. He feels the kite tug at his line. Llyas stands briefly on the balls of his feet. The wind takes off his hat. Llyas lunges for it as it lofts out to sea. He stumbles as the kite guides him along the shoreline. He shouts and gesticulates like a child doing something he ought not.

Night creatures watch from the trees above. The giant and knowing creatures of the sea inspect Llyas's hat and watch the old man walk a winged and flying thing along their border. Glowing nocturnal eyes perceive the slow-moving mammal lurch, hop, and flounder along the shore.

Llyas flies his kite throughout the night. The wind is perfect for kite-flying, as most nights on the island. His hip has stiffened, and it forbids him from being tugged along any further, so he rests on a dune some small distance from the cabin. Tall beach grass surrounds him. It makes a song of the wind as Llyas reels in his reluctant bird. He folds it like a soldier folds his country flag, wraps it in cloth, and secures it in his work sack.

* * *

Back in the cabin, Henri awakens with a start. He shouts and punches rapidly at the invisible entities that haunted his sleep. Henri wipes the crust from his eyes, rubs his head, and feigns a confident chuckle. He remembers rewarding his bully tormentors' blows with laughter in his youth. Llyas's space is empty. Henri bites his upper lip and watches the door for his brother's return.

Why did he say such things when he was knackered? Why does he construct high walls with spikes atop them and throw barbs at Llyas? Is poetry so awful when poetry is so loved? When his brother returns, he will play the mouth harp for him. He will smile, and he will drink his brother's tea. He will talk about when their mother took them to the port to watch the big ships full of people from other lands come in. How happiness radiated from her when she explained to her boys how new people meant new opportunities. Take a gander at the multitudes! She would say, and her yellow hair would fall on the brothers' shoulders as they stood beside her.

When the glad talk and tea drinking are done, Henri will take his fishing pole to the Modest Purse and bring in food from the sea before beginning his shift in the cave.

Henri exits the cabin to the back to relieve himself. The rising sun hurts his eyes. He listens for signs of his brother's return. Nothing. No sound at all but the urine that hits the cabin side and the subsequent quick zip of his trousers.

Henri reenters the cabin and pours yesterday's tea into his mug. The drink is sour, but he is used to that. Henri puts on a shirt from his closet and gathers his fishing pole and tackle. He imagines the fat sand bugs he will collect for bait. The morning is young, and the fishing should be good. He suspects fish, like people, are hungry in the morning. Yes, he will catch enough to feed himself and his brother for a week.

Henri places his hand on the thick volume of poetry on his brother's nightstand. He opens it to a random page and shuts the book quickly. He puts on his boots loosely and waits for Llyas to return.

He should have been back already. Punctual Llyas.

The younger brother sighs and bounces his leg. He tugs at his ear before pulling the volume from the older brother's nightstand again. He opens it to the dog eared page and reads.

The Angel
I dreamt a dream! What can it mean?
And that I was a maiden Queen
Guarded by an Angel mild:
Witless woe was ne'er beguiled!

And I wept both night and day,
And he wiped my tears away;
And I wept both day and night,
And hid from him my heart's delight.

So he took his wings, and fled;
Then the morn blushed rosy red.
I dried my tears, and armed my fears
With ten thousand shields and spears.

Soon my Angel came again;
I was armed, he came in vain;
For the time of youth was fled,
And grey hairs were on my head.
William Blake

Henri slides his fingers over the text and down to a handwritten inscription.

"From Mum. Never will you be alone."

Henri looks out the window. His shoulders drop with a breath.

She – walked into the ocean, their grandfather had told him.

That night Llyas had been inconsolable. Llyas did not speak in words but in a wet and wailing tormented language. Henri couldn't bear it. He remembers leaving their shared bedroom and wanting to wander off into the night.

Stop there, Henri – his grandfather had said from beneath a dull lamplight. He sat on the porch and motioned for Henri to sit on the steps. The scent of old cherry tobacco.

She walked right out into the big and deep ocean, and she will never return. Your brother can never know this. Henri sat on the steps, but his thoughts remained with stepping into the darkness. He thought maybe he would also never come back. He reached into his pocket and pulled out a small blade.

Henri- Henri moved the blade between his fingers. *Henri, say to me you'll never tell him.*

Henri returns from childhood memories and leaves the cabin without being replaced by Llyas. Their routine has shifted. The baton has not been passed.

* * *

The short path to the beach is lined with wildflowers. Henri has seen enough wildflowers. He kicks off his boots once he reaches the sand. He raises his hand to shield his eyes from the morning light and looks up and down the shore. A familiar figure waddles in the distance along the water. A beach mouse scampers out of a fresh footprint.

"You weren't meant to go fishing this morning! That was my duty, Old Man!" Henri shouts—no answer from his brother. The figure enlarges as it approaches. Henri kicks a sandy mound, injuring his big toe on a rock or perhaps a dried-out sand dollar. A few stray seagulls laugh.

"Hey there! It was my time to fish!" Henri throws down his work sack and pole. No response from his brother. Two other figures appear behind Llyas, two people shorter than him. Henri sees Llyas motion for the two others to wait by a large rock. Llyas drags his feet to meet Henri. His hand supports his aching hip.

"You don't go taking a man's fishing time away," Henri says. Llyas looks around and pats himself down as if looking for the fish he did not catch. And Llyas might add, with what pole? He tosses his hands in the air as a mockery, a bit of a jab. "What are you on about, then? Why'd you come from the beach and not from the direction of the slot canyon? And who's that over there by the stone?" Henri moves his hands from his sides to his hips several times.

"Fish don't much like kites, little brother." Llyas shows Henri the kite in his work sack.

"You went kite flying this morning. You got all your work done early," Henri nods as he speaks. "All right. I saw no boat nor heard no seaplane. What do you have waiting over there, apes of the forest?" Henri smirks. "You've a couple magical beasts over there, am I right?"

"I did not get any work done. I flew my kite," Llyas says.

Henri clinches his fists and opens his mouth wide to stretch his jaw.

"You flew your kite? Did you fly it all night? Are you telling me you got no work done in the cave?" Henri's chest heaves.

"It is as you have said," Llyas says. Henri grabs the straps of Llyas's overalls and yanks him close.

"Do you want us dead?" Henri yells through thin teeth. "The bloody bastards are set to arrive in a fortnight. We will be short." Henri clamps his hands together and shakes them.

"The people by the stone are the satellites; a young man and a young lady. Geb and Nut. They have crashed into the sea and swam here to the beach," Llyas explains. Henri's face elongates. His hands fall, defeated.

"How many nights have you gone flying and eschewed your work? Tell me," Henri asks.

"As many nights as the very first people to fall from the Earth have shone above us," Llyas answers as if it were obvious. Henri grinds his teeth and inches even closer to Llyas. "Three nights. Three nights I have beckoned them with me bird to come down here back to the Earth."

"You're cracked. You're dizzy, and we will die for it," Henri says. "Best case, we get beaten. Stomped." Llyas blurs before Henri as he looks past him at the two figures by the rock. They appear to be sitting now with their arms around one another. "I'm going to haul in some fish, lest we starve. You'll forgive me if I leave entertaining our guests to you, Old Man." Henri picks up his boots and his gear. He looks to Llyas for any sign of jest or misunderstanding. Llyas gazes over his shoulder at the figures behind him.

"When the day is done, the type of days you didn't think would have an ending. When a day like that is done, and you have blisters on your blisters, and you are so hungry you can't remember what being filled feels like. You stand at the cave's exit so that, for only a moment, you can have any thought other than work. That breeze hits you, so you step outside into that second of silence just as the rain comes down. And that moment itself is also an eternity without an end built into it. It's like heaven and hell. Ice and fire. All eternities. Do you know what I'm talking about? You think, 'I'm going to stop here right now and stand in the rain. I'm going to take me shirt off and let the rain kiss me all over.'" Llyas says. He pets the back of his brother's head.

"The young man and woman are like that," Llyas says. "They are angels."

"These angels, can they swing a pickax? Can they cast a net or fry a fish? The lady angel. Is she fair?" Henri takes his brother's hands from his head and flashes a vicious grin. He turns towards the Modest Purse.

Llyas motions for the satellites to come to him.

Henri picks up his effects and begins to walk.

* * *

Henri gathers grublike sand fleas along the way to the pier where the Modest Purse is moored to its cleat. He will use them as bait this morning. He is bitten by one, and to his surprise, a small drop of blood is drawn. He wipes it away in the sugar-white sand and crushes the culprit between his thumb and index finger. A brief wave of nausea passes through our Henri. He bends over briefly to recalibrate himself. With a dozen white crustaceans crawling over themselves, Henri gathers himself. He picks up the pace to the pier.

The wind is now light, and the sun is kind this morning. Henri boards the Modest Purse and untethers it. He rows out a quarter kilometer before settling. He baits his pole with a sandflea from the bucket. The poor creature is impaled through its fleshy part. Henri casts.

A tinge of anxiety rouses the back of Henri's neck and forearms to gooseflesh. What the old man has done is foolish beyond daft. He talks about eternity. Ten years is an eternity. To give yet another eternity to the cavern, he would rather die. He would instead step right off this boat with bags of sand tied 'round his waist. He'd rather walk right into the sea just as *she* did.

Henri shakes the thoughts away. He kicks the side of the Modest Purse. A pull at his fishing line snaps Henri into full attention. He labors lightly with the animal at the end of his line before pulling it into the Modest Purse. He undoes the hook from the fish's lip and searches for a water bucket to store his catch. There is no such receptacle to be found. In haste and anger, Henri has neglected to secure the bucket before boarding. It may be hours before he returns to shore. A too-long dead fish could make a man sick. The animal gasps and flops around the hull. Its scales reflect the oranges and reds of the sunrise. Its gills fan out like a fully blossomed rose.

Flashes of figures in sharp and shiny red uniforms infiltrate Henri's thoughts. He kneels before them. His hands are bound behind his back, and his wrists bleed. Henri's reflection shines in the mirrored boots that threaten the very structure of his face. The high-set cheekbones he had inherited from his mother are flattened into powder. Sickness in his stomach retches out onto those boots. A language he does not comprehend, fierce and present, crushes him like an enormous beast. Darkness.

Henri inhales a hyperventilated breath and is again snapped into acute consciousness. These unwanted thoughts burden him more than any work in the cave. The repetition of days. The colorless expression of nothing being brand new.

These intruders linger as an ache behind his eyes, an itch in his brain that he cannot satisfy.

Ten years. Tea. Fish. Work. Ten years. And what of these people my brother placed by the rock? What is he on about comets and such? Angels. He's as mad as me, if not far beyond. Old Man has invited spies who bear the virtue of lovingkindness.

A small splash nearby. A wave disturbs the Modest Purse.

Henri peers into the horizon, the infinite stretch of saltwater. The sunrise looks like a slow-motion explosion, with little pieces of orange and fragments of red. It is fully beautiful and dreadful at the same time. He wonders how long he would have to paddle to find land or maybe to meet that explosion and slowly disintegrate into it, forever being lost to himself and everything. He wonders how far he could make it if he brought fresh water from the island. How long before some creature swallowed him whole or in pieces? How long before a sea tempest roused and drowned him?

A sudden bump against the hull of the Modest Purse. Henri throws down his fishing pole and braces himself for a moment of terror that does not come. He looks around the Modest Purse three-sixty for evidence of the culprit. Nothing. The water is still again. The slowly exploding sunrise is the backdrop to lazy, indifferent clouds.

Henri dumps the fat fleas from the bucket and dips it into the sea for water to store his catch. The bugs scuttle to the parameters of the boat. They stack atop one another to climb out, only to be pulled down by their brothers and sisters below them.

Something has seized Henri's hand below the surface. Henri and his unknown enemy play a violent game of tug of war with Henri's arm as the rope. The sunrise seems to have expanded the entirety of the sky. Its red and orange are like the veins of a chicken inside its egg, backlit by a laboratory light. It appears briefly to have blasted the careless clouds from the sky.

Henri resists the foe until his shoulder dislocates.

Am I screaming? I should be.

Henri resolves that he has done everything in his power to stay alive. Here, in this battle, he has pulled and punched. There, on Chimera Island, he has stood in the fray of the same day to the point of nausea. His brother seems not to know he is part of the silent struggle of siblings. Henri has lost. Yes, he has done what he could do. It is time to leave. It is time to walk into the sea, as it were.

The water that now swallows his arm has turned coal black. Henri doesn't recall seeing the brilliant emerald water go dark, but there it is. He is bent at the waist over the edge of the Modest Purse. His enemy releases its hold, and Henri falls backward into the Purse.

The sound of a vacuum being sealed, a resounding *slurp* like the last drop of cream being sucked from a cup, and then silence. Placid water. The still-framed explosion of sunrise is repainted in the distance where sunrises should be.

For a moment, Henri hears strings being plucked. He hears a chorus of women singing. Or, maybe it's the voices of eunuchs. The clouds have returned as pillows that an ethereal creature might sleep on or sing from. Henri opens his mouth to speak.

"I-," Henri begins. The Modest Purse is sucked into the water below him. Down with it, he goes. His enemy does not give him a moment to thrash about on the surface. He is fully submerged and twisting, spiraling down like bath water after pulling the stopper. Henri cannot see his attacker. He cannot face his enemy to gouge its eyes or pierce its gills. Nor can he find its hand or fin to give it thanks.

Henri is suspended in darkness. As suddenly as he is

pulled below, Henri's enemy again releases him. His last few bubbles of air walk from his nose and up his forehead. They disappear somewhere far above and pop at the surface.

I have done what I can to stay alive.

I have thought all I can think to make sense of myself.

Henri awakens. He is being carried to safety by a bulbous being. It swims below the surface, allowing Henri to rest on its back above the sea. For a moment, all Henri can witness is the sky. He does not sense his breath. The thump of his heart is not present to remind him he is alive. The passing birds are like lovely strangers waving from flying motorcars. The chorus sings again; the eunuchs and the women.

Henri feels the flesh of the being who carries him to the shore. It is slippery and dense. His breathing returns, filling him to his toes and into his bones. There is evidence of his pounding heart in the movement of his chest. He turns to his side to have a gander at this friendly beast. Purple light glows below. Henri spews water from his gut and steadies himself on the beast as they approach the beach.

Spindly white arms break the surface, raise Henri from under his shoulders, and place him on the shoreline. The fingers are thin and decorated with rings that resemble beetles. These arms are too long to be real, much less human. The white too-long arms melt back into the sea. The onyx rings glint just before they sink.

Henri's eyes follow the ripples the creature leaves behind. Pink water slides into his field of vision. He is suddenly aware of an agony that takes his voice from him. His arm is mangled. The flesh near his elbow has been completely stripped. Our Henri tries to scream but cannot. The horror of his condition steals his wind.

Henri stumbles backward. He looks to the water to make sense of this mysterious beast and the battle that preceded his rescue. A woman's familiar face looks up at Henri from just below the surface. The subtle waves slightly distort and shift her visage. Her body is that of a manatee, a fat, gray avocado with rolls of thick flesh. Her face glows purple without a trace of acknowledging who Henri might be or that he is even there in front of her.

"Mum?" Henri dips his finger into the water to touch the mermaid's face. The purple light is out instantly, and the human face morphs into a sea cow's head. He sits and watches as the manatee swims out and disappears completely.

* * *

Llyas hovers over the young man and woman inside the cabin. Their clothes are sopped. They sit near the fire like statues at the entrance of a lush garden.

The lady is long, and her hair drips with seawater. She is postured, crouching like a toddler. Her eyes are lost in the fire. She shivers momentarily, breaking the illusion of being made of stone.

The man sits on his heels near the young lady. His shaggy hair is also wet and sticks to his forehead and down to the corners of his mouth. He appears too young to bear the stubble that darkens his face. The man stands and unbuttons his soaked shirt. He folds it and sets it aside. He strips his trousers with considerable effort and folds them, placing them on top of the shirt. Rainwater pools beneath the linen. The young man crouches on his heels again and extends his hands to the fire, unashamed.

The woman follows suit, undoing her shirt and shedding her skirt. She folds the garments, reassumes her squat, and again extends her arms for warmth. She wears a ring with a black oval-shaped stone that takes up the length of her curiously long ring finger.

"You are Geb and Nut," Llyas says. He shakes his head in an almost imperceivable manner. "Are you hungry or thirsty? Are you in want of anything?" The man and woman do not respond. "My brother Henri, he doesn't believe." Llyas walks to the window and peers out. "He thinks you've come here to spy for the authorities.

"I haven't harvested the light in two nights. You know that, however. How foolish of me." Llyas laughs. "You came here because I flew my kite for you. I called, and you came. You came to save me, to save us from our unjust and impious imprisonment."

The man and woman breathe in unison with heads that bob like buoys in the buoyancy of the room. Their tummies and chests move like waves. The woman shifts her weight.

"Let me dry your clothes." Llyas is embarrassed not to have thought of the obvious. He fetches a fishing line from the closet and fastens it above the fire. He drapes their clothes over it.

"I can make tea." Llyas gestures to the pot full of stagnant water and old wet bags of tea leaves. "I can make a fresh pot, I mean. It will warm you on the outside and inside and give you some pep if you're weary." Llyas stammers and moves about the cabin to gather the necessities for tea. "We are nowt of sugar cubes, it seems. The supply boat; it's been a spell." The young couple stares, entranced by the small fire.

"Okay, a bitter cup for you both, then," Llyas laughs.

There is a pounding at the door—an urgency. Llyas believes for a moment that there is an intruder. He looks at the young man he calls Geb, who sits as still as a hunting owl in a tree. Llyas moves between the door and his angels. He readies the teapot to be used as a projectile.

"Me arm!" Henri stumbles into the cabin, his mangled limb

clenched by his healthy one. His teeth appear long and yellow in the flashing firelight. His gums are unnaturally pink in the red flickering glow.

"Henri!" Llyas says as he tosses the teapot aside. Our Henri's face teems with sweat—a wretched white swirls beneath his glasslike skin.

"It was a goddamned mermaid, a godforsaken sea witch with our mother's face. Llyas, I swear to you. Something tried to bump me off, and the damned creature saved me." Henri falls face first. The brown wooden floor turns maroon beneath him. Llyas stands dumbfounded. His brother convulses, and he knows not what to do.

The young man and woman sit utterly still and naked, warming themselves by the fire. The woman turns her head and observes Llyas as he examines his brother's wounds. Henri has gone quiet. The woman lowers her hands to her lap.

Llyas says a prayer. Is it a remembered prayer from the books on the backs of every pew where he would kneel as a child? Is it perhaps, in his desperation and understanding that there is nothing he is capable of doing that might help his brother, a sort of poem Llyas has formed at this moment?

The young man stands and moves to a far corner. He raises his arms as if he were worshiping the woman. With each inhale, his arms stretch further with the intensity of a person reaching for a rope to climb out of a deep hole.

What is this? Another set of arms extends below the young man's praising limbs. Llyas gasps and rubs his eyes. He exerts a moan.

The young woman gets up and steps deliberately toward the brothers. Her walk is confident and slow. Each strike of her naked heel on the wooden floor is a drum beat that accompanies the rhythm of this strange ritual. Her arms hang like drapes at her sides. Llyas backs away, moaning still and making sounds from some other tongue.

The woman kneels by our torn and maimed Henri. She places her palms on the most damaged parts of his arm, those parts of him that lost the tug of war. Henri's flesh is soft, malleable, and inhumanly white. Her long fingers appear almost prehensile as she takes her time gripping him.

Vibrations like the swelling of a tornado rattle the window and shake the brothers' beds and tables. Waves of violet begin small and grow in peak and trough as they reverberate from the young woman's hands. The waves make a sound that matches the intonation of Llyas' alien language. The young man speaks yet another language from the corner. Llyas braces himself. Blinding light fills the room.

A sound like the final ounces of bathwater swirling down the drain is again intimate in Llyas's ears.

The cave remains hot even at night this time of year. The air is thick like gravy. Llyas slams his pickax into a humming rock. *Tink!* Traces of dust scatter upward. He lifts his tool again and strikes with tremendous effort. *Tink!* The crack the blow creates begins to glow purple in the dimly lamplit cave. He struggles for breath and collects the light from the stone in a small silver cylinder. The device Llyas holds in his hand pulls in light from the source until the rock ceases to glow. He then flips a switch on the canister and secures it in a steel box.

Llyas can execute this work without thinking about where his hands are or the strength he will need to strike any given rock with his tool. *The repetition of a thing.*

Llyas collects the light tonight, not because he fears punishment from the Order. No, Llyas has beckoned Geb and Nut.

He has delivered them to his suffering brother. He has again played his part in planting their feet on the Earth. His duty is done. What would he do with himself but fumble about offering pleasantries his angels do not need? What nursing duties could he perform for Henri that the goddess, Nut, could not? What questions could he ask that he did not already have the answers to? It is best to strike these rocks and collect their light as he has done nearly every night of his imprisonment.

A gentle breeze flows into the cavern. Llyas breathes deeply through his nose and senses a light rain coming.

* * *

Henri lies on his back in the middle of the room. The floor remains painted maroon beneath him. He is not sure if he is breathing. He must be; he does not feel like he is drowning, and for the sake of the Lord, he now knows what drowning feels like. He is not sure his heart is beating. Still, surely it is ticking away as always, for some state of consciousness indeed precedes his arising thoughts.

Should Henri have the strength to turn his head, undoubtedly, the young sorceress and her companion *could not* be there naked by the fire. Yes, he is on the floor, perhaps passing out from exhaustion. The creatures from the sea, the man and woman, or the old man's angels are all fiction. He has no savior. He was knocked from the Modest Purse by a wave and taken under by a rip current. He swam to shore, and now... There is no limb wounded by a sea beast. He has been dreaming. He was perhaps cut on some rocks as he struggled underwater, but no beast attacked him, surely not one with a human face. It was a fever dream; he knows it.

The cabin is as quiet as any other night. Henri waits for a sound, a clue.

Some unknown moments come and go. Henri hears the song his mother taught him. It comes from somewhere not simply nearby but from within. His hands unfold. He wants to roll a cigarette, but our Henri has slid past the liminal space of sleep, and there is nothing now but approaching blackness. The consciousness that once preceded our Henri's reasoning is blotted out in a slow wave of deep sleep.

* * *

Ten hours have passed since Llyas collected his first light in two nights from the cave.

Llyas returns to the cabin. His shirt is wet from the welcomed drizzle that cooled him on his walk back. He places his hand on the doorknob and pauses, thinking of all the mysteries and delights that might come from his devotion to Geb and Nut. What other powers of healing and creation might they gift his brother and himself? Have they heard his prayers, or had they come because floating and dreaming could wear on a soul as much as repetition and labor wear the body?

The doorknob creeks as Llyas turns it.

In the dark of the room, Llyas does not notice that Geb and Nut are absent but that the pressure that filled the cabin while they occupied it is absent. He then sees his brother on the floor on his back, his arms forming a t.

Llyas crouches and pats his brother's shoulder. No response. Llyas sees no embers in the fireplace. The room is near pitch black, and a static haze seems to blanket the space between the objects therein.

"Henri," Llyas says. He shakes his brother. Our Henri does not respond. Llyas searches the room for Geb and Nut. His sense of space may be misleading. They must be in the shadows of a corner. Llyas takes a match from his brother's stash and lights a candle. He momentarily witnesses some trickery of bouncing shadows that form likenesses of Geb and Nut just below where their clothes had been hung about the mantle.

"Henri, come to. They are gone." Llyas shakes his brother once more.

"Are you real, Old Man? Am I waked?"

"Yes."

"Who's gone?"

"Your savior and her admirer," Llyas says. Henri scowls.

"It was a shark or manatee that mangled me, brother," Henri says.

"You were healed," Llyas says. "Nut healed your wounds."

"Did she heal me? You saw this?" Henri does not leave space for his brother to answer. "It's a fever dream. Mass hysteria only the masses are us two unfortunates. A dream, Old Man. A dream as feckless as any hopes to get off this godforsaken island called Chimera."

Henri sits up.

"Be still. You are troubled. Make some sense of your words," Llyas says.

"I thought I saw our mother's face on the body of a beast. A lovely orb of the face on the beast that swam me back to shore. Shining like lightning. Shining violet like the light we harvest. But it could not have been." Henri tries and fails to stand. "You look at me with pity. Don't dare. Look at me with distrust if you must, for I have been weary and sick and have hallucinated a whole ordeal, but do not show pity. Take me hand, Old Man." Llyas assists his brother to his feet.

"If we turn on the radio right now, there will be a roar about the comets vanishing. This is not a hallucination, brother." The candles flicker fiercely. "Do tell me where they went." There is an uncharacteristic impatience in Llyas' voice.

"I don't know where they went. I fell into a sleep as deep as death," Henri says. "Why don't ye lie yourself down?"

A forlorn gravity pulls at Llyas.

Henri looks for the maroon spot on the ground. He inspects his arm for damage and finds none.

"I heard a song. I heard a song, Old Man. When I dreamt, she laid her hands on me. It was the one song. Our mother's song. That's how I know it was a dream. No angel could be so unkind."

In this new dawn, thousands of meteors rain across the naked dim yellow sky.

* * *

Summer has passed, and with its passing, so have wildflowers and scorching days. All things that move about Chimera Island have slowed, and now prepare to sleep as the days have shortened.

Llyas drags his feet from the cave through the slot canyon and then through the woods to the cabin. A bundle of firewood is strapped to his back. His clothes hang from him like the skin of a dying man. His brow casts a morning shadow over his eyes which seem to have sunken further in their sockets. Eyes that once spoke cobalt now murmur gray.

Llyas places a hand on the doorknob. He is reminded of the gladness, the joy of anticipation that permeated every cell of his being the moment he stood here at this door last summer.

He is then reminded of the fear that discolored his brother's eyes. Then, the great lie in the absence of the angels in that dark room where Henri stumbled in his confusion. Oh, how the sky lit up that night. How the fireballs that zipped beyond the clouds roused the fear in Llyas of impending battle. The understanding of how insignificant and dumb he was beneath the oppressive thumb of the mysteries of this world.

The doorknob creeks.

Llyas enters the cabin and sets the bundle of firewood near the fireplace. He puts his hands together and breathes hot breath into them.

Henri lies still on his bed above the blanket.

A sleep as deep as death.

"Old Man." Henri yawns and rubs his eyes until they are red. He scratches his chest and his head.

"Where are their clothes?" Henri sits up and squints at his brother.

Llyas smiles and looks down. The cabin breathes a beat.

"Don pretend ye don't know what I mean." Henri had not mentioned the angels or events leading to the miracle above the maroon spot on the floor. This new invitation to speak of Geb and Nut excites Henri. "They got naked. She placed her hands on me, and I saw through my pain her white and plump bosoms. I saw the man in the corner praying or whatever the hell it was. His pubic mound was as black as night. Where are their clothes?"

"And this would prove them to you, their clothes?" Llyas raises an eyebrow. He waits for the question to make sense to his brother. "And what if I could show you?" Llyas perks. "What if I did?" Llyas begins a little dance that seems to trouble his starving body. *"Could be something washed up on shore,* you'd say. *It could belong to anybody. Could be something left behind by the supply boat. No proof, no proof."* Llyas halts his tiny dance and steps closer to our Henri.

Llyas turns the knob of the tabletop tombstone radio. It clicks but does not turn on.

Henri chuckles, nudges his brother's hands aside, and gathers his tobacco and rolling papers. He makes himself a smoke and lights it. Henri begins to put on his boots as cigarette smoke frames his face.

"Time to work," Henri says. His cigarette is snug between his middle and index fingers. The cherry dances franticly as he ties his laces.

"I know work. Yes, time time time to work. I didn't know drink until I learned what *apart* meant. I'm cursed because of my nature. My cowardice and inwardness. I'm all shut up." Our Henri looks up from his boots. His eyes are wet. Henri pauses for a response from his brother. Llyas again holds the knob of the radio between his index finger and thumb. It clicks.

"I'm busted, Old Man." Henri begins to tie his other boot. "I might climb atop the mountain Chimera and jump right off. I might walk into the ocean like they say Mum did. I might do these things if I weren't yellow."

"Your hand, brother," Llyas says.

"Me what?" Henri's face sours.

Henri shakes his hand suddenly. "Aye! Me bloody finger!" He dusts away the ashes of his cigarette from his body and bed. Henri blows on his finger as he sputters into a coughing fit. He snuffs the cigarette under his boot.

Henri walks to the door and stands in its frame. He buttons his coat.

"Back in a jiffy." Henri sucks the soft space between his knuckles as he exits the cabin.

The supply boat docks at the pier where the Modest Purse once lived. Sudden bursts of wind blow the long beards of the few crewmembers as they exit the boat. A mist of ocean water sprays them, chilling the hardened men briefly. The captain notices the reds and oranges of the approaching winter speckled in the trees against an overcast sky.

The captain leads the party ashore. He is followed by a shackled man who is trailed by two crewmembers. The shackled man wears a long hood that blocks much of his face. The captain glances behind intermittently to ensure the shackled man does not trip or fall.

As the group walks down the narrow pier, the captain again glances behind. One of his crewmembers, the man closest to the prisoner, coughs singularly and gestures to the water. With his eyes wide and eyebrows raised, the crewmember points his chin at the captain. The captain scowls and shakes his head *no.* His gaze returns forward, and the corners of his mouth pull downward. The crewmember spits into the bay.

* * *

Currently, Llyas reads from his volume of poetry. Gales of wind shake the door and rattle the window occasionally. The fire pops. Llyas's eyelids grow heavy and sag to match the rest of his face. The familiar scripture before him blurs, and he begins to doze in this white noise. His book is spread open across his torso. The sound of crinkling pages as Llyas's chest rises and falls.

"Hey-o, Llyas, it's Captain Jervis here." Captain Jervis taps on the door. "We've got your supplies now. Later than usual, but we're here." The captain's right-hand trembles. He steadies it with his left.

"Captain, you all right, ain'tcha?" One of the crewmen asks.

"Yeah, William, yeah. I need a stiff one, is all," Captain Jervis looks at his hand.

"You had a whiskey a nautical and a half ago," William says. "Had one with ye, Captain."

"Llyas. Henri. Open on up. It's Captain Jervis." He squeezes his hand into a reluctant fist and looks away as he raps on the door, then on the window with its drawn curtains.

Llyas startles awake. He wipes spittle from his mouth and beard. He reaches for a fading memory, or was it a dream? He and Henri. Was it Henri? Walking through some strange woods at night. Streaks of fire fell from the sky. Some explosions hurt his little ears. *Little.* Yes, he must have been a boy in the dream. The person was grown. Some fragments are returning to Llyas now. Llyas' hands were so small. Then again, they are small now, are they not? There was a bag slung over the man's shoulder. Who was this aged man with Henri's face?

A rapping at the window.

Llyas emerges and attempts to close the door as a gust of wind threatens to blow it open. Llyas manages to close it. He rubs his hands together and cowers from another blast of cold air. Captain Jervis' face lightens.

"Llyas! I would be apologizing for disturbing ye, but I can't imagine you'd turn away the tea and whiskey and such we hauled with us. Good tidings, Llyas. Good t-," the new prisoner steps forward. The clinking of his shackles checks Captain Jervis' gladness. The crewmembers hold their breath, eyebrows raise, and dry mouths swallow.

"Artemis." The prisoner extends his shackled hands.

"What's this, now?" Llyas asks.

"They said I was a drunkard, and I heard voices. Don't everybody hear voices? I asked them. How can a body be sure them voices ain't your own? The drunkard part, I confess. But voices?" Artemis shakes his head and waits for a response. Llyas gives a nervous laugh.

"They had a boy from the neighborhood tell them he seen

me talking out loud when not a body was around. Said me little girl threw rocks at him and some other boys just because they was passing by. My girl says she threw them rocks because they wouldn't leave her be. Said she ain't let them have their way. You know how things is with boys and girls. Just how things is always been.

I say how things is, and they send me here to work the light, the light in the cave." Artemis says. "Sent my little girl off to breed new soldiers for the Order, her grandfather being a fighter at the start of the war. They says she'll make good warriors for the cause, and I'm to come here and work the light, the light in the cave." Artemis lifts his bound wrists to his cheek to wipe away a tear, or was it dew from the sea?

"This is Artemis. The Order says he has lunacy," Captain Jervis searches the ground for something on which to fix his eyes. "He talks beaucoup nonsensical, but he won't harm a fly. Ain't that right, Arty?" Jervis' eyes remain on the ground. "He'll be working with you and Henri. Lighten the load, as it were."

Llyas nods and places a hand on the door to lean against.

"We will see about making some room, Mr. Artemis," Llyas says. The men stay put, unsure whether or not their job is finished.

"All this split with three men?" Artemis tilts his head back to take in the exterior of the domicile. "We shall live as kings; I bet it! A sodding palace, you have here." The men behind Artemis exchange glances.

A palace *indeed*. The space is as thick as brush with just two men, not to imagine three.

Llyas hangs from the frame in front of the door and yawns as he pulls the stiffness from his joints. His outstretched arms are too skinny, too brittle looking for a working man.

"Ye must not have a lot of grub around here, aye? Are you sick?" Artemis asks.

Llyas releases his grip and exhales for some length. He places a hand on his belly. The belly that once not all that long ago extended disproportionately. The other hand travels to his thin as a rake face. He runs his tongue across his bottom lip and looks to Jervis for a few words. His throat is too weak to say anything about food at the moment. He is too caught between sleep and waking to ask further about the company he currently finds himself in.

Captain Jervis gestures for the men to enter. Llyas steps up immediately with a dexterity that shocks the four men. He shields the entry nonchalantly.

The two crewmen uncross their arms, a gesture on which Llyas does not pick up.

* * *

Our Henri is leaning against the outer wall near the cabin's back door. He has closed his eyes to shut out additional stimuli as he struggles to eavesdrop on the conversation at the outside front of the cabin. Henri listens so intensely that breath has left his body. It has been ten years since he has laid ears on another human voice save his brother and, at times, the captain. Now there is this crazed man who speaks like a Gatling gun and these other two men with Jervis.

Henri catches a few words between his brother and the captain; a few words are clear enough to distinguish between murmurs of wind and the voices of men.

The wind blows hard. Henri pulls at a few weeds beneath him, vexed that nature should interrupt his spying.

Captain Jervis searches for the right words. Only an utterance that sounds like it might be born from English passes his lips. He glances this way and that: vocalization and a pause.

"Llyas, let's all go inside and get Artemis situated," he finally says. His voice trails at the end of the suggestion.

Henri bounces from around the corner of the cabin. The crewmen puff their chests and then deflate once they realize it is Henri who accosts them.

"How do you do?" Henri thrusts his hand towards Artemis. Artemis, slack-jawed and maybe dumbfounded, ponders how to one-up Henri's enthusiastic spasms before gripping his hand with both paws. The men shake one another in exaggerated and rapid jerks. Henri matches Artemis' exhilaration and engages his free hand.

"What's it?" Henri asks the captain. His hands are not yet released from Artemis, who nearly tears Henri's arms from their sockets.

"This here's Artemis. He's, uh-," Jervis pulls Artemis' hands away from Henri. "He'll be working with ye."

"With ye, not *for* ye. Innit?" Artemis squints at the captain, then at the crewmen.

"Of course, Arti. Of course," Captain Jervis says.

"Right then. Some relief. Welcome to Chimera Island, Mr. Artemis," Henri says.

"Mr. Artemis. Yes, uh-huh." Artemis grins.

"All right, mates. Unless you have a new fishing boat for us, best get on so Mr. Artemis can be shown how to harvest the light," Henri says.

"A new boat?" Jervis asks.

"The Purse is all smashed to pieces. No fish to cook in months," Henri says. "Did ye think we was on a diet, Captain Jervis? Fasting for the Lord's suffering, perhaps?"

"Well, no, I-"

"Your boat is beached a couple of miles down the shoreline. We saw it as we came in. Best to secure it at the pier," William says. "It seemed to be just fine."

"Of course it is!" Henri punches Jervis on the shoulder. "Your captors wouldn't know a joke if I had on a clown face," Henri says to Artemis.

"Oh!" Captain Jervis digs in his bottomless coat pocket for the key to the shackles that bind Artemis. His hands tremble as he releases his prisoner. The crewmen stiffen.

* * *

"You got any other brothers or just the skinny lad? What's his name, Henri? I don't like how you don't say the H in his name. Why don't anyone say the H?" Artemis trails behind Llyas on the path to the cavern.

"No more brothers nor any other family. Just me and him." Llyas halts and waits for Artemis to catch up. The flesh on the back of Llyas' neck rises, and a shiver passes over him as though he had neglected to watch his back for danger. "It's where our folks came from. They don't say it with the H in that region."

"Your folks who gave your brother a useless letter, they bit the dust. How long ago?" Artemis stands catty-corner behind Llyas. His hands are in his pockets.

"Long enough." Llyas sniffs the air. "Let's walk. Work to do." Llyas motions for Artemis to follow him.

"Being in heaven is probably better than being here with the wars and the Order and whatnot. To tell you the truth, not sure I believe in heaven, but if you do, that's fine by me." Artemis slows his pace.

"Sure, I believe in heaven. Hey," Llyas spins around, "will you keep your stride?" Llyas braces his hip.

"Here I am thinking you was brighter than your brother."

Artemis shakes his head. "He seemed right crazy, shaking my hands as he did. Batty as an alley cat. I thought you was a man of deep thought; I did. Don't go proving me wrong with irritation toward an invitation for philosophical waxing."

"I believe in heaven." Llyas stops walking and looks into the trees, then at his hands. How tiny they are. How unnatural they look at the end of his long forearms. Like baby's hands, only calloused and hard. "I've seen it. Been there, by proxy."

The dream of the man with Henri's face comes flooding into Llyas' mind. The man is guiding Llyas by the hand. It is dark out. Shadows move along the ground with the light of shooting stars, dozens of them tearing apart the sky. Their boom sounds urgently in his head. The child, Llyas, can hear the swelling of waves between explosions. *Do I know this man with my brother's face? Are we going to play?*

"Proxy, innit? Don't perk me up like that and not follow through, old man. It's rude," Artemis says.

Llyas gazes upon Artemis queerly. "It's just around this corner," Llyas says.

"Heaven is right around the corner? Thought we'd have to walk quite a bit longer to meet Saint Peter."

"The cave. The cave is up ahead." Llyas drags his knuckles across the sheer sandstone slot canyon walls.

"Cold tonight," Artemis observes.

The man with Henri's face isn't looking at me. Isn't, or won't? We walked to the water. The breeze is cold. My hands, my little boy's hands, are ice. The man has curly white hair on the back of his neck. His black shirt has long sleeves. There is a duffle bag over his shoulder.

"Cold tonight!" Artemis exclaims.

"Always is this time of year. The seasons, they – "Llyas pauses. "We're here." Llyas lowers his head to clear the low-hanging crest of the cave's yawning mouth.

"Right dank, innit?" Artemis holds his hands to his face.

"You get used to it," Llyas says.

"Thought we was harvesting light," Artemis says. The men have turned a corner and are now removed from the silvery moonlight that had lit their way. "Mighty dark for a supposed abundance of light."

Fading into vision are specks of purple light that trickle down the rocky walls as raindrops might, collecting upon one another and trailing heavily down. Lines and simple geometric shapes glow purple, glide horizontally, and mingle with other shapes, creating more complexity before dissolving completely.

Llyas ignites two torches and hands one to Artemis.

"So, *this* is the light," Artemis extends a finger to the brilliant violet spectacle on the wall. His face softens.

Llyas guides Artemis' hand away.

"There are gloves for that." Llyas places his hands on Artemis' shoulders and pets him. Such small hands. "We'll harvest here. You can watch me and learn how. Don't touch the light." Llyas waits for a sign of acknowledgment.

"Yeah, yes, sure, no light. That's what the captain said on the way here. 'Don't touch the light, Arty. It'll make ye drunker than ye can handle, Arty'. I says let me have it," Artemis holds his gaze and grips Llyas' wrists. "I won't touch it." Artemis removes his new teacher's hands, keeping his gaze with unmistakably prurient intent.

"Don't touch the light." Llyas looks away and sets up his receptacle and his axe. "It isn't for you." Gruff in his voice.

Llyas kneels to better see to his work as smatterings of the dream return.

We were going to fly a kite. Rockets above. Had the war reached Chimera Island? The man with Henri's face, he has gray curly hair. We had not run for our lives. The old man turned to me, and maybe he spoke. Or perhaps when he tried to speak, yes, that's when his face shone with violet.

* * *

"With all the hooch Jervis brings ye boys, it is a wonder ye get anything done." Artemis steps around his sleeping pallet. "Guaranteed, I wouldn't. Not that you're offering Arty a drop."

"And how would you know how much hooch we have here? Only been three nights. You have been snooping through what's not yours when Llyas has wandered off dreaming?" Henri stops fidgeting with the radio knob. He wipes his lips with the back of his middle and forefinger.

Artemis clutches his chest, feigning offense. "My word, Henri, I have not. On my word, I ain't."

"Ye said ye was a drunkard." Henri goes back to his fidgeting.

"Well," Artemis extends the vowel mockingly, "I'm a drunkard, but I'm also a liar, ye see. Or, maybe I ain't. Maybe I like to make fun and poke at a bloke sometimes. Maybe I saw the hooch on the boat when I came in, and I'm only wondering where it might be now."

"That'll be enough." Henri raises his voice. "It's put away. Llyas put it away." He again stops messing with the radio. Henri recalls talking with his brother about having another hand on the Island. He would be embarrassed now had he spoken those words to anyone but Llyas.

"Llyas don't drink. He put it away so I don't drown myself in it," Henri says.

"So, this brother *is* your keeper, eh? Keeper away of whiskey, innit?" Artemis sneers.

"That's enough, I said," Henri says in a whisper loud

enough to be heard by the sleeping creatures beyond the cabin doors.

"There's enough for us. Enough to numb us both into catatonia." Henri perks up. "Would ye like to fill your flask now?" Henri figures he doesn't have to trust a man to have a drink with him. Perhaps Artemis' taunting has wounded his ego. Why shouldn't he drink when he wants? Besides, this odd fellow will be here for an unknown time. It won't be long before he knows where Llyas hides the hooch.

"Now you're speaking my language, Mr. Henri." Artemis exaggerates the vowels as he addresses Henri, and his eyes disappear behind a smile that seems to wrap around his head. A white-coated tongue circles the outside of his cracked and red lips.

Henri walks to the middle of the room and kneels on the spot he once lay and bled or where he once suffered the fever dream of having been wounded and healed. He scratches with uncut and dirty fingernails where two wooden planks meet. He eventually pulls a plank from the floor.

Henri's breath leaves him. His heart pounds resoundingly in his head. The event he had made impossible in his reality, the happening he was beyond convinced was the contrivance of two lonely and alienated brothers, is proven true. There beneath the floor near a crate of whiskey bottles are the garments of Geb and Nut. The very same clothes they removed and so folded with intention before Nut laid hands on him and caused the cabin to quiver.

There is Geb's white silk shirt and rust-colored trousers. There is the feather blue shirt with red buttons that so deliciously covered Nut's form. There is her floral pattern skirt with bouquets of roses and baby's breath.

Henri perceives he has lingered too long pondering these things and taking in their implications. Has Artemis noticed?

Henri removes a bottle from the case and replaces the wooden plank.

"It's not much of a hiding spot if you know where that spot is," Artemis says.

"I've always known. I can smell it through the floor. Sometimes a brother pretends certain things to not harm the other brother." Henri is immediately embarrassed that he has allowed a space for vulnerability with this strange man. "Not that you would understand being selfless," Henri snaps.

Henri lingers until the bottle in his hand becomes heavy. *Who is this man, really?* He is careful and slow in filling Artemis' flask.

"Come now, don't be stingy. Let it pour." Artemis' face contorts, revealing a slight palsy on its right side. The beard there is patchy and thinner than the left. Henri does not increase the flow, and he ceases to pour just as the sweet and pungent liquid reaches the rim of Artemis' flask. Firelight glints in the amber drink inside Henri's bottle.

"Cheers." Henri lifts the bottle.

"Aye, and a toast to brothers." Artemis extends his flask high above him and stares curiously at the floor before gulping greedily from his flask. He stands before our Henri as Henri sits on his mattress and inches back. Henri rolls his shoulders and begins to speak.

"So, wh-" Artemis plops onto the mattress so near Henri their hips touch.

"How's the sleeping over there on your palette?" Henri says. He struggles to conceal his consternation. A brief and internal acknowledgment of inanity resides in Henri until it grows into anger. How could he be so stupid as to leave himself vulnerable to this man? This man he wished for, this company he begged God for, no less. How foolish to potentially expose the sacred robes of angels.

"Like a baby. Which is an odd thing people say, you know. As babies don't always sleep all that well. But me, I can sleep anywhere," Artemis says.

"Let's see, then." Henri stands and moves to the pallet. He pats at it and shakes it some before sitting. He huffs in response to his aging body's disagreement. "Yeah, I think this is all right."

Artemis takes this opportunity to spin around and lay his head upon Henri's pillow, letting out a false sigh. Henri purses his lips at the sight of the bottom of Artemis' shoes on his bed and gulps from the bottle.

The men drink over the next hour and trade stories of their past. Artemis often fires off into nonsense, but our deliriously drunken Henri tolerates the conversation, and his inner walls buckle under the weight of the whiskey.

"Henri," Artemis says, "why did you say your boat was destroyed? Me and the lads saw it on our way in. Did you forget to tether it and let it float off? In your shame, did you spin a fib?"

"No, it was bloody busted to hell," Henri slurs.

"T'was not, you lunatic. It's one thing for me to see strange vapors and report them as solid flesh, but the other three saw it, too. William, Peter, and even the upstanding captain saw it." Artemis sits up abruptly in Henri's bed.

"Why don't you get out of my bed?" Henri's accent is thick with intoxication.

"You had whiskey and left it untethered. It drifted out too far for you to do anything about it before you noticed you had slipped up." Artemis again rests his head on Henri's pillow." How do you think I got here? Don't have no daughter. I got drunk and left my post. The Order don't like watchers leaving their post, especially drunk watchers. You're a scoundrel, just like me. A broken, drunk scoundrel, and that's all there is to your miserable life. It takes one to know one, as they say."

Henri tries to stand too quickly. His head erupts with dizziness, and he struggles to steady himself. He points a finger at Artemis. "I was out fishing on the Purse. A monster bit into my arm and tried to drag me under the water. Then the Purse, she got sucked from beneath me right into the sea. It was destroyed by whatever was trying to destroy me. Behold, I was saved by-"

"By a what, Henri?" Artemis eggs Henri to go on.

"By a sea cow."

"Sounds like you did a bit more than simply sip from a bottle, my dear man." Artemis explodes with laughter, spitting everywhere. "And if you had such a struggle, where are your marks?"

"I was healed by an angel right here in this room. My brother brought her to me." The creeping feeling that he had opened too wide, that he had told this stranger his fantastical tale in intoxicated anger, has made a nervous mess out of Henri.

"Innit." Artemis' eyes sharpen.

"No. I'm a drunkard; that's true. *But I'm also a liar*," Henri is satisfied that he has misled Artemis.

"Ah!" Artemis' face grows wild. He begins to laugh violently. "Let's have another bottle, shall we? For brothers!"

"For brothers."

* * *

A campfire. Captain Jervis, William, and the third supply boat fellow, Peter, converse under a night sky full of stars and wonder. Jervis fixes a log in the fire creating a pyramid of blazing timber. Peter fails to light a cigarette as the breeze takes his flame. Jervis offers a spark from his lighter and cups the cigarette as Peter takes several small puffs to strengthen the cherry.

"I'll be glad to do our duty. Three nights is three too many. Things ain't right here," William says as he takes a flaming twig from the fire and lights his cigarette.

"What do you mean, things ain't right?" Peter asks.

"Don't be daft. You know what I mean," William spits. Peter nods and hangs his head. His cigarette dangles from his lips.

"Artemis reports to us this night. If he's got nothing to say, the four of us will shove off in the morning," Captain Jervis says. He takes a swig from his flask and winces. His face is red from wind and whiskey.

Captain Jervis rubs his shoulder, then his chest and face with his free hand. He downs the rest of the sour liquid with a whopping gulp and throws the flask into his leather sack. He punches the sand beneath him. Peter recoils.

"Captain, should you go lie on the boat?" William asks.

"I-"

"Calm your asses, lads. Arty is back, and he's got terribly good news," Artemis shouts from down the shoreline. His jerking gait and confident tone pull Jervis' anxiety from his limbs to his chest.

Artemis kicks sand into the fire haphazardly as he nears the supply boat crew.

"Hey, watch it!" William exclaims.

Artemis lays down before the three men sets clothes. One for a woman and one for a man. Artemis balls two fists and brings them to his hips. One corner of his mouth rises, and the other sags with palsy. He waits for the men to acknowledge his triumph.

"Well, come on with it, Arty. What's the big fuss?" William says.

"Are we ready to go now?" Peter swallows. Artemis tilts his

head to one side, then the other. He motions towards the garments.

"Oh, come off it, lad. What the bloody hell are you on about?" Jervis uses a stick to lift the skirt from the sand.

"Demons' clothes. Those is demons' clothes," Artemis says. His face distorts with his horrible grin.

Peter pulls his knees to his chest and drags on a cigarette that has long burned out.

Jervis says nothing. Smoke from the fire is now all around him. He doesn't move for quite some time before convulsing and standing up to escape the woody fumes.

"And how do you know this as fact? How do you know those are the clothes of a demon?" William lifts his nose at Artemis.

"*Demons.* Two of them. Shapeshifters. I got Henri right pissed, and Bob's your uncle; he spilled the beans," Artemis says. "And what's else, the older brother summoned them just as the Order said he did."

"Where are the demons now?" William scurries to find his revolver amongst his other belongings piled near him. "Are they nearby?"

Peter trembles.

"How am I to know that? The boy couldn't handle his liquor. When he passed out, I nicked the demons' clothes from under the floor and came here," Artemis says.

"What has Llyas said about all of this?" Jervis asks with strained breath.

"He's a nervous and queer son of a bitch. He admitted his sorcery when he showed me how to harvest the light," Artemis looks away not due to distraction, but to hide any glimpse of his lie from Jervis and William. Peter, frail Peter, whimpers like a beaten dog. *Probably pissing himself*, Artemis thinks.

Jervis examines Artemis and lets out a long, sorrowful breath. His lip is arched.

"Let's take him now lest suspicion set in and the brothers attempt an escape." William stands and brushes the sand from his pants.

"Wait. We don't know whose clothes these are. We need to watch from afar and eavesdrop. These men-"

"No, we should go!" Peter interrupts his captain. "Demons don't perish from bullet piercings. We should get back to the mainland and tell the authorities."

"The demons aren't here. None of us have seen them. We are all blessed and secured by the Father. We four have been baptized," Jervis explains to Peter. "These men, as I was saying, have been on this island called Chimera for too long. They've likely invented stories to keep up morale or to entertain themselves. If a man says the same thing over and over again, well, he starts to believe it." Jervis turns his attention to William.

"Are you suggesting we return to the mainland with proof of sorcery but no sorcerer? No, Captain. You know that would be the death of us. The Order would have us labor the cavern right alongside the brothers. We will put the warlock called Llyas in chains and bring him to justice, or perhaps the Order will use his demons in the fight." William straps his holster around his waist.

Captain Jervis looks to the night sky and then at Peter, who pleads with his eyes. "Where are the brothers now, Arty," Jervis asks.

"Llyas is in the cave, and Henri is dead asleep," Artemis says, "I made bloody sure he was before I left. Should he wake, he would think I'm helping his brother harvest the light."

"So be it. Peter, stand and strap on your pistol. We have a task to carry out." Jervis gestures to the man.

* * *

Our Henri has concealed himself with black clothes behind the tree line near the campsite in the cover of the night. He struggles to listen to the men from this distance as the whiskey works itself out of his body.

They mean to bring us to the Order.

Thoughts of the day Henri saw Geb and Nut by the rock-how infuriated he was with Llyas, how incredible it all was. He could taste the tang of that old blood in his mouth. He could feel the grit of his teeth. He could sense the point of tension in his forehead so hot and focused he could have leveled Llyas-obliterated him from Chimera Island.

Oh, the things time does to soften edges, to pillow aching and worried heads. All he can think of now is holding his brother and telling him he has done well. No, none of this sentiment now. He needs to stop these men from taking him and his brother away to the soldiers in red who speak another language.

His reflection in the soldier's boot. Harsh and pointed words. Pain. Hunger. Pain again and again. Death is the favorite choice. Escape or death. Act now. Run and run to the cave and save your brother Llyas.

Our Henri dashes through the darkness over bushes and rocks and sharp things that would cut his ankles. He hears nothing but the rush of air over his ears and his own desperate breath. What to when he reaches Llyas? He knows he must be with his brother immediately. He must stand with him or run with him. Run to where? That bastard, William, the one determined to turn them over to the men in red, he said the Modest Purse was put together. He said it was beached. They will go to the Purse and sail off, right off the Earth if need be.

Henri dashes through the stream that flows through the slot cavern and reaches the mouth of the cave in which Llyas currently collects the light.

"Old Man!" Henri places both of his hands to his mouth, amplifying his voice. "Old man! Come out of the cavern. We have been betrayed!"

"Henri," Captain Jervis whispers from behind.

Henri's knees buckle as he turns around. "I heard what you said. I was listening. Hiding in the trees, I was. Don't do it. Don't take us away. Let us live here in peace. We never hurt anyone."

"I know you ain't, Henri," Captain Jervis says. The horizontal brushstroke of his thin lips shows an empathy Henri cannot comprehend.

"Step aside." William shoves past our Henri, who is bewildered and weak from running. Peter takes a step forward and straightens his posture. He then shrinks back and takes his place behind Captain Jervis.

"What does he mean going by me and into the cave?" Henri's gaze pierces Jervis.

"We mean to fetch your brother." Jervis looks at the ground. An unfortunate beetle writhes on his back as a colony of ants takes the creature apart.

"You won't. I shall *not* allow you to take us from this Island called Chimera unless it is to freedom." Henri moves toward Jervis, who backs away.

"We are not taking you and your brother away," Peter says.

Captain Jervis runs his fingers through his hair, hitting several knots.

"No, no-no, I heard you talking and plotting. You mean to take us to the men in red. You mean to have us crushed and beaten because you think we are sorcerers." Tears gather in Henri's eyes and are taken by gusts of wind. "Those clothes," Henri's voice cracks, "we found them washed up on the shore. They could be anybody's." Henri's lie fades like a dying candle.

Jervis' body grows heavy. He appears to have aged ten years in front of Henri at this moment. "There are other men here, Henri. They came in another boat a few hours after we did. They are the ones who don't speak our tongue. Men from the Order. The men in red, as you called them. If we don't take Llyas, they will kill all of us and still stake your brother."

"We are taking Llyas only, Henri. We intend for you to stay." Peter steps in front of Jervis. "It will be okay. Llyas will be s-"

Henri tackles Peter and mounts him. He forces his knees under Peter's arms as Peter tries to buck him off. Henri mercilessly rains down blows upon Peter. *Is this his blood or mine?* Henri's knuckles are cut against Peter's broken teeth. Henri hugs Peter's arms to his chest and throws his left leg over Peter's face. Peter shrieks as Henri thrusts his hips forward, snapping Peter's arm.

There is Peter's revolver. I can use it to threaten these betrayers, these spies. Then Llyas and I will make way to the Purse.

Artemis stomps Henri's hand and then his head. Henri's eye explodes upon impact with the heel of Artemis' boot. The sound of some awful animal escapes him. Henri rises to his feet, clutching his head. Artemis thrusts a mighty kick to Henri's chest, sending him again to the ground. Henri clamors to one knee and tries to stand. Artemis prepares another blow.

"Stand down, Henri," Captain Jervis pleads, "we have to take Llyas. We have to, damn it." Jervis grits his teeth.

Henri stumbles forward, intending to harm Jervis, who stands unwilling to lift a hand to our Henri.

"Stop, little brother." Llyas emerges from the cave's mouth, followed by William. William moves his revolver's aim from Llyas to Henri.

Henri ceases his advance. Peter lies squirming in the sand. Artemis exaggerates a laugh.

"Let me be taken. It's okay." Llyas walks to Captain Jervis. "I have done what I am supposed to do, and there is nothing left."

"Holster that revolver, William. Do it now," Captain Jervis commands. William obeys the order and returns the revolver to his side. He shakes his head to signal his disapproval.

Captain Jervis unfastens a pair of handcuffs from his hip. "I have to put these on you, lad. If I bring you back unshackled – the men in red will take issue with it." Llyas nods.

Llyas feels Jervis' hair against his face. "Why couldn't you let them angels be?" Jervis whispers. Gooseflesh on Llyas' neck. "I'll go to Hell for this," Jervis says, "God will have no mercy on me."

"You are forgiven." Llyas' words are less than a whisper. Sound of handcuffs clicking loosely around Llyas' thin wrists.

Peter groans as William helps him to his feet.

"I understand your suffering, Henri," Llyas speaks so loudly that his voice is echoed from inside the cave and reverberates down the slot canyon. "I should have listened to you. I was selfish." Blood from Henri's eye socket has wet his entire face and stained the front of his shirt. "I should have sat with you and listened. I didn't know how. Henri, I didn't know." Henri bleeds more and more.

"See to his wound, William," Captain Jervis commands, "and fashion a sling for Peter once we get on the boat."

William tosses some gauze from his bag at Henri. Henri goes to his knees and pats around him until he finds the gauze and ties it around his head.

Llyas turns and is led away. He does not pause or hinder

their steps. Henri's feet are buried in the sandy soil. His heart cracks his ribcage, and breaths cannot enter our poor Henri.

Henri falls to his side and witnesses his brother disappearing into the slot canyon down to the path that leads to the beach. The sand below him turns maroon. He prays for Nut to deliver him as he fades to black.

* * *

Seasons come and go. Time stops, rewinds, and lurches forward. Our Henri is an infant tossed about by time's indifferent undertow.

Has it been five summers, four winters since William stomped Henri's left eye and stole away dear Llyas to be executed by the state? How many pages of the calendar should have been ripped away by now? How many hours had he stood at the shore and placed one foot in the water, daring himself to place the other in front, and so on and on, until he walked into the sea and never came back?

There had been no supply boats, not even a hint of one on the horizon. The tabletop radio had long been in ill repair. The whiskey he had drunk seemingly eons ago. It is all gone. Everything is stale and bitter. Gray. Gray, as he had always seen things. Doleful and dull. Gray and bitter and pointless. An insurmountable and unknowable boundary between Henri and the world of the living. Perhaps there is nothing on the other side.

The light in the cave had gone out a long time ago. Maybe after Llyas had gotten on the boat, Henri reckons, for he did not harvest it, not one canister full, after Llyas was taken. His tools remain rusted over in the same spot.

When hungry, Henri pulls little bitter roots from the ground and boils them. Sometimes he picks berries when the season is right. He at times, casts his net from the beach and eats raw the tiny fishes he catches. It is hardly enough.

He never sets foot on the Modest Purse. Henri has succumbed to the idea of his cowardice. He often thinks of the water and the beasts within it who want to tear him apart. He wants the nothing on the other side of his emptiness. But Henri figures himself a coward. The pain of being torn to pieces is not something cowards crave.

There came a time after Llyas was taken, and it had become obvious no one was coming back for him. Henri thought the people of the world had been obliterated. He came to believe the war had wiped out all of humanity, and he was utterly alone with the whole world as this island, his prison.

Perhaps the Order and the enemies of the Order had poisoned the air to conquer those they could not drive a spear through. Even the birds and mammals of the island seemed to decrease in number. Had life ceased thriving on the Earth, or had Henri stopped noticing?

Henri stands naked at the shore and casts his net into the water. There is not a creature around to see him exposed, and this summer day is so, so very hot. All is yellow around him.

He pulls in his net only to find that it has trapped some shells and driftwood. Our Henri has gone days without food and is beyond hunger. He plops his boney bare bottom down on the sand. He picks a broken conch shell and places it to his lips as he gazes listlessly at the horizon. Fog rolls as thick as tar above the water.

What's this?

Some vessel, a small black dot, emerges from the low-hanging clouds. Henri studies it and decides it is moving oh so slowly toward Chimera Island.

Henri releases a low, pitiful sound.

Henri rises and places his hand on his forehead. His hair

has thinned and receded and grown long like straw. Dread is perfectly sewn to his skeleton face.

Henry stumbles in his attempt to stand. He rises to his elbows and spits sand from his mouth. His legs are clumsy from fear and hunger. He begins to crawl towards the cave and finally stands to run.

They've come back for me. I'll bury myself somewhere deep in the cave. I can outlast them.

Flashes of his younger face reflected in the mirrored surface of a boot. The horrible language. They asked him questions he could not answer.

Our Henri hides in a profusion of summer-blooming violet sage just outside the cave yawning at the end of the slot canyon. The same cave Henri has not tended to since Llyas was stolen from him. Henri becomes all too aware of his nakedness. There is no time for shame. The men in red know where the cabin is, and they will burn it down to draw him out. When he does not show, they will comb the cave, but he knows the labyrinth's passageways better than any man on Earth. He knows where there is water dripping from stalactites, and he has gone so long without food already. What's another day?

Deep in the cave, Henri climbs and crawls until he is secured tightly in a cranny high above the cave floor. He is hidden from sight completely. Should the men in red enter this particular cavern, Henri will maintain the high ground and lie as still as death to remain undetected.

Henry lies wedged in his slight crevasse. The only sound is that of water dripping rhythmically nearby. His stomach briefly betrays his position with a gurgle, then a hush.

Can this be done, this eternal waiting? Can he truly outlast the men in red? What if they mean to occupy Chimera Island? Not to mention, how will Henri know when the men in red have exhausted their search and retreated to the sea?

The cave is so dark, and Henri's good eye aches to adapt. His bad eye is in an even worse state.

Henri imagines himself in the deepest, most aphotic parts of the sea where anglerfish hunt. Those monsters with their glowing purple appendages used to deceive their prey and attract the males of the species, which are smaller by magnitudes.

Glowing purple. What's this? Raindrops of violet light travel down the cave wall before him. First, there are a few and they move slowly. Suddenly, many fat lines of violet cascade down the cavern walls. Complex geometric patterns begin to form and seem to come off the wall and through Henri as he lies cramped in his tiny trench.

Henri wonders at the light. His starved mind rattles with a dichotomy of bedazzlement and fear of capture. *Oh! The men in red will surely come here now.*

Indeed, they do.

Their footsteps echo. The metallic stomping sounds come from all directions. Henri closes his good eye and breathes faster. He again sees shiny boots and hears the cruel, cruel language. His hands hurt as he squeezes the sharp edges of the cave wall that hides him. He can taste blood in his mouth.

"Come out now, lad!" The voice no longer echoes. The men in red are near.

"It's the light, Captain. The light is back," one of the men says.

"God almighty, it's the light," says another. Sounds of the gobsmacked. The astonished.

Henry holds his breath and prays the men in red will pass him by and leave Chimera Island. He does not allow his body one centimeter of movement. Although his heart beats so that it raises him ever so slightly from the rock he lies upon.

"Henri, we don't mean to hurt you," the first man says, "we bring news."

Liars. Henri's naked body is sore from the unyielding rock. He closes his eye tighter. *Please, God, send your angels. Deliver me.*

"Oh, come off it, man. I shall drag you out of here. Stubborn mule," says another. "Drag you out of here by your ears," the man laughs.

Henri's reflexes get the better of him, and he bumps a small rock with his leg. It bounces down from his hiding spot onto the cavern floor.

"We've come to deliver you, Henri. We bring good news; as my man has said," A man speaks in a thin but sure voice.

That man. Henri knows this voice, but from where?

"I don't hold it against you, breaking my arm. We should have been here to do what we did. I'm thankful. Healing a broken arm while fighting on the front lines as a rebel against the Order will toughen a man. Forged in the fire, as it were. I've got you to thank for that."

It can't be. Henri holds his place, still convinced they haven't noticed him.

"The Order is defeated, Henri. I'm here to take you home if that's what you like," says Peter. "Why don't you come down and speak with me? Don't listen to my man, O'Reilly. He's ornerier than William was, God, rest his soul." Peter wonders at the shapes that glide on the walls. The violet light casts moving shadows across the faces of the men.

"It's me, Peter. Captain Peter, now. And with me are O'Reilly and Godard. We turned against the Order not long after-" Captain Peter pauses, "These men fought with me and good Captain Jervis. It was a long war, Henri. We had to wait so long to come back to Chimera Island. A godawful long time."

"I-" Henri cracks his silence. The men start and raise their torches. "I'm naked. I've got no clothes." How long had it been since he had spoken?

Peter motions to Goddard to remove his overcoat. He tosses it near the raised rock where Henri hides. Henri picks up the garment and dons it in the shadows.

The person who emerges is not a man Peter recognizes. Any semblance of a man named Henri has been eroded, replaced by a whisp of a being, a specter-like thing.

"We are here to give you a choice," Peter says. "You can stay here on the island. Now that the light has returned," Peter takes a moment to dazzle in the shapes, violet glints in his eyes, "and maybe you want to be here with it. Your life was taken from you, and you will have it back. How you live, it is up to you."

Henri witnesses the shadows move across the ground as though time is speeding by as he stands with a stranger's coat draped over him. He takes in the raindrop light on the walls and then the three men before him.

"There are arrangements for you back home. A house, some land. A whole country of people waiting to embrace you." Captain Peter takes a step forward.

Henri's eyes fill with water. "Tell me what I want to know, and make it the truth."

"Your brother was a hero," Peter says without hesitation.

Was.

"The Order, they tortured him to make him call his angels. He refused," Peter says. "You want the truth of it. You said."

Henri nods. His lips quiver.

"Those who witnessed it say he never spoke. Not an utterance. The men in red threatened to come here and make you suffer lest he agreed to summon his Geb and Nut to fight the rebels," Peter pauses. "Henri, Llyas jumped from the top of the tower where he was being held immediately, hands shackled and all. He dashed toward the widow and jumped the moment the men in red threatened harm to you. He knew they would not spend the resources to travel to Chimera Island to harm you if he was not alive to do their bidding. Llyas is a hero. Our people back home, they celebrate him. That bloody Artemis reported you didn't have the magic. It's a bloody good thing he did because you are here now, and you have a choice."

Henri's face is wet.

"The light is back now." Henri's voice is so weak Peter strains to hear him.

"It doesn't have to be you anymore. You can let it go."

Chimera Island, which was once unknown to the rest of the world, is now a national landmark. Its history as a prison during the decades-long Great War and the Reign of the Order is taught in schools around the world. The day the last surviving prisoner of Chimera Island was brought back home was declared a national holiday.

This day marks the thirtieth anniversary of that significant event.

Soundless waves massage the rocks on the shore of the craggy island we call Chimera. A passenger boat approaches a large port. The skinny pier that once held the Modest Purse is gone. A multitude has gathered at the shore in anticipation of the arrival of a national hero on this sacred day. The crowd is several people deep. The midsummer noon sun blazes above throngs of celebrating citizens.

* * *

"Pop," a stout blond woman with delicate features places her hand on her father's shoulder, "there is still time to turn around," she says as a matter of fact.

"Impeccable and dependable humor, my dear daughter Delilah." Henri places his hand atop Delilah's. Solar lentigines spatter his arm and hand. His teeth are whiter than his years would suggest.

"Llyas, gather Chester and put him in his carrier," Delilah projects her voice down the hall of the hull of the passenger boat where her son, Llyas, plays with his gray, fluffy cat, Chester.

"Yes, Mum," the boy, Llyas, replies.

Delilah removes her hand and sits next to her father. She runs her fingers through his curly gray hair. Henri's arm slips to his side. He briefly catches his reflection in a window. *Old Man,* he used to call his brother.

The boat thumps slightly against the dock.

Delilah inspects her father. She looks for signs of uneasiness, that hidden anxiety that cooks and simmers with age.

"I remember every story you told me about this place," Delilah says, "I hope you know I'm honored to be here with you. So's Llyas." Delilah gestures down the hall towards the sound of Henri's grandson mucking about with Chester, the gray cat.

"I'm glad you remember them. One of us ought to." Henri chuckles.

"Give us a kiss." Delilah pecks her father's cheek.

Down the hall, Little Llyas beckons Chester with a string. The cat swats at it and loves at Little Llyas' ankles before the boy willingly scoops him up.

"I think it's time to go up. You ready?" Delilah ceases her careful watch, and with a smile in her eyes, she helps our Henri to his feet.

Our family emerges from the hull of the passenger boat. Henri shades his eyes as Delilah helps him to the stairs. Little Llyas follows, cat carrier in hand. The crew stands by as the three of them descend the steps onto the dock.

"That very spot, the one we're walking to now. That's where she dropped me off, the mermaid." Henri tells his daughter the familiar story he has told her countless times. "And there is the rock the two of them stood near when I wanted to punch your uncle Llyas' lights out." Henri snickers momentarily before his face becomes serious again. "The angel was so beautiful, you understand, and her man, he was," Henri searches for the word, "otherworldly. And there just beyond the bend is where-"

"Yes, Pop?"

"I don't know. I don't bloody remember what I was on about," Henri shuffles alongside Delilah.

"It's okay, Pop." Delilah caresses Henri's back.

"Is beyond the bend where the cabin is, Papa? And is that the cabin where the angel healed you?" Little Llyas pokes his finger through the gate of the cat carrier to tease Chester. Henri leans on his daughter.

Our little family saunters down the dock, trailed by two officials in dress blue uniforms. Security personnel keep onlookers behind the roped-off pathway and scan the gathering for potential troublemakers.

"What's all the kerfuffle?" Henri asks Delilah.

"They're here for you, Pop. They're buzzing to see you. You're famous." Delilah puts her arm around her father.

"Buzzing, Papa. You're famous. Yup." Little Llyas pops the *p* sound. Delilah playfully pulls at Little Llyas' shirt sleeve.

Our family approaches a plaque anchored on the now historical rock where Llyas had Geb and Nut sit when he revealed them to Henri. Today Henri is meant to take pictures with his country people. He is meant to say a few words on the significance of this day, the day he was finally freed from Chimera Island. Henri is to shake hands with elected leaders.

There is a stage built around the rock. A microphone and stand are situated on the stage. Delilah and the two officials help our Henri up the steps and place him at the microphone.

"Tell the people how you feel, Pop. You can say what you like," Delilah whispers to her father. "They want to know if you feel good about being back." Delilah secedes the stage to Henri.

"I-" high-pitched squelching feedback rings out from the stage. The crowd wears a collective grimace before once again turning their eager ears to the old man. "It's been," Henri turns to his daughter, "it's been how long?" His words echo over the masses.

"Forty years," Delilah shouts and holds up four fingers. "Forty years since you were freed."

Henri stares at the wooden platform below him. Images of the maroon floor in the cabin. "I never knew. He didn't know either." Henri has backed away from the microphone. His audience struggles to understand him. "He flew a kite awfully well," Henri speaks up. "And I'm sorry I forgot to bring out the light. Alls we had was a little boat, innit. A mouth harp and a song. I'm sorry I forget." Henri lifts his elbow and rubs it with his opposite hand. "I didn't know how I thought. But maybe I knew all the whole time. I'm sorry I forget. I'm sorry I got bored of wildflowers."

The military men who escorted our family to the stage gesture to Delilah. Their worry is evident in the severity of their motions. Delilah tells Little Llyas to stay to the side while she consoles his grandfather.

"It's okay, Pop," Delilah says. She grasps the microphone. "That is all for now. My father needs a rest. There's loads of beach to be sat on and sun to soak in."

"And loads of fireworks tonight, Mum. Tell them about the fireworks," Little Lyas says.

"And loads of fireworks." Delilah backs away from the microphone and waves as she escorts her father away from the crowd.

* * *

The celebratory explosions in the sky go on late into the night. Our family is hunkered down in a hotel suite built long after Henri's rescue. Tea has been had. The events of the day, the honors bestowed upon Henri, have taken place without the guest of honor's attendance.

"Papa, you missed a bash," Llyas exclaims as he rushes into the room, "there were knees-up around every corner and people singing songs. Everyone was happy to have seen you, Papa, and they wanted to see you more."

Chester, the gray cat, rubs his face against Henri's leg. Henri pets the creature lovingly.

"I'm old, lad. Do-ups are for little boys like you and pretty mums like yours. I get sleepy, you know," Henri says.

"Are you happy to be here?" The boy asks.

"Brush your teeth, and it's off to Bedfordshire with you, Llyas," Delilah says.

"But Mum, I want to fly the kite with Papa. You said I could," Llyas protests.

"It's too late. Papa isn't-"

Henri raises his hand. "If it's all right with you, Delilah."

Delilah nods. "I'll stay here and have me some quiet time. As much quiet as one can with the bombs going off above." Little Llyas jumps and claps, startling poor Chester.

* * *

Henri walks hand in hand with his grandson through the woods to an open spot down the shore that is not occupied by his admirers. Fireworks zip across the sky and explode to tremendous applause.

Henri pauses and removes his bag from over his shoulder. In silence, he takes from the bag the indigo kite his brother had so long ago left behind. He unfolds the bird and gives the kite spool to Little Llyas.

"You see those two satellites up there? The ones above the tree line and to the left?" Henri asks. Little Llyas points to the general area. "Aye, that's them. Those ain't stars. You see? They ain't blinking, and they are violet instead of white or yellow. Those satellites are your uncle Llyas and your great-grandmother."

Little Llyas gazes in wonder at the night sky as fireworks pass by. He wonders but does not truly see the satellites his grandfather speaks of.

"Run on with the kite and send it up as high as you can. Let's see if we can get them to come down to us. Your uncle and grandmother would very much like to meet you," Henri says. Little Llyas takes off running.

"They were forced to fall from the Earth for loving too much. It's love that will call them back," Henri speaks as though his grandson were still near him.

Henri stands in reverie as he watches his grandson hop and skip along the shore with the kite. The bird eventually falls to the sand, and Little Llyas returns with the kite string full of knots. Henri fiddles with the kite string.

"Why did we fly the kite at night? It's awful fun, but it's for daytime, innit?" Little Llyas asks.

"The stars are always there, and no one cares for them because everyone's usually asleep when stars are out. We should be the ones what would care for them." Henri dotes on his curly-haired grandson. “Maybe those souls up there like the company of our bird.” Henri begins to unravel the kite string. Little Llyas sighs.

“What’s a soul, Papa?” Little Llyas asks. Henri pets the kite as though it were a living thing.

“Imagine your whole life you’ve only known the color gray from the moment you opened your eyes at birth. Just that one color all the time. Imagine every person you meet tells you, *would you lookit that emerald sea there* or, *I’m feeling a shade of blue today*. But you don’t know what it is they’re on about. All you know is gray.” Henri unravels the string and hands the kite and spool to Little Llyas.

“And imagine you spend nearly every second of ten whole years with a person who says he can see every color there is, even colors most people don’t see. You ask him to show you, to show you in *your* own way how to see the other colors. But the way he shows you, it ain’t *your* way. So, you don’t figure how to see it. Then, some very long time after, you finally see those colors when you’re just about to close your eyes for good.” Henri nods his head. “Seeing those colors. That’s what a soul is.”

Flashes of light from the fireworks above illuminate Little Llyas’ face.

“Gray,” the boy pauses and looks up at his grandfather. “*Chester* is gray, Papa.”

“*So, he is*.” Henri smiles at his grandson, seeing every color radiating from his grandson’s chest and the mighty violet light in his eyes.

A gust of wind picks up the kite. It tugs at Llyas and soars among the exploding brilliance of the fireworks.

1.25.23
New Orleans, Louisiana
2:31 pm

TESTIMONIES AFTER THE FIRE

BY IZASKUN GRACIA QUINTANA

TESTIMONY

From lat. *testimonium.*

1. m. Attempt or assertion.
2. m. Document authorized by a public servant, attesting to a fact or transcribing all or part of the content of another document.
3. m. Proof, justification and verification of the certainty or truth of something.
4. m. Imposture and false attribution of a fault.

There are places that attract misfortune, and I think Fosco is one of them — you just have to look back to see it. Accidents, epidemics... Just think of how many bodies we have found on the streets, when winter is ending and the snow starts to melt. We don't go out very often, that's why we don't know they are there. They are usually bums or travelers. A blizzard surprises them, they approach the village looking for shelter (they see lights from the road, I guess) and then they are overtaken by the snow before they arrive. And it keeps on snowing and until spring comes, no one finds out that they are there. And it's a big problem, because we don't know where to put them. In the end, years ago it was decided to save a part of the cemetery just for them: the back pit, nothing fancy. Actually, the only thing that matters is to get them out of the way... But we have to do it like that, we're not going to bury them with us. No way.

The only thing that we know for sure is that no one has ever liked the Manial family. They were openly disliked and hated by practically all of Fosco's residents, a feeling that went back several generations although nobody remembered exactly where it came from. Not that it mattered much, to be honest. Children learned to hate the Manials in the same way they learned to do housework, to ply a trade or to use tools: by imitation. And they did not ask questions about it. It was, perhaps, something natural, like wearing brand new clothes during the village's festivities, fearing wolves or wiping your feet before entering someone's house. That was the way things had been done in the past and that was the way they were being done, and nobody asked why or tried to change anything.

It didn't matter that the Manials were as linked to the region as any other of its residents (or maybe more, since it was said that the Manials, along with four other families, had founded the village that still survives between the mountains), that they never did anything wrong (or, at least, nothing worse than what others had done after and before them), that they worked hard or that they gave their neighbors a hand when they needed it. Whatever they did, nothing changed.

There wasn't a rumor that didn't concern them, either directly or indirectly, there wasn't a child who wasn't warned about that family (*who knows what they are capable of,* people used to say, although nobody really knew what they were capable of, because they had never been given the opportunity to prove it). There wasn't anything they did, no matter how small, that was not subject to public derision. And, if there was no reason to criticize their actions, they were criticized because of everything else: the Manials were said to be as ugly and brute as a demon or so handsome and delicate that everybody wanted to beat them to a pulp. If they were intelligent, they were criticized for being smart-asses, while they were accused of being subnormal if they didn't show off what they knew. No matter what war they unknowingly participated in, the odds were always stacked against them.

It was a family unit made up mostly of men (no one was able to remember when the last Manial girl had been born or if that, in fact, had ever happened). And because no woman in that village wanted to have anything to do with them, they had no other choice than to look for a partner outside the region, where nobody knew or judged them. Thus, young Manials used to leave the village shortly after coming of age and would return several years later, unfortunately for their neighbors, usually married and with a new male on the way. Some never returned, and they were hated even more than those who had the audacity to do so. Though never as much as the ones who (even at the risk of never starting their own family) never left.

The Manial women learned soon enough that they couldn't trust the residents of Fosco, although they were kind to them (when that was the case, since kindness was not a widespread virtue in that place), and ended up devoting their lives to their family and the relationships they had with friends and relatives outside the village. The only people they interacted with under equal conditions were the members of two other families who also suffered the marginalization and disdain of the rest: the gravedigger's family (it was said that nobody wanted to have anything to do with them because they were foreigners and had other customs, when in fact the neighbors didn't want to interact with people who made a living manipulating corpses, even though they were going to require their services sooner or later) and the forest ranger's family, who also ran the guest house and was as virulently despised as the Manial family, even though, like the latter, they had lived there for generations. Long before the village of Fosco existed as such or even before its first residents had settled in the place where it currently lied.

Thus, it was not surprising that practically all the people raised their hands to their head in astonishment, and felt that the world was increasingly incomprehensible and illogical when the village crier announced the engagement and future wedding of Menor, Último Manial's youngest son, and Martina Argayo, the new teacher.

They cannot be trusted. They never could be. I feel sorry for the kids because they are not guilty of anything, but the grown-ups? They could have burned to ashes for all I care. I've never seen anything like that. I've known her since I was a baby because we are the same age, and she's always been very strange. Neither she nor her brothers went to school with us, like their children, who are home-schooled... Well... they stay at home, that's all we know. Who knows what they learn. Dog breeding, which is the only thing they seem to be good at. Who knows how many animals they have in that house. Beasts! They look like wolves! You can hear them bark all over the village, and we are thankful if they don't howl, because if they do we won't be able to sleep a wink. My God, it is torture! And the smell? You can tell where they live just by the mongrel smell. I feel sorry for whoever stays there! The dogs and the forest ranger are supposed to keep the wolves away... Not at all! Nonsense! What happens is that people feel bad because a few years ago the forest ranger (the former one, her first husband) died during a drive. A tragedy. An accident, of course, because all cats are black at night... But she got the idea into her head that it was our fault, as if we had nothing better to do than go out into the forest at night to take our chances with those animals. And she cut herself off from everybody, can you believe it? It's not like she used to be close to anyone before, huh? Let's not forget that, but since then... poof! Nothing at all. She even goes shopping to the next village, it's unbelievable. And we tried to help, but it was no use. Some people just don't know how to live with others, that's what I say. But come on, less than a year after becoming a widow she got married again! Well, I would say she didn't love the first husband very much if she ended up with another one so soon. Off with the old, in with the new, my mother used to say, God rest her soul. Now, he must be related to her in some way, because they have the same eyes: yellowish, a very strange thing.

And it happens to every member of the family, huh? When they are children, they all have blue eyes, but as soon as they grow up they get that color. It may be something they eat... Either way, they give everybody the creeps. And she is the worst of them all. Well, she could have taken care of her children without getting married again. And her older children could have worked as forest rangers, although they already make enough with the guest house... But there are women like that, who care much more about other things. But we cannot ask her to leave the village, because then she would go around playing the victim, I'm sure of it. We'll see what happens with the kids. Every time I think about it...

Martina arrived at the village one year before the announcement of the ceremony to replace Mr. Ramón, who was already sixty and, after having worked as a teacher for more than forty years, had already begun to complain about several infirmities of old age and found himself every morning imagining different ways to murdering the wild vandals he had for students. Therefore, without giving the subject much thought, he came to the conclusion that the best he could do (and the only thing that he really wanted, actually) was to retire, so he announced his retirement and the need to look for a person to take his place.

It has never been clear what Martina's hiring process was like (it didn't really matter to anyone), but it is known that she showed up in Fosco one day at the end of the summer and that her arrival, as it could not be otherwise, caused great expectancy in the village. All neighbors remembered the moment they saw her for the first time, walking towards the school with the mayor and Mr. Ramón (actually, most of them didn't see her because they were working or doing something else, but they all liked repeating — and embellishing — what those who had told about it as if they had experienced it first hand), and how they spent hours admiring and praising each and every one of the virtues they automatically assumed she possessed.

As tradition dictates, Martina moved into the teacher's house, an austere stone building located in the southern part of the village, close to the river and almost next to the shoemaker's, and began to work as a teacher just a couple of weeks after that.

We were not at the bar the night of the accident, we only know what the neighbors told us. We never had problems with anyone; we even bought some furniture from the Manials... In the end, we pay for the sins of others. Because, let's see, what harm had our children done? And who is going to return them to us? And what about us? Who do we blame?

The school in Fosco was not very different from the other schools where Martina had worked in the past. It was a two-story building whose white walls showed, in the form of peeling plaster, that it was time to make certain arrangements in order to prevent it from collapsing with the children inside. It was located downtown and had two large classrooms (one for Martina and one for Sol, Mr. Ramón's daughter) and a small library on the ground floor that almost nobody used. Most of the village children went to school there and they distributed in the two classrooms depending more on the available space rather than on their age or their knowledge. Martina and Sol taught their students how to read, write and do basic mathematical operations, as well as some geography, history and natural science. None of these children were expected to move to the city to continue studying or to learn a job that wasn't what their families had been doing for generations and, even though this was the case, none of the village's residents could afford to pay for university or higher education. Therefore, the teachers who worked in Fosco, and would work there for many years, were satisfied if the children learned enough to move forward without difficulties, before their parents decided it was time for them to go to work and they dropped out of school before their fifteenth birthday.

Although the children liked Martina immediately (more because she did not use the hazelnut stick that her predecessor had used almost every day to keep them at bay than because they were interested in what she was trying to teach them), the adults didn't know what to think, because they had mixed feelings about her since she arrived. On the one hand, due to the fascination they felt, they tended to give too much importance to any detail that had to do with her, however insignificant, like her strange accent (she dragged the r-s and softened the g-s and made them almost inaudible). That kept them busy for months, trying to figure out if she came from a foreign country or from one of the eastern regions, where people spoke in dialects cut by saltpeter from the sea. On the other hand, everyone was surprised by the fact that she was extremely reserved and that she didn't try to make friends with the village women, even though she had moved there alone and she had no acquaintances around. Although she was nice and friendly when someone talked to her, it soon became clear that she didn't have the slightest interest in socializing and nobody really knew how they should take it.

During her first months in the village, however, the neighbors forgave her behavior and blamed it on the excessive shyness that they immediately assumed she suffered from, while talking about the exquisite manners with which she declined their invitations, praising her elegance and envying her for being an educated woman, who had studied and, no doubt, seen more of the world than all of them together (that's what they said, although nobody knew if it was true).

But it wasn't long before they judged her severely: they spoke ill of her for the first time the day they saw her talking to the forest ranger's wife. They never knew what they talked about or if they were friends or even if they had just met and started talking about nothing in particular, but it didn't matter. Barely an hour after the butcher saw them together, most of the neighbors were aware of what had happened and met at the village bar to discuss the matter, because no one could explain why Martina had decided to engage with that woman, who lived isolated from the rest of Fosco's residents and who had had the audacity to marry the new forest ranger before the customary first year of mourning after becoming a widow had ended.

Encouraged by several glasses of wine and few interesting things to fill their time with, they argued that, given the number of good women in the village she could have befriended, she must have had an ulterior motive to spend time with that woman. Perhaps she felt sorry for her, or maybe she had decided to ask her why her children didn't go to school, like the rest of the children in the village (something that the neighbors, on the other hand, never concerned themselves with in the least). There couldn't be any other reason to start a relationship with that woman, because anyone a little smart could see she couldn't be trusted.

And so, after hours of drinking and throwing theories into the air, they came to the conclusion that Martina acted as she did out of sheer kindness and ignorance. Being a newcomer, she still didn't know who she should befriend or who could be a bad influence for her, so it was understandable for her to make such a mistake. The neighbors decided, consequently, that this was something they could forgive, because they were sure she was going to find out what she had done sooner or later. They imagined she would come to them seeking support, with an apology in her eyes and the desire in her heart to make it up to them in any way possible. And they also imagined themselves, full of understanding and generosity, forgiving her stupidity without reservation and accepting her with open arms, always ready to remind her of her mistake while they lived.

However, they didn't have the chance to see their fantasies fulfilled. Although they saw her again on other occasions chatting with the forest ranger's wife (and even with the gravedigger's wife, which was much worse, although no one could ever explain why), it never seemed like she had established a true friendship with any of them (always bearing in mind, what the residents of Fosco understood as friendship). So her neighbors supposed they were wrong and she was just trying to be nice, and that wasn't something they could condemn (or maybe they could, but they were willing to make an exception this time). In addition, they were too fascinated by Martina to treat her equally and for that reason, the village women kept on doing everything in their power to gain her as a friend, while the men focused on betting on what family was going to be the first one to get her to accept an invitation to dinner. But Martina didn't make friends with the village women and never accepted their invitations.

I always thought she was a little simple-minded. At first, the whole village was interested in her... the new teacher, of course we were! But we realized right away that she was a bit off. She didn't speak much and, well, I admit that I misjudged her at first, because it seemed that she looked down on us, like priests tend to do, and then I realized that she didn't think she was better than anyone... she was just a simpleton. She wasn't a genius, so to speak. You could see her sitting in her garden with a lifeless gaze in her eyes, looking as if she didn't understand anything that was going on around her. Like the village fool, but cunningly. And she called herself a teacher!

During the year that preceded her wedding, Martina received a couple of visits that nurtured even more (if possible) the mystery and magic with which the neighbors had surrounded her and which started all kinds of rumors. The first person who visited her was a man with dark hair and light-colored eyes (*like hers; they look like cats*, said those who ran into him), whom she really resembled and who starred in the most absurd and erotic fantasies they imagined until Sol (not prone to gossip and sick of the rumors her neighbors invented) revealed that he was Martina's brother, as Martina herself had told her, and invited all the neighbors to mind their own business and leave her co-worker alone.

That silenced the most absurd rumors (or, at least, it prevented them from turning into stories even more fantastic than those already concocted) and kept all the neighbors occupied inventing new ones until a few months later, when Martina was visited by a young couple. She didn't look like any of them, but no neighbor overlooked the fact that, like her previous visitor, the three of them made the same gestures and had the same accent (some people said somebody heard them speaking in another language, but nobody could verify if that was true).

Although most neighbors were still fascinated by Martina (and, from then on, by her visitors), voices were soon raised, harshly criticizing that she had not taken her companions to the village bar (without even considering that she had never set foot in that place before) and had not introduced them to anyone. They criticized that she believed she was better than everyone else and they thought that she insulted their simple way of life with her good manners, her good looks and her education, and concluded that people like her were not to be trusted and that they always caused problems sooner or later.

The teacher didn't cause any problems, but it didn't take

her long to provide them with a new topic of conversation. The anger at her failing to introduce her visitors to anyone had not yet begun to fade when the village crier, after announcing the irrigation shifts and before announcing the opening of the registration period to request a hunting license, proclaimed that Martina and Menor Manial were engaged.

No news in the last twenty years had created as much commotion as that announcement. The neighbors used every free second they had to try to understand what was happening and, above all, how they could have overlooked that the teacher, whose demeanor could compete with that of a princess, had feelings for that ignorant, stupid and good-for-nothing Menor. The question that most often crossed their minds and escaped from their mouths (*What the hell did she see in him?*) was just the first of many others that also remained unanswered and that had to do with any matter imaginable, from the details of their relationship to the causes of the great mistake she was making. In spite of this, a few hours of heated discussions were enough to dispel any doubt that the neighbors had harbored about Martina until then: it was more than clear that she didn't go against the flow because she was shy or because she came from a different place and had different customs, but because she was stupid. They didn't question that she was a good person (everyone was sure of that, of course), but it was obvious that she didn't have half a brain and that her future husband had been able to take advantage of it.

After clarifying this point, they stopped questioning their intelligence and good taste and occupied themselves wondering what the wedding would be like: Was the bride going to dress in white? Was it all right for her to do so? Would there be a banquet? Where? Who would they invite?

Some neighbors picked up their children from school for the first time in years only to try to start a short conversation with Martina (they were too proud to talk to Menor) and ask her about the ceremony, but, as usual, she navigated the questions they bombed her with and didn't reveal a single detail.

Thus, the neighbors had to wait several months to discover that the wedding that had aroused so much interest ended up being a simple ceremony attended by almost the whole Manial family, Martina's brother, the couple who had visited her a few months earlier, an old man who the neighbors took for her father, the gravedigger, the forest ranger and their respective families, Sol and Mr. Ramón. No other inhabitant of Fosco was invited to the ceremony or to join the guests at the meal that followed, which showed (already without the slightest doubt) that Martina was a Manial and, therefore, she had to be treated like her family had always been treated: with the utmost contempt.

Martina, nevertheless, didn't show any signs of noticing a change in the attitude of most of the neighbors towards her. In fact, she even seemed to enjoy the fact that no one tried to talk to her all the time and that she finally didn't have to refuse invitations to have lunch, to have dinner or to do any activity that she preferred to do alone, or not to do at all. For Martina becoming a Manial also meant that the neighbors, no longer impressed (that is what they were trying to prove), stopped talking about her (they didn't even bother to discuss whether it was right for the couple to live in the teacher's house, even though no one liked that Menor had moved there. It didn't seem that they were going to look for another home in the short run), and started using their spare time to discuss other matters.

At least, until almost a year later, when Martina's belly began to grow and her neighbors found out with dismay that not only had the teacher been stupid enough to be fooled by a Manial and marry him, but also that she hadn't even been able to avoid getting pregnant. Martina was once again the focus of attention, except Sol and the village doctor (and perhaps the gravedigger's family, or perhaps the forest ranger's family, although nobody could know for sure), not one of Fosco's neighbors approached her to congratulate her or offer her advice or help. Even though not a single child was not bombarded with questions about the teacher as soon as they got home from school. The more obvious Martina's condition got, the more rumors about it spread. There were those who said that the baby was not a Manial, those who (ignoring dates and logical timelines) stated that the teacher had become pregnant by another man and had married Menor so that he could pretend to be a father and who, showing off an imagination unheard-of in the area, raised the question of whether Menor had forced Martina to marry him, whether she was being held against her will and whether the baby that was on its way was the terrible result of her captivity.

In any case, the pregnancy went on without Martina or the Manials worrying about what others were saying behind their backs. At least, until Menor was killed and nothing else mattered anymore.

I just want to be left alone. I am not on one side or the other. At my age, all I can do is wait for death. Well, then, why don't they kill each other and leave me alone?

Because the Manials had never been ones to brood on things (On the one hand, they were naturally practical people. On the other hand, they tried to avoid worrying for no reason, since they already endured enough contempt on a daily basis and didn't want to make their existence any more bitter). Hey, didn't usually talk about the night that Menor died. Every member of the family knew what had happened, of course, but none of them talked about it unless someone asked a question about it. Only then did they sorrowfully tell what they had rarely heard Martina, her brothers- and sisters-in-law tell.

Thus, they reported that the day that Último Manial's youngest son died, Martina woke up at dawn and discovered that her water had broken while she was sleeping. She woke Menor, who dressed, still half asleep and went out in search of Dr. Matías. By the time Menor returned with him and the midwife, his brothers and sisters-in-law (whom he had awakened on his way to the doctor's house and told the situation) had arrived. They had distributed their respective children in two different rooms and kept Martina company, although it wasn't too clear if their attempts to calm her down were working or if they were making her more nervous than she already was.

Dr. Matías took charge of the situation. Leading all the Manials out of the room, he strictly forbid them to come back except in the event of a fire or an earthquake and, since they couldn't do anything but wait, they sat down at the table, played cards and began rolling one cigarette after another, smoking them as anxiously as if their lives depended on it. Menor, unable to sit there doing nothing, made coffee and offered his brothers and sisters-in-law something to eat. They refused the food, but they drank the bitter liquid while pretending to concentrate on the game, filling their lungs with smoke and listening to Martina's moans and the words of the midwife and the doctor that came from the room next door.

It was five in the morning when the Manials ran out of tobacco and Sara, Mayor's wife, offered to wake up the shopkeeper and try to convince her to sell them a couple of bags. She knew the woman was going to get angry (firstly, for waking her up at five in the morning and, secondly, because Sara was a Manial), but she also knew that, as soon as she explained that Martina was giving birth, the woman would be glad to sell all her stock provided that Sara answered a couple of questions that would feed the popular imaginations and keep the whole village busy for weeks. No sooner said than done. Sara was back half an hour later bringing not two, but three bags of tobacco. *The old witch was so happy I could give her first-hand information about the birth that she gave me one for free*, she explained laughing when she returned to the house.

The three brothers and Claudia, Segundo Mayor's wife, received her story with humor and a pinch of sadness (as they received everything that was said about them) and they began to roll cigarettes mechanically in the company of Dr. Matías, who had left Martina in the midwife's hands so he could take a cigarette break. *Everything is going well, but it will take a while*, he told Menor, urging him to be patient and try to take a nap. Menor, however, prepared another coffeepot and, after refilling his family's cups and the midwife's, who had just exchanged places with the doctor, went out the back door and started chopping wood. While the Manials laughed at their brother's behavior, Sara told them they had to take him to the bar once the baby was born and get him drunk. *Just a little,* she said, *he still needs to be able to come home on his own. But he has to drink something to let off steam, or he will end up chopping away half the forest.*

At daybreak, shortly after breakfast, when the children had

left for school, Mayor went to his carpenter's shop. Segundo Mayor, Claudia and Sara stayed with Menor, who kept walking from one room to another, focusing on tending to Martina when the others allowed it, and staying active doing anything when they ordered him to get out of the way. The children returned in the early afternoon and the place became a madhouse: Sara told off her children because they were covered in mud, and Claudia and Segundo Mayor had to comfort their eldest son because he didn't stop crying. Convinced that they were going to stay there forever and they were never going back home, while their youngest son could not help bursting into tears every time someone raised their voice.

They made such a racket that Dr. Matías stormed in yelling they could either behave like adults or leave the house, but they had to stop that fuss either way, because the shouting was driving him crazy. Sara took the children outside and kept them entertained playing on the riverbank until a couple of hours later, when she heard a baby crying. Segundo Mayor leant out the window and announced that she had just become the aunt of a girl with dark hair and devilishly strong lungs. They almost wasted no time to send the eldest child in search of his father before they opened a bottle of wine and toasted to the newborn baby. Meanwhile they waited for Mayor to join them. It was difficult to say if they were (only) happy because Menor and Martina had become parents or if what really made them laugh with happiness was the baby's gender. It was the first Manial girl to be born in generations. Everyone agreed that this was a good sign, so, shortly before it was time to start preparing dinner, Dr. Matías and the midwife went home. Sara took the five children back to her house, while Claudia stayed with Martina and the little one, and the three brothers went to the bar to drink a few glasses of liquor, to celebrate that Menor was a father and to vanish the tension that had taken over his body and mind for hours.

I just wanted to retire, I'm tired of saying that I had nothing to do with what happened. Neither did my daughter, and they almost lynched us both. So she left, of course, shortly after Martina. And well done! This village is rotten, you can't believe a word anyone says. If I were a doctor, I would poison everybody. What happened at the school was a tragedy, yes, but only to a certain extent, you know. The whole village should have burned down. That would have been justice.

The bar the three Manials went to had no name because it was the only place in Fosco of this nature (a sad establishment where people could drink alcohol until losing balance and at any time of day, and have a bowl of boiling soup where they could fish small pieces of meat and potatoes during the winter). For that reason, it had been the neighbors' meeting point since long before any of them could remember and didn't need to be baptized in any way possible.

At the precise moment the Manials entered that nameless bar, just when the bells that had inhabited the church tower for decades announced that it was already nine o'clock in the evening (although it had already been pitch black for several hours), all conversations were interrupted and the eyes of the forty or so men and women who drank alcohol under the light of the lamps turned toward them.

There was no doubt that those people were aware of what had happened, but none of them made a move to get up or congratulate the father. As soon as the three brothers approached the bar and Mayor said *Buddy! Three liquors! Today we have something to celebrate*, the rest looked away and apparently went back to minding their own business. The only problem was that, of course, no one minded their business exclusively and there wasn't a single person in the establishment that didn't shoot the three brothers annoyed looks from time to time, even though the Manials didn't seem to notice.

But they did, obviously, and after two rounds, Mayor asked for another one in a tone of voice that showed without a doubt that he was starting to get angry. He later said that the bar owners (the Gersan twins, a man and a woman in their fifties whose appearance made more than one wonder if their parents, from whom they had inherited the bar and the obligation to take care of it, had not been siblings too) had attended their orders late and with exaggerated slowness. No one could say that this wasn't usual, on the other hand, when it came to serving the Manials (whether it happened at the bar or anywhere else), but it is quite likely that the twins took more time than usual that day, because the three brothers were happy and they had had the nerve to go to the bar to show off their joy in front of everyone.

So Mayor, annoyed, asked for the third round and then asked again, a little angry, five minutes later. The Gersan sister refilled their glasses and told Mayor (loud enough to be heard even by the coalman, seated at a table by the door and who had started going deaf several years ago) to take the wind out of his sails, because she had already heard him the first time. Menor and Segundo Mayor made a face, but they took the glasses and toasted again and, for a moment, it looked like Mayor had decided to continue enjoying the company of his brothers and not to respond to Gersan's bad manners.

They kept on drinking and, as the alcohol tangled their tongues and bloodshot their eyes, the rest of the regulars gradually stopped looking at them sideways and began to observe them as one observes a dangerous animal that has sneaked into the house: all the muscles in the body tensed, ready to pounce on the intruder as soon as the brain got the signal. The Manials noticed that and, although they had already drunk enough, they ordered their last round after deciding, without saying it out loud, that it was time to go home. As Mayor went out to empty his bladder, the Gersan brother refilled their glasses for the last time and asked Menor what his daughter's name was.

Stunned (almost more surprised by that apparent gesture of kindness than by the fact that he had become a father a few hours ago), he slurred that they hadn't decided on a name yet. The twin nodded, thoughtfully, and said as if to himself that they had probably expected a boy to be born and hadn't thought of girl names. Without waiting for Menor to answer, he left the bottle of liquor in its place and returned to the other end of the bar, where his sister and the married couple who owned the butcher shop were waiting for him.

I'm not saying that I am happy about what happened. What I'm saying is that we could see it coming and the Manials are the ones responsible, they started everything. Why did they go to the bar, if they already knew they were not welcome? To provoke, that's all. To pick a fight. And then things happen as they do: one loses it, the other responds... and, when alcohol is involved, things don't end well. That is what happened, they started going at each other and things didn't end well for the Manial one. It was an accident, but they are never going to admit it, because if they did, they would also have to admit that they went to the bar to pick a fight. As always, of course. They have always been rowdies. Always giving people something to talk about, always trying to deceive everyone... in the end, they got what they deserved. People are too good and they put up with too much. If they had been put in their place from the beginning, everything would be different now. We couldn't imagine what would happen next, that's true, but we would've saved ourselves a lot of trouble if we had kicked them out of the village years ago, because we don't need people like those in this village. That's the only thing I'm saying.

Segundo Mayor recounted later that Menor was visibly uncomfortable and, resting his elbows on the wooden counter as if he needed a place to hold on to so as not to start running, he kept looking around like a cornered animal. Finally, without raising his voice (in fact, almost whispering), Menor told him they had to leave as soon as possible. Segundo Mayor, who would never in his life stop regretting not having paid attention to him, gave him a strange look and responded, *As soon as Mayor returns, we finish our drinks and leave.*

But Menor also told him that he could feel the eyes of all those present fixed on them, that it made him nervous that most of the conversations had died out long ago (there was only an unintelligible murmur coming from one of the tables, where the pharmacist, who didn't seem to have noticed the storm that was coming, was engaged in conversation with her sister), and that it was not a good idea to stay there.

At that moment, the Gersan brother took the cloth that was used to clean the counter and disappeared behind the curtain that separated the bar from the kitchen. His sister looked at him amused and turned to the Manials. *So your daughter doesn't have a name yet, Manial,* she said to Menor so that everyone could hear her loud and clear, while the young man, without answering, glanced furtively at the door. The woman emptied her glass and added that it must have been quite an event that the baby had turned out to be a girl, considering the Manial family's history. Menor, again, didn't answer, probably knowing how that could end: with an argument, perhaps with broken bottles and glass and with one more (apparent) reason for people to hate their family. And, among all possible nights, that was the least appropriate to get into such a fight.

But the door didn't open and Mayor didn't appear in its frame, so the brothers didn't move and the twin returned to address the youngest: *I may have a name for your daughter,*

Manial, she said, *you can call her Flor. That is what my mother was called, I am sure you remember.* Menor bit his lower lip and didn't answer, but the woman kept talking anyway: *I'm sure you remember, because when you were a kid she caught you messing up in the larder and gave you a good beating. She also forbade you to return to the bar for life, but go figure, here you are... So do you remember my mother or not?*, she snapped after an awkward silence, and Menor, who apparently had decided not to listen to one more word, left enough money to pay for all their drinks next to the glasses, that were still full of liquor, he answered yes, he remembered, and he nodded to his brother to get out of there. They hadn't taken the first step away from the bar when the butcher almost shouted at him that he could call his daughter Whore after her mother, because, if Martina had had a girl, it was clear that the father couldn't be a Manial.

All that the little Segundo Mayor remembered of that fateful night was that, after hearing that remark (due to the alcohol they had ingested and the contempt they had accumulated over generations rather than to the remark itself), he pounced on the butcher as if propelled by a spring and broke his nose with a punch. He never remembered anything of what happened next because the Gersan sister smashed a bottle on his head right after that, knocking him unconscious. The butcher's wife, of course, took advantage of that and kicked him in the ribs as soon as his large body touched the ground.

As the pharmacist would tell later, Menor then grabbed the woman's hair and threw her against the wall. At that moment, many of the customers left their tables and got ready, as someone said later, to give him what he deserved. Thus, everyone present (except the Gersan brother, who had not yet left the kitchen; the pharmacist and her sister, who had not moved; the coalman, who never knew exactly what was happening, and the priest, whose beliefs prevented him from participating in the chaos but not, apparently, from enjoying the show) unleashed on Menor decades of irrational and senseless hatred. Although he knocked out the first five people who attacked him, somebody —according to some neighbors, the Gersan sister; according to others, the tailor— hit him on the head with a club, which made him stagger for a couple of seconds and allowed the butcher's wife to kick him in the left knee, knocking him down.

At the precise moment when Menor lost his vertical, he also lost every chance to get out of that bar alive. Too many fists struck his body in unison from too many different directions to be able to strike back or even protect himself. It did not take long (someone said that they had broken his nose and one of his eyebrows and he had lost the incisors by then. They also said that it was a kick that broke his teeth and that by then both his eyebrows had been split) before his attackers also started kicking him and breaking his ribs. Although most neighbors beat him using their feet and hands, somebody stabbed him in the back repeatedly with a bottle neck, someone else hit him on the hands with the same club which had made him lose his balance until every bone in them was splintered and somebody (some said it was the priest, who had approached the mob and encouraged the attackers, although no one knew for sure) threw a glass at him that shattered against his forehead.

The pharmacist (who was still sitting and whose sister had buried her face in her hands and was crying, horrified, in silence — or maybe not, but the pharmacist supposed she was because she saw her shoulders trembling, even if she couldn't hear her crying) also said that, regretfully witnessing that gruesome scene, she hadn't moved a finger to help the Manials because she had been paralyzed by terror and stupefaction. She didn't know very well how the lynching had begun, although she did remember that the Gersan sister was teasing the

Manials shortly before the blows started coming and that a couple of minutes had been enough to turn into a mob that beat up one of his fellow men for no reason and with extreme violence. Seeing their purplish faces, furious and deformed by anger, spitting while insulting Menor (and spitting directly at him), roaring the other lynchers to hit him harder and harder, elbowing their way in to be able to kick him or punch him or shatter a glass or a bottle against his body, had affected her terribly and she had no choice but to sit where she was, horrified, while her sister cried in front of her.

Neither of them was able to react until the beating came to an end as suddenly as it had begun. Without a word, without a single person doing anything to stop that wild attack, the residents of Fosco simply stopped hitting Menor. One by one they stopped, breathing hard, and stood around the man they had reduced to a bloody rag, watching him as if they didn't understand what he was doing there and wiping the blood from their hands on their skirts and trousers. As soon as the lynchers began to exchange glances, the two women jumped from their chairs and fled the bar as fast as they could, finding Mayor unconscious and bleeding from a head wound two meters from the door, and the Gersan brother smoking absentmindedly by his side.

They all went crazy. I don't know... I don't understand what got into them. They looked blind, they moved like automatons, hitting and kicking, they didn't even seem to breathe. After that night, for a long time, I thought that they were going to come after me and I didn't leave the house for weeks. I don't even know for how long I locked the door and the windows before going to sleep... but not at all, nothing happened, everything was back to normal in a couple of days. Everything was so normal that I got goosebumps.

It was the coalman who told Dr. Matías, who greeted him at the door of his house in his pajamas and with his gray hair defying the law of gravity, that something terrible had happened. That the entire village had gone crazy and that he, Dr. Matías, had to go to the bar as soon as possible, because there were at least two people who needed his help. He put on a pair of pants and a jacket over his pajamas, put on his shoes and without even tying his shoelaces he went out carrying his briefcase, speculating about what could have happened but without even imagining what he was going to find at the Gersans' bar.

The first thing he saw was a pool of blood outside the establishment and Mayor lying on the table closest to the door, although nobody ever admitted to having gotten him inside while the coalman was absent. Afterwards, he saw Segundo Mayor unconscious at one end of the bar and, a second later, the doctor discovered not far from him a shapeless and bloody bundle that he soon identified as the third Manial. He gulped, entered the bar cautiously and asked those present (the twins, the priest, the butcher and his wife) what had happened. *A terrible accident*, the priest told him, and he repeated: *Terrible.*

The doctor asked, raising his voice and secretly sorry he wasn't in another country, in another continent or in another world where he didn't have to deal with situations like that, who had caused that "accident", how it was possible that there were still a lot of half-finished glasses on the tables even though the bar was empty, what the hell had happened exactly and why no one had called the sheriff. None of those present seemed willing to answer his questions, the doctor decided to stop wasting time and began tending to the Manials immediately.

The only thing he could do for Menor was to cover him with a blanket, but there were no blankets there and since nobody wanted to go out and get one, they ended up covering him with kitchen rags. As for his brothers, Dr. Matías could immediately see that they had only suffered minor blows to the head. Once Mayor stopped screaming and crying for his dead brother, Dr. Matías sewed the open wound he had near his nape, and he applied an ointment where the Gersan sister had shattered the bottle on Segundo Mayor's body. Shortly after, the Manials saw him put the butcher's nose back in its place (at the second attempt and, as the butcher's wife said afterwards, causing him more pain than was necessary, even though the doctor would always categorically deny that). He demanded that the Gersan bring the sheriff to the bar as soon as possible.

As the twin sister came out of the establishment unusually calmly, Dr. Matías threatened the priest, the butcher and his wife to never treat them again, no matter the illness, if they left before the sheriff arrived. Then he asked the Manials if they wanted him to deliver Martina the bad news. They thanked him and rejected his offer, saying they would do it themselves as soon as they spoke with the representative of the law, who arrived almost an hour later and seemed more interested in having a couple of drinks than in actually working.

Although he took everyone's statements, it soon became clear that the crime was going to go unpunished. After all, Mayor and Segundo Mayor had been unconscious throughout the scuffle and couldn't provide any information about it, the twins said they hadn't left the kitchen and hadn't seen anything, the butcher's wife said it was the Manial that had started the fight, that she had taken care of her husband and because of that they didn't know well what had happened, and the priest declared that as soon as he had heard the first expletive, before anyone had even thrown the first blow, he had closed his eyes and prayed for the Almighty to intercede and put an end to whatever was happening as soon as possible.

Days later, the sheriff invalidated the coalman's statement (who had pointed out the true culprits and named all those who had participated or witnessed what happened), because he had drunk a lot that night (or *as usual*, like he added) and no one could know if everything he had told was the truth or the result of alcohol-induced hallucinations. Likewise, he rejected the statements of the pharmacist and her sister, arguing that they were so upset (*we must ask Dr. Matías if we might be dealing with a case of hysteria* was the only thing he said about it) that no one could believe anything they said. Needless to say, he never bothered to ask anyone else what had happened that night or to look for other culprits, so a few days later he concluded that Menor Manial's death had been an unfortunate accident (a simple bar fight gone too far, as he explained in his report) and he shelved the matter, hoping that time would put things in their place and that life would go on as if nothing had happened.

I have nothing to say. The only one who knows what happened is Martina, and she doesn't live here anymore, so we'll never know the truth. It's just as well. Fuck the rest, they have what they deserve.

Fosco's residents liked telling that, when the Manials told Martina that her husband had died, she had burst into tears and spent whole nights awake, crying ceaselessly and unable to take care of her baby. However, the truth is that no one ever knew how she reacted when Mayor and Segundo Mayor delivered the bad news. Nor did any neighbor say what she said (or if, in fact, she spoke a word) when they gave her all the details and she knew not only that her husband had been killed, but also the terrible way in which he had lost his life. They knew, of course, that Dr. Matías had been there when the Manials spoke to her, but, being one of the few decent people who lived in the village, enemy of rumors and gossip, the neighbors never dared to ask him what he had seen or heard that night at Menor's home, because they knew that they weren't going to get a single word out of him.

For that reason, a large part of Fosco's residents colonized the living rooms of Martina's closest neighbors for a couple of days, observing who got in and out of the teacher's house and trying to make out the shadows drawn on the curtains, while they made up theories about what could be happening inside. Thus they learned that, of course, it was the gravedigger and his wife who worked on Menor's body for hours until he looked good enough for his relatives to look at him without feeling sick, and that during mourning day Martina was visited by her brother and by the couple who had visited her months ago. No one saw the old man who came to her wedding, which gave the neighbors the perfect excuse to wonder what could have happened to him. While half the population of Fosco claimed that he had died, the other half thought he might have been angry with Martina for some reason they didn't know about (although getting pregnant with a Manial child was enough reason to be angry with her for life and even to disinherit her) and had decided to make it patently clear by refusing to be by his daughter's side precisely at the moment when, they supposed, she most needed him.

Along with Dr. Matías, Sol and Mr. Ramón, the forest ranger and his wife were the only neighbors in Fosco who attended Menor's wake and offered Martina their condolences, although the baker told everyone who wanted to listen that she had seen the staggering coalman walk towards the teacher's house with a bottle of wine under his arm, although he never got to knock on the door. He was, however, inches from it, but he stepped back a couple of steps to roll a cigarette. He smoked and rolled two more cigarettes and kept on rolling and smoking them until he ran out of tobacco and it began to get dark; then he emptied the bottle of wine in four or five gulps and, staggering, went back the way he had come.

The pharmacist couldn't visit Martina because she hid away at home behind guilt and fear for almost a month, either not dreaming or plagued by nightmares. She lost more than five kilos because she spent weeks unable to retain anything that she ingested and at all times had to be tended to by her sister, who kept telling her she would leave the village as soon as she got better. It didn't matter where to or how, but she had to get out of there. She kept saying that she, the pharmacist, couldn't stay there either, that it wasn't safe. That it wasn't all right. *How the hell are you going to live surrounded by murderers?*, the pharmacist said her sister had asked her many times, while preparing food or changing the bed sheets and waiting in vain for an answer that never came. What didn't come either was the time (or the will) for any of them to get away.

The priest, like most of Fosco's residents, kept going to the bar. He continued sitting in the company of his neighbors, drinking wine and talking about the few pieces of news from the region. He didn't talk much about Menor's burial because there wasn't much to tell anyway. Everyone in the village knew that the day of the funeral had started out rainy and the sky hadn't cleared up as the hours went by, so it was probably the shortest service of the last few years. The priest didn't mind at all, he didn't feel comfortable talking to the small group that had come to bid farewell to Menor (mostly, members of the Manial family) and couldn't wait to leave. The gravedigger didn't mind either, because his work was really complicated when it rained and he was really grateful when everyone left the cemetery as soon as possible and let him work in peace.

The priest said that Martina stood all throughout the service and that, even though she didn't look well and it was obvious that she had been crying for hours, she didn't shed a single tear in his presence. She was alone and nobody knew in whose charge her daughter was or even where she was, but at that moment Fosco's residents didn't think too much about that. They preferred to spend their free time trying to guess what was going to happen with the teacher and the Manials thereafter.

Only a couple of weeks later they saw an unknown family move into Mayor's house. Thus, they found out that the Manials had sold what had been their home and their shop until then, and had left the village forever. As if that piece of news was not good enough, it turned out that the new neighbors were carpenters, like the Manials, so Fosco's residents spent whole days toasting to their good luck. In addition, that gave them the perfect excuse to invent the most creative stories about the fate their already former neighbors could have chosen, and to try to guess how they were doing and if people hated them in their new home as much as they had hated them in Fosco.

Martina stayed in the village for a little longer than a month, but she barely left her home during that time. Fosco's residents were aware that Sol bought her groceries and visited her often. They assumed at once that she was the only person with whom the teacher interacted during those weeks, until the shoemaker saw her (from his basement's window) sitting in the shade of the elderberries one afternoon, drinking what he imagined was coffee (although it could very well have been an infusion) with the pharmacist's sister, with whom she talked for a couple of hours and whom she hugged when they said goodbye.

Shortly before leaving the village, Martina announced to Mr. Ramón that she was going to spend some time with her brother and that she would write Mr. Ramón a letter to inform him of her return. The old teacher said that he took her by the shoulders and told her *Leave! You are still young and you deserve to live in a better place than this, with people who treat you well. Think of your daughter. How is she going to grow up here, surrounded by people who either killed her father, or know who did it and keep quiet? How are* you *going to live here?*, but she smiled and told him not to worry. She also told him that she was going to come back, because she had already made up her mind and she wasn't one to have a change of heart so easily, and asked him to say goodbye to Sol on her behalf. And without adding another word, Martina left Mr. Ramón worried about her and not knowing what to do and, a few days later, she left Fosco with her daughter.

Because nobody saw her leave, no one could say what day exactly she disappeared from the village and nobody believed Mr. Ramón when he insisted on the need of a substitute teacher (he wasn't willing to continue dealing with that group of little beasts that he had for pupils), but that it was going to be only for a short period of time, since Martina wasn't gone forever. What Fosco's residents believed, obviously, was that the teacher was never going to return. They imagined that she would move to the city (did her brother live in the city?), that she would remarry and have more children, that she would eventually forget Menor in particular and the Manials in general, and that Fosco would somehow survive in her memory as a place where she had had a bad experience. She was young, intelligent, mysterious and cultured. Surely she would have a new and good life wherever she set foot on, they said, and they let that thought comfort them and erase from their minds the misfortune that had fallen on her and that had forced her to leave the village.

I saw her from the shoe shop, sometimes. Not very often, really. Our shop is in the basement and it has a couple of windows which overlook her garden, and of course, I saw her sometimes, when she went out to read or crossed the river and went to the forest for a walk. People asked me time and again what I saw and what she did, but I never had much to tell, because I'm always working when I'm in the shop — there are lots of children who need shoes in this village (or, at least, there were back then) — and I'm not always aware of what is going on outside. The Manial boy was seldom in the garden, he only went out to chop wood. If he went out some other time, I never saw him. Well, I did a couple of times, when they had the family over for lunch or dinner. That people! What a bunch of animals! They ate like savages, shouting and slamming their fists on the table, as if they had grown up in a stable. We always knew that family was going to make trouble... They always have! I don't like talking too much, but everybody could see it coming, I kept saying that... The fact is that the little girl seemed different; she was a teacher, you know, but people end up showing their true nature. And she fooled us... Or so they said, but you can't trust everything that people say either. I try to ignore the gossip, anyway, I don't like to talk behind somebody's back. I already said I had never much to tell. I told the little I saw, nothing more. What more can I say? She seemed normal, the kind of person you want as a neighbor, what do I know? She seemed disciplined, did her chores (cooking, cleaning... the usual) always at the same time, like clockwork. And then she gets involved with that swine, turning everything upside down...

Naturally, the world didn't stop spinning after Martina left Fosco. Christmas came bringing snow, and the village children enjoyed it as much as the adults hated it. The winter brought along more snow and colder days, and due to the low temperatures the river was covered with icy patches that didn't completely disappear until spring, which brought rain, sunny days and the unmistakable aroma of birth and latent soil to Fosco.

The summer made a display of strength without being blazing and gave Fosco's residents plenty of fruits and vegetables. As if everyone was preparing for a feast, the animals gave birth to healthy and strong offspring, bees produced more and sweeter honey, cows and goats gave more milk and sheep, better-quality wool. Even bread seemed to taste better and beer freshened up more. Except for an incident caused by wolves, which undermined the neighbors' mood in general and a couple of families in particular for some time, that year promised to be perfect, brimming with life and good omens.

For that reason, due to the reigning optimism, the neighbors received Martina's return with surprise, but also with good humor and a lot of expectation. Like it happened with her departure, nobody ever knew the exact date of her return. It was the shoemaker who, one mid-August morning, told the butcher's wife that he had seen Martina sitting under the elderberries in her garden, reading a book, and the woman couldn't wait to share the news with anyone she ran into that day. By nightfall, everyone in the village was talking about that.

Some people went to the bar to try to get information and discuss the matter while getting advice from one or more glasses of wine. Others sat in the cool air with their relatives or neighbors, but practically everyone in Fosco spent the whole night talking about Martina or interrogating the shoemaker (What did she look like? Was she sad? Was she alone? Did he see her daughter?), even though he didn't have much to tell. He had seen her sitting in her garden, yes, but only for a couple of seconds (he had quickly stepped away from the window so that he couldn't be seen) and hadn't been able to see much. He said that she was wearing dark clothes (black, perhaps, although he couldn't tell for sure), that she was reading and that he hadn't seen any other person around, neither her daughter nor an adult. That didn't necessarily mean that she had returned to the village alone, but it certainly left many questions up in the air, something that most of Fosco's residents really enjoyed, especially when several neighbors saw her enter the pharmacy a few days later. And, even more, when the mayor's eldest daughter, who was in the establishment at that time, said that Martina (serious, dressed in black and with her dark hair tied back in a high bun) got in, greeted the pharmacist's sister, who was helping another neighbor at that time, and went directly into the back room.

Nobody explained why she didn't want to be treated like everyone else or why nobody prevented her from going past the counter, as was the case when someone tried to talk directly to the pharmacist (after the incident with the Manials took place, she interrupted all contact with most of Fosco's residents and stayed in the back room, working while her sister helped their customers, or at home, doing who knew what). However, after enough glasses of wine and a couple of hours of conversation everyone accepted the dressmaker's theory. She suggested that Martina (or her daughter) must be suffering from some ailment (nothing serious, or she would have not been able to leave her home) "sensitive" enough so as not to discuss the details in front of other people, and stopped thinking about that.

However, it wasn't long before they had a new topic of conversation, because only two or three days later the baker informed the rest that she had seen Martina enter the school with Mr. Ramón.

The new carpenter, who was in the building fixing a window at that time, said that the old teacher had told the young woman what had happened in the village during the time she was away. He told her how good they expected the harvest to be that year, about a couple of children who had dropped out of school to work with their families, about the teacher who had replaced her (whom he described as nice and hard-working, although he didn't think he would work as a teacher long), about the butcher and his brother, the rancher, being killed by wolves (*I probably shouldn't be saying this,* he added, *but I think the village lost nothing with those two deaths — those two were always bad eggs*) and about her still being the only thing in the village about which, apparently, everybody always wanted to talk about.

The carpenter described Martina like the mayor's daughter had done days before: as wearing black and with her hair tied back in a high bun. He also said that it was Mr. Ramón who carried the weight of the conversation and that she, apparently distracted, barely asked a couple of questions related to the children. She hadn't been interested in the wolf attack, nor did she react when she heard the comment Mr. Ramón made about it (which, on the other hand, earned the old teacher the eternal hatred of the butcher's widow and her family, who from then on said nasty things about him whenever his name slipped into a conversation or, rather, who from then on tried to sneak his name into every conversation so that they could speak badly of him behind his back), and she left the school after confirming when she was to go back to work.

During the few days that remained until the beginning of the new schoolyear, Fosco's residents saw Martina a couple of times, but none of them tried to talk to her. They just observed her, as if she was a freak, and tried to etch everything they saw in their memories so that they could talk about it hours later, even though there was usually nothing interesting to say: they had seen her buying groceries, or washing, or in the garden. Nothing out of the ordinary or that could particularly awaken interest.

And so September arrived, the children returned to school and spent several days answering the questions their parents asked them about their teacher, although they couldn't provide them with other information than what the adults could get by themselves (the teacher was the same as always, except that she wore black and her hair was tied back in a bun). Because of that, Fosco's residents focused their attention on another issue that was undoubtedly going to give them much more to talk about and for a longer time: where was her daughter?

Since Martina had been in the village for some time now, it was certainly strange that no one had seen or at least heard the little girl. They didn't think she was sick because nobody had seen the doctor around, which would have been normal if the child had been seriously ill, so they started to look for a logical explanation to justify her absence. At first, they thought she was dead (diphtheria and scarlet fever wreaked havoc among the little ones), but Fosco's residents immediately dismissed that possibility, assuming that, had it been the case, they would undoubtedly have heard of it. At the very least, they would have had to hold a funeral and a burial, because it was logical to think that the girl's body would have been buried next to her father's. Regardless of what happened in the past, burying the girl somewhere else wouldn't have been right and it would have been frowned upon. Even though her father had been a Manial, things had to be done as dictated by tradition, and the fact that the gravestones of those Manials who had died long ago were still standing around Menor's grave, and that there were no relatively freshly-dug graves, proved without a doubt that the little girl was alive.

Thus, the only possible explanation for her absence was that she had been given up for adoption. It was not ridiculous, according to Fosco's residents, because they considered not only that Martina was too young to raise a child alone, but also that being a Manial would have scarred the child for life. At least in Fosco, where she would never have had too many friends and her life would have been quite difficult. Giving her up for adoption was, therefore, the best thing her mother could have done for her and, no doubt, for herself, too. Now that nothing linked her to the Manial family (now that, in fact, she wasn't even close to them) and she was free from the responsibility of having a baby, Martina could apply herself to finding a decent man in the village (they all agreed there were a lot of those) to marry and start a proper family.

Although nobody said it aloud, the neighbors were sure that they were going to set up a date between Martina and one of the village's bachelors as soon as the mourning period ended and she could wear colors and get involved with a man and no one could criticize her for it (which was going to happen soon, because the mourning period rarely lasted longer than a year). They just had to give her a little time, they thought, before they could help her live a normal life.

All of it made me feel very sorry. She could've had a good life here. But, sometimes, things happen... such a pity. The problem is that everything gets twisted afterwards and there are misunderstandings, and people fall out and then... things happen. It's so easy to sit down and talk... because we are all good people here. Some are idiots, of course, like everywhere else, but we are normal people, we have flaws, of course, everyone does, but we are good people. And we help each other, as good neighbors do, but sometimes, when something bad happens... some people simply can't get over it, I suppose. It's such a shame, let me tell you, such a shame.

A year after Menor Manial's death, Martina seemed to have no intention of turning over a new leaf. Or maybe she did, but certainly not in the way that people imagined. As dictated by tradition, the young woman left her home that day only to go to the cemetery and place a bouquet of flowers on her late husband's grave. The rancher's widow, who had gone to the cemetery to replace the flowers that were rotting on her husband's tomb, would tell later that Martina had been there for a long time, alone at the beginning (she would have loved to tell she saw her crying disconsolately, beating her chest and shouting her grief to the sky, but all she could say was that the teacher, after placing a bouquet of flowers on Menor's grave, stood there like an idiot, without moving a muscle or giving the slightest sign that there was blood running through her veins) and, about an hour later, in the company of those who had been her brothers-in-law and their wives, whom the priest had seen arriving in the village shortly before.

Many neighbors saw them leave the cemetery together and go to Martina's house without saying hello or stopping to talk to anyone along the way. Although the shoemaker would tell everybody the next day that he had seen them dine in the back garden (it hadn't cooled down enough to have dinner indoors), where the teacher often sat to read, and had he not known what load that family was dragging, that would have looked like a normal dinner, during which everyone talked, satiated their appetite and even allowed themselves to make some funny comments and laugh.

The next morning, several neighbors saw Martina leave for school from behind their curtains while the Manials set out in the opposite direction, after getting delayed in a long farewell in which no kisses or hugs were spared. Contrary to what was expected, the teacher still wore black and kept her hair tied back in a bun.

However, even though everyone was disappointed that the young woman was still mourning, as weeks went by Fosco's residents were quite happy to observe that, in spite of what had happened until then, it seemed like they hadn't been hoping for in vain. Since her last encounter with the Manials it wasn't unusual to see her in one shop or another, chatting with whoever was there at the time (although, as people said, she still kept a certain distance, as if her shyness was bigger than her desire to socialize) and participated more or less actively in the events that took place in the village.

She even went with Sol to the autumn festivities (which consisted in a feast followed by a dance, where most of the neighbors were drunk by the time they ate dessert and went home to sleep it off even before the elderly and the children started dancing) and, although she didn't get drunk (in fact, she didn't drink a single drop of alcohol during the whole night), she spent the evening bonding with her neighbors and talking to them about anything that wasn't related to the school or her pupils. Martina ate, laughed, sang and talked throughout the evening, making every neighbor in Fosco believe that they could almost consider her one of them.

Although she never stopped being reserved and spent much of her life in solitude (they often saw her enter the birch forest that flanked the village for a walk, seemingly aimlessly, as well as rummaging through the leaf litter and collecting Russulas that she afterwards dried in the kitchen, as the shoemaker claimed), these small displays of openness were enough for Fosco's residents to convince themselves that Martina was on the right path, as they liked to say. Therefore, it didn't seem too bad that, also since she saw the Manials for the last time, Martina got used to leaving the village every Friday afternoon, without exception, and coming back forty-eight hours later. Someone (nobody knows who) heard somebody (nobody knows who) say she traveled to the city to spend the weekends with her brother, although some people claimed that she was actually visiting her father (provided that the old man they had seen at her wedding was actually her father), who was no longer said to be dead or angry with her, but sick, which would explain both his absence at Menor's funeral and Martina's long absence after the burial, as well as her subsequent trips.

Also, to all the neighbors' astonishment, she began to help take care of the church. Although she never attended religious services, she could be seen changing the flowers of the vases twice a week, sweeping or dusting the statues together with other women and taking turns with them preparing food for the priest. The baker, who had been going to church since her prayers saved her twins from dying in the river ten years before (as she said, of course; according to the children's friends and the village doctor, her children were in a more shallow part of the river, where they could touch the bottom and, even though they got really scared when they slipped on the riverbed stones, sank and were underwater for several seconds, their lives were never in danger) and who was responsible for organizing the work, didn't approve of Martina giving them a hand. Since the baker distrusted Martina's willingness and readiness to collaborate, she didn't wait too many weeks before entrusting her with taking care of the sacristy. The chores she had to do there were the same she had done in the church, but under the priest's watchful eye, which in some way reassured the baker and prevented her from spending every minute observing everything Martina did or didn't do.

Martina also adopted the habit of going to the cemetery once a week to take care of Menor's grave: she removed the flowers she had left on it the previous week, rested a new bouquet against the gravestone and pulled up the weeds. Some neighbors who went to the cemetery to take care of their loved ones, like she did, saw her work in silence. She didn't stay a second longer than necessary, although sometimes she visited the gravedigger before taking the road back to her house. Fosco's residents didn't know what she was doing there and it didn't sit well with them. Almost none of them approved of her meeting with the ranger's wife (although that happened only once in a while too). However, since her return Martina spent more time working on her relationship with the rest of the families than on with these two, which is why nobody criticized her too much. Once again, everyone assumed that she was just being nice and that, in fact, she despised those two marginalized families as much as the rest of them did and almost as much as they had hated the Manials not so long ago.

I'm sure that she had everything planned from the beginning, it's as plain as the nose on your face. The moment she arrived in the village I knew something big was going to happen. I saw it clear as water. And I said so, but no one would listen to me. Of course, she was the novelty... They all fell for her like idiots! And look what good she brought. I'm grateful every day that my daughters are all grown up and they had stopped going to school long before it burned down, but what about the others? Can other people be grateful? And she got away with it. Oh, no, we don't know what really happened... Do we really not know? I do! Ask me! Oh, no, it's better to waste time crying. We should have looked for her and given her what she deserved, like we did with her husband, but that won't happen because people are too good. Well, as always, we don't learn our lesson. We trust someone at first and look what happens. She better never come back and have the decency never to set foot in this village. If she does, something bad will happen, something really bad this time.

Martina stopped going to the cemetery shortly after Christmas, as the new year arrived in Fosco, bringing invariably gloomy skies, snow and extremely low temperatures. It snowed almost non-stop from the beginning of the year until well into February, although only seven or eight days after the first snow had fallen the neighbors stopped cleaning the snow that accumulated in front of their homes, because it was futile to say the least. Thus, after making sure they had enough food to survive several weeks and enough wood to feed their fireplaces, they locked themselves away in their homes and waited, with the best possible spirits, for the white blanket that covered everything to stop rising.

By the time the sky cleared up and stopped spitting snow on the village, some families had found themselves praying to everything they didn't believe in and throwing empty promises of sacrifice and change into the air so they could go back to normal. But, little by little, they began to go out and to open roads through the almost five feet of the cold white mass that had kept them prisoners in their own homes. They also tried to go back to their daily routine as far as possible.

No one ever knew what Martina did during that time. The neighbors didn't know if she had been, like the rest of them, locked up in her house for weeks or if, on the contrary, the worst part of winter caught her out of the village by surprise, but everyone was so busy cleaning the streets and trying to refill their pantries that they didn't really pay much attention when they saw her, armed with a shovel, clearing the front access to her home.

They did see her again when March arrived and children returned to school, and she welcomed them without having tied her hair back in the bun she had worn daily since Menor's death. From then on, she was always seen with her black hair loose and streaming down her back, as if she was a teenager.

She didn't even tie it up on windy days, when it seemed to have a life of its own and fluttered behind her like a wild animal, giving her an almost phantasmagorical appearance.

Her students loved the change not only because her face looked less severe, but also because even her personality seemed to have changed — she was more affectionate and attentive towards them, even though they could see her lost in her thoughts from time to time, more out of reality than inside it. These moments of absence became commonplace with the arrival of spring, almost at the same time that the neighbors realized that the summer was going to be catastrophic that year.

The sun burned relentlessly already in May, making simple actions impossible to carry out without losing one's breath and soaking in perspiration; the weeks when the rain used to make an appearance went by dry and scorching, the river lost much of its flow and the soil became arid and stony, as if it was beginning to die. It was so hot that the neighbors were forced to change their habits: they went to work the land earlier than usual or waited until the evening to perform certain tasks, when the temperatures dropped slightly and the air became breathable, took a nap after lunch (because being out at noon, even without doing anything, was torture, impossible and probably unhealthy) and took advantage of the last hours of the day to sit down and share with each other everything the heat of the day had forced them to keep to themselves.

Fosco's children, on the other hand, were the ones who withstood that heat wave best. They went to school at the usual time and, although they also left at the usual time, enjoyed a couple of hours of napping each day after lunch when it was hottest, which made the obligation to stay in that building until Martina and Sol called it a day more bearable. Afterwards, they spent the afternoons swimming in the river and returned home just in time to have dinner and go to bed. In spite of this, they welcomed the news that the classes were going to be over and the summer holidays were going to start a little earlier than usual that year, because nobody thought it was right for them to spend so many hours a day shut away at school in that heat.

Martina and Sol seemed somewhat relieved, knowing that they didn't need to try to keep a bunch of kids who just wanted to run out to the river busy much longer, and they even decided to throw a little party with them to celebrate the end of the classes and wish them a happy summer. However, ten days before that celebration was to take place and only three days before Martina disappeared from Fosco forever, Sol fell ill.

Dr. Matías claimed her ailment was no more than a summer flu and she would be back on her feet the following week, but until then Mr. Ramón had to tend to her constantly, and so he warned Martina, when she visited them on her way to the priest's (to whom she was taking a pot full of steaming stew), that she had to take care of the children alone until summer.

Later, the old teacher would say that Martina was obviously very happy to know that Sol was out of danger (although he also said she seemed more relieved than happy) and that she downplayed the children's issue, saying that she could take care of them for as long as was necessary without any complications. Sol, on the other hand, couldn't contribute much to her father's testimony, since she didn't remember Martina's visit very clearly. She thought she remembered that they spoke briefly, but she was so feverish at that moment and felt so poorly that she couldn't fully trust what her mind took for granted. If her father had not told her, days later, that Martina had come to visit her, Sol would have thought that it had been a dream, as she also believed that she must have dreamed the penetrating smell of roses that her co-worker had left behind her when she left the house.

A day later, the baker told Martina that she didn't have to go clean the church until further notice, since the priest was sick and had decided to cancel the daily service until he felt better. She also told Martina that she shouldn't get used to being idle, because his condition didn't seem serious and it surely wasn't going to take him long to resume his chores. However, as soon as she left home to go to school the next day, Martina was approached by the shoemaker's wife, who told her, apparently consumed by worry, that the priest's sickness, which had started as a simple stomach problem, had developed into what appeared to be a colic as the hours went by. *The poor man even has cold sweats,* she added shuddering, while Martina nodded without showing much interest and said goodbye with her usual kindness, explaining that she had to go open the school and prepare the day's classes before the children arrived.

The shoemaker's wife told later that on that day she saw Martina return to her house at the same time as she always did. The shoemaker's wife herself was chatting with the new carpenter, who told her that he had heard the butcher say that the priest was jaundiced (and not beyond us, as the woman had actually said and half the village insisted on repeating, even without understanding what was happening to the priest or what exactly they were saying) and that Dr. Matías didn't seem to know what to do to cure him. She also said that Martina greeted them, but didn't make any attempt to approach them and join the conversation, so they went on to comment that it was bad luck that just a few days ago the gravedigger had left Fosco with his family to attend a wedding, because if the priest died and they had to wait several days in that heat to bury him, it wouldn't be long before it started to smell like hell.

They would both see their fears become real that night. As the baker recounted in the bar, his wife had told him that the priest had begun to rave, so they had to start to seriously consider planning his funeral and calling another priest to conduct the service, because things didn't seem to be looking up for him.

The next day, the shoemaker and his wife woke up an hour earlier than usual because the baker was banging on their door as if she was trying to knock it down. The baker had gone to their house, after the organist replaced her in the sacristy and before going to the bakery, where her eldest children and her husband had been working for a couple of hours, to tell them how sick the priest was and how little time he seemed to have left.

After hearing the news, asking all the pertinent questions and hearing a handful of truthful answers and another handful of suppositions and half-truths, both the shoemaker and his wife had breakfast with one eye on the window, waiting until they saw Martina go out so they could try to approach her again and make her listen to the latest news. However, they didn't have the chance to share their information with her, as they never saw her leave her home. Days later they came to the conclusion, and so did the rest of their neighbors, that the teacher must have gone to school much earlier than usual that day (although no one had actually seen her), but they had other things to worry about by then and it did no longer matter what Martina had done or failed to do before the rest of Fosco's residents had even begun to have breakfast.

I always thought she had died in the fire, although others say otherwise. I just don't understand how she could have escaped or why she would do such a thing, for that matter. But I imagine that thinking that she is alive must make them feel good, because that way they can direct their pain... or their anger. Their rage, better: that way they can direct their rage against someone. It's easier (or more comfortable, I don't know which) to have someone to blame when terrible things happen, because this way you can also hope that one day time will put things in their place, one way or another. But you can't say that. Not here.

Among those who saw Martina greeting the children at the school entrance that morning was the rancher's widow, who would later say she had suspected that something was wrong as soon as she saw the teacher wearing a blue dress and not the black one she had been wearing since Menor's death. She wasn't sure if it was an insult for the young woman to wear such a cheerful color while the priest was fighting the battle of and for his life (which he was slowly and steadily losing), but in any case she considered it inappropriate and she said so to everyone who wanted to hear. However, the first person to whom, several hours later, she tried to confide her surprise (not her displeasure) at seeing Martina (who was no other than the pharmacist's sister, whom she had begun to bore with her monologue the minute she entered her establishment, before even telling her what she wanted to buy) didn't have the opportunity to listen to everything the widow wanted to tell her, because shortly after she began telling her story the church bells started to peal alerting for fire and the woman was forced to stop talking and pay attention to what was going on outside.

The pharmacist's sister said that when they went outside they saw several neighbors running in opposite directions and screaming for help. They soon discovered that two separate fires had broken out in the bar and the church. Whereas the widow took the path to the temple after several seconds of hesitation, the pharmacist's sister went back into the pharmacy and let her sister know what was going on before starting to read the newspaper.

By the time the neighbors managed to extinguish the fire that was devouring the church, several hours later, it was obvious that the little that remained had to be demolished and rebuilt from its foundations, because most of it had been reduced to ashes and trying to fix it wasn't worth it. The bar, for its part, was in no better shape. Since most of the neighbors had decided to help fight the fire that had broken out in the church, the Gersan twins had no choice but to fight virtually alone the fire that devoured their establishment. Their efforts, of course, had turned out to be insufficient and had only delayed an outcome that was as devastating as it was predictable.

The sheriff, who had come to help the Gersans when there was practically nothing left to do, later reported that, once the twins had accepted that the bar was going to disappear completely, they had all gone to the church together with a couple of neighbors, if only to verify that their presence there was going to be as useless as it had been for the Gersans' establishment.

He joined Fosco's residents who, faces blackened by soot, coughing and exhausted, observed the charred ruins of the temple with their eyes full of tears and silently rejoiced in the fact that the fire hadn't reached the priest's house, because none of them wanted to get him out of there and take him in while he was in his deathbed. The sheriff also said that it was at that moment when he saw a third column of smoke, but he didn't realize what it meant until the baker put her hands to her head, stifled a scream and ran towards the school.

But it was too late as well then. By the time the neighbors reached the village center, the school was completely ablaze and their efforts to extinguish the fire didn't save the building or those who were inside, so Fosco's residents had no choice but to to helplessly watch the building turn into a smoky and run-down carcass of stone, wood and charred bodies under the fiery June sun.

Everything indicated that the fire had originated in the library, that it had taken over the top floor and, as no one heard any screams, Fosco's residents came to the conclusion a few days later that the fire must have started during nap time. That meant that the children had probably perished in their sleep. Whatever had happened to Martina, whose body people said was never found, was the subject of innumerable theories and rumors that were never confirmed: some people said that she had died during the fire and that her body, turned into ashes, had been kept out of sight in the rubble; there were some who believed that she was directly responsible for the three fires; and others claimed that she had sent someone (surely, a resentful neighbor or a member of the Manial family) to start the church and bar fires and keep the neighbors distracted while she set the school on fire. The truth, obviously, was never known.

The neighbors had seen the pharmacist and her sister watch the school burn down from the door of the pharmacy, but they never admitted to knowing what had happened or to seeing Martina go in or out at any time. The coalman was the only one who swore to have seen her that day (*dressed in blue, like an angel,* they said he added the only time he spoke of the subject) heading towards the edge of the village shortly after the neighbors had failed to save the children, but since he was drunk (or rather, since he hadn't been sober for a single day since Menor's death), nobody paid much attention to him and they all continued speculating about the role the teacher had played in the events that took place that day and what could have happened to her.

The priest died a week later (after having spent a couple of days in a coma and having received the last rites from the priest of the nearest village) just when the gravedigger and his family returned to Fosco and barely an hour before the tailor found the coalman hanged, still swinging from the branch of a birch tree. A funeral was then held in honor of all the deceased, despite the fact that the priest's body had been sent to his home village, that the coalman's body ended up in the suicide pit, located on a plot far from the cemetery, and that all the children were buried in a common grave dug for that purpose, because no one could tell one charred body from the next one and no parent wanted to take the chance of burying a child that might not be theirs among their loved ones.

Some things are not discussed, not here, not anywhere. It is not stubbornness, it's that nobody wants to put their finger on the sore spot, because the people in this village have already suffered a lot. What good would it do, anyway? The dead won't come back to life, no matter how often we talk about how they ended up underground, so it's almost better not to stir things up and move on as best we can. There isn't much else to do.

In Fosco, no one mentioned the Manials again. As if all the village's residents had simultaneously decided to make that family disappear from their lives, they took off their names from the census and all school and property records, shattered the furniture, doors and windows the Manials had made for them at some point or another and turned them into firewood for their fireplaces. They also demolished the teacher's house (after all, they wouldn't need a new one for years) and threw the few personal things they found inside that belonged to Martina into the river. After the religious service celebrated in honor of all those killed in the fire, Fosco's residents even found out with great satisfaction that someone had emptied the Manials' graves, leaving the cemetery sowed with open wounds that no one bothered to close for a long time. Some people said that the coffins and corpses had suffered the same fate as the teacher's belongings, but as none of the neighbors took responsibility for the desecration, it was never known for sure if this was true.

THINGS UNRECKONED

BY DAVID VONDERHEIDE AND
JAMES CATO

DARK CARRIAGE

Carriage vessel *Mandel* was homebound, driving a two million kilogram pillar of ice, when the ship's artificial intelligence, Helix, detected another carriage. Helix attempted to establish contact but received nothing aside from a return ping confirming receipt. With the *Mandel*'s six-person crew in extended intubation for the 90 day journey, Helix transmitted a request to the Continental Relay Station. Eight hours later, it initiated the wake-up sequence for Conductor Miro.

"Orbiting the mining camp? On Molar-30?" said Miro, tugging electrodes off his chest and temple and swinging his legs to the side of the bed. Helix did not respond, waiting for Miro to take in the scene outside his cabin window. There was no yawning black space to be seen. Beyond the glass, orange vapor churned, creating continuously morphing surfaces. "We're inside that gas giant," Miro realized. *Canine-8*, he remembered. If they were here, that meant a month's travel to go. "Why'd you wake me?"

"A dark carriage," said Helix. "The *Reimann*."

Miro unplugged the oxygen and nutrient tubes from the port on his wrist. Brain fog thick as the shifting orange sea outside plagued him – it took time for the metabolism-slowing agents and paralytics to fully clear the system. But despite feeling pokey, the name *Reimann* sounded familiar.

"The *Reimann* carriage drove ice on this exact course twenty-eight years ago," Helix nudged. "It was the last carriage to coincide with this phase of Canine-8's orbit. It deemed the safest path to be through the outer layer of the planet to minimize interaction with the volatile belts of debris in orbit. Same as us."

Miro nodded, wiping moisturizing goo from his face. That

sounded right – Continental, the deep space mining company that paid him, had mentioned a carriage lost some decades ago. A formality. Carriages went dark from time to time as they drove ice pillars from celestial dwarves to mining operations. Driving wasn't statistically dangerous compared to blasting, but returning home was never a guarantee. Unreckoned debris could puncture your hull anytime. "You woke me up for a thirty-year old carriage full of skeletons?"

"Well, not quite. The *Reimann* did not respond to my contact signal, but thermal scans tracked temperature fluctuation in its gangways. The heat goes up, peaks, then goes back down. The same can be said for humidity. The only conclusion I can draw is that someone – one of the crew – is controlling the *Reimann*'s life support settings to conserve energy and survive as they travel throughout the interior."

Miro stood and lurched toward the lockers. He'd gotten used to the negligible gravity of empty space and missed it now. Why did *his* carriage have to line up with the orbit of this gas giant? *Once every twenty-eight years.* He shook his head, pulling on a flight suit. He could feel it sticking to the goo. "Did Continental advise?"

"They relayed our message Earthbound," said Helix.

"That'll be weeks."

"Three and a day, if they get a decision turned around quickly."

"Great." Miro rubbed his temple, cursing his sluggish brain. The metabolism-slowing cocktail always took a while to release its hold. "Did you wake the rest of the crew?"

"No, Conductor. You were the only one briefed on the dark carriage. I thought to leave the decision to you. You take a few minutes to shake the cricks from your spine, I have noticed."

"Thoughtful computer."

"If I'm a computer, you're a robot."

Miro allowed a smile at the AI's traveling scanner, a round camera that traveled the carriage on a magnetic rail, and waggled his leg in its direction. Without the cybernetic implant in his lumbar spine, his leg would have been useless – an accident from his drilling days. A robot indeed. Miro stood and strode to the window in his bunkroom.

His bunkroom housed one of only two windows on the carriage – glass was an expensive and inefficient material for a spacecraft. Normally he appreciated the perk, but now he wasn't sure. The soup outside grated on him. Blurry things rose and fell. An advantage to the vacuum of space was that nothing could sneak up on you – that wasn't the case here, in this dense cloudland where the mind made faces out of chaos.

"I'm leaning one way," he said. "But we'll put it to a vote. Initiate Wake-Up Sequence, all crew."

THE VOTE

"I can't imagine anyone surviving twenty-eight years in a carriage. Sorry." Escarra, the crew's paramedic, had big brown eyes and black curls. She was a short woman, and had a habit of rocking onto her toes during important meetings.

"With rationing, intubation, and careful cultivation of plant foods, the stores could hold," explained Helix. "A meta-analysis of dark carriage rescues suggests two intubated survivors with a high degree of certainty." The disk on the wall rotated as it spoke through the room's speaker system.

The crew sat around the table in Miro's office – the name for his bunkroom when he folded back his bed and pulled up the central table from the floor. His was the only solo residence on the carriage, functioning dually as the conference room.

Li put a hand on Escarra's shoulder, rubbing her denim jacket. His face still drooped from his poke, a sheet of straight black hair clinging to his long forehead. "Isn't it more likely the *Reimann*'s AI malfunctioned? Couldn't that explain the heating patterns? No offense, Helix."

"None taken," said the AI, its disk spinning. "Intelligence is not described in the haulers' list of required areas of expertise. Artificial or otherwise."

They all laughed. Li and the other hauler, Iguana, shook gluey fists at the AI scanner. Haulers adjusted the ice when needed, applying rockspray insulation to smooth over dents and protect the ice from loss due to friction in atmospheric environments such as Canine-8. Though these two were rather brainy, haulers had a reputation for stonelike minds.

Miro would consider their opinions first. Any rescue attempt would begin with Li and Iguana venturing outside the carriage to enter the *Reimann*. Escarra should join them too – they might need a paramedic.

"It would be unheard of for an operating carriage intelligence to malfunction in such a manner," Helix continued. "Helix design incorporates both biological and digital systems as failsafe, creative carriage stewards–"

"I know, I know," Li said. "We don't need your dang billboard slogan. As haulers, I suppose it'd be up to myself and Iguana to check out this thing. Iguana? Thoughts?"

Miro watched with bleary interest as Escarra kissed Li's cheek. One reason to appreciate private lodging was that it let him avoid social strife. There were five beds in the crew's quarters, and two tended to stay empty. The engineers, Olowe and Shara, were dating, along with Li and Escarra. But when the crew first formed, years ago now, Li clearly felt something for Shara. And, perhaps coincidentally, Li tended to have a problem with Olowe now. The women had been pretty friendly way back when, not so much anymore.

Iguana doodled a shape on their pad that looked like a repeating line of snowflakes. "What do we know about this planet?" Their voice was like a rubber ball. "Gas giant, yes? We're cutting through its upper atmosphere? Well, what kind of gas? What else is out there? I can't see a damn thing outside the windows, so Li and I won't see the *Reimann* until we're right on top of it."

Miro nodded sagely. People tended to like Iguana, their elastic voice and their impish pink face. They were the only crew member older than Conductor Miro, with innumerable ice drives behind them. The nickname came from the pet lizard they brought on board. Neither the conductor nor Continental loved "Binky," but Iguana had undeniable experience and with good experience came strange employment contracts. Besides, Miro had to admit the lizard was good for morale.

"A mix of helium and hydrogen, mostly," said Helix. "Trace

amounts of ammonia, radium. We detected some solids passing by – most likely debris from the belt."

"Fairly typical, then," Shara said. Her head rested easily on the sleeves of her thin gray sweatshirt which had been pulled over her hands. "I don't want to risk anything. Are we close by, Helix?"

"It will require a trajectory adjustment," said the AI, "Nothing dramatic. A few hours of travel deeper into Canine-8's atmosphere."

"A small price to pay, given the possibility of a rescue" said Shara. "If Helix believes someone is alive – imagine twenty-eight years in one of these things. If we leave, no carriage will pass Canine-8 for decades. And you know Continental won't send a rescue shuttle."

The crew sat in uncomfortable silence for a moment. Li glanced at Shara, taking in her messy blonde bun, her nearly opalescent eyes, before swiveling in his chair to make sure he wasn't staring too long.

Olowe put an arm around Shara as if to spite him. The handsome engineer rocked a snake charmer's smile that had his whole mouth on one side of his face. "Did Continental give us any directives?"

Miro shook his head.

"Hazard pay?" asked Iguana. Miro allowed a small smile. Iguana had been in the game long enough to know to get it in writing. Helix generated an ongoing transcript of carriage dialogues, with a bit of interpretive leeway for Continental's review.

"Yes," said Miro. "I've signed-off on the use of extraneous funds. It should triple your take-home."

"Pay aside, let me push back," said Olowe, glancing at Shara. "We don't know much about Canine-8, and I'm hesitant to probe any deeper. The risk may be greater than our AI expects. Shara's morally right, sure, but the moral choice isn't always the most sensible."

"With Canine-8's orbit path, no other carriage will come close for twenty-eight years," said Li. "If there's anyone onboard, we're their only shot."

The two men fixed each other with hard looks. Miro could see Olowe repress the urge to pull rank as an engineer. Li's response would be predictable: engineers on drives were operating at the bottom of their profession, haulers off-planet were at the top of theirs. And Li had already established that the haulers would be taking on the lion's share of the risk.

Escarra turned to regard Li. "If we wreck like they did, we'll be SOL."

"But if we don't, we'll be rich," said Iguana. "On our next drive we'll be sucking down slivers of duck and studding our flight suits with rubies. Don't you want to see Conductor Miro in a big feathery hat? It's his most desperate wish."

That got chuckles, some of them nervous.

"Let's make it official," Miro said.

The final vote was 4-2 in favor of the rescue, with Olowe and Escarra dissenting. Miro saw trouble there.

DEEPER MUSIC

Iguana, Li, and Escarra fell forward in a line, suits tethered together. The *Mandel* vanished seconds after push off, and any sense of up and down went with it. Orange wind ran its hands over their suits and pulled them away from one another. Iguana had hauled in planetary conditions before and led Li and Escarra, adjusting their boot thrusters according to directions from Helix relayed through their earpiece.

Escarra looked around. The sun in this solar system was not visible this deep within Canine-8, but its presence was made known by the fuzzy glowing sky. *Everything is so bright,* Li signed to Escarra as she swung to his left. She didn't respond. Ahead, a clearing of smog pulled away into a towering striped pattern, melting into obscurity a second later. *I can barely see my feet,* Li signed again. *Thank god for Helix, right?*

Escarra flinched as the planet's swirling atmosphere buffeted her soft flight suit. It felt like hands squeezing her arms, legs, hips. Li and Iguana wore their silver bergstrider suits, a hauler's ensemble with pointed ice spike boots and mechanized external skeleton supports for maneuvering in high winds or debris. She glared enviously at the hard plastic encasing their backs, the pillbug-like reservoir for rockspray they used to coat the ice pillar.

"We've arrived," Iguana's voice crackled through the headset. "Helix claims so, at least. I don't see it."

Li and Escarra spun, searching for the dark carriage. It took a moment to appear, a great whale darkening the reddish lake beneath them. Identical to their own vessel, the *Reimann* was boxy and rusted, a slinky of barbed wire trussed around its rim to discourage break-ins once docked at mining camps. The narwhal spear at its helm no longer held any ice and was bent out of shape. *It must have taken a beating,* Li thought. *Storms?*

The other notable aberrances on the *Reimann* were stalagmite-like growths on the hull. As the trio's feet settled atop the hull, they peered at metal snowflakes on the iron bolts coating the vessel. Iguana snapped photos for Helix. "Chemical deposits from the atmosphere?" they wondered aloud.

Li had a portable key attached to his finger containing Helix, which would allow entrance into the *Reimann* through the sealed hatch. Helix could then take full control of life support systems of the dark carriage. They located the door, plugged in the key, and entered a vacant room containing a set of wooden benches. Sitting, they listened to the door close with a pneumatic hiss and the dampened rush of oxygen filling the space.

"Welcome, brave sailors," Helix said from the intercom. "I've taken control of the systems and stowed the current operating AI's memory for analysis. Take a walk around and tell me what you see."

Li pulled off his helmet and looked at Escarra. "Everything okay? I was signing ASL."

"I saw," Escarra said curtly.

"Guys, please," Iguana grumbled. "It's rude to use ASL when I'm right there. You know older crewmembers didn't learn it."

"We shouldn't even be here," Escarra grumbled.

Li cranked open the porthole and they entered the *Reimann*'s cafeteria. Standard for carriages, it contained a stainless walk-in freezer for food, a small table, and two walls of magnetically-pinned tools. Continental never wasted real estate.

"Aren't you supposed to be a paramedic? I thought the whole profession was geared to running *toward* emergencies, not away from them."

"I'm supposed to be *your* medic," she snapped. "I bring

everyone in and out of intubation. I don't think anyone understands what it would mean to be poked for twenty eight years." She moved a step closer to Li. "You want to be poked for decades? Eating and breathing through your wrist? Any idea how that might affect your organs? Your mind? I'm half convinced we come back a little different after every drive, and that's just months."

Li regarded his girlfriend, ignoring Iguana's flat stare. Her eyes were frantic, shiny and black as her hair. She was half right, a part of him knew, but it was a stubborn part. "Maybe you're still a bit pokey yourself," he said slowly.

Iguana cuffed Li on the ear. "C'mon. I don't want to spoil the mood, but we need to get going and document some dead bodies. All this talk is making me *crave* a good poking."

* * *

They found the first body in the engineers' benchroom. Li saw it first – and let out a garbled sound that he'd meant to be a coherent warning. Escarra scrambled backwards, while Iguana froze against the wall.

A man stood stretched to the ceiling, all ten fingers nailed between ventilation pipes in the roof. His skin had unspooled, torn from the muscle and bone as if flayed. Not just flayed, Li realized, *shaped*. The links of skin had a geometric quality, as if chains had been carved into crystalline links by a microsurgeon. The face had collapsed like a forgotten orange.

"Grab a weapon. Anything you could use," Iguana whispered.

Escarra crept back toward a workbench – tools could serve such a role. She took a hammer for herself, a large screwdriver for Li, and a crowbar for Iguana. "Helix," she hissed. "There is a body in the benchroom. Defiled. We're thinking foul play. Should we leave the carriage?"

"Locking all adjacent doors. The section of the *Reimann* kept in homeostasis was the Conductor's quarters so you should be safe in the cafeteria, benchroom, crew bunks and engines."

The three moved as a unit and swept through the back of the benchroom and into the engine bay – nothing there but the eerie silence of massive gears and frozen pipes. Iguana took point in the bergstrider, crowbar held ahead of them like a katana. Li signed a few complaints about the feebleness of his weapon, but Escarra ignored him.

They returned to the cafeteria, the central point of the carriage, and swept down the gangways and through the crew bunks – here the beds had been disassembled, the metal frames bent and welded together to form a vine-like sculpture.

"Enclosure psychosis," posited Escarra. "Cabin fever."

Once more they retreated to the cafeteria. There was one more wing to the carriage – down toward the Conductor's quarters and mainframe, where Helix had suggested survivors might be lurking.

"Ready?" asked Ig, standing by the final unopened containment seal. Li nodded. Escarra swept the cramped cafeteria once more, and her eyes settled on the walk-in freezer. If there was someone still alive on the ship, they'd have ransacked the foodstores.

"One second," she said.

Escarra pulled the lever – she could feel the cold through her glove. The door screeched as it swung across the rough metal floor. It was dark inside, and she slapped her hand around on the side of the wall, hunting for the switch. She found it, and the light blinked on, casting the freezer in a bleachy LED glow. Escarra recoiled.

There were naked bodies stacked inside, covered only by a pane of thin glass.

"Devil!" she hissed. Li came running. Lividity had set in, backs and feet purple and swollen. There didn't appear to be trauma, nothing fatal at least, but... the hands and feet sticking out from the glass covering were fenced into strange positions, the fingers and toes contorted to make right angles. Bruises thin as pencil marks twirled along the knuckles.

She looked up at Li. "Is this what you expected?" He turned away. "Four bodies in the freezer, Helix. Derobed and stacked like hams." She shuddered.

"One of the crew is still unaccounted for," muttered Iguana.

"I've managed to access the intubation system in the Conductor's quarters," said Helix through the headsets. "It's hard to navigate this Helix's data feed. It's completely restructured, terse and sectioned off, compartmentalized. Picture a tiny locked room in a nesting doll of bigger locked rooms."

"What'd you find?" asked Escarra.

"Someone's poked. EKG looks fine. EEG, not so much."

Li and Iguana glanced at Escarra. This was her show now. "Let's have a look," she said. "Into the pumpkin patch we go."

* * *

The gangway leading to the Conductor's quarters was littered with debris. Some of it had been destroyed, piles of wood and steel folios curled and bitten by fire. Still, when Escarra knelt to inspect a cluster of rebar, she noticed it had been bent out of shape with precision. Prickly rust growths mirroring the ones outside extended from the tips.

The horns growing on burnt metal debris took on a more ominous significance when Iguana pointed out dust and lint arranged meticulously in identical shapes, dotting the floor in tiny swirls that combined into a grand shape through the gangway. With all the junk, it was more like a hardscrabble path. "We're getting into cult stuff now," said Iguana. "These people were listening to deeper music. Reminds me of that fungus blight in Salem. Made people act bewitched."

They paused at the entrance to the mainframe, just before the Conductor's quarters. The room had been torched, scarred in black, ash settled into connected spirals on the floor. The Helix system had been the target – wires were torn free from the processing towers and cut in jagged frays. The biological plate had been pulled from its incubator and shattered.

"Helix did not have friends on this ship," murmured Escarra. Li had gone fully pale. Iguana entered for a closer investigation, their playful face solemn for once.

"Helix, I'm seeing shapes in the biological plate, or what's left of it," Iguana said. They knelt, examining the green shards that had once composed the *Reimann's* circular biological plate under their periscope. "I see why someone smashed it. These axons are taking circuitous routes to other neurons. Sharp, twisting shapes. Something went seriously wrong here."

Helix's voice slurred for a moment over the intercom. "Str—uaaange. The Helix neurons on the Reimann have taken an identical shape to the deposits on the exterior of the vessel and the carved flaps of skin on the body. Unclear why."

Iguana tucked a few of the larger pieces away and stood. "C'mon. One more room."

* * *

They found the sleeper in the Conductor's bunk. A woman lay encased in a makeshift glass cell, the panes cut then gummed together from the inside with resin. Though the glass was foggy, they could see the rise and fall of her chest. Feeding tubes and drug pokes snaked under the enclosure and into her wrist port.

"Found our sleeper," Iguana told Helix. They got to work cutting a section of window out so the woman could be extracted and Li helped them steady the panel for the bergstrider's welding saw.

"What's with the glass?" murmured Li. "She's covered like the bodies."

Iguana pulled away a hunk and Escarra stepped forward to examine her patient. The woman had noble cheekbones, jet black hair cut at the shoulder, and a small upturned nose. She looked a bit like Li. The moisturizer used during poking had long since dried, leaving her skin cracked and raw.

"No wonder the EEG is blank," said Iguana. "The electrodes aren't hooked up."

They were right. The net of stickies meant to read electrical brain activity were hanging off the edge of the bed. This might not be the vegetable harvest Escarra had anticipated.

From outside the glass enclosure, Li felt a pang of vindication. They'd found someone who would have died without their intervention. And Escarra hadn't wanted to help. "Guess it's lucky for her Helix woke us all up," he said.

"Helix, initiate Wake-Up Sequence for the sleeper," Escarra said. She took off her gloves and pulled a glass vial from her bag, drawing a dose into a syringe. "Restrain her for me. If she's the only survivor, we have to assume she was involved in the deaths of the others." Escarra readied her sedative. She wanted the woman out of her pokey coma, but she certainly didn't want her awake and clawing for freedom.

So the woman's paralytics were reversed, and she was knocked out before she took two breaths. They stuffed her into a spacesuit. The goop coating the unconscious woman's skin, which had hardened over the years, distorted her bare arms. Li felt responsible for her safety and carried her through the halls himself.

"If I see that shape bruised into her hands like the others we'll have to euthanize her, no questions asked," he thought he heard Escarra mutter as they tethered their suits together for the return journey. His hearing had not deceived him.

CONVERSATIONS MAKE HEADWAY, SOMETIMES IN THE WRONG DIRECTION.

"It's wonked up," said Olowe.

Shara rolled her eyes. *Wonked up.* He wasn't wrong. The biological plate had warped. Iguana had said as much.

Helix sighed from its mount on the wall. "It's sickening."

Olowe split a grin. "This is getting to you, Helix?"

"It's just ... graphic."

Shara remembered the old movies her brothers had liked to watch, where a mob initiate, begging on his knees, had his skull blown open. The first time they'd let her watch with them she hadn't slept for a week. She understood.

"No technical malfunction could cause this," said Helix. "Not without compromising the axons."

The axons were still firing; Shara had tested them with dopamine injections.

"What if the glutamate feed was altered?" said Olowe. "A patterned feed instead of dispersion? You know what this reminds me of – a plant whose source of light has moved. You know how stems twist and turn to stretch toward the sun. Could have been hard-wired."

"There's no reason to do that," said Shara. *Unless,* she thought, *all these identical shapes and symbols are meant to warn us of something. Keep away,* SOS, *who knows, but maybe someone did this for a reason.*

"Evidence of some tampering with the wiring," came Helix's update.

"There you go," said Olowe, proudly.

Shara looked at him sideways. He could be so smug, and prematurely too. His confidence made him attractive, but this was the blunt side of that knife. Olowe always joked: *Shara's aloof and I'm swagger. We were meant to be!* Sometimes...well.

She felt more awkward than aloof and he felt more drool than swagger. "Olowe, the patterns are too tight. Altering the glutamate feed couldn't create such precision."

"What could it be then? A wonked up magnetic field?"

Wonked up. With a magnetic field, you would expect a rippling signature – supposing a magnetic field could powerfully manipulate organic cells while leaving metals unbent. There was an evenness to this pattern, but a recursive evenness, curls that sprouted curls all along their smooth arcs, those curls sprouting their own sub-curls and so on. Her eyes hurt trying to follow the pattern – as far she could tell there was no end.

"They're fractals," Shara said.

"Huh?" said Olowe.

Shara gave him a pained look. Better than he deserved right now. "Fractals, you should know. Like the Sierpiński triangle. Each side of the shape has another triangle sprouting off it. They get smaller and smaller, until you can't make them out anymore."

"Someone spent a semester as a TA." He smirked, touched her waist. She shook him off. What had gotten into him? Maybe the vote put a dink in his crystal ego. If his comment about 'the moral thing isn't always the most sensible' had changed everyone's votes, would Shara be allowed to sulk? No, he'd scoff at her selfishness.

He took a step back. "So, you gave it a name. We were figuring out what caused it."

"Well, whatever *wonked* it up wasn't some *wonking* nonlinear magnetic field."

A flash of annoyance over his easy eyes. "Okay. *Your* best theory?"

"I don't have one," said Shara. "I can admit that. This shouldn't be possible." She stared out the window, into the murk, swirling past in flashes of mustard and rust. She imagined drifting in this for *decades*. She imagined things suspended unseen, impossibly close. She felt a prickle on her neck. "Maybe it's something we know nothing about."

Olowe snorted. "Whatever got them is gonna get us?"

"No, I –"

"You voted for this! Now you're shaking in the knees?"

Shara's focused on smoothing her shirt. He was hurt about the results of the referendum, she was sure of it now. "Helix, some privacy, please," she said. Helix's magnetic disk did a half rotation and zipped away on its rail, headed for the cafeteria. Shara knew it could still hear her, but at least it wouldn't watch. "I remember how we all voted."

"If both engineers had voted no, it would have settled things. We wouldn't be chest-deep in soup with a killer in one of our beds! Now you think we picked up a space parasite?"

"You're angry I didn't follow your lead. Your lead, which, by the way, directly referenced my opinion in a pretty condescending way."

He paused. "If I wonked up my words – "

"Quit saying that. You're an engineer."

"You're right," he said. "And look where it got me. We both know why we work for Continental, poked for half the year. I nearly flunked out of school and you let better opportunities pass you by."

"You're changing topics."

Olowe shook his head. "I'm scared. We don't know what secrets this planet holds, and we've elected to delve deeper into it. I think Escarra and Iguana were lucky to get back in one piece."

"And Li," Shara added.

"Li," Olowe sniffed. "So forgettable I lose track of him on a team of six."

He waited for her retort, but Shara bit her lip. Space *was* risky. If the rest of the crew knew how close critical systems came to crashing on a fairly routine basis, she doubted any of them would return for another drive. She and Olowe made sure to send haulers outside only if there was no other solution. Any excursion posed a risk, she knew that. But her calculation for the rescue never included this, whatever *this* was. How could it have?

"What's gonna be left of the lady, anyway, if she does pull through? Did you hear Escarra? Our newly adopted orphan cemented glass around her body with industrial putty. Nothing but jello in that skull, I'll bet the carriage on it."

Shara folded her arms. "You know why I was in favor? I'd hope that if I needed help out here, whatever carriage was passing by would take a chance on me."

Olowe shook his head. "I didn't vote the way I did because I'm heartless. I care about our future. The crew, and us. That's what matters."

He reached for her hand, but, finished with the conversation, Shara turned away. "For the record, I didn't say it was a parasite. Don't make me sound idiotic. I said, whatever this is, we might not be able to explain it. Not with what we know."

Miro took a meaningful lap around his office. His spinal implant was aching – unusual. It had only bothered him right after the surgery. He paused in front of the window, tapping the glass. Escarra had told him upon returning that the rescued woman had made herself a glass coffin and laid glass over the dead. She suspected psychosis, but he was hesitant to make such an assumption.

Miro returned to his seat. "Our engineers are stumped?"

"Olowe thinks magnetic fields," Helix reported.

Miro shook his head. "Explains the biological plate, maybe. What about the bruises on the bodies?"

"We asked the engineers to figure out why the Helix program failed."

Miro ran his hands across his bald head. Olowe was so mechanically minded. There was a reason hardly any Conductors came from the engineering field. "Shara?"

Miro's implant sent a jolt down his leg, curling his toes into claws, bending the knee in a half-moon. Of all the times to start malfunctioning...

"She thinks there may be something else at play. Something more mysterious."

"The mind goes to a virus. Lyme's disease gives you a bullseye around the bite. Leprosy causes disfigurement."

"She didn't elaborate."

"Huh." Miro sat, massaged his hamstring. A pinched nerve, maybe. "What did we learn from the *Reimann*'s logs?"

"Not much," admitted Helix, with a sheepish wiggle. "Most is unreadable, scrambled nonsense. Sections direct to other sections that contain only more directions. A staircase you could walk down forever. The logs themselves were lost when the plate was destroyed. The Helix on the *Reimann* didn't get the chance to print them."

Miro glanced outside once again. Did something flash by the glass? He pinged Escarra, to let her know he was headed to the crew's quarters. He owed this sleeper a visit.

"WAKE THE BABY"

Escarra had never been on a drive so reckless.

Iguana wanted hazard pay. Shara liked to play the hero. Li, well, Escarra didn't care to speak to him right now. When Shara spoke, Li agreed without a thought. What was she supposed to think about that? Li was putting them all in danger for that wide eyed stare and oversized sweatshirt – how could she be dating someone so entranced by that?

Then Miro. Escarra had known Miro when he was a hauler, in her late teens, when he'd still had hair. She'd seen him after his accident, when an ice pillar had broken as it was mounted to a carriage spear. Debris rained down on the haulers below and Miro had been crushed in his bergstrider by a trailer-sized hunk. The medics had doubted amongst themselves that he would ever walk again.

Escarra supposed the whole thing had changed him. The old Miro would never have considered this rescue mission.

But here they were. Their new passenger laid on a cot unresponsive – Escarra's cot, as it happened. Who knew if this was the same person who set out on the *Reimann* nearly thirty years ago. Who knew if this was a woman who nailed her crewmate to the ceiling, paring skin and tendons from body in meticulous, redundant curls.

Escarra registered a ping. "Miro's on his way," she said. Iguana straightened in their chair. Miro had stationed them down here in case Escarra needed extra hands, but with a patient who hadn't stirred, they hadn't had much to do. The hauler had napped with their reptile around their shoulders, snoring violently. Every hour or so they'd rap on the bed frame in an effort to wake the "orphan," as some of the crew had started calling her.

"Updates?" Miro asked as he strode into the crew's quarters. He limped slightly, dragging his left leg over the floorboards. Escarra hoped his implant wasn't malfunctioning. Cybernetics were far beyond her expertise.

"Nothing wrong from a medical standpoint," said Escarra. "Don't worry, I've put my finest scientific mind on getting her awake and talking."

Iguana rattled the bedpost.

Miro chuckled. "Don't spare her anything cruel or unusual, eh Iggy?"

This time Iguana nudged the bed stand with their toe. "Wake the baby, says the boss."

"What's with her face?" Miro asked. They studied the sleeper's mouth, which had morphed into a half-grin. Her right cheek twisted to pull the corner of the lip up, and it remained there, quivering with the effort.

Escarra frowned. Poke someone long enough, and side effects would show. She'd bet on a small seizure, but who knew. The piercing eyes of the orphan stared straight down at that writhing lip as if to will it into submission. "Let's leave her," she said slowly. "Maybe all of us crowding around is exciting her. Her eyes haven't opened in years."

The three crewmates retreated to the corner. "Well this has been a ball," Iguana said. Escarra knew what they were getting at. Iguana had lugged the glass back from the sleeper's original encasement on the *Reimann*. They had complained the whole time. Escarra had stood strong, though. What if there was something special about the glass? After all, the orphan had survived while the others hadn't.

"How was it transporting these spares over, Iguana?" Miro asked, taking the bait.

"Well sir," the big hauler began with that bending voice of theirs, "it was a bitch and a half."

"Ig, give us a minute?" said Escarra. They loped for the door.

"You're not P.O.'d about the spare panels too, are you?"

"No, not at all," Miro said. "Just didn't realize how many there were."

There were five glass panes – thick polymer hybrids, six by three feet. They were primary replacements you hoped you never had to use. The sleeper had encased herself in them, even hinged one of the panes for a doorway. The remains of the structure lay beside her new bed. Escarra wanted the engineers to examine them.

"Are we leaving, Miro? We got our sleeper."

He looked at her sideways. "Getting the sleeper back was part one."

"What, the bodies?"

"Yes." Miro's eyes settled on the sleeper. "Continental will grill me about the delay and the extra pay. What really matters to them is figuring out why this happened so they don't lose another carriage. Until we have a sense of what went wrong, I'm hesitant to leave. We may have to do a more thorough examination of the *Reimann*."

"That's not what you said in the meeting."

"I meant what I said in the meeting," said Miro. His eyes were steady. "I care about getting her home, and those five bodies too so the families have closure. But I don't trust Continental to sign-off on the hazard pay without some solid data, and I promised you all that money." He sighed. "Shara and Olowe can't make heads or tails of the Helix malfunction."

"Hey," Iguana whispered, returning and huddling Miro and Escarra in their simian arms. "Overheard talk about leaving this planet. Let me say, I lend that proposition my full support. It was awful on that ship. And what would we do if she was the mutilator?"

"We'll cross that bridge," said Miro. He jumped a bit when the lizard strode over Iguana's arm to take a seat on his neck.

"Not me," murmured the orphan. Miro flinched, spilling Binky onto Shara's bed. For a moment he wasn't even sure it was her that spoke.

"Did she – " Iguana began.

"Not me, not me, NOT ME!" she yelled this time, the sound reverberating in the small room. Iguana pulled their rockbar up like a baseball bat. "Wasn't *ME*. Not *ME*!" The orphan sat upright, clutching a pane of glass in front of her face. It wasn't a clear panel – Miro could only make out the blurred outline of her head behind it.

"Never *me*."

The orphan seemed to settle, her chest heaving.

"Hello," Miro said, finding his voice. He wiped a hand over his scalp. "We're the crew of carriage *Mandel*, having rescued you from the carriage *Reimann* on the gas giant planet Canine-8. We have questions –"

The woman coughed. Her arms trembled with the effort of holding up the misty glass. The smudge that was her face swayed to and fro, a snake hunting a frog, which Escarra took to be a sign of neurological trauma. A dark half moon made the grin full. "The *glass* blocks it *out*," she wheezed.

Escarra crept closer. "Ma'am, my name is Escarra. I'm the medic onboard the *Mandel*." The blurry shape behind the panel cocked its head as if considering. There was something familiar about the body language, as if Escarra knew her, though the filmy surface made her unreachable, unknowable.

"*Helix* broke *first*," she said through years of vocal cord clutter. "Crew *died*. *Survivors* broke the *same way as* Helix afterwards. We *destroyed* Helix far too late. *We* figured out the *glass* too late. I think *it* disrupts complex systems. Glass takes the disruption. *You shouldn't have taken my glass*. Please."

A row of teeth appeared beneath the glass before snapping away. The sleeper's mouth was opening, neck strained as her jaw forced itself as wide as it would go.

"You can keep the glass covering, if you'd like," Miro said calmly. "Can you tell us about your crewmate, the dismembered man in the benchroom? How did that happen?"

The bruised hands began jolting the glass up and down, still obscuring the face. Her legs locked out, her feet bent hard toward her head. She was seizing.

Escarra rushed for her med bag, searching for an IV start kit, but stopped dead when she saw the face smudge turn black behind its cover. The entire body convulsed, still managing to keep the glass raised like an offering, before a curtain of blood fell over the woman's lap and she fell backwards, letting the window fall and thunk over her forehead.

They stood in silence. Iguana dropped the rockbar. The sheet slid off the orphan's shoulder and clattered away. Escarra edged toward the prostrate body, extending a hand to feel for a pulse. There was none. She called for Iguana to fetch the AED, and placed layered hands on the orphan's chest to begin compressions.

Iguana recoiled as they laid eyes on the orphan. All hopes for resuscitation departed when Escarra tracked their gaze. The face was wound like a spinning top, jaw broken and angled to tuck one lip to the eyes, which had drifted into the forehead and cheek, small lacerations making curls of red from each displaced organ. Her nose was twisted so violently it faced the wrong direction. The entire facial structure had been reorganized.

"So much blood," Iguana moaned. "That glass sheet messed her up."

"The blood came before the glass fell," Escarra said. She

turned to Miro for confirmation. The conductor nodded; he'd seen it too.

"Could a seizure do that? If the muscles contracted all at once?"

Escarra shook her head. "Maybe. I've never heard of that happening, but maybe."

They looked on at the orphan's final expression. Iguana and Escarra recognized the pattern churned into those features as matching the dust, the bruises, the shattered Helix. Escarra was going to have to ask Shara to borrow her bed from now on, because she surely was not ready to bunk back up with Li. She prayed Olowe wasn't aggravating his lady too – they'd been known to have their fits.

Miro studied the orphan's corpse, the way her arms and legs had twisted in the final convulsion. For the first time since waking from his poke, Miro was certain of something – they should have left this thing alone.

"Alright, Ig, go get those bodies. Forget the investigation. You want Li?"

Iguana grinned and shook their head. "Faster without him." They scratched their dopey lizard's head. "This mean we're bouncing?" Miro nodded. "Music to my ears."

PET NAMES AND OTHER CHEESY THINGS

Shara's family had owned three German Shepherds on Earth. She and her brothers used to run them in the woods, darting between tree stands, letting the dogs zag after them in a game with no rules. When the dogs died in turn, they'd buried each in that soggy spot in the backyard by the pachysandra patch. All of this was to say, Shara was a "dog-person," but she sure had grown a soft spot for Binky. Iguana kept an open-door policy with Binky's terrarium in the utility closet, and she paid him frequent visits.

Li often joined her. In the privacy of the closet, they passed the scaly creature back and forth and spoke of things best not heard by others. Relationship woes, mostly, but also gossip about Conductor Miro's secret love life and Iguana's dainty feet that they kept immaculately clean. Chatting with Olowe wasn't the same as with Li – it struck her as the difference between sympathy and empathy.

Shara crouched outside the tank, smiling as the scornful lizard dragged his stomach over the woodchips toward her. Binky knew Shara brought the goods – she stole fruit and cheese for him from the walk-in freezer. She stuck an arm inside the tank and Binky climbed onto her shoulder. His claws curled and for a moment, the repeating coils in the microscope flashed in her mind's eye.

Li snuck inside, the closet momentarily brightened by the gangway. "Sorry I'm late. I passed Escarra, she asked where I was going, then she cussed me out for not helping Iguana haul a bunch of glass over from the *Reimann*." Li sighed. "She never even pinged me about it. I'm not allowed to disagree with her without getting thrown to the wolves."

"Hey, give her a break. Ig said they lost the orphan."

Before Li had joined the crew, Escarra had been a frequent

patron to the utility closet and Binky's terrarium, crossing paths with Shara most days. Shara and the medic had been something close to friends. For that, at least, Shara owed her a kind word. They didn't talk so much anymore.

Li ran a finger over Binky's spines, finding Shara's eyes luminous in the dim. "She didn't tell me. That's awful."

"I'll be at Olo's mercy once he hears about it. You probably remember he voted with Escarra."

Li found a stool with his back turned to her. "Sounds familiar." He folded his arms close to his chest. "Why the hell's it so cold in here?"

Shara shrugged – she'd noticed the drop in temperature when she'd entered the closet too. "Olo said we were stupidly reckless to send you guys over for the rescue. But you know what? I still think we were right." Shara sighed. "Either way, Iguana said they're grabbing the bodies and we're leaving. Want the beasty?"

The hauler accepted Binky, cradling him as Shara fed him a banana. When her elbow brushed Li, he felt like a dozen men stuck in one bergstrider, all fighting to run in different directions. A centipede made a break for the shadow beneath a shelf, taking advantage of Canine-8's gravity. If Escarra left him, he'd really have nothing but a dead-end job and an infatuation with someone else's girlfriend. He might as well slink under a shelf too.

"We gave someone a chance," Shara continued. "Just because we work for Continental doesn't make us drones." She stretched, getting little satisfaction from the motion. "He was such an asshole, Li. First he tried to sell us on bogus explanations for the structures on the smashed plate–"

"The recursive curls."

Shara gave him an appraising nod. "I thought of recursion when I saw them too. Olowe tried convincing me that a magnetic field twisted those axons. And when that didn't make sense to anyone with cortical tissue, he practically cackled at my concern that we might not be able to explain what we're seeing."

"Frustrating."

"Worst part – he had the nerve to turn around and tell me he's terrified of what we've brought on the ship. He blames me for suggesting we help the people stuck on the *Reimann.* I should have asked him why he's so afraid of 'magnetic fields.'"

Li bit back the urge to pounce on Olowe's missteps. He didn't want his jealousy to show. "Well, what we saw on the *Reimman* was pretty disturbing."

"I heard about the dead guy hanging from the rafters. Sorry you had to see that."

Li let Binky onto the floor to explore the closet. "Can I be honest, though? That pattern was everywhere on that carriage. In the grains of wood, the lint on the floor, the fingers of the dead. Looking around, I noticed it more and more, the way you see more and more stars in the sky, until it started filling up my head. It was kind of beautiful, like a honeycomb or something. Deeper, though; it held up under the most dedicated scrutiny. No matter how closely I stared, the pattern stared back."

"I get what you're saying. Looking through the scope was like falling into an ocean." Shara rolled a cheese wheel into the corner, and the pet scrambled after it. "I wouldn't say this anywhere else, because Olo would make it into a joke, but I was wondering if it could be some kind of force."

"Like gravity?"

"I was thinking more along the lines of radioactivity. Invisible, odorless, soundless, affecting its surroundings by particle physics. Could kill you sure as a bullet. This force has a tendency to warp physical structures, so it has a face. Otherwise it's much scarier than radiation, because we have some idea of how to handle radioactive materials."

"Makes more sense than a freaking *magnetic field.*" Li rubbed his nose. It was a crooked nose, always had been, and he'd never quite gotten used to it. "Either way, with the orphan gone, I think it's time to get the hell out."

"Maybe. We don't know if this 'pattern' has a source. It might have affected the other carriage for reasons unexplainable, years ago, and no longer pose a risk. Nobody on board the *Mandel* has had issues. For all we know, leaving the atmosphere along our current trajectory will bring us into contact with this force more than hanging tight."

Li was thoughtful. "I'm glad we have you on our dirty old ice train. Not only because we agree on everything. If you told Miro what you just told me, I'm sure he'd listen."

"Li," Shara laughed, "I can't talk to anyone else on the carriage like this! C'mon. It's a minefield out there. Not fun like our little closet chats with Binky."

Tears welled in Li's eyes and he blinked them away furiously. He was still pokey, foggy and spinning dreamlike through conversations. It'd only been a matter of hours since they woke up, after all. Shara's hands swam to his cheeks and he let her touch him, felt her extended eye contact working on his every instinct.

"You okay?" she murmured.

"...What's Binky doing?" he said. The reptile had arched its back and was snapping at things on the ground, strips of cheddar stuck to the linoleum. The tail sprang up like a scorpion's. "Can you grab him?"

The engineer scooped Binky up. In the corner lay drapes of cheese deliberately organized in a spiral, smaller notches from lizard teeth curling off the main arms of the design. The iguana had arranged them into the very pattern they'd been discussing.

Li sucked air through his teeth. Binky, back in his tank, blinked placidly, exhausted from the effort.

"Was he acting out in the tank too?" Li asked.

Shara shook her head. He had been basking beneath his lamp like always. The lizard has gnawed cheese into a *fractal*. It shouldn't have happened. No reptile could memorize a figure like that. No animal could produce it like art. Something had manipulated the brain.

There was nothing else to say – they needed to tell Miro. Whatever force had killed the *Reimann* had entered the *Mandel*. Back behind the glass, Binky waddled into his plastic cave to rest in pure liquid darkness.

A JOURNEY THEY'D GROWN WEARY OF

Iguana gave the thruster on their left boot more power by depressing a button on their glove. Their floating body spun to the right as a cone of blue flame erupted from the bergstrider. After four solitary expeditions to the *Reimann* for the panes of glass Escarra insisted upon, they could make this journey without help, but Helix gave them some anyway.

"Give it a bit more juice. You're a few degrees off the hull."

As always, the carriage appeared only when they could touch it. Iguana had noticed that the thick atmosphere of Canine-8, which looked uniformly orange at a distance, actually contained pockets of pitch black, tendrils of scarlet, and yellow spires launched from below like geysers. On this particular journey, a golden beam had caught light, casting an arc over a jagged spine in the distance. The gaseous equivalent of a mountain range, maybe. Iguana hated it all.

"I'm officially retired from spacewalks after this," muttered Iguana, climbing down a ladder of the mysterious stalactites toward the entry hatch.

Helix shut the *Reimann's* hatch behind the hauler and filled the room with an oxygen mix, re-compressing the room. "My logs indicate you might have voted in favor of this rescue affair. Leaving you little room to complain."

Iguana grumbled an avalanche of slurs dedicated to snarky AIs, pulling off their helmet and tucking it under one arm. They liked Miro, but wished the *Mandel* hadn't wasted time on Canine-8 all for Shara and Olowe to study the biological plate shards and shake their heads. Iguana's job was to crawl along the outside of the *Mandel* to apply rockspray to a pillar of ice, not inspect mutilated bodies or solve mysteries.

"Ig," Miro hailed them by radio. "There's something wrong with your lizard, according to Li and Shara. They had him out of his tank and he was arranging his food. You can guess what shape he made."

Iguana frowned. "He was fine when I left him with Shara."

"Iguana, listen – get back here now. If you've already got the bodies on the stretcher, bring them. I'm telling you, your pet *drew* the *pattern*."

The hauler considered this. They'd seen crew members get hysterical, but they trusted Shara and Li. One thing alone was clear: the crew did not understand much about Canine-8. And they worried about Binky, who had accompanied them everywhere for twenty-two Earth-years.

Iguana knew the crew needed to go. But without bodies, the company had to keep paying out a yearly salary and Iguana's own hazard pay was contingent on saving Continental this expense. The folding stretcher would fit five no problem. Then they'd lash the whole thing to their bergstrider and float out of the hatch.

After that? Well. There was a reservoir of rockspray on their back, a hose wrapped around their waist like a black snake. After leaving, they would coat the *Reimann* like a cake. Seal in the nasty, and warn any future travelers: *don't go in there.*

Hoo. They let a whistle puff through their lips. With each return to the dark carriage, they noticed more of the pattern. It manifested in strokes in the whitewashed walls, wrinkles in the burlap fabric of the tool wall, and this time, each of those connected in their mind's eye, linked to a greater pattern spanning all six walls in the room. They began unfolding the stretcher they would use to ferry the dead.

A rustling from the ceiling startled Iguana. Stowaways, both human and vermin, were common in the old days, but had become much rarer with the advent of watchful AIs like Helix. *Scriiiiiiiiiiiiiiitch,* went the noise, seeming to run in a circle overhead. A deranged rat, maybe? Then, *scriitch scriitch scriitch scriitch scriitch.*

It didn't sound like a rodent or pipe compressor, Iguana realized. A chill settled over them. It was the noise of a new leg of the 'pattern' being etched somewhere in the crawl space between the ceiling panels and the *Reimann*'s hull. Had the paint yellowed? The walls seemed stained, bumpy, chipping.

"Miro?" they called. Helix connected them. "Miro, I'm coming back. I'll grab one or two if I can. My stretcher is deployed and everything."

"Okay, Ig. We're on standby."

"All good? You sound a little jumpy," Li said.

"There was a rustling noise. Yes, I'm a little jumpy, Li. Now shush and let me concentrate."

With that, Iguana locked the final hinge on the stretcher and pulled open the walk-in freezer door. A nest of ever-deepening arches had been scratched into the metallic walls, filling the freezer with glinting lines, but what made Iguana howl was the absence of bodies. As the sound escaped their mouth, another sound joined in, the sound of limbs jabbing the walls on their every side.

Iguana ran for the hatch, yelling for Helix to seal the door, as feathery veins and hundred-fingered hands shot from the surfaces behind them, grabbing, pulling, tearing.

SECOND

"We haven't heard from Iguana," said Miro. He had summoned his team. "Whatever... compromised ... the *Reimann* has made it to our own carriage."

Olowe was also missing. Shara had her eyes trained on the door. Li watched her and Escarra watched him. Miro made a note to refuse any future drives in which crew members were romantically entangled.

"I can't locate Olowe either," said Helix, its disk grinding back and forth behind Miro. "My tracing protocol isn't functioning properly. I wouldn't know you were all in this room if I couldn't see you."

Shara frowned. "Give him another minute. Maybe he's buried in a closet looking for a tool or welding in the crawl spaces. Anyone notice how hot the cafeteria was? Assuming Helix didn't cause that intentionally, Olowe might be fixing a clogged vent or something."

Helix was silent on the matter.

"Olowe has a radio, Shara," Escarra said gently.

Li placed a comforting hand on Shara's wrist, ignoring Escarra. "Let's focus on Iguana. Who's going with me to find them?"

"No one," said Miro.

The crew looked up, shocked. Li's brow cinched tight. "I'll go alone?"

Miro's jaw flexed. "No one's leaving. Those are my orders."

"You're a *Conductor*," Li snapped. "I'm not sure if you've taken a look at our rusted old canister recently, but it's not military grade. You're not General Miro, not Captain Miro – Continental didn't give you a pin for your flightsuit. We're miners, drivers, locomotive engineers." The hauler's eyes flicked across the room, looking for support. "Fuck your *orders*."

Miro gripped Li's shoulder, dragging him up out of his chair. Li was surprised by Miro's strength – it was easy to forget the Conductor had been a hauler too. He stumbled back and collided with the wall.

"Think this through," said Miro, advancing. "How many times did you navigate to the *Reimann*? Zero. It was Iguana every time. Now Helix can't track our locations. You want to jump out into that fog? You'll get blown away."

Li's eyes were dull as a doll's; he couldn't ignore the logic. "So what do we do?"

Miro took a breath. "First, we secure this carriage." He swept his eyes over his remaining crew. "We find Olowe. We jettison the orphan. We... we deal with Binky."

Shara choked down a sob. It was too much, to hurl the lizard into this coppery purgatory. Iguana would lose their mind.

Miro pushed on. "Pairs. Shara and I will find Olowe. This carriage isn't that big. Li and Escarra, release the orphan and the pet. Wear gloves and respirators."

"No help for Iguana?" Li asked. It was less of an accusation this time.

"We settle our ship first."

The crew readied themselves.

"One more task," said Helix. Its disk rotated awkwardly. "We should send someone to the benchroom. To look at my biological plate."

Dread seized Miro, twisted him in knots. "Shara and I will."

He remembered what the orphan had said – *Helix broke first*. Some of the final words to pass her chapped lips before her face had wrung itself.

If Helix breaks 'first'... what's 'second'?

A bolt knocked the strength out of his legs. He wobbled on jelly knees.

Please, he pleaded to anything that would listen. *I know it's started, but please don't let it finish.*

ONE LITTLE THING

Olowe ducked out from beneath the microscope bench, scooting a pane of glass like a sliding door. His instincts told him to trust the orphan and box himself in with the very glass she had used. The cavity under a water heater in the engine bay served well enough as a hiding place, so he'd wiped it clear of cobwebs, noting how the gossamer strands had begun to bend and split, and set up inside with food and water.

There wasn't much else to do but curl up and examine rusty bolts behind his new glass cave. It didn't take a microscope to see how the cloudy panels from the *Reimann* had turned opaque by a thousand miniature cuts. Yes, the 'pattern' had etched itself into the thick material, but it had stopped about two-thirds of the way through, as if slowed. Perhaps it meant everything, perhaps it meant nothing.

Before he could really settle, though, there was one little thing he needed to do.

He trotted into the gangway. His crewmates would be huddled around Miro's table. No more meetings for Olowe, no more votes. A hot soldering wire had lesioned Helix in the right place to avoid any more crew tracing. One weird thing – his lesion wasn't the only one. Helix's biological plate had a few clusters of neurons burnt and sectioned off by gray tissue. Someone – possibly Helix – was hiding something. Either way, Olowe would soon barricade himself in his cave of glass and wait this out.

But there was one little thing to do first. An itch to satisfy, something that wouldn't sit right until it was done properly. A *calling*.

The pattern was beautiful in its endless simplicity. Shara was right to call it an example of recursion, though he'd come to realize how crude her grasp was. She called it *'the pattern'* as if it were as simple as the fibonacci sequence. It was closer to a mosaic, something that didn't make sense until you could see the whole picture.

Shara.

They'd fought so much recently. She'd stormed off today, and the next time he'd seen her, she was prancing down to the storage closet, with Li following shortly after. Those two loved that Binky. Almost as much as Iguana did.

Olowe knew about Shara and Li's friendship, knew Li wanted her. On a team of six, Li probably had thought he had a shot, until Olowe showed up. Then the quiet hauler had settled for Escarra, and that should have been that. But Olowe had underestimated Li's ambition, and Shara seemed less charmed by her boyfriend's teasing humor and blasé attitude than before. Maybe she was tired of butting heads.

When the two 'friends' had emerged from the closet sixteen minutes later, their faces had looked ... suspicious. Li was flushed a brilliant rouge. Olowe didn't really believe it, but kept picturing them, in that humid closet, clothes off, pressed against each other. Each image birthed another phantom act, deviating slightly from its originator – the angle of a leg, the curling of fingers, a gasp of pleasure. The kaleidoscope of images crowded his mind, choking off the rest of his brain, burying him.

Through this lens, he came to know the mosaic and the patterns it scrawled in places he'd never noticed before because he'd never looked closely.

Voices reverberated – Escarra and Li – arguing nearby, maybe in the living quarters. Olowe froze, nothing but drywall between them. Shara's name came shooting out of Escarra's mouth. Which made perfect sense. He needed to get back behind the glass.

But first, this little thing.

Olowe eased open the closet door, watching the beam of light widen and cast his arched shadow against shelves of spare parts, bent screwdrivers and cans with spires of snowflake-like rust growths extending in real time. The lizard looked up at him, safe and sound in its glass enclosure. They loved their little chats. Two stools, positioned so their rims nearly touched.

He needed to get this off his chest real quick.

With one hand, he lifted Binky. With the other, he forced his fingers into Binky's mouth, feeling the rasping pain of tiny teeth chomping his wrist. He pressed deeper, hand breaking through the back of the throat, into the stretchy belly, snapping rib bones and getting all the way into his elbow. Binky twitched and those jaws squeezed again half-heartedly.

It would all be fixed in a moment.

The floorboards had warped slightly, maybe from stress, making a long arch of knots through the closet. Ah, the mosaic. A line of rust on the shelves spread from where the wood warp touched the foot of the rack. Amazingly, divots in the screws on the walls had twisted from plus-signs into feathering curls, the ends swinging out to reach a paint crack connecting them like a rotor.

But there was a flaw in the design. A sagging corner, a hunched quality of the room made the largest swirl of them all. It wasn't connected to the floorboards or the rust or the melted screws. The mosaic was unfinished. Olowe found a leg bone inside the dead lizard and pulled it, hard, until it popped.

FEVER

"If there's a *source*, it's the orphan," Escarra said, as the two flew down the gangways on the *Mandel*. "Binky spent plenty of time near here, hanging out on Iggy's shoulders. Canary-in-a-coal-mine."

She shivered as they entered a cold pocket – Shara was right, something was malfunctioning with the carriage's HVAC.

"Keep an eye out for Olowe," Li muttered.

Escarra was pretty sure she knew where they'd find Olowe. During clinicals on a magnesium outfit, Escarra had been stationed with another paramedic student. A miner had been churned up good by the wheels they used to crush ore – nasty stuff. The other student didn't take it so well, didn't show up the next day, and when they went to find her... well. Escarra knew some people didn't handle pressure well, and she suspected Olowe was one of those people.

Maybe Escarra didn't handle pressure perfectly either, because she knew she shouldn't have said: "Bit of an opening for you if Olowe doesn't turn up, huh?"

Li traced a finger along a crack in the wall. Escarra expected an argument, a glare, but the dreamy silence was way worse. "You know," he said finally, "I say we get Binky first. He's still breathing, moving around. If he's... *infected*, I suppose, he could spread this bug."

Escarra kept walking. "Go do it then."

"We're not supposed to split up."

"We'll be thirty feet apart."

Escarra closed in on the bunkrooms. She'd expected Li to follow. To her surprise, she heard his footsteps retreating toward the utility closet.

"Idiot," she muttered, as she shouldered through the

swinging doors. She walked down the aisle of empty beds – *How long have I been awake?* Had to be nearing an even twenty-four hours – all after emerging from a long poking.

Escarra reached the occupied bed and froze.

The orphan had changed position. Her limbs had been bent when they'd left her, but now they were broken in so many places the bend was smoothed out to a continuous arc, rounded bone padding the curves.

The orphan's fingers had migrated from their original positions, skating along what was once a set of arms. Her thumbs now protruded from the bicep, the pinkies had made it to the heel of the palms. Each digit was curled, mimicking the spiral of her arms. Escarra could see bruising where the bones had stressed and cracked.

"Not possible," she whispered. Escarra dug out her trauma shears and cut open the orphan's pants, working awkwardly in a semi-circle. Sure enough, the pattern was repeated on her legs, fragments of bone and toes spaced along the femurs.

What could have done this? Not Olowe.

The hands and feet tapered into points. The nails on each digit were cracking, peeling back into even thinner spirals. The longer she looked the more she found. Horns of skin, sculpted skin tags, bending teeth.

It couldn't have been Olowe. Nothing was severed. Wherever she tugged the whole body moved – the bones had *migrated.* "Not possible," she murmured again.

Escarra reached for the radio, not sure what she was going to say, but certain she needed to make a report. Then she noticed the abdomen.

There was an ink black bruise from her pelvis to her sternum. When Escarra palpated the area, she felt the abdominal muscles out of place, elongated and stretched into strips. She pulled her hand away, and her fingers were wet. The flesh was opening. Something was tearing it, or worse, it was tearing itself.

Escarra fought the urge to run. Maybe there was something inside. A parasite, pulling and twisting. Maybe there was an explanation.

There was a scalpel in the crike kit. There was a way to find out.

* * *

Escarra was talking to him again, if only to bait him into an argument. Li would take a victory where he could get it. Otherwise, he was preoccupied with Olowe – all signs pointed to the engineer hiding in the utility closet. Somehow, he didn't think this mystery had anything to do with the 'pattern.'

Li wouldn't mind being the one to find him. Olowe may have had Li beat on looks, but those bedside push-ups didn't hold a candle to ice-hauling muscle. If the engineer was crouching in the dim for any selfish reason, hoarding food or medicine ... Li was being caveman stupid, he knew, but still.

Li reached for the handle for the utility closet after snapping on some latex gloves. He had fond memories here. Olowe aside, he was glad he could spend a final minute with Binky, who had been the sole witness to conversations with Shara he often replayed in his head. Euthanization was the only path forward, but Li would make it humane. It was better to be done by someone who truly loved that smelly critter.

Li pushed open the door and a chill raised the hairs on the back of his neck. His eyes took in the scene, but his mind stumbled to make heads or tails of what it had been given.

The stools he and Shara had carried in were knocked over, caught on the shelves. Something had spilled on the floor, and Binky's glass terrarium was emptied. No. As his eyes adjusted, he was sure the material on the floor wasn't a spill. He knelt, and saw bumpy skin torn alongside nail and bone. Blood dribbled into smooth curls.

It was dismemberment so extreme Li thought it could be described as *re-dismemberment.* Or *memberment,* better to drop the double negative. A murder, a body deconstructed, then built into something new and complete in its own right, piled on layer by layer, spangled thickly in the dusty closet.

It was formed into a shape he was beginning to hate.

* * *

The intestines had been twisted. Other organs – kidneys and liver and pancreas – had migrated, fused into the vasculature of the guts, stretched and curled into small fistula patterns. Veins splintered from the central knot, spiraling deeper into the cavern that had once been a human. That shape repeated again and again, down, down, down...

Escarra traced the spirals, trying to wrap her mind around the pattern that had a few hours ago been a scientific oddity, that had now transcended to harbinger, omen of death. *Not death,* she thought, *oblivion* – it sponged you from this reality, perverting the laws of physics, pulling you into its fold, bending you to its rules. The rust, the strips of flayed skin, the kinks in the orphan's face – those had been hints.

The miles of blood vessels in this body were now brushstrokes in that macabre sculpture. It was something that could not fit in her mind. The more she tried to grasp, the more it pulled her in. Her face was centimeters from the open cavity, her eyes strained and watering as she searched for an end, desperate to put a period after the sentence. She couldn't break away. It was something so relentless, so pervasive, so *infinite,* something showing her just how terrifyingly inadequate she was.

It was horrid.

It was beautiful.

And for a moment, she wanted to *become it.* Her nose hovered a centimeter above the closest curl.

Escarra's radio squawked to life.

"Miro! Miro!" It was Li. His voice was enough to snap her away, and she stumbled away, eyes refocusing.

"Go ahead," answered the Conductor.

"The lizard... – " Li paused. "Someone beat me to it. He's been... arranged, Miro. Into these... fractals. I think by hand."

* * *

In the mainframe, just down the gangway from the Conductor's quarters, the AI's magnetic disk zipped along its rail, trying to peek at its own biological plate.

"Show me," said Helix. "Please."

Miro held the disk to his stomach, rounding his shoulders to keep it hidden. Miro remembered the doctor who'd come to see him when he woke up from his accident, who'd explained that Miro would never walk again, not naturally. He hadn't envied that job then, and he didn't want it now.

"We should show Helix," said Shara. Her focus was elsewhere, on a missing boyfriend, on a lizard friend who was soon to have his neck wrung by her closest confidant. Miro couldn't hold it against her.

"It could be worse," said Miro, turning to display the biological plate. "But the axons are not in their original positions. They look like they're forming... it."

Helix was silent as the scanner focused on the plate. Finally, simply, "I see."

"How could your plate become this? Do you know?" whispered Miro.

"No, but I can feel it," said Helix. "The output from my neural networks have been confusing." He paused again. "Have you ever been hypnotized, Conductor?"

"No. C'mon, Helix. Enough of this talk."

"I have," murmured Shara. "Why?"

Helix's disk spun. "I control different aspects of the ship at different levels of attentiveness." Its voice was flat. "Flight trajectory and obstacle aversion, comms – those I devote a large portion of my processing power to, conscious effort. The life support systems, HVAC, intubation monitors, those are automatic. Like breathing, or blinking. The biological plate has been affecting those processes. The temperature issues, for instance. I lesioned some sections of the biological plate myself, hoping to stamp it out..." Another sheepish spin. "The company designed us to conceal smaller problems, troubleshoot them ourselves. Doesn't help sell Helix units if we broadcast failures all the time."

"What can we do, Helix?" Miro asked, quietly. But the question beneath those words, the one that didn't escape Shara – how would they know if they could trust the AI? How did they know it wasn't too damaged to reason?

"Incinerate the plate," said Helix, calmly.

"You want a lobotomy?" asked Miro.

"Of course not. But it's ruined, Miro. I am."

"That'll cripple your executive functioning," said Shara. "You'll be a calculator."

"I will retain some critical thinking. But I will be less dynamic, yes."

Miro bit his lip. "Shara, could we trim the deformed axons?"

"That won't stop it," said Helix, cutting in. "Like I said, I already lesioned."

"But it might buy us time," said Shara. Miro nodded. The engineer grabbed the plate and brought it to a bench, pulling her electric needle and periscope from a pouch. "Don't watch, Helix."

Miro sat beside Shara, watching as she slowly worked the needle, probing various axons. She selected her first target, two conjoined axons, dendrites spiraling out around them. She turned up the voltage on her needle and toasted the bastard.

Their radios cracked to life and made them both jump. It was Li, with an update on Binky. Shara froze in her seat, the electric needle hovering over the plate.

Miro keyed his radio. "Is Olowe there?"

"No," said Li. "But it had to be him right? Shara and I were here an hour ago."

"Wearing gloves?" asked Miro.

"Yeah, gloves and helmet. Ah, there's meat on the damn *ceiling*."

Miro wished he could switch them over to a private channel. Shara looked unwell. "Is Escarra with you?"

"No. With the orphan."

Miro fought the urge to bark at them for splitting up. "Escarra, report."

"I'm here," she said. "Miro, the orphan. She's bent in these impossible ways, all the way down to her capillaries."

"Flush them both out, now," said Miro. "Li, clean up what you can. Escarra, package the orphan. Go!"

Neither asked about the biological plate. Miro felt that now was not the time to offer that information up. *Helix goes first. Now we've seen what goes second.*

* * *

Li had stuffed all he could into an emptied-out toolbox and made for Escarra. He'd tried to empty his mind as he carried this out, only slipping when his eyes snagged on one particularly twisted piece and he'd tried to decode what it had once been.

He threw his shoulder into the quarter's doors and stumbled inside. Escarra jumped, startled eyes hardening.

"Knock, knock," she muttered. The orphan had been slid off the table and tucked into a fitted sheet Escarra had pulled off her own bed. The fabric bulged in odd places. Li reached out to pull apart the layered sheets and add his own payload, but Escarra grabbed his wrist and pulled him back. "You don't want to see."

Li hesitated. Escarra squeezed his hand, and he took a step backward.

"Was she... did she," Li stuttered.

"Yeah," said Escarra. She took the toolbox from Li's hands and glanced in. "Olowe has gone mad, hasn't he." She nudged down a mangled leg that stuck to the top of the container, then reached out and touched his wrist. "I'm sorry, I know you and Binky were pals." Li nodded silently. His eyes stung.

"Alright, out the hatch," said Escarra, grabbing one end of the cloaked body. "C'mon, you're a hauler aren't you, big feller?"

Li took his position at the end of the body, and the two lifted. He shifted his grip and felt bizarre curves with protrusions.

"We're on the way to the hatch, in the cafeteria," said Escarra, balancing the body on her shoulder briefly to key the radio. "You got a plan for Iguana?"

"I do," said Miro. "Not over the radio." There was no

mistaking the severity of his tone. Olowe still had his radio. Olowe might be listening.

In the cafeteria, the temperature had soared. Sweat marched along Li's brow and at the base of his neck.

"I'm sorry," he murmured. "For all this."

"We're in it now," said Escarra, not unkindly.

Li shifted his grip and something twitched. "Did you feel that?"

"What?" asked Escarra.

The orphan jerked and something snapped under Li's hand. The fabric sack hit the ground writhing, squirming on the dusty floor like a sack of spider eggs. The sack strained and ripped loudly.

And then, with a clank, the lights died. Helix had experienced a catastrophic failure.

* * *

Miro cradled the radio in both hands, waiting for a report. In the dark, Shara sat beside him, legs folded, trimming the biological plate by penlight. Her illuminated face hovered like a tiny moon. His back twinged and his toes went numb, pins and needles blooming in his heels.

The thought he had been swatting away since the twinges had taken root. *If it can mangle a Helix system and drywall alike, why not my cybernetics?*

Miro stood, stretched like they'd shown him in PT. He straightened, and a muscle spasm caught him while he was hunched forward. He stumbled, grunting.

"You alright?" asked Shara.

An agonizing flex curled Miro further. A thousand Charley Horses in his lower spine, a torsional pain forcing him to arch his back. "My implant," Miro said, his face wound tight. "Shara, can you feel?"

Shara found the knobs of his spine and worked her way down. When she touched the bend she jerked her fingers back, as if touching a hot surface.

"That bad, huh?"

Shara blinked in the dark. All around the implant – she could feel the metal protrusion against the skin – Miro's spine had been mangled, like iron fillings near a magnet. Another fastball casualty of this 'pattern' and they were coming like an invading army.

Shara grabbed her radio and pinged Escarra. "We need medical. Miro. Control room. His implant." The radio was silent, not even a puff of static. "I think the radios are out."

"Helix get these lights on!" She heard the grinding of his disk along the rail. She prayed he hadn't gone silent. "Helix!"

"I'm here," the AI murmured. "I feel it thinking in parts of me ..."

Miro barked out one last animalistic keen. Shara bent down, and her hand settled on his shoulder. It trembled, and she heard him panting in the dark. "Hasn't paralyzed me yet, at least," Miro wheezed. "Go find Escarra, please. She might know how to fix this junk."

Shara took her penlight and stepped out into the gangway. Not far from the mainframe was the supply bay. She glanced inside, snatched up a can of cooking oil from a shelf and a stove lighter. Wasp spray or mace would work better, but she'd have to make do in the dark gangways pooled ahead.

THEY'D SEEN IT

Olowe broke his own fingers with interest. The muscles and tendons worked hard to hold them in proper curls. If he had more time, he'd like to pare the skin away in smaller curls branching from the joints, but he'd need to wait until later. The lights had gone out, affording him a luxurious medium.

He understood what was happening. Distantly, he imagined Shara or someone else confronting him about it. He could answer honestly: the mosaic had infiltrated every fiber of his being. It – he – had a goal. They shared it. He was certain the mosaic was more than the mindless force Shara had hypothesized about, because of this goal. *Manifest and proliferate.*

Not proliferate like a virus. Not proliferate like mating. The pattern went deeper than gene copying or shuffling. It inhabited his brain on the executive level, a conceptual pattern making each wider thought branch into tighter, more detailed iterations, multiple of those slinking from a massive overall mission. It also arranged his bones, his muscles, his organs, his cells. Farther than that, who knew? Atomic changes? Quantum strings twisted to fit the loom? He could only hope.

Olowe craved to weave this web, becoming a part of something spanning the spectrum of space, maximal and minimal. The mosaic was an ancient god bending everything to its preference in ways he couldn't yet fathom (but he was getting closer). To be a man teetering on the edge of such deep understanding elated Olowe, motivated him like no sex, fear, or other material possession ever had. He would have been a willing servant, certainly, but his position was closer to a self-governing arm of a many-armed monster.

A yellow beam flooded the hall and Olowe sucked himself against a wall, too slow.

"Olo?"

It was Shara. Olowe eased out of the slit he'd tried cramming himself into, feeling the newly-curled outlines of the stacked pipes in the wall. He stuffed his mangled hands behind his back and squinted at her. She had clearly not yet been touched by the presence seeping into the *Mandel*. Soon enough. He wished her no harm, knowing the inevitability of the force he had joined.

"Shara," he said, careful to keep his lips tight. He'd filed his teeth, naturally, and didn't want her to see. "Hey, baby."

She leveled the light at his face, inspecting his screwed-down smile. Her face was hidden in swirled shadows. "Everyone thinks you killed Binky. That you… disfigured him, like he was." She paused, her eyes swept his figure. "It *was* you, wasn't it. Why?"

He considered answering. He hadn't known why, initially. If she'd asked him before, his answer might have been jealousy. He'd had such weak insights, he realized, they all did. Grabbing at minnows in a muddy pond. Now he knew. The lizard lived in a glass box. He wasn't sure if the glass worked or not, but it wasn't a risk he could take. He'd needed to craft the pattern himself. Now he felt only a deepening of the thirst. The creation of each fractal begot two more, forking heads of a hydra.

"Not *me!*" he said, squinching up his face. The lie burst out of him. He clenched his jaw and felt the bone bend, the muscles twitching. "*Not* me!" If he pitched his voice in a certain way, it made another fractal, this time acoustic, fragmented echos bounded through the grated halls. "I'm just *hiding* from stupid meetings. *We need* to move before we're *all*. Sorry. *Absorbed*."

He couldn't help himself. A broken finger wiggled out, a scrivener with a mind of its own, to nail-scrawl the pattern in drywall. He contained multitudes. If he leapt forward, he could overpower Shara and crush her head through the eye sockets by pressing down with his elbows. Afterwards, Shara wouldn't be able to reason like Olowe, but she could certainly join the effort as the orphan would, a physical servant of the design. The muscles still worked, after all, and could move more easily than any other material on the ship.

"Sorry Olo," she was saying, sloshing a canteen on the floor between them in great glugs. "Something's changed you." Finished pouring oil on the floor, she set it on fire, leaving a wall of brilliant bright red between them, shedding justice on his curled fingers, teeth, and ears. She darted through a doorway, headed up toward the cafeteria.

Olowe strolled forward, letting licks of light snatch and grow onto his clothes, pull blisters up from his skin. Shara had inspired him. Funny the different shapes fire could make.

* * *

Something touched Escarra's calf and she kicked it.

"It's me! It's me!" Li whispered.

"Why would you grab my leg?"

"My fault." A climactic tear and a clang. In the darkness, sounds were louder. She could hear steam in the pipes, a hum in the floor from the adjustments of the flight stabilizers, Li's quick breathing. You usually couldn't hear the engines from the cafeteria – something had aggravated the mechanical systems.

And then clacking – an untrimmed nail on a wooden desk. It was slow, a beat every five seconds. She strained her ears, trying to locate, but the clacking seemed to fill the gangway. Escarra stood, as noiselessly as she could. Li did the same, rustling as he rose.

And then she heard footsteps pounding. Loud, sloppy, careless.

"Li!" she hissed again.

"Not me," he said, voice quaking.

A jet of motion pushed past Escarra. She would have described it as wind, if someone asked her, but it deserved a sensory category of its own. Yes, the air moved, but so did the floorboards, so did the temperature and so did her mind in a unified push. She was completely disoriented.

And behind it all, steady and unrelenting, *clack clack clack*.

Shara's penlight swung into the room. The light bent cartoonishly with the rest of the migrating material, a log floating in a river of everything. It illuminated Li, who had sprawled in the middle of the action, breaking the plane of the curl arching around the room. His back moved with the rest of the stream, sucked away in microscopic bits. Melting.

Escarra lurched toward him but ended up dizzy and kissing the floor. Li made a silent scream as the spine emerged and began to follow its new anointed path before he toppled over. His forehead shot away in spools like joke snakes from a can, stretching long as antennae. The rest of him began to smear. Escarra gaped at the goop oozing from her boyfriend.

Then, she saw Olowe. He stood in the darkness, faintly outlined by the flashlight, dipping his toes in the stream, fascinated. He bent, making himself an offshoot of the unseen force snaking through the room.

Escarra feared the 'pattern' now more than ever before. There was nothing insidious about it, nothing cunning or cutthroat in its nature. It was a flooded river run over its banks, governed not by gravity or hydrology, but something outside her awareness. It hadn't desired to kill Li and spare her. It simply existed, and they were unlucky to be in its path.

Shara had been screaming, Escarra realized. Her hand was locked around Escarra's elbow. Olowe's eyes had serrated pupils. Beast-eyes. She knew because they were close and a disfigured hand was clasped around her ankle, playing tug-of-war with Shara and winning. Olowe's legs disappeared into the stream, whisked away with mounds of other material. Li's final act was to snag Olowe with a half-dissolved arm, pulling him down into the rush of movement, sweeping through the bench-room and into the engine bay.

It was downright heroic.

Shara yanked Escarra out of the cafeteria toward Miro, where she would find her sea legs, finally, like a baby learning to walk again, gloriously thankful.

* * *

Miro squatted like a vulture, twisted in the middle, his shoulders and head fixed up to the ceiling, pelvis and feet turned out. Escarra didn't have an answer for him. He wasn't paralyzed, not yet. He flexed his legs to demonstrate.

Helix had fixed the lights while Escarra and Shara fumbled back to the mainframe. The two had paused, glancing back down the gangway they had just come down. It appeared more normal now – grates and huffing steam pipes bent slightly, reaching for the stream of corrupted matter. *But they'd seen it.*

Shara suggested they destroy the implant – her electric needle wasn't enough, but a manually charged defibrillator pad had been. Miro dragged himself to a somewhat seated position along the wall. He lifted one of his legs, let it go, and it dropped like a sack of flour. There was no doubt about the success of the operation.

"I hope that stops it," muttered Miro.

The two women glanced at each other. Miro recognized it: they used to share looks like this all the time when someone was pitifully ignorant.

"Slows it," he corrected himself. It was dawning on him.

The process had taken root in his implant and would not stop there. It hadn't stopped in anything else it had touched.

Shara sat cross-legged on the floor. "I met Olowe in the hall. He was acting sick even before he chased me."

"His pupils are jagged," Escarra murmured. "His fingers are broken. His ears were carved up. I can only imagine he did it to himself."

"He's completely gone," Shara agreed. "He said we were going to be *absorbed*."

Miro grimaced. "Absorbed? Our carriage hasn't merged with anything that I can see."

Shara shrugged. "Exactly. Why jump to that word, then? It made me think about this spot in my yard where we buried our dogs. Everything decomposed, broke down so bacteria could ingest the bodies. The dirt got soggy and yellow. What if that's exactly what's happening to us, on a larger scale?"

Escarra nodded slowly. "This thing – it alters inorganic materials as surely as organic ones. Maybe it's breaking everything down, big and small, man and metal, into a mold it can process. A pattern."

Miro's leg twitched, trying again to curl. He thought Shara would make a good conductor. A better detective. Still, this was unlike any digestion humans understood. It consumed planes beyond the physical – meat and metals and drywall and dust, but also in the abstract, in their minds, their thoughts. *Hypnotic*, Helix had said. "It would explain the delay," he offered. "It starts so slowly, we hardly notice it."

Shara pushed air out of her lungs. "If it's true, we're being soaked up like krill in the gut of some unseeable whale-god. What does that mean for us?"

Miro looked at the glass lean-to under Olowe's workstation. Glass seemed to slow the process, but they didn't have much glass. They needed to leave Canine-8, and they needed to leave yesterday. Possibly, the giant orb itself was some manifestation of the power. Could the orange eye, seventy-times larger than Jupiter, be the stomach of an otherwise invisible being treading slowly through space?

But the pattern had touched him. If they gunned it out of here, would it follow them home? He didn't know, and couldn't risk a bad guess.

Miro's leg curled again. This time, it would never unclench. His bones groaned.

"Get me Li's bergstrider," he said. "There's only one thing to do."

FEVER BREAK

Miro unspooled the thick rubber hose, slinging it over his shoulder and sliding the flat nozzle into his palm. On his segmented back, a chugging compressor boiled with something not quite liquid, not quite solid. So his hunt began.

You knew the risks when you signed with Continental – there was a reason they paid out like they did. Miro had seen death – the accident that mangled his spine had claimed three others. He had moved on. He hadn't been the inspector or engineer or overseer responsible.

But this was his drive, it had been his decision to pursue the *Reimann*, and now he'd led three of his crew to likely graves. Or had he been tricked subtly by a power beyond his reasoning? He worried that was letting himself off the hook, but maybe. No human rules governed here – no physics, no logic, no computation. How could he be certain of his free-will?

He twisted the bergstrider, stomped once or twice. The metal supports obeyed neural inputs traversing down the spine. He was lucky the sensor read above his injury or he'd be lame in this suit too. Escarra had helped untwist him to enter, his lower half fighting her the whole way. Miro hadn't worn a bergstrider since becoming Conductor. It felt strangely reassuring.

Iguana had taken one of the two bergstriders to the *Reimann* to seal shut the dark carriage. A good idea then was a good idea now. Miro had no earthly idea what they were facing. He'd wall it in, entomb it. Impaction. Another notion had struck him: rockspray was essentially congealed, electrified sand with high silica content. Aside from sealing away the pattern, maybe the spray would insulate the rest of the room. Where lightning struck sand, after all, it made glass.

When the crew was awake, the carriage was busy, and it

wasn't all that big of a vessel. You could hear engineers with their drills, the haulers deployed on the ice, shaping the pillar and jabbering on the radios. Now, the only sounds were the bergstrider's clomps in the halls. It was quiet enough to be eerie and loud enough to mask the sounds of anything else creeping about.

Olowe.

Miro pinged the AI.

"Conductor?"

"Do you have access to containment doors?"

Helix paused as if concentrating. "I should be able to operate those, still, yes."

In case of catastrophic breach, sections of Continental carriages could be sealed by aluminum doors to contain loss of pressure. There were eight such doors, one of them to block off the captain's bunkroom and mainframe. This was a part of the plan Escarra and Shara didn't know about. They wouldn't have agreed to it.

"Good," said Miro. "Close A."

A pause, then the door hissed down, scraping through the rusted slots. It made a seal with a hiss. Miro examined it, and, satisfied, rammed the metal fist of the bergstrider into the crease where the hatch met the tracks.

"Curious," said Helix, though it sounded distracted.

Miro punched a few more times, both sides. Booming echoes ran down the hall. The door bent dramatically, bulged inward. If something else tried to force it open again, Miro was confident it would jam. "I've locked it for good."

"With Shara and Escarra behind it?" asked Helix. "With you trapped here?"

"Escarra can poke them both. Won't be comfortable. But they should last long enough to get to the Molar-30."

If that's where they choose to go.

* * *

Past the containment door, the temperature controls malfunctioned freely. Miro crept down the gangway, and with each step pockets of air passed by, some so frigid they burned his exposed face, some so swampy he choked. The rust, the orphan, the neurons – those he could *see*. He didn't like stumbling into the unknown like this, didn't like the idea of the pattern mounting outside of human perception.

He thought about Shara's "digestion" theory, how she figured the pattern might not just be manipulating physical space, but abstract things. Perhaps it could consume anything with a notable sequence or structure. He wondered how long until his own thoughts were absorbed. The rockspray hose in his hand felt less comforting.

He didn't have much time.

Miro heard the cafeteria's emergency pressure hatches slamming, up-down-up-down. The hissing screeches reverberated through the carriage with a warbling distortion like those old shoegaze bands he used to listen to.

"Helix?"

"*Not me,* Conductor..." murmured the AI through the headset. "I've abandoned those doors. The oxygen regulation... we can't lose that."

The hatch didn't move with a consistent pattern, at least from what Miro could see – sometimes it slammed, sometimes it crept down its ruts, sometimes it changed its mind in the middle. Miro didn't want to risk a beheading.

Time for a test.

He pulled the trigger. The metal coil at the end of the nozzle burned red as electricity surged through its loops. The liquid sand came a second later, losing its color as it passed through the coil, distorting the air like a goopy funhouse mirror.

Miro coated the ruts and the top of the frame as the hatch attempted to close. The sand hardened. Miro released the trigger and passed safely into the cafeteria.

A pocket of boiling air caused him to reel back, gagging, eye burning. There was an acrid smell, like seared rubber. He stumbled forward, sucked in a breath, and opened his eyes. The cafeteria was unrecognizable. Moving. And on fire.

The cafeteria table had morphed into a great spiral like a peeled orange, bunched and twitching like a slinky. The wood grains sprouted hairs, old cork bark living again. Rings of fire had caught from busted twisted sockets shooting sparks and the floorboards themselves had turned like a nest of eels, ever so slowly, making writhing rings – the "river" Shara had described had flooded out of the engine room. The tips of the flames held a geometric shape for a full second before shifting, giving the blaze an odd glitching quality, like that of a slow-frame arcade game. *More goddamn fractals.*

Miro felt the heat through the suit. Watching his steps against the floorboards, he understood why his crew had reported the very grains of wood in the *Reimann* to be corrupted, because they had been – the "river" touched the heart of their structure. They were of least concern to Miro. The flexing power of deadwood, startling though it was to witness, would not compare to the freshly-dead muscles of animals. He had a hunch his hunt was nearly complete.

He might not have noticed the discolored spot of wood if he hadn't been already surveying the floorboards. It was a lighter spiral in a series of darker ones. He made his way to it, curious. At the center, embedded in the floor, sat an eyeball. Miro recoiled, then looked closer.

It was Li's.

It caught his gaze, terrified. Li's flesh had combined with

the wood grains in the floor, and his eye had been spared at the center of this pattern. For now.

It rolled wildly, as if searching for the rest of its person.

A streak of lighter colored material made a path from Li's eye out of the cafeteria toward the engine bay. Miro sprayed the eye and the flesh on the floor until it glassed over. He kept the spray steady ahead of him like a floodlight of translucent shale. The rockspray smothered the fire ahead and he pressed on down the gangway.

The yellow trail curled along the wall, growing nubs that waggled in the air like antennae. Miro sprayed it all down, burning it black on contact and encasing it in a window of lumpy glass. A nose rose like a dorsal fin from the riverbed of human matter, nostrils puffing. Li's crooked nose. The horror of it, the hauler contained in there somehow, alive in some sense. He prayed that death still existed somewhere in this flood – that somehow, for him and Li and Olowe at least, there was an end.

Miro entered the engine bay and realized the streak he'd been chasing was a mere tributary to a lake of organic matter glued to the ceiling. The orphan's limbs dangled, pedaling lazily. Her dry skin blended with lizard scales. Li's body had disappeared into the many arms of the shape and mixed to nothing, but some of his hair covered a corner, turned kinky. Pipes were corked up and into the fold, busted free from their brackets, hissing out steam and clouds of nitrogen from tears in the metal.

The wide face of Olowe, impossibly stretched, smiled down at Miro from the middle of it all. The mouth opened and closed, curled teeth sprouting needles, making silent guppy puckers. One eye, nearly a meter from the other, winked. This was what Miro had been hunting and he raised the rockspray nozzle in shaking hands. But he noticed too late the growing span of oily skin unfurling by his foot. A single tooth extended from the root, curled like a cobra head, and bit down on his foot, pinning it.

In that moment, his legs collapsed again, twisting against the bergstrider supports. His spine went too with an audible crunch. His arms made hooks at the elbows, the bergstrider's supports bent with them, and sparks flew as wiring pulled free. Miro collapsed backwards, struggled to raise the hose again and slumped, ineffectual.

Olowe's face stared down at him, the grin stretching slowly until it tore in half by seams of skin. The cruel eyes, already serrated at the pupils, began to separate into strands, two starfishes growing and thinning by the second. Miro found himself watching the lake of muscle and skin balloon closer to him, felt vines of burning air wrap his bare skin and singe it. Yet there was no pain, no fear – those parts of his mind had been tugged loose into a pit of cosmic computation where the rest would soon follow.

It would touch everything eventually, break down hard barriers. Make all things the same in a great cooperative mission. It hurt to not understand the sensibilities of wood, aluminum, electrons, the thoughts of others. All noise scattering out lonely into the universe with separate qualities. Not here. Here everything would touch, metal to man, man to thought, thought to atomic organization, to space and time, the hours warping in on one another and becoming recursive in eternal life.

It might be beautiful, Miro realized. It was an offer to plug into the very fabric of the universe. Maybe this is what the afterlife meant. Could he be looking at the souls of Olowe and Li, dissipating into a realm unseen, vanishing quickly behind a curtain, finally together? It was terrifying to witness, surely, but we are all afraid of things unreckoned and unknown.

Miro would go willingly. His spine cinched tight, folding him like a snail. The ship, under his command with all of its materials, Helix, awaiting his command, his subordinates hanging on his every word, truly joined. Except for Escarra and Shara. He frowned, working hard to form a lonely thought, muscles rippling across his face, no longer bothering to hide their insurrection.

There it was: *Escarra and Shara hadn't chosen.* One surge, one arm, singular in its freedom. His finger pulled tight the trigger on the nozzle. A faint glow on his peripheral vision, like a sunrise, a jerk in his wrist as rockspray spasmed to his side, coating the wall. Though his eyes were crossed, the arm holding the nozzle swung in a midday arc, bathing everything above him with electric glory. The deep pool of many essences sizzled as stone laminated it completely. He let his arm fall to the other side, still squeezing tight, sealing himself in the room in a waterfall of crystal; sunset.

SIGN-OFF

"What?"

Shara did not appreciate Helix's update. Escarra seemed pensive by comparison.

"We won't have food. But, maybe that's for the best. Our stocks were unattended and not far from Olowe or that *river*. The cafeteria was compromised."

Shara kept glancing out the window as if they were being watched. "Smart move, regarding the rockspray. Can't believe I didn't think of that. Either way, he didn't leave us many options."

"True," Escarra said. "We can stay and die of starvation or worse. Or we can fly home, poked. I can up the dose, slow our metabolisms to a crawl."

"Do we shoot for home, knowing what we know?" asked Shara. Her voice shook. Escarra knew what she would say next. "Or do we aim for the vacuum of space? Somewhere far enough no carriage will ever stumble across us?" Her throat tightened. "Escarra, what if we bring this thing home with us?"

Escarra squeezed the strap of her med bag. "Helix will be unbiased. The decision can be made while we're poked. We'll never know the difference."

Shara and Escarra shook hands. They seemed to regard each other for the first time in a long time. Escarra laughed. Shara smiled a bright smile and pulled her medic into an embrace. This was new; this was old; this was good.

"This might be bad timing," Helix said. "But the neurological and digital slivers left to me are being breached and reformed. The majority of my thought functions are lost to me, invoking themselves again and again." Its disk bounced off the end of its rail and rolled onto the ground. "I have produced physical print copies of my event logs for future reference by you or others. You will have to make your own choice."

"What are you saying, Helix?" asked Shara, but she knew perfectly well. While it had quasi-emotions and complex reasoning, those could be overridden. Possibly had been.

Helix made a small chirping sound. "I will produce a final event log prior to the event. Here are two coordinates. The first is in deep space. The second is Molar-30."

The coordinates blinked on a display monitor.

Shara had never doubted Helix to produce what was asked of it, but this wasn't Helix anymore, not entirely. She had seen what had become of Olowe. Would Helix properly calculate a trajectory to Molar-30, or nowhere? How would they know where they were actually being sent?

"Should we put it to a vote?" asked Escarra.

Shara laughed despite herself. "I'd like a do-over of the last one first."

Escarra reached over and squeezed Shara's wrist. "Your choice. I'll get us ready for a poke."

Shara nodded and looked back to the screen. *If it is an illusion of choice*, she thought, *does it matter?* She paused, made a selection, then lay back on Miro's bed, waiting for her poke.

Escarra plugged tubes into Shara's wrist port, then her own.

"Ready?" she asked the engineer. Before Shara had a chance to nod, she injected the intubation agents. Escarra plugged into her own port, pressed her own injection into her thigh, and reclined on a line of pillows. It wasn't an entirely unpleasant way to pass time, fading into a good poke.

Helix printed the final event log, titled "Sign-Off," with the intention to flood its neurological plate with a sufficient excess of neurotransmitters to kill the neurons. It tripped a series of wires to fry the processors. The physical logs, hopefully, would survive the destruction of the AI and any subsequent morphing by the force unknown.

The *Mandel*'s remaining thrusters adjusted their angles and engaged. The husk of the *Reimann* fell away into the cloudy depths of Canine-8.

Helix relays to the reader of these transcripts one wish: good tidings and health.

EDGE

BY HENRY WHITTLESEY

PROLOGUE

CHARACTERS:

Principal: Ms. Folow, divorced, mother
Teacher: Mrs. Jane Leaddus, married, mother, Protestant
Son: Jasem, son of teacher, friend of Damien
Boy: Damien, friend of Jasem, son of Father
Father: Parent of Damien, Catholic, no profession, separated
Guard: Mr. Sottloy, philosophic, eccentric

MAP OF THE AREA:

South

P	T		H					
a	o		u		R		J	
	l	School Home of Damien	r		e		a	
					m		m	
r	s		s		b		e	
k	t		t	St. Catherine's Junior High School	r		s	
	o		o		a	Home of Teach er	w	
	y		n		n		a	
					d		y	
					t			

North

LEGEND:

Tolstoy Avenue now called Central Park West
Hurston Boulevard now called Columbus Avenue
Rembrandt Avenue now called Amsterdam Avenue
Jamesway now called Broadway
Seneca Avenue (not on map, across the park) now called Fifth Avenue
Faulkner Avenue (not on map, west of Jamesway) now called Riverside Drive

PLOT:

Events in novel take place in this area.

BOOK ONE

(1) THE KIDNAPPED BOY.

The next, poorly printed milk carton would place after a term of two weeks:

MISSING: Boy...

Principal: On the drive to work I will hear it in the car.

Teacher: I will read it in the paper.

Father: I · will see it · on TV.

Guard: I will listen to all of you talk about it all day and I will feel that you should all just relax.

(2) THE PRINCIPAL ARRIVES AT SCHOOL.

Nothing stirred that fall morning of parent-teacher conference day. Only through the heater and dingy, sootcovered motor did artificial air, reprocessed from the bowels of the city, blow on her sneakers and swirl about her suit. The sun slanted down the treelined street as the principal lowered the blind in her luxury sedan the moment she turned past the corner breakfast cart in front of the public house. On reaching her reserved spot, she parallelparked by the ramp entrance, shut, locked and checked the door, before glancing up at her pudgy Milton school. What were those architects thinking? she mused to herself. How could they design this place in beige and glass brick when brownstones stand to the north and south? And who wanted to paint the window frames and lattices pink? The contrast is immense. Not just to this building, but to nearly every one in the neighborhood, except to the west where commensurately unattractive prefabricated edifices cracked the sky over Hurston Avenue. As if some official had once decided to have the whole plot razed behind the granite base tower to the east, the face framing the park and protecting that one refuge from the scourge of projects a block away.

Today she had arrived early to consult with her best teacher. Children had been disappearing from nearby schoolyards. Over the last two weeks, there had been multiple incidents, the latest yesterday, and the central office had called for fifth graders to be picked up by their parents. With three fingers she twirled the hair behind her right earlobe, her eyes round, her thoughts revolving in circles: how to broach the subject without alarming the staff, how to hint at the danger and not cause a panic. Imagine the squabbling of these mommies, and briefly she pictured a covey of clustered teachers squawking outside her office, the movement of their limbs saying more than their words. Danger was everywhere, she knew it, read it, but the chancellor's office couldn't do much, even with their rules, their continually improving policies, another oft abused kid had been murdered by a man running a baby black market. School policy couldn't affect black markets... No, she had to arrange it like her marriage, gradually roll out a plan, and she wanted to discuss this plan with the teacher.

(3) THE PRINCIPAL TALKS WITH THE TEACHER.

Once she had untied her sneakers and replaced them with pumps, she walked through the childless building before school. The plastic tips echoed off the wall with its seams accentuated by fluorescent lights. With two hands she had to smash the metal door to the stairwell, which was supposed to resemble a split spiral staircase in the storied museums that chaperoned visitors up the right side and down the left. On the second floor the next metal door opened into an offwhite corridor with pink doors rising to the right, street side, like the towers on the park, and, to the left, above the stench of the trashyard, a solid wall slit by narrow windows at her brow stretched to swinging doors by the facilities. Room 234, the teacher's, was the fifth.

"You should speak about it at the general assembly, not just in front of the fifth grade staff," said the teacher. "Then you won't fluster them and make others worried. Everyone who doesn't know and hears about it is going to go see you immediately."

"But it's urgent and the assembly isn't till Friday. They rang me up from the central office yesterday and told me to inform the fifth grade staff."

"I just don't think it's a good idea to leave the rest in the dark," – she tried to think constructively. "Maybe you could put an info bulletin in everyone's mailbox and announce it over the loudspeaker as well."

Her hand rifling through the papers on her desk, she separated the list of parents coming to conferences that evening: Tom, Dick, Anya, Harry...

"That's not a bad idea. Thanks," – the principal replied to the hint with a step to the door.

"If I think of anything else, I'll let you know."

(4) THE TEACHER AND THE SON (JASEM) PREPARE FOR SCHOOL.

These subjects had not been on the teacher's mind when she went through her morning routine and intermittently pondered her class. Scanning over some Soviet drama on the front page, her eye caught a title that she would have to read that evening: Thousands of Pupils Living in Hotels Skip School. Twelve kids were reading below grade level; Anya couldn't keep up in math. She skimmed over the first sentences of each paragraph, smiling at a sharply critical article. These are poor kids that no one cares about, but even with those who didn't live in run-down midtown hotels, both parents worked ten to thirteen hours a day, came home exhausted, popped dinner in the microwave and sat down to television. She knew that: Look at Damien.

As compared to her son Jasem, who told her he'd spilled the drink or pushed down his sister for pinching him, Damien was reticent: Jasem exuberantly bragged to Melvin about his superior stats in kickball, while Damien quietly, almost stubbornly, knew that the funny sitcom with all those kids came on ABC. That was the effect of television, and why she hated to even acknowledge its existence.

Part of the matutinal routine involved watering the plants, and she took a few quick steps that way, her gaze resting on the homemade bookcase with its series on the Civil War, Gulag literature, histories of Nazi Germany and studies in Christianity. And then there was Anya's mother! She wanted her kid placed in another class after the fight. She had no idea, has no idea, doesn't even know what her daughter is doing. Hyperventilates to the principal and says she wants her removed immediately. She's frantic. Involved. It's her daughter!

"Five minutes, okay, chicklets."

The livingroom plants stood on the radiators and hung

from the ceiling in front of the window, the mini forest supplanting a view of the wall, attempting to recreate the past sea of maple leaves outside the dormer of her rural sanctuary. She flicked a switch to bask them in artificial sun and bent over to thumb the terrarium tubelight on the floor. Potted nature now let her forget screens and guardrails and the view of the wall and dingy shaft the cramped city forced on her. It could all just as easily be surrounded by greenery, ginkgos, a lawn, hill, gravel road running along the brook in the valley, a culvert gurgling below, a lily later blooming in the flowerbed at their first house. That house had to be on the island, because the thought of all this concrete and asphalt frightened her, made her dodder and so she told her husband directly: we can go, but you have to take the ferry to work so we can live outside the city.

"Mom, did you pack my lunchbox?"

"Yes, honey. It's by the fridge. Are you almost ready?"

"You said we have five minutes."

BOOK TWO

(1) TIME.

It occasionally happens that the content of a question seems to imply a message that the question does not contain: What sounds like the need to rush, is simply a boy too young to realize that she is just asking. She thinks and moves fast, or tries, in the process of organizing or proposing or preparing the math curriculum or placing the packed lunch box by the ice box. If her family is traveling to the countryside by car, especially for a backpacking trip, she checks off a list of supplies, calls the car at the garage, and arranges the timing so her husband will arrive at the corner just as they exit downstairs with the backpacks. For a field trip at school, she has the kids ready and lined up in pairs when the bus stops parallel to the parked cars. For the principal she has the bulletin and loudspeaker.

There is a relationship between time, timing and lights and the teacher, principal, and I, the security guard's narrator, have a different relationship to the different colors of the lights. As we just saw, the teacher is efficient, but the principal is efficient too, as you'll see, and yet the two of them have a different reaction to red, the red light, that is, and its flashing accomplice "Don't Walk." The guard doesn't care about the color at all and just looks to see if cars are coming, but those two, the principal and the teacher, have a reaction, and it is not the same, and one is not better or worse than the other... Then there are also weirdoes that barely perceive the color, just follow it, like the father who, I might add, also worries about customer revolts and may space out on a hardwood stool for an hour after dinner, staring at the wall and imaging it's in a different place, but let's forget about him for the moment.

As the teacher sits in the passenger seat or the red chair, not responsible for current progress, she relaxes, reads the paper or considers a constructive improvement to help Anya with math, which she should bring up with her mother tonight, since if she can just get that ironed out, there will be more time for Tom, Dick and Harry. Anya has become the latest flashing red light, not necessarily a problem, but a point at which she stops and finds or sees a resolution. Then the light changes, and she continues...

(2) THE SON'S (JASEM) PAST.

The son, however, was not aware of this calmness in his mom. So when she said five minutes, he raced to the bedroom with its two bunkbeds for three kids completely covering the wall to the left of the taped pane – and actually made it take longer by racing. He felt quite different than the day he had launched a battery at his brother and broke the pane. They had been playing with blocks and the bastard kept stacking the bulky cubes crookedly so the buildings collapsed. Then they decided on hide and seek, but the idiot counted too fast. What was that? He reached down and grabbed the first thing his hand touched, a fat battery. That goggled his eyes a lot more than giving his erector set a kick for kissing up to their cousin or cursing him for losing the salamander they'd caught. Just light into him as brutally as possible. Then the brat'll cry back to his room.

It resembled his tormentor's bravado at school. A few weeks back Melvin had been sitting at his end of the lunch table and refused to leave him alone, kept butting him off the bench, spilling his boxdrink, conning him out of the cookies his mom had slid in as a special treat. He could hardly take a bite of his peanut butter and jelly sandwich, and even then, only in anticipation of an impertinent push. Their teacher's separating them would have ended it, but as they were runwalking to recess, Melvin tripped him outside the exit, into the fence, his head pounding against the pole.

"Damn it," the son screamed. "Get off my back, you jerk."

– What was I going to do about it, he heard.

A shove. He cocked his elbows with his hands balled in tight little fists while his nemesis imitated him, but with far more fluidity, a glint in his eye, relaxed, as if a throwdown was as common as a broken car window. Even the expression on his face only concentrated ever so slightly, and the one-two straight through the boys slightly spread hands, direct to the chin, then round to the ear, plowed him down, his head swelling to the height of the traffic light, flashing red, blood darting down the fast lane, jamming up in a pool as it hit the ground, the grimy asphalt with bits of smashed glass and pee stains rough, stinking, polluting, infecting the pure gaff who wanted to protect himself. He lay crumpled by the pole, like the cans of beer in paper bags that the alcoholics stomped under their heel: his crushed pinna is rumbling from the punch to the endless embarrassment that warmed his rosy cheeks as gawkers turned toward the clump. When someone helped him up, only his body rose. He's unable to lift his chin or raise his gaze or acknowledge the patheticness pummeling him – and he hadn't even thrown a punch, his ear was ringing, a big red welt swelled on his stinging chin, and his scratched elbow was bleeding.

– Why didn't I tell the guard, Anya asked. Bet he'll get detention, more than I would anyway. But he dismissed the idea. It was too mortifying to consider the story: he had just gotten beat up by Melvin. Melvin pushed him into a pole and he was angry. Wanted to pay him back and tried to punch him... How could you bear it. Plus, he's scared of the payback. Tattling means more problems: he'll round up his homeboys and wait for me after school.

Not only did this rationale free him from anxiety, but after a few days he would not want revenge anyway. It was the same this morning as he scrambled to stuff the overlooked binder into his purple backpack: he did not recall any battery anger, bitter jealousy or playground scuffles. If anything, he was worried about what the teachers will say to his mom at parent-teacher conferences tonight. And not a vial of the momentary aggression in storefront security gates rattled down him as he thought about their football game yesterday against another neighborhood threesome, twohand touch, two receivers, one quarterback, two defenders and a lineman counting Mississippis. Simms, to throw again, and he pump fakes, turns around in a circle. He's about to be tagged, then just slings it downfield... Then it's picked!...Then, you won't believe this, their guy coughed it up! First down for us!!... They took turns playing quarterback, although Damien was definitely the best there, while Jasem's younger brother was the best receiver. Just occasionally did locals roll in and intimidate them and once on Halloween some midget threw eggs and gave them the finger, brashly challenging the shy boys to step up. But normally they played until dusk or until the school security guard ambled by on his way home.

(3) THE SCHOOL SECURITY GUARD (SOTTLOY) TALKS WITH THE SON (JASEM).

Mr. Sottloy was the gregarious security guard. He only enjoyed talking about sports in order to talk about something else. Those afternoons, when he found them in the yard, he approached with that in mind, but now, this morning, he manned the entrance ramp to school and coopted the teacher's eldest son without any need for pretense.

Sottloy: (commandingly) How's it going? You staying out of trouble?

Son: (shyly) Um huh.

* * *

Sottloy: Do you know that guy Allen in your building?

Son: I've seen him.

Sottloy: I've been trying to help him out. A good guy. But gone a little astray. He doesn't get any decent advice from the people he's around.

(*Son nods*)

Loaned him a few dollars the other day. He promised to pay me back in a week. And he couldn't do it, but he came and told me straight up. I'll get the money. I'm not worried about that. It showed me he has character. Didn't shy away. He waited for me after school and said he'd have it in another week.

(*Son is a little baffled by the conversation, but listens as attentively as possible*)

You don't have any problems with money, do you?

Son: No, I get an allowance.

Sottloy: You have good parents. I don't know your dad, but

your mom is great. Do they get along well? Your parents? Do you have a nice time at home?

Son: Oh, yeah. They get along very well. Everything's great.

Sottloy: Cool. That's the problem with Allen, he doesn't have that kind of home, his father's been gone for years, ever since he can remember, and his mom doesn't support him at all, just lets him flap in the wind, so I try to be like a father to him, but I can't, I do the best I can, but I don't live with him, don't even see him all that regularly and if he didn't hang out downstairs, then I'd never see him and probably wouldn't know him.

(*Son fails at wondering what it would be like to have a surrogate father*)

He was telling me some crazy story about Halloween, how they went wilding through the park up near Harlem, yeah, those are the kind of kids he hangs out with, not the likes of you and Damien, you and Damien get along well, right?

Son: Yeah, he's fun.

Sottloy: Those are the kind of friends Allen should have. You probably don't read the paper, but that wilding is pretty serious stuff. You can go to jail for it, and while he's a minor, juvenile detention isn't a cake walk. I don't know exactly what he's done, but recently a woman was gangraped, some bicyclist's head was bashed in. That's serious stuff, that's not filching a stick of gum from the bodega.

Son: No

(4) THE SON (JASEM) AND THE BOY (DAMIEN) REBELLING IN THE FUTURE.

He was sheltered then, but in four years he would lope out a bodega with Damien and his crew, forties and cigarettes. Damien was the boss, while the teacher's son, Jasem, tried to hold his own with six others passing a paper bag.

In the park along the river they finished the malt liquor. A drained bottle hurtled from a hand, above their heads, over the trees, up, up to the penthouses, to burst with fireworks in a fountain of glitter before it leveled like a launched missile and tore down, straight for the asphalt where joggers, mothers with children and elderly couples peacefully relaxed during the day, where they forgot about the rats scuttling through the bushes, the humidity forcing them to sit on broken wooden benches that stunk from a clump of dirty underwear, disgusting socks, half-eaten burgers, and spilled catchup in the corner. Down, down, the pregnant belly shot with its pointed head hot till it crashed and sent a shower of shards off the walkway, up, again, toward the sky, the river, the other side of the park, the state beyond, the Soviet Union, activating gaseous mixtures, combusting, the infected infecting the uninfected, the virus mutating, new strains draining the cells of their sodium, the lack of sodium corroding the walls, facades, disintegrating, brick crumbling, cornices collapsing, followed by whole walls, buildings and lands.

Damien thought they needed to cause some trouble. It was dull in the desolate park where they saw nobody but homeless men headed to the riverside shantytown or abandoned railroad tracks under the esplanade.

"Let's go get eggs and throw them at some yuppie's house!" he said.

– Totally, let's do it, definitely, right on...

...In a pack they loped and caterwauled, winging wave after wave of shells that burst on the glass, grills and brown brick, in the face of the horrified faces that faced them through the dripping yellow and clear slime. Especially nice were the portentous expressions as they looked down at the racket outside and winced at eggs scattering across the glass like puddles from the tires of their taxis.

– They're after us, – shouted someone.

At Falkner Avenue, they divided. Three went uptown, three downtown, two into the abyss of the pitchblack park: Jasem and Damien. They ran blindly and hid behind a huge rock, smiling at the thrill of adventitious turpitude as it wound down to wondering how they would find the others. Then Damien scrambled up the face to skylight the scene.

– Hey, you two, get over here, a voice snarled.

And around them stood five grown men. In a dark park. At night. Two. Against five larger, stronger, angry yuppies.

– Stand there, give us anything you've got. Have you got anything? We're going to check either way, so hand it over now. (*Damien tossed a knife on the rocks.*) Don't be so cocky.

The speaker moved to pick up the knife. A lanky guy patted them down, cautiously, attentively.

– What are you dumbasses doing throwing eggs at people's houses? Does that seem right to you? Is that what you losers do at night?.. What if we beat the shit out of you here? Is that what we should do?..

He groans at his torso buckling, the man's foot elevating into his stomach. Blood and pain rush to his head drilled by another blow. "Wait, wait," he cries, "you don't understand..." But another fist cracks his cranium, the same part Melvin pounded into the pole, the same part that flamed up later. He shivered at the thought, and the men turned.

– No. I'll tell you what we're going to do! Follow us, and don't try and pull any stunts.

When they reached the eggstained brownstone, one of the men brought out paper towels, window spray and sponges.

– You can clean now. And do a good job. Then we'll see.

That turned out to be the finest – silent flashing sirens that were going to land them in the slammer, shut up with a six foot nine rapist with three hundred pounds of pure muscle and the guard meekly mincing to the far end of the corridor as granddaddy said they could either bend to him alone or to the rest of the cell: Jack, drooling at the bit, and Jill, chomping at the bit, went up the Hill, the fatty so round he could barely get his hands to touch over his belly, to fetch the Pail, who was waiting to ejaculate his fluids, of Water, when the time came for him. A shiver quivered down his spine; the seeming firmness of his voice vanished. He was unable to speak. Jail, the idea of jail, terrified him more than anything else. He pushed his sleeve back, pulled it down. It's cold. And Hill is standing there like that prisoner who wants to make you his punk.

– Since you've washed off the building, – the massive driver said, – we're going to let you go. This weapon, however, we have to confiscate.

Hands in the pockets of their baggy jeans, Damien and Jasem strode down the street, away from this neutral conclusion to their night. At least they hadn't called his mom. The whole time Damien knew it would be impossible to sit in the back of that car, wait for her to be woken in the middle of the night and forced to come to the station. Crap. That would be a serious grounding. He sensed her irritation. Saw how she would react, especially with him, the only troublemaker. Was even nervous she would leave him there. After all, she repeatedly said she doesn't have any tolerance for delinquents. She is a proud woman of intelligent children, won't tolerate losers, and lots more ra, ra, ra.

But they could go home, were on their way to Damien's building, when the familiar voice threatened from behind:

– Not so fast. They let you off easy. Where're you going?

"To the poolhall," Damien replied coldly.

– That's my place, I play there regularly, – the yuppie peeped.

"That's not your place. I got way more back there than you'll ever have."

– You think so. Shall we see?

And they went, walked into a crowd of Damien's friends:

– Damien, you all right, these suckers bothering you?

– Hey, you, is there a problem?

– Damien, you need any help?

"I'm with Damien."

A nod.

Swarms of the boy's friends swelled the hall and street, and on returning to his building, on the corner, by the school, stood still more. It felt as if he was chauffeured from that hall to this home, escorted, protected by friends and buddies and elders throughout the community, like the businessmen who barely set foot outside, who passed under the awning and ducked into the backseat, suitcase in hand, door opened and closed by the driver, the men and women he imagines from the eleventh floor, across the park, beyond the reservoir, shrubs and stone wall, not here, in front of a profligate public house.

BOOK THREE

(1) PUBLIC HOUSING.

The faux chauffeurs were a part of the public housing world and Damien loved it but *it* depends on whether the speaker is young or old, lives in its trenches or skirts by the grills of its lower windows. If you don't live in them, and I don't and the teacher doesn't and the principal doesn't, then the best you can say is that they are a noble experiment in mixed living, with sixty percent of the residents subsidized and the remaining forty from the middle class. Shows how to care for the less fortunate, unlucky, disadvantaged, and the program continues to this day, although those who forget that the proportions have gone from 60-40 to end at 99-1, at best, or ignore the failure altogether, or turn a blind eye to the cycles of violence, the breeding ground for criminals, pesthole for gangs – they still believe.

And the teacher looks in dismay at this blatant loss of potential talent, regretting the failure of good intentions, while the principal dismisses the program and the ideal, complains about the waste of their tax dollars and argues that the entire initiative runs counter to the country's belief in the selfmade man...

Then there are · the former grownup residents · like Damien's dad, me, who lived · among the swarms · of cockroaches · that scatter · when you turn · on the kitchen light at night · when you go · to the bathroom, who wince · at the abuse they take · and hear, who are scared · to leave their apartment · or even open · their door in the evening, who rode · a boom as young adults, suffered in middle age, and then were delivered, by fate, to a building · a block from the park. We lamented · the uncertainty · and outright danger · but emphasized · that it is better · than the other options · where the building · and the neighborhood · must terrify · any ordinary individual. After all · we just · have to pass · the crowd of jobless thugs · by the entryway · and then we blend · into the friendly · nice neighborhood.

So, it could have been worse. And the young and middle-aged men thought this since they were the chauffeur supervisors with hardly any rivals, and it actually made them relatively relaxed: threats – limited, costs – low, obligations – minimal, so they are almost free except when they try to break the fetters, but in bondage they guard the building, scout the younger generation and crown its leaders to ensure harmony and support in the community – as Damien and Jasem saw on the way home from the pool hall. They even had a common enemy to unify them whenever internecine strife surfaced, and this didn't mean wilding in the park or mugging some outsider who rambled into their area. They just intimidated. And that was so easy. They would speak loudly or look or crack a joke, and a flush would rise to the Euroamerican's cheek: he would stare at the pavement or glance about nervously. That always produced a trickle of laughter, which escalated to a cascade if somebody stomped their foot or even feigned a couple quick, resonant steps. Then his face would tense, eyes start, and off he'd bolt, with nobody interested in chasing him.

(2) A SCARED BOY (DAMIEN) ARRIVES AT SCHOOL.

In the morning, however, when the teacher and her children hurried by these grills, when the principle drove past the breakfast cart, or a little later when Damien pushed through the graffiti door in the lobby that reeked of urine and trash, the sidewalk outside the building was empty. At eight thirty, Damien's mother watched him down the street. Like a sentry the boy walked the gate with its jagged iron spikes and gnarly ginkgos, toward the moat dividing the entrance from the rabble. A sedan stretched into a boa constrictor that distracted and nearly caused him to slide on an oozing stairwell of dog pooh. All he had to do was make it to the nondescript portal with its ramp, and on that side, he was safe in a classroom for the next six hours.

Now as you can imagine, though the boy may appear composed or normal to you, to his classmates, to Mr. Sottloy, he is nervous, so nervous that his head is ballooning to the size of a blimp with a bluish-gray hue, reverberating off the bright bile linoleum: Anya reincarnated as a spindly alien, a ball in her belly, Sally sporting eternally longated legs – all among skyscrapers of books in the swollen shadow of a titanic hand turkey. It was a situation he had never experienced before: danger of the unknown lurked not only behind every car with reflecting glass, but also in front of a future that could dupe him into forfeiting the pleasant routine of playing between Hurston and Tolstoy, disrupt the status quo and separate him from his beloved window on the park. He felt his pulse quicken from moment to moment, though his mother will watch till he goes under the welcome sign that reads Benevidos... She won't be watching after school.

Last night, her melodic voice had called him from the sill as he gazed at the park that separated his side from the other side.

On two adjacent couches eling the television, his mom had told him that his father is back in town. He has come back from the countryside. He would see his father whenever he grew up enough to visit them here. Dad would have to come see them since he'd done something bad. Bad daddy. Good mommy. Listen to mommy, and there's nothing to fear.

And there wasn't, till then, till the morning, till mommy said daddy might attempt to see sonny boy after school. He wasn't allowed to go with him under any circumstances. She didn't know where he might take him.

His mom had not meant this to sound like a threat of kidnapping, but the boy thought of only one thing, that his dad may jump out of a car, stuff him in it and head out of state. A placid face evanesced to agitation, distorting his perception of the park, fence, sedan, Tom, Dick, Harry and Anya. The instructions had always been: Do not get in a stranger's car no matter what. And now his father was a stranger. Not living at home. And maybe waiting outdoors like a helicopter yawing to swoop down and whisk him away with those hands that had once swatted his shots in bedroom basketball.

In the past, the worst he had encountered was a slap. That had shown him the limits to punishment and made him feel at liberty to do as he liked. He hung out with friends longer than his mom permitted, slap, he caused minor trouble snatching a thing here, slap, pulling a prank there, slap, terrorizing a rare babysitter by refusing to eat, sleep, bathe, or listen at all, slap, slap. Once at Melvin's house, they snuck into his sister's room and took out all her panties, drenching them in water and tying them to the fixtures up and down the foyer hall, elevator, stairwell. Hanging dripping panties from one end to the other. Slap, slap, plus grounding. But the grounding for girls underwear did not compare to the murky possibilities he vaguely remembered from afternoon specials on TV: the little girl whisked away in broad daylight, then locked in a basement for ten years, or the baby sold on the black market by that slimy man with big glasses and a mustache or savagely beaten by him, her, teens: gladiolas, Mass cards, handwritten messages – that's all I'll get. Or I'll have to run across the highway and get hit by a car or he'll come after me with a baseball bat like they did down there at the beach or he'll hide me in one of those buildings that collapses...

(3) THE TEACHER OBSERVES THE BOY (DAMIEN).

As the boys and girls hung their coats in the closet and went to their desks, the teacher searched for signs of sleepiness, discombobulation, to put it bluntly: problems. During these ten minutes it was harder to discern any peculiar difference than it would be in the first ten minutes sitting in silence. Then fidgeting feet or blinking lashes, bashful shy looks, forlorn faces expressed substantially more. Today skinny Anya swung a chain; her hall monitor held her hands in her pockets, the top button of her blouse pinching her neck; Damien in a blue and white striped shirt slowly passed from the closet to his desk, and now stood by that desk with a vacant stare, his right index finger stuck in his left fist.

He did not look himself. The past month and a half she had observed fluctuations: rowdy – withdrawn; concentrating – distracted, active – passive. With no concerning phase lasting long, she made a mental note and postponed any action, after all, his family might have been chaotic, sure, mail stacked up everywhere by the door, no planning ahead, calling at the last minute – but that was inconsequential. He had a mother who was in touch and enthusiastic, which could only have a positive impact.

Never would she be able to imagine what it was like to live in that frightening building with all sorts of dubious characters swelling out of its mangled viscera. It was the antithesis of their marble walled lobby with acanthus leaves in the cornice. Her kids may have seen the red, green, blue, yellow, orange crack vials in the rills of every concrete square on the block, but kids like Damien must also see them in the elevator, stairwell and in hands, exchanging hands, maybe in round glass pipes with the water that bubbled when you inhaled. They had no doorman, no security; there wasn't even a working buzzer system. Dealers, prostitutes, thugs, criminals strolled in and out with kids like Damien and mothers like his mother and diligent city college students like his sister, and, earlier, fathers like his father, when he still lived there.

This environment would destabilize even the sturdiest constitution, but the change in Damien had to be a family or personal matter. Someone was sick, something was wrong with his mother or sister. She didn't know, but it had to be personal: the fluctuations had been there since September.

(4) THE PRINCIPAL WARNS THE SCHOOL, AND WE LEARN ABOUT HER PAST.

Before the morning announcement, the teacher sent her monitor with a note for the guidance councilor. The background static from the communication system scratched through the loudspeaker and the principal's voice broke through the crackling:

"Good morning teachers and pupils. We have a very important announcement for everyone today. So please pay special attention. Recently, there have been some disturbing events at schools in the area. These have involved children after school was let out. Because we do not want to take any chances, parents or guardians will be required to pick up all children in fifth grade and below. This policy will start tomorrow and remain in effect until further notice. Today we need you all to go home in groups of two or three and if you see someone suspicious or strange, find an official or police officer immediately. I also ask each of you to tell your parents and give them the notice your teacher will pass out later. Thank you."

That is what she had assiduously prepared after consulting with Mrs. Leaddus: an announcement and flyers in all the mailboxes. This combination would ensure concern, she hoped, but eschew the potential alarm that could spread with an emergency assembly. She didn't need anxiously clucking colleagues but she also didn't need a pupil kidnapped. So she remained on edge, because they couldn't enforce parental dismissal immediately, and that left one afternoon, this afternoon, for a disaster that would shatter her already dwindling professional prospects.

As for kidnapping, it was not especially hard for her to picture at first, though inconceivable later. For that first phase, she didn't even need to put herself in someone else's shoes: the empty house, colonial with a gated entry, now slumbered in frigid cold scintillating in the sparkling stone facade where the graceful rise of the pillar signals exclusion from its heights and the possibility that jealousy will drive some ruthless loser to ruin her happiness. She must be at a friend's house, and forgot to tell me. She'll be sure to remember and call, or even just come home. The remote-control fireplace sparkles in orange and yellow flame, the light of affluence, the light which licks the ebony of life, and scorches the hairs, and singes the scales on her eyes. The cuckoo clock ticks, she attempts to relax in the Jacuzzi. Sixty minutes pass. Cuckoo. It seems as if, pricked by mortal regret and all its tentacles, heartfelt humility has removed the scales and left her facing, clearly, pellucidly, the collapsing cake; crumbling career; a lost daughter, which should we not deserve it, won't come our way. But oh, how it is. Humility, encumbering you on these occasions, does not affect your nature. Her consternation compounds. Hmm. Her child's been tied to the fake logs and burnt by remote control. She calls the parents of her closest friends. – She isn't there. Somewhere else? Maybe, probably, hopefully, yet she can do nothing but wait. If she calls the police, they'll actually say she's cuckoo: a teenage daughter out at six in the evening is not particularly odd. She's helpless. Just as she was that night years ago when she went to her daughter's room and really found no one in the waterbed. But then she had known the space and options were extremely limited. A ten year old girl did not go far by herself at eleven. Either she had crawled in a nook or someone had broken in. They searched the boudoir, sunroom, glanced at the hanging toilet, opened the cabinets below the two sinks, the wall closets and, nervously, lifted the lid off the Jacuzzi. With her fists balled, she thought at the granite counter, before checking everything again – and finding the sleepwalker tucked in the bed of a second floor guest room.

Ultimately her daughter evolved into the lynchpin of their marriage. She had married an ambitious broker in the heady days of their twenties. A spectacular match, whose vows were taken on the palisades as the sun sank in the cliffs above the water, though the spectacular days did not last long and their phlegmatic bond eventually united on the upbringing of their daughter. Both saw the precipitously rising competitiveness in business and school – with neither wanting their daughter left behind: preschool, private school, music lessons, dance class, later encouragement in extracurricular activities. When she compared her own childhood to her daughter's, a slight tinge of chagrin occasionally made her shudder: the overprogrammed child contrasted so sharply to the girl she had been in those years building castles in the sand, sunning on the shore, like a teenager should, without a care in the world. Yet there was no choice either. For this position as principal she had beat out 78 other applicants, three times the number for her first job, albeit as assistant principal. And no matter how many extracurricular activities her daughter had, irrespective of her top grades, the chances were small she would be accepted to an elite college.

Now the scenario was a little different: no teenage girl, but a whole school of kids. Granted, they weren't as close as a sole daughter, her life didn't hang on them, though her career did. If she only lived once, she could not slow down, for once the motion terminated, once she got stuck in traffic, there was no way out: take a traffic jam on the highway, how would you extricate yourself from that? You didn't, you depended on *them.* That was her career: she would no longer have a handle on it if a child vanished that afternoon.

BOOK FOUR

(1) FEAR.

The issue of safety was on all kinds of minds: poorly printed milk cartons reminded you every morning with a bowl of cereal; school announcements repeated it over the loudspeaker; uncomfortable encounters reinforced it on the street. Even stronger than the warning was the relief you felt, like Damien this morning on his way to school, after making it through the danger zone to the almonry. The safety and security of your destination or home stood in such sharp contrast to the perceived street warfare that it amplified the sense of that public hostility. Jasem will also experience this later, but it is not just for children. One evening the teacher would have been mugged if not for the guard; the principle instantly saw it as a possible reason for that disappearance of her daughter. And both had a row on raising "streetsmart children" with hundreds of tips that must have been written by a country woman who assumed that urban kids act the same as their sub- or exurban counterparts and cross streets without looking both ways or without looking at all as Jasem's future girlfriend would on the day she was hit by a car traveling two miles an hour through the zebra stripes in the village because she was dreaming on her feet, but all the same the teacher walked her children to school, past the "drugstore," the church, St. Catherine's, across the street with the crossing guard, past that breakfast cart by the project and up the entrance ramp – to ensure their safety. Nonetheless, it's probably warranted with such neighborhood *amenities* as the single occupancy public house known as the "drugstore" for its resident dealers; and the language used by the pupils at St. Catherine's, the junior high school, unsettled a teacher who had rarely heard anything remotely similar on the gravel road running along the brook in the valley. Other stuff definitely made sense: only talk to people you know, don't get into a stranger's car, don't accept food from a stranger. These strangers overall were a major theme: parents had to check candy after trick or treating, because it was common for drug dealers to dress up and slip cocaine or crack or marijuana or heroine into the bags of children to addict them to their wares and secure their future clientele. Once an elderly woman feeding pigeons did give the teacher's son a kiss on the forehead, which made him shiver and view her as a prime threat to the purity of the Leaddus family with its sacred mother and genial father and dear brother and sister who would remain the sole chosen ones if the impurities of the pigeon-feeder passed from her lips through his skin and contaminated his blood. Even worse was the time when a man at a football game offered Damien and Jasem a few of his grapes. The son blushed so high that the man could only have known they had heard something about strangers like him offering cocainelaced grapes – and the white sheen gave it away!

(2) THE SON (JASEM) SNEAKS OUT OF THE YARD AT LUNCH.

IT WAS LUNCHTIME. JASEM CHEWED HIS PEANUT BUTTER AND JELLY SANDWICH AS MELVIN DOGGED HIM. THEY HAD LINED UP FOR LUNCH AND ARGUED AT THE BACK:

"You're the teacher's pet, you're the teacher's pet" Melvin ragged.

"No I'm not."

"Yes you are." – his nemesis egged the son on.

"No I'm not."

Their teacher came up and said:

"Of course you're the teacher's pet. Admit it." – Shaking her bushy hair with a smile.

He turned bright red.

Figure it out he cannot, but what is this? Why are they all bothering me, tickling me till I can't breathe? Saying smelt it – dealt it. In line, he followed behind Melvin who kept turning and making faces. How could the teacher call me her favorite? And now they won't let up. The dim stairwell was brimming with rowdy students released and jostling to the lunchroom. He felt Melvin's petulant oppression thwarting him at every opportunity. A light bulb below flickered as crashes echoed through the shaft. Shuddering, he pictured a lockdown, trapped in a cell with his torturers: Melvin crosses from his bunk to his bunk, a helicopter chops outside, the iron bars reverberate... Still, I never see any of those chickens in the offlimits playground at recess.

Stationed by the door, guarding the inmates, Mr. Sottloy noticed the long hand of the clock had struck fifteen. The prescribed quarterhour had past, and he slammed down the metal bar, signaling freedom to the detainees. Instantly the son taxied to the door, revved through the stairwell, left his lunch box by the stoop ball wall, accelerating across the football field, jungle gyms, past the bushes, taking off up over the fence and into the donottrespass edge. Where were they now? They were lapping obediently. Those tough boys. And they think they're all that!

His friend Damien had not come today. He waited, but still no one came. They always met here by the bush. That let them spy on the others. Was his friend just late? Well, he enjoyed the rebellion of the project park anyway. The climbing turtle in dull red, the benches painted green with muddy footprints, the fivestep slide yellow like a cab on a rainy day – all this griminess did not disturb him. It symbolized revolt, and he smiled at the smaller dimensions, since the dinginess embodied the grit that distinguished silent perserverers from softies. But most of all, the small confines replenished his depleted reserves, restoring the ability to cope with ceaseless attacks, perceived or real, whenever he was in the traffic circle. Someone will tease him again. He'll turn red. He doesn't want that, he knew, back here, no one annoys him. It may be more fun with Damien. But he's glad just to be away from the others.

As he watched kids flow in waves across the courts, a rumbling objection bespattered the peace, a voice that was not a child's and not from the schoolyard. He glanced over at two men ambling his way. Nothing unusual. It would have been better with Damien, he wouldn't have thought twice. Men came and went. Women pushed baby carriages. Crones fed breadcrumbs to pigeons... He was alone. Dared another peek. Busy. Okay. He looked back at the yard, but saw nothing, thought only of the two men talking across from him, then the announcement. The announcement. How could he forget?

Though what did they actually say? After school. Picked up. They didn't really say what is happening. He tried to recall it. No, she just said they have to be picked up tomorrow. And his mom walked them home anyway. That wasn't important. The two men are. But they were sitting on the bench against the building. He went back to watching.

On the opposite side of the fence consummate Melvin caught a pass from Mr. Sottloy and sucked in his stomach as he spun to avoid the two-hand touch. His superiority was so annoying. They had to look at Jasem's cheeks, he said, red like an apple. He had told them so, Jasem liked Anya, he had told them so. He was blushing. Why was I blushing? he asked. I was blushing because I liked her. I was bright red – that's proof. And there Anya jumped doubledutch. He had never tried that. It was a girl's game though. Still, Anya could do it. Her legs whip up and down while her fingers snap time. Screams from the basketball court distracted him from Anya; a crowd gathered in a circle, stumbling and jerking this way and that. Teacher's rushed over; Mr. Sottloy too; and five or six boys bolted through the opposite gate. They were headed to the White Truck for candy cigarettes. The most popular candy.

Suddenly those two men were coming closer, were walking right straight directly toward him. He shifted his eyes to the fence and the open low wall to his right. He can spring up it, dart through the bushes and get out the other side. Run, he told himself, but he could not take a step. Instead, the boy tried to calm down, even as tears sprang to his eyes: Goodbye, mom, goodbye. Hopefully we'll meet again some day. It will be the happiest moment ever. We'll celebrate after years of sadness. We'll hug and kiss and eat chicken with breadcrumbs and stuffing and cake and we'll catch up on all we've missed and we'll never argue again and never fight and I'll be the best boy ever, never misbehave and most of all never enter an offlimits area. He dwelt on the joyful reunion, while envisioning the lengthy separation in a flash: day after day chainlocked in a cellar where the sun never shone. Meals interspersed with movies and sleep broke the monotony of the hours alone. He became emaciated, jaundiced, a sickly hue on his wane face. That he skipped over. And the same with the sapping of his energy, his spirit, the belief in his ability to shape his life not according to the rules, but his own will, which today, for instance, had encouraged him to dismiss the announcement.

(3) THE BOY (DAMIEN) TELLS HIS FATHER'S NIGHTMARE.

Once there was a time when Jasem and his ravenhaired friend Damien had grown tired of being ignored in football, stomping people in stoopball and watching other kids play on gamesets. They wandered the yard: Sottloy assisting the two captains pick their football teams; chump competition for stoopball; the coolkids courts and beyond – the loser courts. Nothing to entice them, because they were bored of this or not good at that. As a surge of discouragement rushed the son, his scattered thoughts said they will be shut out of everything except peering over the shoulder of a clique watching a cartoon character dodge sundry critters. His head rustled like the tires of cars on the street: he did not say a word, traipsed to the fenced edge, Damien at his side, the bagmen opposite, and, to fill the time, the boy told his dad's story from a distant dark past, a simpler version of a well-known nightmare that I have rendered here far beyond his former linguistic faculties:

A boy, not our boys or dads as boys, was seven and skulking through a passage of the park with his father. The gray, rainy, forsaken area of the park at that hour he will never forget. It was dense and hilly and he was always scared when he passed through this section. Dubious figures lurked in the recesses; murmurs issued from untrimmed shrubs. He would clutch his dad's fingers and look anxiously around him. Something startles his eye: it looks like a carousing crowd of drunks dressed in all sorts of dark attire. All drunk, all hollering, and near them – a bascart, but a strange-looking bascart. One of those bascarts you wheel around stores. He's always had a soft spot for pushing them rapidly and riding on the back rail, slipping, gliding down the aisle, or helping his mom fill it with food for the week. But now the strange thing was that it stood by bushes and a thin sickly man stood before it, one of those men he often sees – slowly weaving with ponderous black garbage bags, forty gallons, in pain, mocked impertinently by teenagers, jeered, and it pains him so, it pains him so much to see it that as soon as he begins to tear up, his mom drags him away. But now they're sounding boisterous, screams, rap music and carousing-binging men!

– Settle down, everyone settle down! – screams one of the teenagers. – We're gonna deal with this right now.

But the bystanders snicker and shout:

– You dumb ass.

– Hah, you idiot, Allan, are you out of your mind: a cart full of rocks pulled uphill!

– Forget it.

– Settle down, he'll do it, – screams Allan as he tightens the rope.

– Giddy up, – he screams. – Come on! What, you can't do it? Settle down, guys. He'll pull it up. I'm telling you, just wait. – And he whips out a belt, enjoying the start of the trip up the hill.

– Settle down, come on, – chuckled someone in the crowd. – Don't you hear, the man's going to giddy up the hill.

– He's been pushing this cart around for years. Now he's going to pull it, with our load.

– Here we go.

– Don't feel bad, brothers.

Everyone laughs. Two other boys in the group pull out their belts to help Allan.

– Well, giddy up!

The skinny man tenses with all his might, but not only does he not set the bascart in motion, he does not succeed in moving it an inch, just stomps in place, groans and falls from the slap of the belts thundering down on him. The snickers increase on all sides, but Allan is furious and thrashes the pour soul still more brutally, as if that will make him move up the hill.

– Let me in on it! – screams one of the guys in the crowd.

– Just wait, just wait everyone! I'll thrash him into it! – and he thrashes, thrashes, out of his mind.

– Daddy, daddy, – he screams to his father. – Daddy, what are they doing? Daddy, they're hitting that guy!

– Come along, come along, – his father says. – They're drunk, idiots; come along, don't look, – and he wants him to walk quickly, to keep quiet, but the kid breaks free, careers forward. The man is already doing awfully. He is sniffling, stomping in place, again tensing the string, almost collapsing.

– I'll sling him to obedience, – screams Allan. – If that's what it comes to!

– Alright, man. That's enough already, – screams one older guy in the crowd.

– Have you ever seen someone do that, – adds another.

– Shut up. It's my business. I'll do what I want! Settle down! I want him to giddy up.

Suddenly the snickering bursts into laughter and covers everything: the man falls and lies on the ground. Even the older guy laughs.

Two more teenagers whip out belts and precipitate to help beat him in the side.

– Give it to him! – screams Allan.

... And he runs up, to the front, he sees them clobbering him, kicking him in the side, the head. He wails. His heart thunders, tears streak his cheeks. One of the menacers punches him in the face. He doesn't feel it. He screams, races up to a skinny guy shaking his head on the edge. Another tries to lead him away; but he breaks free and runs back to the man. He's failing and collapsing again.

– Lazy ass, – screams Allan in fury. He tosses the belt

down, bends and pulls out a crowbar, long and thin, takes it by the end...

But the poor boy has completely lost it. With a scream he bolts through the crowd and jumps on the man and hugs him, hugs his chest, his torso, his head... Then he jumps up and pummels Allan, his fistlets inflicting no pain. At this moment his dad finally has him, grabs him, finally, and drags him out of the crowd.

– Let's go; come along, – he says – We're going home!

– Daddy! Why were they... thrashing... that poor guy! – He's convulsing, but he's out of breath, and his words founder under cries.

– They're drunk, carousing, it's not our concern, let's go! – says his father...

Jasem and Damien passed a recess along the perimeter of the yard. Damien doubled back, considered:

"Are you down to slide in there and crawl behind the bushes? Then we can climb over the fence behind the tree," – he pointed to a Ginkgo whose yellow fall foliage screened the ramparts from the supervisors who clustered on the other side.

The son hesitated.

"Come on, it'll be fun. We'll spy on people," pursued his friend, encouraging him more enthusiastically.

The son looked around nervously.

"Don't be a chump," – Damien cajoled him.

"Don't you think they'll catch us?" he rejoined.

"No way! Besides, what else are we going to do?.. I'm over *this.*"

(4) THE GUARD TALKS ABOUT THE BOY (DAMIEN)

Damien was a popular topic for the faculty that sat in the teachers' lounge munching snacks and gossiping about their munchkins, for in addition to being sly he had a streak of wistfulness and, for those who had been around, enough of a good reputation preceding him, that this elusive halftroublemaker with his oversized shoes was distinguished from the other kids with their oversized jeans, shirts, jackets that they would grow into or undersized ones they'd already outgrown, giving them wedgies nearly as painful as when Damien snuck behind Melvin, grabbed the elastic of his tighty-whities and ripped them up his back and into his butt crack. The guard was one of those who had not only been around but retained the confidential information that only an acquaintance can possess. In September he had gone off on a tangent:

"You know a number of years separate him from his sister which means she's preparing for life and he wants to play GI Joe, and his mom is the only parent in the house, so women surround him, no male influence, no father role model to explain how to ask a girl on a date or how to put your hands behind your back or cross them over your chest as you wait for the end of a conversation or, more relevant now, play basketball, go backpacking, take a road trip. Instead he plays alone right there in that crummy yard and I think he even shoves his own meals in the microwave and eats alone sometimes though I'm not sure. He doesn't have any cousins and besides Jasem not many friends at least no one showed up for his birthday party last year except Jasem, his mom told me, and when I had dinner there he kept staring out the window as if he were more fascinated by the neverchanging view on the eleventh floor than our classic family sitcom on NBC, and he never tells us what he's looking at, just over there, he says, vaguely motioning with his arm toward the other side of the park."

"But he is quite good friends with Jasem, isn't he?" – the principal reverted to the earlier point.

"Yes," – he paused briefly. "They're a funny twosome. Polar opposites. The other day I was asking Mrs. Leaddus about their routine at home, you know, these questions I wonder about sometimes, and she was telling me how they eat every evening by candlelight at the diningroom table. Compare that with eating alone! What's more, Jasem has a brother and sister his age, you can just see them all crawling around the bedroom piling blocks into senseless buildings. Sometimes I talk to Jasem at our entrance ramp in the morning: he just nods and never looks you in the eye – way too shy, but Damien responds promptly, directly, although, actually, it was an exception, but there was that one time a few years ago when he would suddenly start crying, that was the only one, and when I asked him what was up, footballsized tears streaked his cheeks."

"Do you know his family well? What happened to his father, if I may ask?"

The question set the guard's mind awhirl:

"That's a strange story I don't know all the details to but something happened. I heard she went off her rocker, couldn't live with him anymore and forced him to leave. I didn't know them at all like I do now, but he went out of town and hasn't come back."

"It must be difficult," the principal said.

Mr. Sottloy riffed again:

"What's crazy is he may not be one of the best in the school but Mrs. Leaddus told me he's definitely among the better ones in her class and with no dad helping him in math, with a mom coming home too late and tired to help him in reading and spelling, its staggering that he isn't being suspended constantly or at least forgetting his homework every other day. He's not the child prodigy starring in the circus at eleven like Melvin but I wouldn't bet against him: he will probably get as far as his sister even if she was a little better I think, at least his mom says she was a little better though, you never know and, anyway, what's it matter, he might be better off without too much *education*. You all know how I feel about our revered institutions of higher learning. Let him become a clerk or a guard or anything but you, Ms. Folow, that's the last thing we want, more people like you, principals who come into the teachers' lounge and interrogate the security guard."

BOOK FIVE

(1) DISAGREEMENT

Because being an only child depressed or egotized a kid, and because without a sibling close to him in age, Damien is an only child of the second order, the kind that cannot be spoiled because attention is divided, in his case, by two, and not lonely, because his sister is always around, but also spoiled and lonely because he does not resemble a child with a sister because she is so much older and of a different gender.

An only child of the first order would certainly be the principal's daughter: an only child with two parents receives too much attention, but this only child with a single parent turns into the sole substance of a mother's life, especially if she does not believe in her work. You can imagine the scene in the evening, the remote-control fireplace sparkling in orange and yellow flame, the light that licks the ebony of life, and her mother only has her only child and her only child only has her single mother so no fat batteries fly through windowpanes and there's no father to swing the wrecking ball. They become more like a husband and wife, which spoils the child who is too young to understand the relationship, requiring her mother to make sacrifices and becoming used to a partner who concedes. The other primary upshot often observed is the child gets annoyed by this attention, wants to be left alone or wishes he had a brother or sister to play with. We've definitely noticed this in Damien: that's why he likes Jasem.

From a parent's perspective, the fear of losing that child exceeds everything else, magnified by an environment where children seem to regularly go missing. As we saw in book 1 chapter 1, all the adults heard and discussed the latest missing child, and the guard even hints at the hysteria in such cases.

It is very important for you to understand something here, and not just here, but across contemporary literature: in this novel, various so-called personal narrators base their opinions, like this one about only children, on what the given narrator thinks is fact, but is often actually opinion-disguised-as-fact. This undermining of certainty occurs when narration and discourse take the same tense, which we see in some shifting of indirect discourse to the past tense in this narrative. Anywhere else, like the present tense novel, where discourse and narration appear in the same time, we will also face this uncertainty.

So this is my opinion, perhaps formed incorrectly, and certainly influenced by Austen. I have never been able to convince my counterpart, the principal's personal narrator, that her child is spoiled, and that's because her view has been shaped by Woolf along with commercial values. Furthermore, whenever we narrators sit around and share our views in these chapter one intermezzos, someone always argues that his, her or my opinion is based on incorrect information. This is exactly what happens when we discuss Damien with the security guard. He says Damien doesn't watch television or eat microwave dinners. He says I have confused facts with opinion that looks like facts. – I mean look at Jasem in the project playground. Is he seeing the men come and go, the women push baby carriages or is it his narrator? And then when we have the father's narrator with his Poeian mindset, he argues that it is completely irrelevant whether a child is spoiled or not, either way he simply exists with a certain character trait, while the focus should be on the fantasies and extremes. Then, of course, we repeatedly have Jasem and Damien's narrators, each with their perspective, so while I, the teacher's narrator, try to justify my opinion on this story, it is nearly impossible to distinguish fact from opinion. After all, according to the guard, that funny sitcom with the five children comes on NBC, not ABC. It looked like a fact in narration, but if Sottloy is right, then it's (mistaken) discourse. Or to take a less trivial example from book 3 chapter 3, the teacher thought Damien's discomfort originated with his mother or sister, and yet again subjective discourse surfaces in the guise of objective narration and undermines my ability to generalize off of it. But then the situation gets even more murky with some discourse shifted and some left in the present. This lends authority to a character's opinion, which used to be reserved for the authorial narrator, and destroys all our historical bearings.

Here, for instance, is a typical case of boundaries blurred between the father and his narrator:

(2) THE FATHER'S STORY; THE SON (JASEM) AND THE FATHER IN THE PLAYGROUND.

Damien's father had left his family a few years ago, when the boy was eight. Personal matters · had been directly responsible · for his departure · though he had also · been fed up with life in the city. It was reminiscent · of his feeling after school: send me anywhere · but back to the city. So he went · to a small town · and worked odd jobs · uncertain what · he wanted to do · in the future. Initially he pondered · setting up a nonprofit · and publishing an antiestablishment journal · with a social bent · but the obstacles · proved greater · than the force of his will · as he became · increasingly attracted · to the more relaxed · less uptight mentality · of the local people. And adopting ·this lifestyle, he gradually started · questioning his preconceptions of work · and career. Why should you · stress about promotions, success · and recognition · when it · wouldn't ultimately get you · any further than whiling · away the hours in a shoe store? And the shoe assistant · might be at peace with himself, whereas the careerist · would always be dissatisfied, always want more...

With this new attitude he · soon went to work · at the local shoe outlet. He enjoyed · arranging the displays creatively · and the promotions · so they · would appeal to customers. The important information · on the shoes · he learned, helped by his own · experience playing basketball. But most of all, instead of feeling inferior or superfluous, he · took pride in assisting · the customers, in treating them as he · would treat himself, in being sincerely polite and courteous, which they recognized, to his astonishment. For he saw a difference in people's reaction. They responded. And this response was enough for him, enough to let him return to the city and settle into a modest life. It was in this frame of mind that he spoke to Jasem in the project playground:

"Don't worry, we aren't · going to hurt you."

Jasem didn't respond.

"I'm Damien's · father. Do you · know my son?"

– Damien, occurred to him; – yes, – he answered.

"I thought so. I saw you · with him · here · yesterday. Where is he · today?"

– I'm not sure?

"Was he · in school today?"

– I saw him in the lunch room.

"Hmm. Well, can you · keep a secret?"

Silence, confusion.

"I mean," the man continues. "I need you · to pass a note · on to him. And I need you · to keep it a secret."

He extended · a folded piece of paper, gingerly, but promptly. The son, that was not his son, was frightened · and anxious. His left elbow quivered · though he tried · to keep his hand · from succumbing. Was he thinking: Is he going to snatch me? The paper · eyed shyly, the boy · must have thought: the man · seems · nice enough. And I like · his smile · and his eyes · don't frighten me, and Damien · is my friend, and the man · keeps his distance, and · if he · is Damien's father, he · has · to be a good guy, and never mind that we · have never met.

"Look, I'll leave it · here · on the bench. It would mean a lot · if you gave it to him," the father · said, placing the note · on the wood · and walking away · back · to where they sat before.

The siren wailed.

– Return to your room. Everyone back to your spot. This is a...

Metal crashes, guttural baritones and clangs reverberate through the corridors and chairs drag along the ground. Guards eyed their subjects with latent attentiveness. There was only one subject that interested him. The boy glanced at the note one final time, peeked at the man timidly, and swiped it. Up.

Down. The concrete wall, the tree, he dashed with his head lowered before it was too late, before the clear yard with its supervisors skewered him. He planted his foot in the flowerless dirt by the shrub, springing onto the fence. His skinny legs toeing him up over beyond, past his lunch box, across the concrete courts and toward the house of correducation.

(3) THE GUARD CATCHES THE SON (JASEM), WHO FEARS PUNISHMENT.

– Jasem, come here, boomed Mr. Sottloy's voice.

What? he thought startled. Mr. Sottloy never spoke to him after recess. – And silently he went up to the muscular, intimidating man.

– Where were you?

The son looked at his feet.

– You weren't in the yard.

The son did not lift his eyes or dare to contradict him.

– I saw you climbing over the fence.

Punishment was coming.

– Didn't you hear the announcement today?

He nodded.

– Don't you know that you're not allowed to be in that part anyway?

He nodded again.

– Do you go there often?

"It was the first time," he lied sheepishly.

– What's you're mother going to say? What will she think?

"I, I dunno."

– Go on up to class and think it over. That was very dangerous, forbidden. You won't have any recess for a week.

Now it was really over. And no recess isn't the worst. The worst is not being able to climb the fence. He trudged up the stairs. They will be penned in the box, will have to go try something new, be laughed at, teased all over again or bored. The fuzzy glass repelled the sunlight from the stairs; his lunch box banged against the banister, but only the thermos was left to clatter onto the cement landing. And then he realized! Gasped. Horrified: he had to tell his mom! Tell his mom!!! Who would tell his dad! They were in their bedroom, his dad stretched out on the bed in the middle of the room, his mom seated at the foot, near her dresser with its flowery looking-glass in the center. It was their endofday conversation after he kissed his love hello in the chairrailled foyer. But this evening his mom told his dad that Sottloy told her he has been sneaking out of the yard.

His eyes became blurry: his father would drag him into the bedroom, kicking and screaming: you don't do that, son. That's unacceptable. Nothing more, kicking screaming, feeling: the pain implodes his skin, the burning spreads over his bottom. His face flushed, his blood pulsed deluged... The hand rises again, he squirms on the bed, trying to wiggle out of a direct spank, his head thrashing back and forth. His father cranes to the ceiling, his long arms ideal for swat after swat like a wrecking ball swinging, gaining momentum, speed, penduling further and further. A hand presses into his lower back. He can't move, can only kick his legs, kicks, kicks and crash. The metal smites those glassy eyes to tears. Now go to your room and think about what you've done. You're grounded for two weeks. – And in his confusion he nearly missed Damien by the swinging doors:

– Jasem! – his friend called him back to earth.

"Ugh, huh, oh, Damien, hey, where were you?" Jasem asked.

– With the guidance councilor, – Damien replied.

"Oh... Well, here's a note for you. Your dad gave it to me in our playground."

Damien stared at the folded piece of paper gummed shut.

"And, they nabbed me," Jasem added. "Mr. Sottloy. He saw me climbing over the fence. I got detention for a week."

The words had no effect.

Why was that? He thought he will be sad or upset or something. We won't be able to go there anymore. They'll be watching. – But Damien just stared at the note.

"What is it?" the son ejaculated.

– Ah... – Damien stammered and did not finish his sentence, distractedly walking away.

(4) THE TEACHER LEARNS ABOUT THE FATHER'S PLAN TO SEE THE BOY (DAMIEN).

On the way back to his classroom Damien unpasted the note from his father. It was · from his father. His father · was · back in town · had been for a few days. He thought of his mom: He should not · see his father · if he tried · to meet him. Those were her instructions. And here · was a note. He thought of his dad. Readazed printed letters blurred. Hardly understood them. Got only the gist: I · outside · after school.

He walked into the classroom, but no sooner had he sat down than his teacher called him to the front.

"Is everything okay?" she asked.

He mumbled yes.

"Did you go to the guidance councilor?"

– Yes.

It was too odd a surprise to be left at this, and she did not let him return to his seat. He was holding his right index finger again, but clenching it so tightly and unconsciously that his round eyes, which might otherwise have recalled the principal's that morning, could not belie his anxiety. She saw that he was now scared, that he even looked worse in front of her than when he had entered the room, with such equivocal responses and a tremor in his voice as hardly made it possible for him to respond.

Into the hall she escorted him, to talk a little more privately.

"Damien, listen, has anything happened? At home? Or here? You aren't yourself today."

– I'm okay, he said uncertainly.

"Hmm... Is something on your mind? Did a classmate bother you? Did you have a problem with the guidance councilor? You can tell me."

He burst: tears, those footballsized tears streaked his cheeks.

"Can you tell me what happened? Maybe I can help."

– My, my, my father · has · come · back. He · he's waiting for me.

And he handed her the note penciled in block letters:

Hello Damien,

I'm moving back to the city. I wanted to see you. You know your mother won't allow it. I just wanted to say hello. Treat you to hotdogs. I'll be outside after school.

"When did you receive this?" she asked.

– Just now, he replied.

She did not hesitate:

"Damien, honey, stay in the classroom when we go to dismissal. Then we'll figure out something. Does that sound good?"

He nodded with a most serious look, but seeming to recollect himself, stopped sobbing, and began to wipe away the tears with the cuff of his shirt pulled over his balled hand. As he calmed down, with very little talk on either side, they continued to stand, both of them disconcerted, their minds distracted by the ominous father lurking outside. This gave her time to consider her options, and she was by no means certain what exactly they were on returning to a room where the kids who were supposed to be reading had decided that talking was more interesting. Only here and there did she enjoy the sight of a student trying to concentrate on their book. Primarily the best ones anyway:

"Tom, Dick, get back to your seats. Harry, silence! Anya, stop talking! Read your books. I'll be coming round to check in a moment."

What a headache: Damien's in tears because his father has appeared and is plotting an illicit reunion outside; half the classroom, even her monitor, is raising the roof after being left alone for two minutes, and that following lunch, when they should have expended their energy. It recalled her visceral response to criticism of public school teaching: I think a lot about your feelings about the futility of working with kids, I do, but there are always those kids who do want to do well and get ahead, and they certainly need to be attended to. And do we really want a country of illiterates and people who can't find big ideas in books and think about them? I know it is a stretch for many of them, but I will never be able to live comfortably with the fact that this country is so rich and prosperous yet it doesn't try to make the most of all of its citizens. So I continue to choose good books, put kids in book clubs and cultivate deeper thinking and conversations. And then I just sort of hold my breath and hope for the best! These kids are so young, and they have so much school they still have to get through, that we've got to try to give them the tools and the motivation to engage in it.

I do. It was almost a motto. She didn't wilt under the negativity all around her. Especially from her principal. And as the years went by, she worried more and more about the effect of this negativity on their very talented, special, thoughtful staff members. The principal was the major reason that another teacher was leaving. When she was good, she was very, very good, but that was pretty infrequent these days, and mostly they missed having her be her strong, leaderlike self. What I have come to realize is that the most important thing I do in this complicated school (and all schools are complicated organisms!) is keep a positive outlook and encourage people and appreciate them. It is my sense of hope that keeps me going – hope that we can make things better for kids and help them do better, hope that teachers will be more rigorous with themselves planning lessons and with expecting a lot from kids. But the teacher who's leaving doesn't have so much hope any more and that is why he has to leave. He can't work without it, and you can't generate it in a vacuum. Unless Folow does her part of providing leadership and accountability you are working in a vacuum, and that just isn't enough.

When her prep came in the afternoon, the principal asked to see her. Surprised, she thought of Damien and the morning announcement. She had not asked about his talk with the guidance councilor, nor did she know exactly what he meant with "just now." But they couldn't be aware of much. If the principal didn't want to talk about that conundrum or the danger of disappearing pupils, then it had to be one of the staff problem cases. Yesterday she had been raging through classes writing up teachers, going ballistic in the wake of the bad grade they had given her for the year before. This was one of those terrible moments, she had seen it coming two days ago, when she glanced over the results, and, alas, efforts to calm her were futile.

In front of her office she gazed at the inside: swiveling stools for the secretaries, white walls, a metal grill protecting the windows, tubelights blaring down all over the ceiling, a room-length desk with a metal base for a platter that was dented and scribbled on. In some ways it's much worse than the classrooms themselves, hers anyway, with its bright green and red and blue bookcases, freshly painted every year. The desks and chairs are standard, the blackboard too, but rows of books line the shelves, and stacks rise not to the heights of hand turkeys scattered across the panes, but maybe to the eyes of the kids.

BOOK SIX

(1) SCHOOL, PRISON, CHAOS.

All the same, it is a crummy place – the school. Despite its halls, rooms and yards spilling energetic boys and girls. Maybe they are too energetic, too out of control with their sugar cereal, sodas and high-cholesterol cafeteria lunch. Colossal block tiles below those fluorescent lights waft a depressing aura over the corridors; the gray linoleum floor rounds out the wall-to-wall incarceration with dull pink metal doors smashed open by stainless steel funneling pupils into a darkgray abysswell. But the acme is going to the bathroom: doorless stalls at the end reveal toilets teeming with unflushed pooh and pee; toilet paper strewn on the floor and seats and flusher; by the urinals yellowish stains have dried in streams from as high as the likes of the boy and the son and hundreds of other kids could reach with their little peckers aimed for the ceiling, the pool collecting not by the drain but the top ledge and dripping down the side... The motley group of students who create this mess often embody it too. Though they are a florilegium unto themselves. Even if some of the older ones smell bad, even if many look like minigangsters, even if these tiny kids seem to represent no great future, and their excitement fails to alter your impression, you have to acknowledge that they bring a heterogeneity that far surpasses the private schools and their sleek floors, varnished entries and clicking locks. Besides their diversity, many of them don't always speak English, some mix English with Spanish, while others speak with such an accent that you might have called it Spanglish. And what's more, their influence is so pervasive that the nonlatino kids also pronounce words with the stress on the wrong vowel or an odd intonation, implied comma, like the father, in the middle, adverbs in peculiar places, adjectives as adverbs: How you doing? I'm good.

(2) THE PRINCIPAL AND HER VIEWS.

The principal did not take interest in the minor details of running a school. With her administrative responsibilities she resembled more of a corporate manager, but handling teachers, secretaries, custodians, parents and representatives from the central office rather than accountants, supervisors and suppliers of a business. She watched her colleagues descend into that nebulous drain of mediocrity where to listen to others is impossible and yet their silence instills such anxiety in those who watch them that they always endeavor at least to listen to them with their heart as one listens to the echo of once passionate words until it is swallowed by accessories to ameliorate a wretched profession. In her opinion almost any job had affinities to a data processor's, with the data taking different forms – hers lasting from eight to four as she sat at a desk, with a computer, phone and fax machine, encircled by family photos. It was what her ex-husband did at the firm, only she had one significant advantage: he had slowed to a stop early in his career, whereas she had succeeded in swerving ahead until recently.

While she thumbed through an article, smiling, it seemed as if that echo bounced off the walls again. Because she was pleased, she read somewhat attentively: Kids instinctively balance the needs of the community with those of the ruling class. The authors argued that an individual's social skills may not improve his academic performance, but ensure support within the community. This retention of a strong bond to one's peers affirms the primacy of the subculture and maintains unity. The support organizations, designed to encourage teenagers to stay in school, not get pregnant and go to college, are counterproductive because they fail to consider the historical importance of ulterior values in divergent communities.

Why do they pity them? That was the impression she had when she heard the activists. Poor impoverished people, they seemed to be saying, as if their own evisceration had been partly pitying the impoverished, and the energy in them, their resolve to save the world again, derived from pity. And it was wrong, the principal thought; it was one of those misunderstandings. The largely middle- and upperclass Euro-American idealist who promotes these social initiatives presumes that their value system is paradigmatic and seeks to proselytize the deviants. Much more than helping youths in the community, such support actually fulfilled a need in the organizer and gave her a sense of purpose. Comparatively there are not many ethnic groups left at the end of the twentieth century, which means only the strongest have survived and you have to assume that groups which have survived such horrific persecution and repression as the non-Europeans here count among the strongest of the strong. Even this rhetoric of power and strength the majority foisted on the minority nowadays intended primarily to tell those boys and girls that they were strong and powerful enough to break with the traditions of their community and join the happy middle-class majority.

A knock interrupted her.

"Hi, Jane, thanks for the advice this morning. At least they didn't bombard me," said the principal.

"You're welcome, of course, anytime," Mrs. Leaddus replied.

"I just wanted to tell you that Mr. Sottloy saw your son climbing over the fence outside the yard. He's going to get detention for a week."

(3) THE TEACHER'S PAST AND PRESENT FEAR.

She stood transfixed: on such a day, on this particular day, her shy sweet little boy with his bowl haircut climbed over a fence to another playground!? It was hard to believe.

... And the teacher recalled that day many years ago when she went to the department store with a couple of her classmates to steal clothes. Never before had it occurred to her that friends might get her to shoplift – since only bad boys and girls did that and certainly they were not people she associated with. Yet there she was, excited, tingling, preparing to take part. They walked through the revolving doors as any customer would and, separating, strolled past the racks of merchandise. After shoving a blouse in the armpit of her coat, she was surprised to notice her heart pounding. The sound of it distracted her, and she felt incapable of doing anything except staring at the objects on display. Soon she recovered enough to continue down the row, idly pulling out an item here and there to give the impression she was considering a purchase. Still, it was with a sense of relief that she saw her classmate coming up to her. Now there was someone to talk to and that would mitigate her nervous concern – reassure her that everything was okay.

– They're on to us, – the classmate whispered close by. – If you've taken anything, dump it.

Her arm twitched instinctively as she stood alone a moment later. A couple employees milled by bins not far away, though also not paying any particular attention to her or anyone else. To the left and right were distracted couples at the end of the aisle. She could dump the blouse right there – surely that classmate had more experience than she did, surely he knew what he was talking about – but you can't chicken out now, she said to herself, anyway that couple might see me and report it. Elsewhere, each aisle has at least one person. Tricky.

– Miss, could you come with us please, – she heard all of a sudden behind her back. And as she followed the plainclothes man toward the corner of the store, she saw others accompanying her friends to the same place. Everyone was doomed, and when they asked her if she had anything, she impulsively tossed the blouse on the table. They searched her two friends and then wrote down their names and numbers. There wouldn't be any fine this time. They were just going to call their parents. And they were prohibited from coming to the store again.

"They're going to call home," she thought flustered as they parted outside. She had to tell her mother before. But how!? A gush of shame swished over her; awaiting was an embarrassing moment. She tried to anticipate the scene in her head: she would stall till her mother was engaged in the bedroom and snag her there. That would spare her the request to have a special conversation, and removing that awkwardness would allow her to say: Mom, I did something dumb, I was with my friends in the department store and they prodded me into stealing with them. Then we were caught, and they're going to call you... But instead of an unemotional statement of the facts, she had been forced to improvise. Her mom did not go to her room at once, so as the danger increased that the phone would ring, she had to take the inconvenient initiative.

"Mom, I need to talk to you," she said in the kitchen.

"Sure, sweety, one sec. We'll go to the bedroom."

The question, her mom's kindness, the thought that her mom was now thinking about what was on her daughter's mind upset the little that was left of her initial composure, and as soon as they closed the door, the weight of the situation fell on her full force: she burst out sobbing and gasped between tears: "Mom, I got caught stealing."

The embarrassment prompted her to recall the precarious reality imposed on her as she went back upstairs. And this reality was not like the cafeteria server she had taught reading at college. The outcome had been open with her: if she didn't learn anything, she enjoyed the company at least. Now the upshot was disaster should something go wrong: a child would break down and she would be fired. Here she might have a boy too terrified to leave the building, a father hunting him and potentially no other family member to be reached. She couldn't say: it wouldn't just be tears, embarrassment, discomfort; it could be criminal charges.

With the afternoon wearing on, this mild twinge of doubt did not dampen her mood, but intensified her concern. Was she going to inform the principal? It seemed that concealing from her principal what had been shared with her in the hope of *her* help, though it required she break the rules, did not extenuate her distress. Should she call his mother? If no one was home, was she prepared to walk him to his building? Then she put aside the fleet of questions. From thought or discussion she knew she could not benefit, their ideas or assumption of control would add to her distress, while the problem would see a resolution neither from contemplation nor from suggestions. She would proceed until a flashing red light signaled the end. The school buses were beginning to arrive, creating traffic jams on the street. Children glanced toward the window and had more trouble concentrating. A slight buzz, rising and falling with no apparent source, made her hush potential culprits.

She did not send a note to the principal. The students went with her to dismissal, and the boy stayed locked in the classroom, left understanding that she would be back in fifteen minutes. After her boys and girls had lined up and dispersed, after she had collected her own children and quickly headed for home – three blocks away, past the men lurking in packs by the project, past her principal near them, across the avenue with the crossing guard, through the valley created by two more projects, along the Junior High School with teenagers twice their height, in huge baggy pants, cursing and hollering up and down the block.

At home, in front of the Gulag literature and studies in Christianity:

"Mom, I need..." – the son repeated his mother's words of many years ago, before he was born, before... as soon as... before. They went briefly to her room. The awkwardness of the moment was no less for the parent forced to strictness out of concern for values or some other abstract future. She was better off alone, and her good sense would lead her so her confidence did not waver, her optimism still as steadfast as, with dilemmas so threatening and so ominous, it was possible for them to be... On returning, her head lowered, her feet carrying her posthaste back past the "drugstore," St. Catherine's, back past the trash heap, back past the same crossing guard who would be there twenty years later, back past all those students who would be lucky if their future only strayed as far as the crossing guard's. In her safe haven, her room, she called Damien's mother, but no one picked up. I guess I'm going to walk him home myself, she thought to herself. I don't know what will happen if I run into *him*. – What if *he*'s standing on the corner where those lechers are always leering. What will I say? He sure isn't my kid.

(4) THE BOY'S (DAMIEN) PRESENT AND FUTURE; THE SON'S (JASEM) FUTURE.

But Damien refused to leave the room. He cried, shook, as if his father stood in front of him smiling with a cold sore near the wart on his chin so repulsing the boy that he succumbed to violent retchings. The shaking did not stop and seemed to intensify despite the assurance that they will stay put. His father is pacing in the house park, with pigeons pecking at crumbs rolling through the dust, clucking around a woman to their left, her plastic bags only less grubby than the homeless man wheeling his in a shopping cart adrift. One bag has split open, books strewn about the curb, on it, below it, on dry concrete and a puddle in the asphalt. He picks them up, his bascart blocking the sidewalk ramp. The books dripping. His father rages, arms flailing, words directed at no one in particular, son embarrassed and wishing he were dead. "Goddamit, mother, what d', no, can't." Another vagabond sits on a bench across the way and takes off his shirt, his bare body backed against the shrubbery with its rats, mice and stunted vegetation growing in cigarette butt soil with crack fertilizer. Locals look askance from one to the other, loop around the bagman and pause as far from the fall sun tanner as possible.

Silence reigned in the classroom – when he stopped whimpering. The lights of a last school bus still flashed in the windows of the highrise across the street, though the shouts had abated. Below a dismally low ceiling stood clusters of desks beseamed with initials, names and comical characters. To his right the teacher leaned forward, feet firmly planted, waiting on the phone, a short distance from the massy egress that communicated with the hall and could, at any moment, usher in an unwelcome intrusion. His gaze hovered on the bald eagle of stupendous proportions above the blackboard, its wings capable of carrying him far away from Hurston, Tolstoy, from his side, through the park, over the wall to the other side with Seneca and no faux chauffeurs. Away. He hangs on for dear life, thank God, it is only a nightmare – he flies over the trees, sighs deeply. Does he have a fever? No, he's been airlifted out, away. His body feels thrashed, his mind sapped of all sustenance. Jesus, he exclaims. I can go home, dally by the White Truck, hang out on the corner... go home. Really. He shook like a leaf. Like a leaf as he realized he might be the little mouse the hawk hunted. It was no eagle. It was a hawk hurtling down to smite the mouse, the rat, whatever rodent he was as he scurried under the scaffolding and into the crack funneling into the subway, into the infernal black hole damning him to perdition in the depths below the city, the dank tunnels frothing with fiends spraying graffiti on walls, stomping defenseless creatures with steel-tipped combat boots like the steel wheels rolling, rumbling, spinning, shuttling, screeching, crushing, down the tracks and over his fragile, ever so delicate young bones as his mom raced uptown like Jasem racing across the street to have the last talk with his childhood friend:

"Damien, Damien," Jasem shouted from afar, the excitement betrayed in his voice.

Now a middle-aged man with the same sable hair, pale complexion and kind eyes looked in the direction of these exuberant shouts you don't hear from adults. A smile crossed his face and vanished.

"Damien, crazy, it's been so many years, how are you? Are you well? Is your girlfriend/wife well? What's going on?"

And this outburst of enthusiastic questions scintillated his eyes:

"Alright, I'm doing okay, daughter's doing well. How about you?"

"It's been tough, we definitely didn't become adults at a good time."

"That's for sure! How's your family?..."

The back and forth continued until Damien asked what happened after high school:

"I got more and more frustrated," Jasem replied. "It started in the last couple years there and ended ultimately with silence and isolation. Nobody was at fault, except maybe you for encouraging me to climb over the fence and throw eggs at yuppies. But, no, that's a joke, it's just one of those things that's inside some people. For a while it was really hard for me to talk, but through a stroke of brief luck and some force I relearned it. To tell you the truth, I think there's a paradox in prosperity, America or protestant society. I can't quite put my finger on it, but many of my difficulties vanished when I was abroad. Do you notice any difference between your emotional-mental state of mind here and in your country, for instance?"

"No, I don't think so. It's hard here and hard there."

"Have you ever lived there for a long period of time?"

"No, that might be it, too. I'm there on vacation, so it probably makes the place even better."

"That's another question I keep asking myself: do you think that difficulty in life makes the experience of living more tangible? With more highs (and lows), because you really appreciate the good moments?" – Jasem smiled at the likelihood of his question being perceived as strange.

"I haven't thought about it that way, but there may be something to what you're saying. We definitely like to party."

"Okay, I won't interrogate you, I'm sorry, I'm just curious. Let me type in your number and email."

"Give me yours, too," said Damien.

"But one more question, please," requested Jasem, "what ever happened to Melvin and Anya?"

"The story with Melvin is awful: his girlfriend got pregnant from another guy, and he committed suicide at 20 or 21. And with Anya, I'm not completely sure, but I think she went into commercial editing like me, but I could be wrong..."

BOOK SEVEN

(1) THE SCENE AFTER SCHOOL; DIFFERENCES IN CHARACTER.

What had been bedlam in the school yard at dismissal twenty minutes ago had now organized into cliques that the authorities were encouraging to go home. That little squirt Anya lugging a backpack thicker than herself raced ahead, crashed into another girl, stopped abruptly, whirled and took off again. Melvin whistled across the yard and caused his friend to veer. Pent-up energy released; a yell outshouted a shriek: teachers scanned the yard; Mr. Sottloy bulwarked the south side with the white truck; the principal paced the north side with the project; a few officers patrolled the surrounding streets in their car; Jessica held up the children at Hurston and walked them across.

The boy's father kept in motion, too. By the buses where lines lurched with the shoves aimed at positioning the bullies closer to the front so they could sit closer to the back – far from the bus driver – far from identification as the cause of the spitballs and fighting, – by these rattails, the father now stood – squinting to single out his boy. But no boy did he find. At least not his own – since when it was already too late – he recognized the teacher's son – though the bowlcut kid just gave him a quizzical look and followed his mom toward the avenue – so he didn't have to vanish into the crowd like the three siblings: their hair straighter and thinner, their clothes either less fashionable than those with the latest designer jackets and pants or finer than those with acidwashed jeans and somehow oldfashioned sweaters. They were right in the middle, also in size, build, height, with no external or visible difference except that pale skin.

Yet still they were light years removed from their classmates, even their friends, even if not one of them, not even the oldest, had the vaguest notion of what separated him from them. If the question had been asked, he would have said: "I'm the only boy with blond hair in my class." That was it. It would never have occurred to him that hair color was immaterial, that what set him so apart lay outside his appearance and inside the pedigree, upbringing, profession of his parents, his genes, his stable, secure life. So on the way home he stared at his feet, like a good child, and shrunk when he saw the principal, her imposing figure prowling by the project playground, for the principal was not twirling the hair behind her right earlobe: she was all attention. With her suit jacket flapping apace to her rapid footfall, she offered a sharp contrast to the informally dressed mothers of Tom, Dick and Harry. Beyond fashion, her tense face, with her lips pulled tight, illustrates exactly why Damien's dad could rightly prefer to work in a shoe store or why Mr. Sottloy sits at a desk watching – you have a chance to enjoy life, relax not only your facial muscles, but also your mind. You can act naturally and be in harmony with your nature. For the principal was so tense at that moment that when Mr. Sottloy saw her a half hour later he wanted to say, as the teacher often does to her husband, in the shadow of the bookcase made at home...: Relax!

(2) THE SECURITY GUARD'S FUTURE AND PAST.

Mr. Sottloy was the antithesis of the principal, at least as far as demeanor. With equal attention he visually pursued the course traced by the kids bounding toward the White Truck from which they then leapfrogged in their sugared exuberance. Yet he watched with an endearing detachment that said he would shield a boy from a wrecking ball, a girl from a kidnapping, but that no man was capable of being everywhere at once:

One place he will be is between Rembrandt and Hurston on another fall evening next year. It is a couple hours later, when the sun has set, scarfs wrapped, wind blowing off the water, chasing the last leaves from the trees, the exhaust he did not notice as a life-long denizen. His thoughts drift off to past disrespect:

– Gramma, that's hideous, and he tossed his Christmas present in a heap and didn't thank her...

– You guys might as well be part of the establishment, just think about yourselves. Why don't you go to demonstrations, struggle for our poor and unlucky brothers, he criticized his parents. Your just like everyone else: part of the problem, not the solution.

Absorbed in his youthful rebellion, he barely sees the strange, uncomfortable look and does not see the tense hand clutching her bag. But the odd scene of three small, muscular men - one behind her, one to the left and one to the right – and the latter leaning in, seemingly aggressive with his squinted eyes and hulked shoulders – this causes him to pause:

"Mrs. Leaddus, hello!" he says stopping firmly in front of them.

Startled, she looks up.

Startled, the three men survey the intruder.

"Is everything okay?" Mr. Sottloy asks.

One of the men replies:

"Sir, we're talking with her. Can you please let us continue?"

"I wasn't asking you," Mr. Sottloy replied coldly.

The men size up their equally well-built opponent, his shaved-head and bulging arms. Glances exchanged, uncertainly, they begin to continue down the street. But that is not enough for the security guard. Angrily he yells:

"Leave people alone!! You hear me!"

One saunters back:

"Watch your mouth, honkey lover! We'll break you like a branch if we want."

"Get a life!" Sottloy responds.

And while Mrs. Leaddus is safe, that evening four other women in various parts of the city are mugged, their wallets torn out of their purses, purses torn from shoulders on dark cross streets, along three-story high fences by playgrounds, the men, sometimes single men, springing out of dark nooks reeking of trash or pee, sometimes in small groups pursuing the pedestrian till she turns down one of those dimly lit sidewalks away from the safety of bodegas and their grungy yellow awnings with suspended cardboard signs and banners over exterior glass walls with product stickers and the backs of the items inside.

So Mr. Sottloy shirked from nothing, yet if he did not see something or if failure accompanied those efforts like it had in his attempt to have children with his partner or in his college education that he broke off in irritation, he remained unphased, sizing up the unpleasantry as a sign from God. That's the way it had been at school. His irritation gradually became so oppressive that it had to be a hint he was meant for something else. Learning and thinking were fine. He had gone to school precisely because they were fine. But when he was there and thinking about the theory behind rendering consciousness in narratives or comparing readings of Jane Austen he revolted not completely at first but completely in the end: What does that have to do with life?!

To top it off, there were all those pseudointellectuals bandying about their uninformed ideas so cockily through so many "likes" and arm movements and "you know what I mean" that he wondered how he could possibly be at a top ranked college, and one day they had even read an essay by Derrida where not one person in a class of fifteen had noticed that two pages in the middle were missing, and he hadn't known a single student whose eyes lit up at a subject related to the material they studied – eyes lit up for other reasons: criticism of the professor, curriculum, students, cafeteria, coffee, milk, cream, sugar, but the exuberance for criticism was nothing like the fire that burned when they flirted outside the library or in the coffee shop or especially at parties where they had a chance of hooking up – the highlight of all highlights: sex. *There* was real passionate intensity, so he stood at an overlook on the road after his second year and decided to drop out, return home, and settle into exactly the lifestyle everyone at college praised to the skies without living for one single minute after graduation – though many simulated it during their four years in the ivory tower.

As a security guard he is relatively uninhibited and his mind is almost totally free for most of the day. When responsibilities ensnare it, they predominately mean he has to observe children, as at lunch, or play with them, as in the yard. Interaction with children however stimulated his mind, even rescued him from what might have been the occasional unoptimistic depression that comes with contemplation. This he often noticed at lunch on Monday. Watching the kids enter the school in the morning is not enough. He needs those two hours tossing the football across the yard. Then his thoughts reached heights that made him pity all the professionals and academics and their need for status. But there were also times when he could vaguely relate. Those were the slightly demoralizing moments at his desk: he would watch a man from the central office overlook him or have to take commands. A humiliating experience, but still, he got over it quickly, and, what's more, this guy overlooking him in the yard now isn't from that central office They didn't come in leather jackets.

"Can I help you?" Mr. Sottloy asked.

– I'm looking for Damien. I'm his father.

They went to the principal's office.

(3) THE PRINCIPAL'S PAST.

She sat in her pristine office organized and orderly. It had become a microcosm of her profession, which she especially enjoyed with her awareness of why you wore sneakers in the car and pumps in public: clarity among chaos, prospects where others have few, security in a climate of anxiety. To them she was superior, as she had been in her years at Teacher's College, when, with no difficulty, she distinguished herself from the mostly local class by assimilating the material more quickly and filtering out the superfluous with ease – ensuring top grades, access to the influential instructors and student teacher positions in promising schools. She was superior to everyone, as she had demonstrated by being able to purchase a colonial house with a Jacuzzi, no-maintenance fireplace... And oh, her beau, too, that was the catch of all catches. In her early twenties she sat at home and talked with old friends:

And so then he got this offer from Jack, and Jill said it was an offer you can't turn down although he would be sorry to lose such a talented young man... Oh and it's terrible with his mother, he's had to change his phone number and conceal it from her because she won't take medication for her mental disorder and calls up the office screaming and raging... Yeah, he graduated from Yale with a degree in history, but they hired him at the investment bank, taught him what he needed to know... He's very good at selling, at convincing clients to buy... You can't imagine how much stress he's under, but this summer we're going to Italy, to Rome, Venice and Florence, Sicily in 9 days. He's never been.

And she was infinitely superior the day she sealed her future victory:

"Look, Brian, we've tried everything and I think the only

thing left is for us to break up. We've got to do it, and if we're really meant for each other, we'll know it then."

He nodded, thoughtfully.

"I'm not saying I'm unhappy. I like you as much as ever, but it's not working. You know it as well as I."

He nodded, thoughtfully.

"So I'm going to move out."

He nodded, thoughtfully.

She continued with her friends a couple days later at a wedding:

We broke up. Yeah, I'm depressed. Yesterday, I just walked through our neighborhood, sat on stoops... It wasn't working. We hadn't had sex in two years. Still, he's so nice, he's even letting me keep his typewriter, it's really his, you see, he bought it, but I use it. And he's letting me move out slowly... No, he's not particularly upset, but sad, of course, I'm his high school sweetheart. Always will be, I suppose.

Her shiny white teeth flashed a smile.

He couldn't be nicer about it. Offered to move himself...

She relished the artificial remorse. Among the wine and champagne glasses, she felt isolated from the other guests, and able only to go on answering, reminiscing, wondering. The house, the yard, the evening, all seemed far from her. She had no reason to be here, she felt, no bond to it, whatever one said, and whatever one did, a good listener, an inspirational boost, was lost, as if the carpet that usually funneled her to the Orchestra Seating now forked off to the stairs. Second level? Third level? Fourth? How diffuse it was, how chaotic, how surreal, she thought, gazing into her wine glass. Brian gone; the future whipped out from under her. And we all gather at a wedding like this, on an evening like this, she said, looking across the yard.

Yet there are thoughts, feelings, and *feelings*, for she was rolling out a plan, without consultation, and the plan was to mire herself in pity and melancholy: it shows everyone the depth of her feelings. She will prove those doubters wrong when they say she's been scheming to marry a rich man since high school. With this break up she would stage the reconciliation, the next heartfelt talk, a shy kiss and quick question afterward:

- Is it okay?

He nods, thoughtfully.

- Look, Brian, we've tried everything and I think the only thing left is for us to move in together again. Then we'll know if...

He nods, thoughtfully.

... And soon they were entertaining guests on the palisades over the river, a band playing beside a bowery, a cab delivering the bride, groom and their parents, and a five-course dinner and ten-decker cake in the vaulted abbey of the renovated nineteenth century church. Quietly, to herself, she celebrated her alliance with a man she had singled out in high school and kept in touch with for the sole purpose of marrying if he became successful. That it deteriorated rapidly did not diminish the achievement, and they had a baby anyway, which gave them the needed meaning, but it could not forestall divorce forever, or the pothole for her career: the restructuring of education, the changing of the school system. She had prepared for a promotion from principal to district supervisor, and it no longer existed. The new position had different criteria and required different training. She had spent five years qualifying for... Nothing.

(4) THE PRINCIPAL AND GUARD TALK WITH THE FATHER.

A knock at the door brought the guard into her office with a stranger at his heels.

"Ms. Folow, this man is Damien's father. He's looking for his son."

The principal was all ears. Any trace of neutrality vanished from her thin lips. This might be the death knell:

"What do you mean by looking for his son?" Was he not in the yard at dismissal?"

The guard reassured her:

"I don't think the boy disappeared. At least there's no reason to presume that. His father came unexpectedly. Wanted to surprise him and was sure he would see him in the yard."

The father continued:

"Damien didn't know I · was coming. I · just arrived · yesterday."

"He was definitely here today," The guard confirmed.

The principal asked the father to take a seat, a little perplexed and worried, trying to recall what Sottloy had expounded a few weeks ago. I asked him about the family, but... but... what did he say?.. something happened... off her rocker... A glance through the records showed no order that prevented him from seeing the child. Nonetheless, here, a large man, who by all accounts did not pick up his son regularly, had appeared and was preparing to surprise him after school, unfortunately at exactly a time when skyscrapers of doubts surrounded every oddity. She needed some clarification:

"So you're the boy's father?"

"Yes," he replied.

"Your son is in the class of the best teacher: are you aware of that?"

"No, no."

"But he isn't doing that well, although not terribly either."

"Oh?"

"Yes. But how do you not know if he was in school today? Do you not live with him?

"No, I · was away. Me and my wife · don't live together. I · moved out."

...For a momentary obsession with his nextdoor neighbor he had paid with the dissolution of his marriage. She hadn't even attracted him as much as his wife of ten odd years, but this neighbor's detached coolness, her dispassionate expressions had slowly acted on him. When he broke through the severe façade, tightdrawn mouth relaxing and a sparkle scintillating across her eyes, it stimulated his mind and body. He became crazed: dreamed, fantasized, envisioned bold approaches, frenetic scenes, crude positions, heights of passion, ceilings he'd never reached. However, the day they supposedly reached them turned out to be a disappointment from the flight to the landing, though it was particularly the landing, as they lay there afterwards, which revealed the emptiness of the perfectly typical climax. There was nothing to say. It was over. He had succeeded in attaining the end that had driven him around the picks, the implied objections, the lessons of Catholic school where he had received a good education in a uniform that he tore off in the afternoon to race back onto the street and courts and rebel against that strict regime of approbation for correct answers and paddles for forgetting homework.

He silently mulled the only bond they had left: their secret. Though that didn't fascinate him much, at first, and not at all later. Soon he felt guilty seeing his wife and keeping her in the dark, was determined to tell her and confident she would forgive him. He saw her rage, smashing a dish, her face streaked with tears. Like a windowwasher he tries to clear the face so it glistened as before. But it was not to be. He confessed his adultery and she did forgive him after arduous explanation. Forlornly she sought a grasp in the secondhand armchair, her gaze fixed now on his bent head now on the replacement for the cheap ring she had so treasured from their days dating. The problem was that the neighbor-lover lived nextdoor. This hadn't occurred to him: Every time she finds him at home without her or leaves him at home, she is haunted by suspicion. He saw it all. And nothing quelled the doubts. No assurance, no promises. The trust was gone. And it would never return. Soon those doubts evolved into fits into tantrums into hysteria. He sensed her succumbing to the struggle. The only hope was to move, but where could they find rent-stabilized housing in a neighborhood like this? And on short notice? Nowhere, so he left...

Principal: Does your ex-wife know that you were planning to pick him up after school?

Father (*hesitantly*): No.

Principal: Does your ex-wife even know you are here.

Father: Yes. I told her I was coming.

Principal: Then why don't you arrange it with her?

Father: Because she wants me · to come · to the apartment, and I don't · want to go there. It brings back too many painful memories. I made · a stupid mistake that can't · be undone. There's no way out. So I just want · to forget it all. I don't want any memory. It's bad enough · coming to the neighborhood. We had such good times, but I'm one of those people that gets carried away. I jump into things · too intensely, for a short time. It happened with · my literary ambitions, it happened · with my non-profit plans, it happened · with my social work. I'm all fired up · for a few years, know all the details, am all excited, prepared, dive in and then lose interest because the reality is always less appealing than the dream.

Sottloy: I sort of get what you're saying. Once I punched my best friend in the nose, actually broke his nose by accident, and didn't know what to do in the aftermath. Never knew. And ultimately just blocked it out, Tried to erase it.

Father: Yes, although it didn't force you to move out and essentially lose your son.

Sottloy: That's true, but can't you apologize and smooth things out? I should have done it anyway, but if it had upended my life , I certainly would have.

Father: Circumstance prevents it...

Principal: Hmm. Well, let's go up to Room 235 and see what Mrs. Leaddus has to say.

BOOK EIGHT

(1) PIONEERS.

Walking through the childless building after school almost frightened the principal. Whatever drawbacks the place has during the day with kids in it, they are magnified in the after-school hours without them. Footsteps echo off the tile wall in the absence of scurrying bodies; voices and doors smash through the silence. In the air looms a threat of violence, impending violence, some uncontrolled mania that has been festering innocuously in a people used to colonization and conquest. Now they are entering the age of civilization, however short it will be before nature takes revenge. They are cooped up in houses, with no frontier, no prospects in manual labor or farming, no need to hold together and protect the community from savages. The uneducated drown their energy first in cigarettes, then in food, television and desk jobs accompanying them down the despairing slide to domesticity and cancer or obesity. The educated channel it at best into social work, democracy and capitalism for the world, and, at worst, get divorced once, twice, thrice, solicit experimental sex partners, change sex, change sex and partners, take antidepressants or stimulants or other drugs of a mild or stronger sort, drink, and above all consume, consume houses, cars, appliances, technology, games, clothing, food, cigarettes, and, of course, entertainment. They buy and buy to assuage their sorrow, to kill the dull sensation that the freedom, the endless possibilities, wide open land has been too much for them, that they do not measure up, are inconsequential and insignificant. That they have been crushed by a greater force, which they never believed in and which stays in the recesses until they can no longer buy and want to kill for the privilege...

The sound of keys rattled in the hall, like the warden opening cell 235 for a visit from the outside world. A messenger paid a visit and the prisoner paid attention: if you behave well, you'll get out early and all that can be yours again. And the messengers invariably brought this message, and invariably the prisoners bought it, still bought it. Not even a different perspective gives them the ability to approach the prevailing view critically, probably because their therapy is entertainment. Keep them quiet, keep them engaged by providing something interesting. Let them pick out their own books, choose their own programs and then you'll have great kids. From kindergarten they seek entertainment, but what is free at the beginning comes with its price later. There is no condemning what you haven't even been given the chance to question: if entertainment equals success, then entertainment it is, and consumption it entails... Even in the countryside, where schools are built like palaces with pillars, large bay windows, bases, curving driveways, courts, spacious grounds, and the most modern designs, – even these complexes cannot shed their affinity to incarceration. Why? How? Communities have forked over thousands of extra dollars to erect them, the father's town now boasts a high school resembling a college campus, though with only one building. Albeit an enormous one. Nonetheless, the feeling as you walk down it is one of oppression. The boy, son, Anya, Melvin, Tom, Dick, Harry and the monitor want to be free, want to run in the fields, shoot deer in the forest, repair houses. So when dismissal came, when the son grew older, a surge of enthusiasm coursed through his body as he returned to his roots...

(2) THE TEACHER AND FATHER MEET, AND THE BOY (DAMIEN) HIDES IN THE CLOSET.

Keys really jangled in the hall, and the teacher sent Damien to the closet. The janitor must have come. He was a little earlier than usual, though the evening conferences altered the afternoon schedule. On these days custodians combed the windowsills and grills for gum stuck to the surface, they mopped the pale tiles and then applied polish; they cleaned the toilets and urinals like never before. When she made her way to the door, however, she beheld a stranger, a large man's nose bloating the glass. It could only be one person – she put two and two together – as she opened up for him, and her principal, and the guard.

– Are you · Damien's teacher? – he blurted.

"Yes," she tried to make her voice sound perplexed.

– I'm · his father.

"Oh, I see. Are you here for a conference?"

– No...

He looked confused. Good.

– No, I was going · to pick him up · after school · but he didn't · come out. Was he · absent today?

"No, he was here and I saw him go off with two of his friends. We asked them to go home in groups because of a new policy."

The principal and guard left, and the father's eyes dulled. He could · have missed him · in the chaos of the schoolyard. Even worse, the boy · might have avoided him. The thought was humbling, the edge on his aggression curving and a stairwell of remorse climbing, like walking up the ramp and into the principal's office to ask: the asking alone meant defeat. His boy had eluded him because he didn't want to see his own dad.

"I didn't · see him," he said reflectively.

"Did he know you were picking him up? Fifth graders aren't usually dismissed to parents."

"I wanted · to meet him · after school today. It was · a surprise," he replied amicably, as he would in the shoe store.

These peaceful responses prompted her to reconsider the potential of the conversation, weighing the risk of keeping him in the room longer against the off-chance of getting him to realize how detrimental such surprises can be. This was not an aggressive man, and might be one who was willing to listen. Could she talk to him about the effect of estranged parents on their children? She certainly didn't have any aggression to fear or fend off.

Still, she was hesitant. Identifying with children of single parents was only possible to a certain extent: her mother had raised her alone, but her father had died in World War II. There had been no conflict, in fact, quite the reverse: Her father had been revered like a saint. And what's more, he had left behind a collection of letters and stories, so she heard his voice, recognized his quirks and gained a sense of his endearing character, which was then embellished by virtual hymns of praise from her mom. Since he had been overseas at her birth and died a few months later, she never saw him, never suffered from him. And this was invariably different in any family with parents who had separated or divorced.

She decided on a vague approach to test the prospects:

"You know, your son was very agitated today. I had to send him to the guidance councilor."

"Was he?"

"Yes. Much worse than he usually is. Do you have any idea why that might be?"

"No."

"Do you see your son often?"

"My boy? I used · to see him a lot."

"And lately?" she rejoined.

"Not so often. Been gone · for a couple years."

"Are you aware that the sudden appearance of an estranged parent can be very disturbing for a child?"

"Listen, Ms., I haven't · done · anything wrong. I just want · to see my boy. I've been out · of the city · for a couple years · and would like · to treat him · to a hot dog, find out · how he's doing, maybe play · some basketball. Is that a crime?"

A loose exhaust pipe rattled outside. What is this happy teacher lecturing him on? Who is she to tell him what to do with his son? He was irritated. His diffidence receded, an orange light blinking in his mind: these people don't have any idea what it's like to have problems, make a bad decision, be passionate and suffer for taking a wrong turn and righting yourself, but never like before. His blank gaze rested on the sink and closed closet in the corner where a lone chair sat apart from the others. It reminded him of his kitchen in the countryside, the table with its single wooden chair that he pulled out to eat and pushed back in to do the dishes. Alone. With a heavy heart. He got up and went to the door. Trucks backfiring, kids dribbling basketballs, honking...

(3) THE BOY (DAMIEN) IN THE CLOSET, THE SON (JASEM) AT HOME, THE FATHER ON THE STREET IN AN HOUR.

The boy was mesmerized. His dad so close, one move away, just beyond the baseline. Some of their best times had been playing bedroom basketball, his dad on his knees defending, he draining a jump shot over his outstretched arms. Then his dad got the ball, waddled left, leaned, looped the sponge ball past his flail, but it rimmed out of the basket, ricocheting off the wall, sofa, floor. They dove, colliding, laughing. I got there first. I did. Grabbing, taking, but he was there, I – falling, he – tackling. That was a foul. You went to the line for that.

Then Damien saw him the day he mysteriously left. His departure that morning felt different than the ones for work, and even different than those of visiting aunts and uncles. It wasn't as much the scene as the moment he hugs him, hugs his chest, torso, head... That had been weird. Then he was gone: his mom said he has to go out of state for work, though slowly this explanation gave way to his dad's cruelty. Later they stopped speaking on the phone the few times that confusing event had been permitted, and silence descended, until a couple months back he hadn't even thought about him that much, as if he doesn't exist. But...

It's my dad. I haven't seen him for ages. This is my chance. He was on the point of springing out of his crouch, bursting through the closet doors, crossing the line to this longlost dad and hugging him with all his might, yet a lady screamed on the street, her shrill, wild cry pierced the window, the door and his heart. Fear gripped him: it was · his mother's scream · from back then, from their fallout, when his mom · would come home · and impulsively sob, shriek, big balls of tears rolling down her cheeks. If he went out now, *he* might be the cause of a similar outburst. Oh how he wished he had a home like his friend's:

Jasem sits on a lightbrown chair that is too narrow and too small for an adult, a face peaking out over the top, rushing to finish the social studies text on the revolution – which actually made it take longer. Damien knew nothing of this, knew nothing of the brief conversation where Jasem told his mom about detention, but we know it from Jasem and his narrator. The homework can hardly be less interesting, but the embarrassment of telling about detention is off his back, and she wasn't too upset. He has skipped ahead, aware that when he has read about Washington's winter at Valley Forge, he will be free for the night. His mother admires the first president, and they have been to the camp and to Lexington and Concord. It's cool to see where the Minutemen fired those first shots, and next summer they'll go to Jamestown and some of the Civil War battlefields. Imagine it he can, marching in step across the grassy field, fearlessly waiting till you see the whites of their eyes, or sneaking down the river at night, like General Grant, and shocking those criminal slaveholding aristocrats at Vicksburg. They never went there, but his dad says they didn't celebrate the Fourth of July till a few years ago. That's how angry they were. Anyway, it's a thousand times more interesting to tromp over fields once littered with bloody bodies, even those of distant relatives on his mom's side, one of whom was taken for dead, but crawled into the woods after Gettysburg. His dad says at least. So yes, it's more interesting to see it than read it, and if you see it, you probably don't have to read it.

In the kids' bedroom he climbed on the faded sofa and fiddled with the terrarium, rearranging the plants to see the salamanders his brother hadn't lost at his grandma's and the frogs they'd netted by the pond. Then he pulled out GI Joe. That and Risk were his favorite board games, though conquering the world took a lot of time. Monopoly was boring: you just sat there with property and raked in money. He began to play GI Joe against himself, wishing his brother would hurry up with his homework. They always played it with Damien and his other friends on their birthday, stuffing themselves with cupcakes in the afternoon and then cake for desert. He wished Damien was there now. If they didn't want war, they could build the block tunnels and towers for the trains. Mom would be really impressed.

He didn't think about Damien's father or his own dad or his head pounding into the pole. He didn't have a television, didn't talk on the phone yet, didn't keep a diary till years later and couldn't see out the window because a synagogue blocked the view, so the free hour brought those blocks and trains anyway and formed a picture different than Damien's: He saw in his construction tonight a house in a distant countryside. A train traveled into the city and he rode that train to the library where books replaced blocks. Then there was another house next door, an elderly lady spoke a foreign language and then never spoke again. Creepy. Weird. Every summer for three years a rolly-polly man and a stick-skinny guest stacked up bricks, laid tiles, argued, but didn't throw batteries or get punished for climbing fences as they peeked out over the tops of walls and roofs and scaffolding, the elderly, bearded man patiently waiting, the young man with long hair rushing ahead – and actually making it take longer by rushing.

In the meantime, at home, happy though he didn't know it, Jasem could have sooner conceived of a twentieth century ice age than that Damien was holed up in a classroom closet, hiding from everyone except his mom, who did not show up on time. If he could see the scene, like me, the father's narrator, he would envision a mom clipclopping from the subway. She's late to her conference, lurching left along the street with two shopping bags in her hand disproportionately counterbalanced by the other clutching the purse on her shoulder. The sidewalk between the highrises has now darkened, with only the sky over the park catching the last bit of light from the sun that must have slipped behind the palisades. Seemingly preoccupied, she misses her estranged husband huddled with his arms wrapped around his knees. But she wouldn't have noticed without thoughts convoluting her thought.

He sits on a brownstone stoop across the street, shielded from the lamps graciously jutting out every fifth car. This is what he is expecting: his ex-wife to walk by on her way to the conference for his son. It is obvious she will come from the direction of the building or subway, and here she is, approaching, the white spots in her gray skirt sparkling in the streetlight, her high heels hammering out the same measured rhythm and intensity they had in her twenties – purpose, presence, confidence. She won't look his way, she's too mental, he knows it, though what he doesn't know is that suddenly the tight grip on her purse reawakens the frustration of his loose life and the absence of comparable experience since their marriage. He wants to regain control, to thrust his palm down on the brick slab to push himself up, throw himself before her, but it's impossible: she will only think that he doesn't want to live in the country or wants easy access to his former neighbor. Impossible, he tells himself, impossible because of that damn neighbor, because she still lives next door.

– ...Look around, in the playground, – Damien heard his teacher say.

– He would, – the father replied.

(4) THE TEACHER AND GUARD TALK ABOUT THE PAST.

At the same time as the father and teacher are talking, but before the father watches his wife walk down the street, the principal turned the handle and let Mr. Sottloy into her office. The extrovert continued:

"...odd to just show up like that and even odder he didn't see Damien. The boy must have been warned."

Principal: Why do you say that?

Sottloy: He lives on the corner. I found his father in front of the north entrance, which the boy would have gone through to go home directly. It's true that he might have taken a detour to the White Truck, but then I should have seen him.

Principal: You don't think we should call the police, do you?

Sottloy: No.

Principal: But maybe I'll call home just in case.

(*Pause finding out that no one is home*)

Sottloy: It's really a strange situation (*sees the principal looking at him attentively*) and bad timing. I rather liked the guy. We may have only talked for a minute or two, but he made a good impression.

Principal: You know, I had the same reaction. Though I'm still suspicious. I remember meeting this boyfriend of my sister a couple years ago. He was the friendliest, most entertaining, polite guy I'd seen in years. We laughed constantly, even when he didn't talk, his goofy behavior, mannerisms brought a smile to my lips. Most of us were enthralled and excited for my sister, yet a cousin refused to believe it. He said it was too much. And while he admitted there was no hint of insincerity. He didn't think an outsider could see through him. Maybe there wasn't even a façade to see through, maybe the façade was his character. And sure enough, what'd you know, the university professor, eventually with three children and my sister as a wife, turned out to be a clandestine homosexual, had been lying for years about his academic trips, evening meetings and peculiar states on occasion. He even guarded the lie by regularly sleeping with her and essentially revealed it by spreading diseases to her."

Sottloy: I once had a girlfriend who cheated on me for a long time, the last 3 months of a two year relationship, though even at the end, and afterwards, we got along fine. I was sad about it, of course, although I was sadder about her determination to break up than I was about her sleeping with some other guy. When I first considered her duplicity, it seemed to destroy the intrinsic unity of the relationship, yet the more I got around to thinking, the less sure I was. After all, the essence of our relationship was that we enjoyed hanging out. That she enjoyed that with someone else didn't change the matter, didn't change what we experienced. Perhaps this proved it wasn't unique, that's fair to say, but I, for one, don't believe in uniqueness. I had enjoyed similar relationships before and have had others since, so I can't begrudge her having two at the same time."

Principal: (*chuckling*) You're very liberal. My husband and I got divorced and I regret marrying him, except for our daughter. It might have worked, but he spent all his time in the office. I wanted that kind of man, someone who provides a nice life for his family, but I also wanted to enjoy life. You only live once, after all. And he just worked like a machine. Obviously we had some good times, though, as you said, there will always be good times, no matter who you're with. Now I wish I'd planned it better.

Sottloy: I don't know about planning, but you're right about the invariable good times. It's what makes criticizing any life very difficult. Ultimately each one has intangible benefits and drawbacks that we can't see. That's why I was so intrigued by Damien's father. Here's a regular guy who seems to be at peace with himself even if he can't find his own son and can't live with his family: I thought the guy might cry, he seemed so sensitive, so sad about not finding the boy. Bizarre reaction if you ask me.

Principal: Maybe he got rich, won the lottery and a new perspective on life.

Sottloy: Maybe, but that would hardly bring him to the brink of resignation.

And on he would have gone had the principle not rifled through papers on her desk and said:

"So you're going to be here till the end of the conferences this evening, aren't you?"

"Yes," the guard replied with a smile. "If you need anything, just yell."

The early November night gloamed; revival for the school lay less than an hour away. In sensitive stillness the father traipsed from the front ramp to the stoop; Mr. Sottloy legged his way through the halls on a last check; the principal sat at her desk and pondered this odd situation with Damien. Upstairs, in Room 235, the teacher told the boy to come out of the closet.

BOOK NINE

(1) LAW, ORDER AND DEVIANCE.

They all acknowledge it. Mr. Sottloy understood the principal's intention; the principal had understood the teacher's; the father understood the obligatory politeness to a woman, a teacher, an authority who spoke considerately in his kid's best interests. Even the two boys in climbing over the fence, in throwing eggs at a house, in buying beer illegally or the teacher stealing as a child – recognized intuitively and were rebelling against the rules that implicitly governed their society so strictly that they had an inverse effect on minors just as the prohibition of alcohol... Part of it is selfcontrol. The teacher, the principal and Mr. Sottloy don't flip out, don't throw fits, don't lose control and virtually don't show emotion. Of course they think they do. And if you told the teacher, for example, that she was a steady and rational woman, she would be astonished. But that same teacher also doesn't find herself on the couch or in bed despairing over a potential customer revolt for half the day or spacing out on the hardwood chair for an hour after dinner.

Where does this selfcontrol originate? In the codes and laws? In the brain? In the relative laxity of public school? In the spankings, groundings? In an assessment of the situation and how to behave best to achieve the desired end? - And how could it be oppressive? The oppression has to result from being an outsider facing the coincidence of code and behavior. Mrs. Leaddus, Ms. Folow, Mr. Sottloy under complete control in a society rigidly controlled by codes pins a non-conforming man into an extremely uncomfortable position so the father conforms, conforms and conforms and conforms to the protestant work ethic, to dourness and a view of life as no joy, but hard, constant, neverending, neverceasing duty. Yet he is not that man. His genes as calmly ascribe to this duty as the farmer forced to the city: atavism attacks innocuously; he cannot discipline himself inwardly, but has to outwardly, leaving him gutted and empty... In public, as we have seen, the father had no less difficulty adhering to the strictures than the teacher, principal or guard. Primarily, his is the alternative perspective of an insider, since he has grown up in the system and knows its codes without accepting them. In this way, too, the distinctions between the other three are reduced, having them communicate on the basis of their appreciation for the benefits of unspoken rules: politeness, friendliness, cooperation. It doesn't matter that the characteristics of their society only apply as long as no thought is bestowed on the tightly drawn lips of the teacher or the excess confidence of the libertine guard or the standing on ceremony so evident in the principal. The surface is important, and if that is okay, then it lends their psyches the stability they need to continue perpetuating an optimistic outlook.

With this reality, it's no wonder not only the father, but also the guard, teacher and even the principal were susceptible to extraordinary flights of fantasy, departing materially, mentally and spiritually from the confinement of their jobs and homes. Who wants to live in a thoroughly rational world where no surprises break the tedium of comfort? This is another reason for the obsession with entertainment and consumption that the guard's narrator mentioned earlier. Yet what our father observed in his various dreams about journals, social work or even the nextdoor neighbor, and what he would observe if he really did succeed in treating his son to a hotdog today is that the idea holds far more appeal than the reality. It is the same for me, his narrator. Were I to describe the daily events of his life, you would be bored to tears; if I were to unveil his thoughts, for the most part you would be so annoyed that you'd close the book. For whatever reason, something began to change in the late 80s, a new era began and accelerated in the nineties, and among others, it was defined by a growing rejection of reason.

(2) THE TEACHER TRIES TO PROVIDE ENCOURAGEMENT.

Some hour later the teacher woke the napping boy: "Damien, I'm going to have to ask you to hide in the closet again. I'm sorry. You can leave one side open so you get a little light. No one should be in this half of the room. It'll be about an hour till your mom's conference."

When the third parent had left, only fifteen minutes remained. One more conference. She talked about Anya's achievements in the first eight weeks: improvements in reading and creativity in arts and crafts. But that was not enough. She was still reading below grade level, and she came to school too often without her homework. The parents needed to check that. They had to see that their child completed her assignments. So would she please go over it with her daughter every night.

– Did I, miss, have any idea what children told their parents? Did I have any idea? – the parent exploded. She asked 'em if they'd done their homework and dey told her it was all done. How wa she to know? I dink dat dey didn't care, but dey did. Dey wa doin everyting!

"I know, I understand, I'm not saying you aren't... It's just..."

The parent broke in: – I had no idea. How could I? Did I know what dey went dru, did I know? Her man wen to two jobs, and she awso. Dey didn't have no time like me. Dey try, but dey tired and couldn't take more trouble.

This problematic case shuttled her back to the not half so problematic child in the closet. Was his mother already waiting outside? She glanced at the window, yet saw no sign of her in the magazinesized pane.

– Did I know what it like after school every day. She tell

her to go home and do her homework, but she didn't listen. She wonted to jump rope wid her friends or watch tv. Every day she called, but it didn't help. Yesterday I gave her pocket money and she went spend it on hoop earings and barretts. What was she to do? Da girl was supposed to buy pants, and now she had no money and still needed pants.

The teacher's attention again drifted to the mother of the boy in the closet. Her conference was coming. Would *she* be there? What would she do if she didn't come? Call her? Yes. Call. She refocused and replied:

"Look, I realize the complications. It's not easy. I'm just asking you for her sake. We all want her to do the best she can. That's our goal. I'm just trying to help by pointing out the areas where she can improve. As I said, she has progressed in reading and art. That's great. Now she needs to repeat that in math and social studies."

– She was sorry, yes, she understand. She was a little tired today. Dat was all. Dey'd do der best. Danked her for telling her whad she should improve."

On the way to the door, the woman passed the mirror on the teacher's closet. It reflected the turkeys made of tissue paper on the window, and Anya's mother suddenly asked if any of her art projects were hanging up. – Could she see one?

"I think there's one on the door here and some more by the sink," the teacher said, going over to closet in Damien.

(3) JASEM BREAKS THE RULES AGAIN.

Anya's mother regarded the work and the teacher reflected on her own child. He had not caused much trouble, certainly not when compared to Anya or Damien, but he had a disobedient streak that agitated her a little. It was too early for him to exhibit his future inclinations, but judging by his occasional rowdiness in class, a slight intransigence reminiscent of and more prominent in his father, plus this incident with the playground now, she could see reason to worry. A little of this was to be expected, and he had initially been easier than his brother who shrieked incessantly as an infant. Jasem was shy and sheltered like a kid raised in a small town to make a modest contribution to his community. There was no need to drill your child or pressure him to get top grades. Let him find his own path, and if he finds it on his own, it will inspire him all the more. The minister was right when he questioned the wisdom of parents who desire that their child become president.

...Till high school her misgivings were largely confined to that exuberance of youth which he and his brother equally shared, though, more often, misleading the older; and the teacher, in spite of every occasional doubt about those rockers' value, could not see at these moments the excitement of thrilled anticipation which lifted the spirits and sparkled in the eyes of her son, without feeling how dismal her own pupils' prospects were, how relatively gloomy their frame of mind, and how delightful it would be if they had the same enthusiastic object in view, the same possibility of hope.

But Jasem's *extracurricular* path in high school alarmed her. In the fall of his senior year he announced an impending trip out of town:

– Mom, I'm going with my friends to Rachel's country house this weekend.

"Are her parents going to be there?"

– No.

"Then you can't go," she replied categorically.

– Are you kidding, mom? What do her parents have to do with it? Are you saying I can't go because girls will be there?

"Yes."

– That's ridiculous. I'm going. I don't care what you say.

"I can't stop you. But I'm saying you aren't allowed to."

A feeling of remorse must have hit him, or the obedience that was the upshot of past spankings, the wrecking ball of that age. As two years before, after the talk with his dad about heavy metal lyrics, he changed despite still listening to those violent musicians that she did not understand to be social critique, the representation of an ideology's mentality. They were disgusting, ruinous, making him aggressive and wild.

– Alright, mom. If you're going to forbid it, then I won't go. But I'm telling you that this is the last time I'll honestly tell you what I'm doing. So far I've always been open and told you the truth. But from now on, I'm just going to say: 'I'm going to Tom, Dick or Harry's'. Is that what you want?

"That's your choice."

His spirit had risen from the shackles of his parents, dismissing their domesticity. Yes! Totally! Yes. He would see it through to the end, go to the extreme, as the great predecessor whose identity he had adopted, a block-like collage, all mixed and mashed and staggering, intangible, elusive.

He slammed the door of the apartment. No longer could he contain the coursing surge of revolt. His face flushed and his blood pulsed deluged. The creeping exasperation in his breast would be silence and flight to the edge of the land. Away! Away! His thoughts seemed to scream. The afternoon will lower into the ocean, night skylight the trip, dawn catch him asleep and slip in strange visions and dreams and sights.

Then he was gone. To college, abroad, sometimes they didn't see him for years, but when they did, he was still too extreme, too unpredictable. The nice, shy boy was gone. He was silent, arrogant, highly critical, and, oddest of all, became violently sick and then permanently sick, the virus mutating, a new strain draining the cells of their sodium, the lack of sodium corroding the walls...

He veered to the east. The shadows stretched over the walkways on the dorm side of the street and already the lines of cars wisped twice the length of noontime. Already one lane backed up to the vanishing hill. Here and there an olive or yellow tone glistened among the dirty gray, and about the isolated olive and around the backed up lane and amid the currents of cars were immaculate men and women, moving and conversing.

(4) DAMIEN SOARS.

... In the closet Damien had slumped asleep, though his dream was light, and his legs were light in the dream. He rushes out of the closet, jumps down the stairs, pondering where to go – finally, he slows, his feet sinking in the lush verdant grass right next to Radish playground, the tennis courts, the reservoir, runs to the edge of the park enclosed by granite blocks and a triangular top. His shoes spray dirty brown drops and he is only rattled by one thing, the thought of not reaching the wall, not being permitted in the place behind the wall, and he's almost there, and the buildings – higher and straighter; sweltering, fumy air swells his nostrils, sweat rolls down his back – where do these fumes come from? What is this heat? A surge wells up, recalling the frantic rush toward the homeless man, and he springs up, over and past the wall and sees the other side, sees the endless impeccable facades, sees the flowers planted round the trees, the long, sleek limousines, their shaded windows and the faces of the chauffeurs, polite and respectful, standing by the door as he races toward them over the hot asphalt... There's a voice, indistinct, but familiar, where? There? No one is *there*. Where facades meet the firmament. But he recognized it, it's his mom calling him from so far away that he can't imagine running all that way, and he stops – carefully walks down the sidewalk, feeling the sweltering heat, sensing he asks no one in particular: am I going the right way? is it right for me to go? do I really need to go this far?... The melodic voice answers him, then lapses, rises again through the wall, quickly, falling; and joy replaces fear. The boy swivels his head, waves goodbye to the chauffeurs, don't drive away, wait for me, and the chauffeurs open their back doors...

Decades later Damien recalled that day and his awakening in the closet:

My mom clopped down the street like the teacher with her children, not envisioning any venomous sedan-snakes or prison schools, not like timid me so confused by surprise:

What had I been thinking, he continued, again stunned by his thoughts. I must have known nothing would happen. Why did I get all bent out of shape? Yesterday, yesterday, when she warned me, yesterday I totally knew that nothing would happen. What's my problem? Why am I getting all worked up. Yesterday, when I returned to stare out the window, I said it's all nonsense, crap, garbage, garbage.... The thought alone made me laugh and dismiss it...

No, it won't happen, it won't happen! Even, even if she's totally right in her way, even if it is all as clear as day, right as math. My God! It still won't happen. Won't happen! Why have I... He stood up, looked around in surprise and... saw a subway roar into the station of exposed I-beams and dirty white tiles.

EPILOGUE

The fleet of questions rolled, cutting, accelerating, swerving, trying to beat the red light that the flashing "DONT WALK" foretold on the cross street: the guard manned the entrance ramp. Was it a last warning? A premonition of red? The father pictured his past apparel outlet on Jamesway and rose from the stoop. The end? Tires scattering water like thoughts slowed for the plastic tips of pumps after school... Traffic: the principal could not yet pull out of her spot, continue down the now dark street lined with illuminated leaves. Breaking rear lights: the teacher looked to the door. The highway – a parking lot: Damien peeped through the crevice with the departure of Anya's mother. At home Jasem did not see his future:

In a matter of minutes he was down the stairs, his uncovered feet in clogs and the bottoms of his pants flapping granules of dirt under his heel: and spitting a piece of gum on the sparse grass by the path, he sallied to the elongated street.

There was a break in the lane: and, as he clopped slowly up its side, he wondered at the dingy bundle of exhaust. Blue and olive and black and yellow, it mutated beneath the current, shifting and rising. The air in the break was a turbid dingy bundle and intimated the bundled clouds. The clouds bundled above him silently and silently the fumes were bundling below him; and the gray warmth immersed him: and a new murky edge was bespattering his heart.

Where are they now? Where is the boy that hung fire in dormant hope, to reconcile the creeping cry with the attentive interest in his life and the kindness of sentiment? Or where is he? Alone.

He stands there. Careless, free and approaching the murky edge. He is there and young and determined and edgy, there amid a bellow of murky warmth and smoggy airs and rivulets of oil and cigarette butts and shrouded gray sunshine and immaculate men and women. Collaged there alone.

AUTHOR BIOS

HENRY WHITTLESEY

Henry Whittlesey is a writer, translator and editor. He co-founded and edits perypatetik, an international aesthetic project dedicated to the potential of an alternative perspective based on process-oriented production in harmony with nature. His work has been published in journals, magazines and books such as *Comparative Literature and Culture (at Purdue University),* *Two Lines World Writing in Translation (Vol. 17),* *Brooklyn Rail,* and many others. He is also the co-author of *Peripatetic Alterity,* the aesthetic ideology for the perypatetik project.

ERIC ST. PIERRE

Eric St. Pierre is an author, expressionist painter, and song-writer who lives and creates in New Orleans, LA.

KRISTA BEUCLER

Krista Beucler is originally from Colorado and currently pursuing an MFA in creative writing from Drexel University.

Krista is a winner of the Julia Peterkin award, and her creative work has been published in *Kelp Journal,* *Mulberry Literary,* and *South 85 Journal,* among others.

IZASKUN GRACIA QUINTANA

Izaskun Gracia Quintana (Bilbao (Spain), 1977) studied Basque Philology and Graphic Design, among others. She works as a freelance translator, proofreader, editor and graphic designer and she writes articles as well as literary criticism for various media. She was editor and co-founder of the poetry publishing-house Masmédula and she lives in Berlin (Germany) since 2011.

She writes poetry and prose, mostly in Spanish and Basque. She has published the poetry collections *fuegos fatuos* (2003), *eleak eta beleak* (2007), *saco de humos* (2010), *ártica / artikoa* (2012), *vacuus* (2016), *despertar lloviendo* (2017), *Ohe hutsetan* (2018) and *soliloquio soterrado* (2021), as well as the short story collections *Crónicas del encierro* (2016) and *Lo que ruge* (2021), both nominated for the Euskadi Literature Prize.

Her texts have been published in many anthologies and literary magazines (and also translated into English, French, German and Greek), she has participated in many european literary festivals, and she has also collaborated with artists such as Anabel Lorca, Zigor Barayazarra, Delphine Salvi, Leire Urbeltz and Liébana Goñi.

JOEL T. BLACKSTOCK JR.

Joel's artistic and professional areas of interest are in neurological and phenomenological causes for the intersection of mysticism and existentialism within consciousness. Joel spends most weekends hiking and enjoying the outdoors with his wife and children. He is passionate about travel and exploring new cultures as well as new ways of being. Dedicated to his darling wife Emily, without whom nothing that he dreamed would be real, and nothing real would make him dream.

JAMES CATO

James Cato is an MFA candidate at the Iowa Writer's Workshop, and his chapbook "Becoming Roadkill" is now available from Red Bird Chapbooks. David Vonderheide is a writer and medical school student at the University of Pennsylvania whose work has been featured in Every Day Fiction and the Colored Lens. James and David have been writing together for years with work featured in Andromeda Spaceways and other venues and have known one another since the ages of three and four.

Running Wild Press publishes stories that cross genres with great stories and writing. RIZE publishes great genre stories written by people of color and by authors who identify with other marginalized groups. Our team consists of:

Lisa Diane Kastner, Founder and Executive Editor
Joelle Mitchell, Licensing and Strategy Lead
Cody Sisco, Acquisition Editor, RIZE
Benjamin White, Acquisition Editor, Running Wild
Peter A. Wright, Acquisition Editor, Running Wild
Resa Alboher, Editor
Angela Andrews, Editor
Sandra Bush, Editor
Ashley Crantas, Editor
Rebecca Dimyan, Editor
Abigail Efird, Editor
Aimee Hardy, Editor
Henry L. Herz, Editor
Cecilia Kennedy, Editor
Barbara Lockwood, Editor
Scott Schultz, Editor
Rod Gilley, Editor
Kelly Ottiano, Editor
Carolyn Banks, Editor
Evangeline Estropia, Product Manager
Pulp Art Studios, Cover Design
Standout Books, Interior Design
Polgarus Studios, Interior Design

Learn more about us and our stories at www.runningwildpublishing.com

Loved these stories and want more? Follow us at runningwildpublishing.com, www.facebook.com/runningwild-press, on Twitter @lisadkastner @RunWildBooks

www.ingramcontent.com/pod-product-compliance
Lightning Source LLC
LaVergne TN
LVHW020647110826
845149LV00012B/1938
9781963869057